TRADING IN DANGER

TRADING IN DANGER

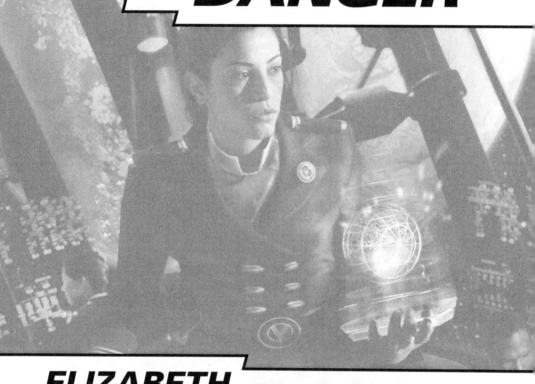

ELIZABETH MOON

DEL
REY

BALLANTINE BOOKS • NEW YORK

A Del Rey® Book
Published by The Random House Publishing Group

www.delreydigital.com

Library of Congress Cataloging-in-Publication Data is available upon request from the publisher.

ISBN 0-345-44760-3

Book design by Susan Turner

Manufactured in the United States of America

First Edition: October 2003

10 9 8 7 6 5 4 3 2 1

To Joshua, without whom this book and several others would not have seen daylight . . . and thanks for all the chocolate.

And to all those involved in the matter of the sword: you know who you are, and you know why.

ACKNOWLEDGMENTS

As usual, this book reflects more than my own limited expertise; friends, family, and acquaintances all had useful suggestions and vital information. Some preferred not to be named here.

Thanks are due to David, Richard, Susan, Julia, Selina, Joshua, Laura, Ellen, and Sean, all of whom made innumerable helpful comments. Also the economist I met on a flight to Tulsa, and whose name I never knew . . .

David R. Watson deserves particular thanks for his expertise with archery and his willingness to help choreograph fight scenes.

Anne McCaffrey, with a lift of the eyebrows, solved a problem I was having when I talked to her about it. Her words were wise, but the lift of the eyebrows had already done the trick.

The regulars on the news group, with their encouragement, helped me over the rough spots. So did the SFWA Musketeers and Musketeer Auxiliary.

The Florence High School faculty and staff (especially the special education folks) had a part in this toward the end, by doing such a great job of easing our son into high school.

Mistakes and omissions are all mine.

TRADING *IN* DANGER

CHAPTER
ONE

Kylara Vatta came to attention in front of the Commandant's desk. One sheet of flatcopy lay in front of him, the print too small for her to read upside down. She had a bad feeling about this. On previous trips to the Commandant's office, she had been summoned by an icon popping up on her deskcomp. Those had all been benign visits, the result of exams passed in the top 5 percent, or prizes won, and the Commandant had greeted her with the most thawed of his several frosty expressions.

Today it had been "Cadet Vatta to the Commandant's office, on the double," blaring out over the speaker right in the middle of her first class period, Veshpasir's lecture on the history of the first century PD. Veshpasir, no friend to shipping dynasties, had given her a nasty smirk before saying, "Dismissed, Cadet Vatta."

She had no idea what this was about. Or rather, she hoped she didn't. Surely she had been careful enough . . .

"Cadet Vatta," the Commandant said. No thawing at all, and his left eyelid drooped ominously.

"Sir," she said.

"I won't even ask what you thought you were doing," he said. "I don't want to know. I don't care."

"Sir?" She hated the squeak in her voice.

"Don't play the innocent with me, Cadet." Rumor had it that if his left eyelid actually closed, cadets died. She wasn't sure she believed that, but she hoped she wasn't about to find out. "You are a disgrace to the Service."

Ky almost shook her head in confusion. What could he be talking about?

"Going outside the chain of command like this"—he thumped the sheet of paper—"embarrassing the Service."

"Sir—" She gulped, caught between the etiquette that required silence until she was given leave to speak, and a desperate need to find out what had the Commandant's eyelid hovering ever nearer to its mate.

"You have something to say, Cadet?" the Commandant asked. His voice, like his face, might have been carved out of a glacier. "Do go ahead . . ." It was not a generous offer.

"Sir, with the greatest respect, this cadet does not know to what the Commandant is referring . . ."

His lips disappeared altogether. "Oh, you can play the innocent all you want, Cadet, and maintain that formal folderol, but you don't fool me." He paused. Ky searched her memory, and came up empty. "Well, since you insist, let's try this: do you recall the name *Mandy Rocher*?"

"Yes, sir," Ky said promptly. "Second year, third squad."

"And you can think of no reason why I might connect that name and yours?"

"Sir, I helped Cadet Rocher locate a Miznarii chaplain last weekend, when Chaplain Oser was away . . ." A dim glimmer of what might be the problem came to her but she couldn't believe there would be that much fuss about a simple little . . .

"And just how did you locate a Miznarii chaplain, Cadet?"

"I . . . er . . . called my mother, sir."

"You called your mother." He made it sound obscene, as if only the lowest criminal would call a mother. "And told your mother to do what, Cadet?"

"I asked her if her friend Jucha could refer me to a Miznarii chaplain near the Academy."

"For what reason?"

"I told her that one of the underclassmen was overdue for confession and the Academy chaplain was out of town."

"You didn't tell her what he wanted to confess?"

Ky felt her own eyebrows going up. "Sir, I don't know what he had to confess. I only know that he was in distress, and needed a chaplain, and I thought . . . I thought it would save trouble if I just got him one."

"You're not Miznarii yourself . . . ?"

"No, sir. We're Modulans." Actually, they were Saphiric Cyclans, but that was such a small sect that nobody recognized it, and Modulans were respectable and undemanding. You could be a Modulan without doing anything much at all, a source of some humor to more energetic sects. Ky found Modulan chapel restful and had gone often enough to acquire a reputation for moderate piety—the level most approved by Modulans.

"Hmmph." The Commandant's eyelid twitched upward a millimeter; Ky hoped this was a good sign. "You had no idea that what he wanted to confess concerned the honor of the Service?"

Her jaw dropped; she forced it back up. "No, sir!"

"That he made a formal complaint to this Miznarii, in addition to his confession, which the chaplain took immediately to the Bureau of War, where it fell into the hands of a particularly noxious bureaucrat whose *sister* just happens to be on the staff of *Wide Exposure*, so that I found myself on the horn very early this morning with Grand-Admiral Tasliki, who is not amused at all . . . ?" It was not really a question; it was rant and explanation and condemnation all in one. "The bureaucrat spoke on *Wide Exposure*'s 'Night Affairs' program at 0115—clever timing, that—and this morning all the media channels had something on it. That's only the beginning."

Ky felt hot, then cold, then hot again. "S-sir . . . ," she managed.

"So even if you did not know, Cadet Vatta, what Cadet Rocher wanted to confess, you may be able to grasp that by going outside the chain of command you have created a very *very* large public relations problem, embarrassing the entire general staff, the Bureau of War, and—last but not least—me personally."

"Yes, sir." She could understand that. She could not, she thought, have anticipated it, and now she was consumed by curiosity: what, exactly, *had* Mandy Rocher said? They weren't allowed access to things like *Wide Exposure* except on weekends.

"You are an embarrassment, Cadet Vatta," the Commandant said.

"Many, many people want your hide tacked on the wall and your head on a pike. The only reason I don't—" His eyelid was up another millimeter. "The *only* reason I don't, is that I have observed your progress through the Academy and you have so far been, within the limits of your ability, an exemplary cadet. When I thought you'd done it on purpose I was going to throw you to the wolves. Now—since I suspect that you simply fell for a sob story and your entire barracks knows you have a soft spot for underdogs and lost lambs—I'm simply going to take the hide off your back in strips and see your resignation on my desk by 1500 hours this afternoon."

"S-sir?" Resignation . . . did that mean what it sounded like? Was he kicking her out? Just because she'd tried to help Mandy?

Now the eyelid came all the way back up. "Cadet Vatta, you have— unwittingly, perhaps—created a major mess with implications that could damage the Service for years. Your ass is grass, one way or the other. You could be charged, for instance, with that string of articles beginning with 312.5—I see by your expression that you have, belatedly, remembered them . . ."

She did indeed. Article 312.5 of the Military Legal Code: failure to inform superior officer in a timely manner of potentially harmful personnel situations. Article 312.6: failure to inform superior officer in a timely manner of breaches of security involving sensitive personnel. Article 312.7: failure to inform superior officer in a timely manner of . . . rats, rats, and flying rats. She was majorly doomed.

"I . . . wasn't thinking, sir." That was not an attempt at apology, merely a statement of fact.

"Fairly obvious. What did you think might happen?"

"I thought . . . Mandy—Cadet Rocher—was so upset that day—I thought if he could see a chaplain and confess or whatever, he'd settle down until the regular chaplain got back. He had those exams coming up, and they were group-graded; if he didn't do well, his squad would suffer for it . . ."

"What you don't know, Cadet, is that Rocher had been avoiding the regular chaplain's cycle; his so-called emergency was of his own making. He wanted to talk to someone outside the Academy, and you made that possible."

"Yes, sir."

"And you didn't tell anyone at all about this, did you?"

"No, sir."

"Easier to get forgiveness than permission, is that what you were thinking?"

"No, sir . . . not really." One of the places where Modulans and Saphiric Cyclans disagreed was about the giving of aid. Modulans felt that moderate assistance should be moderately public—one did not make a huge display of charity, but one allowed others to know charity was going on, to set a good example. Saphiric Cyclans, on the other hand, believed that all help should be given as anonymously as possible. Now was probably not the time to talk about that difference.

"I am so reassured." The Commandant's eyelid quivered. "Cadet Vatta, it is unfortunate that you have to suffer for a generous impulse, but we need naval officers with brains as well as kind hearts. You will not return to class. You will, as I said, present a letter of resignation which does not mention any of this, and cites personal reasons as the cause, by 1500 hours. Sooner, Cadet, is better than later, but first you will go to Signals, and make contact with your family, so that you will be able to leave quietly and quickly when that resignation is approved." The look he gave her now was warmer by a few degrees, but still not cordial. "Staff will pack up your things; they will be at the gate when you depart."

"I . . . yes, sir."

"And yes, you infer correctly that you are not to speak to any of your former associates. Your departure will be explained as seems most expedient for the Service."

"Sir." Not speak to anyone. Not to Mira or Lisette . . . not to Hal. *Only another few months, and we can*—but not now, not ever. Please, please, let no one figure out . . .

"You are dismissed."

"Sir." Ky saluted, rotated correctly on her right heel, and left his office, her mind a blur. Signals. She knew where Signals was. She passed without really seeing an enlisted man in the passage, and another at the head of the stairs down to the classroom level. Halfway to Signals, her mind clicked on long enough to panic . . . She had to call her family, tell her father and, oh heavens, her *mother* that she was disgraced, dismissed . . . Her brothers would all . . . her cousins . . . Uncle Tomas . . . Aunt Grace, worse than Uncle Tomas, who would say again all she had said when Ky first went to the Academy, laced with *I told you so* . . .

She felt the tremor in her hands, and fought to still it. Now, for this short period of time, she was still a cadet, and now, for this short period of time, she would act like one. Even as the dream went down in smoke and ashes, even then . . . her stomach looped wildly once and settled.

At the door of Signals, a uniformed guard stared past her.

"Cadet Vatta, on order of the Commandant," she said.

He stepped aside, and she heard him murmur into his comunit "Cadet Vatta at Signals, sir."

Commander Terry had the watch in Signals; his expression suggested that her family were loathsome toads, and she was toad spawn. "Vatta," he said, minus the honorific.

"Sir."

"Which contact number?" As if having more than one number were also a crime.

"Vatta Enterprises," Ky said. "They have a relay—" Wherever her father was, they could reach him, or give her a link to the senior Vatta onplanet.

"We would prefer that you make a direct call."

She knew her father's mobile number, of course, but he'd often said he hated the damned thing, and would leave it on the bedside table as often as not. That meant her mother might pick it up, the last person she wanted to talk to. Vatta Enterprises would ring his skullphone, which he couldn't take off. She didn't have that number; no one did but the communications computer at VE.

She rattled off the string for the mobile, and mentally visualized the arc of blue, best fortune, of the Saphiran Cyclan wheel, as Commander Terry nodded to the rating who entered the string.

"Name?" Terry asked abruptly. Ky startled. "The name of the person you are calling," he said.

"Sir, my father, sir. Gerard Avondettin Vatta. But if my mother—"

"You are permitted one call, to one recipient, Cadet Vatta." Commander Terry picked up the headset and held the receiver to his ear. Ky waited, the blue arc fading in her mental eye. Then his hand twitched. "This is Commander Terry at the Naval Academy; I need to speak to Gerard Avondettin Vatta." A pause, then: "Kylara Vatta will speak with you." He held the headset out to Ky.

She was not even allowed to speak from a privacy booth. She had known the call would be recorded, but at least a semblance of normal courtesy would have helped. She could feel tears swelling now, stuffing her nose. She fought for calmness as she took the headset and put it on. Enough of this; she turned her back on Commander Terry without permission.

"Dad, listen—"

"Ky, what's wrong? Are you hurt?"

"Dad, no, I'm fine, please listen. I have to leave, I have to leave today. Can you send somebody to the gates?"

"Ky, what is it?"

"Dad, please. I have to resign. I have to leave. I don't have any money for transport; I need a way to get home—"

"What—!" She could hear the explosion building up, the familiar prelude to the famous roar. Then it ended, surprising her into silence. His voice gentled to a soft growl. "Ky, listen, whatever it is, we can help. Let me call the Commandant—"

"No, Dad. Don't do that. I'll explain when I get there, only help me get there, please?"

"When do you need transport?"

She looked at the chronometer. Only 0935. Surely she could write a resignation that would satisfy the Commandant by noon.

"By noon, if that's possible."

"For you, Kylara-mish, five minutes would be possible. Only tell me, has someone hurt you?"

Later, she would consider whether Mandy Rocher had hurt her; now she wanted only to get away. And even if Mandy had, she had made it possible; it was her own fault. "It's not that, Dad."

"Good. Because if any one of those fisheaters had laid a finger on you—"

"Dad, please. Noon?"

"At the gates. On Vatta honor."

"Vatta honor." The signal died, and she handed the headset back to Commander Terry. He took it without comment, and gave a curt nod.

"Get on your way, Vatta."

"Yes, sir." She needed a place to write the resignation; if she was forbidden to return to her quarters, where could she go? Outside, she found the answer, of sorts: the wiry gray-haired senior NCO who had been her year's nemesis in the first four quarters, and an increasingly valuable resource ever since. She had not, she remembered, taken Mac-Robert's advice on the matter of Mandy Rocher.

"Commandant's library is empty, Cadet Vatta," he said now. "Fully equipped."

"Right," she said. She would not cry. She would certainly not cry in front of this man. He turned to lead the way and she followed.

"Right mess you made of things," he said, when they were around a corner from Signals.

"Yes," Ky said.

"I won't say I told you so," he said. He just had, of course, but she didn't answer. "I daresay you feel bad enough already."

A shadow of a question in that. Anger stirred suddenly, beneath the anguish. "Yes, I do," she said, hearing the sharp edge to her own voice.

"Thought so," he said. "Here you are." He opened the door for her. She had never been in the Commandant's private library before; the long narrow room held not only racks of ordinary books and journals, but shelves of ancient books like those in her family's oldest house. A long table ran down the middle of the room, and at one end someone had set out a stack of white paper and a selection of pens. "It's appropriate that a resignation of this type be handwritten," MacRobert told her. "You can use the voice recorder or the keyboard to rough it out, but it's better to stick to the simplest format . . ." Someone had also laid out a copy of *Naval Etiquette: Essentials for Officers*, and the hand reader.

"Thank you," Ky said. It was still not 1000 hours. Her world had ended less than an hour ago. She had another couple of hours . . .

"What time did you arrange transport for?" MacRobert asked.

"Noon," Ky said.

"I'll see that your gear is at the gate by 1130," MacRobert said.

"Thank you," Ky said again. She felt unreal, still, as if this were a dream, as if she were floating a few centimeters off the floor.

"I'll leave you alone," MacRobert said. "When you're finished, you can leave the resignation here—"

"The Commandant said on his desk," Ky said.

"That's right. And so it will be; just tell me when you're finished." He nodded and went out, shutting the door silently behind him.

She put *Naval Etiquette: Essentials for Officers* into the reader and found that someone had already bookmarked the section on resignations. Voluntary and involuntary, sections of the legal code relating to, forms of appropriate and inappropriate . . . She paused there and looked at the appropriate wording for resigning one's commission while in command of a ship, while in command of a flotilla, while between commands, while on leave, while suffering an incurable mental or physical condition precluding further duty . . . That's me, Ky thought. Suffering from an incurable tendency to trust people in trouble and help lame dogs.

She turned to the keyboard—she didn't trust her voice to use the speech-activated system—and copied in the phrasing. "I, [name], hereby resign my [cadetship/commission] for reasons of [reason.]" "I, Kylara

Evangeline Dominique Vatta, hereby resign my cadetship for reasons of overwhelming stupidity and weak sentimentality." No, that wouldn't do. "For reasons of totally unfair blame for something I didn't do." That wouldn't do either. "For reasons of a mental illness called gullibility?" "Softheartedness?" No.

Tears blurred her vision suddenly; she blinked them back. Memory stirred, bringing her Mandy Rocher's image as he sat, shoulders hunched, hands trembling a little, telling her that he had to find a chaplain, he really did. Had his hands trembled with secret laughter that she was so easy to fool? Had he looked down to hide the scorn in his eyes? He was such a little . . . little . . . she searched her vocabulary for a sufficiently descriptive phrase. Insignificant. Forgettable. Boring. Pitiful. Nonentity. And to lose her cadetship because of *him*!

She would get him someday. Vengeance, said her grandmother, was an unworthy goal, but this was a special case. Surely this was a special case.

"I, Kylara Evangeline Dominique Vatta, hereby resign from the Academy for reasons that reflect on my ability to carry out the duties of a naval officer."

Close. Not quite yet.

She looked around the room, squinting to bring the titles of the old books into focus. Herren and Herren's *Chronicles of the Dispersion*, all ten volumes. Her family owned III through X, but I and II were very rare indeed in paper form. Cantabria's *Principles of Space Warfare*, evidently a first edition. She longed to pull it down and check, but was afraid to. A row bound identically in blue-gray cloth . . . logbooks, the old-fashioned kind. Those would be centuries and centuries old; she got up and looked at the names on the spines. *Darius II, Paleologus, Sargon, Ataturk* . . . she felt the gooseflesh come up on her arms, and looked quickly at the last, least-faded volume. *Centaurus*. Not in fact centuries old, not even one century: these were logs that the Commandant had kept, his personal logs from every ship on which he'd served. She'd once memorized the sequence on a dare. Her fingers twitched. What had he thought, felt, done as a young man on his first ship?

She would never know. She had no right to know. The adventures she had hoped to write into such logs herself would never come her way now. She made herself step away from that shelf and look at another. History here, biography there, reference works on all the neighboring states, on the biota of First Colony, on the ecology of water gardens . . . Water gardens? The Commandant studied water gardens?

A sound outside in the passage startled her and sent her back to the table, but the footsteps passed by. She stared at the screen again. "For reasons of . . ." Back to the hand reader. Alternate phrasing: "due to." Clumsy.

Never say more than you need, her father had said; her mother had muttered that Kylara always said more than she needed.

She'd stop that right now.

"I, Kylara Evangeline Dominique Vatta, hereby resign from the Academy for personal reasons." Short and . . . not sweet. Nothing about this was sweet.

She stared at the screen a long time, glaring at the tiny blue words on the gray screen. Then she moved the paper over and copied the words very carefully, in her best script, the handwriting of a properly-brought-up child and good student.

Panic gripped her when she had signed it. She did not want to do this. She could not do this. She must do this. She looked at the time, 10:22:38. Had destroying her life really taken so little time?

A tap on the door, then it opened. MacRobert again, this time with a large silver tray. A teapot, incongruously splotched with big pink roses. A pair of matching cups, gold-rimmed, on saucers. A small plate of lemon cookies, and another of tiny, precisely cut sandwiches.

"The Commandant will be joining you," MacRobert said. He set the tray on the end of the library table, picked up her resignation, and walked out with it. Ky sat immobile, staring at the steam rising from the teapot's spout, trying not to smell the fragrance of cookies obviously fresh from the oven, trying not to think or feel anything at all.

The Commandant's entrance brought her upright, to attention; he waved her back down. "You've resigned, sit down." He sighed. His left eyelid was back up where it should be, but his whole face sagged. "Pour out, will you?"

Ky carried out the familiar ritual, something she didn't have to think about, and handed him his cup of tea. He waited, and nodded at her. She poured one for herself. It was good tea; it would be, she thought. He took a sandwich and gave her a look; she took one, too.

He ate his sandwich in one bite, and sipped his tea. "It's a shame, really," he said. "Here I had a perfectly good excuse to remove your internal organs and hang them from the towers, make an example of you . . . It's my job, and I'm supposed to relish it, or why did I ask for it? But you were a good cadet, Mistress Vatta, and I know you intended to be a good officer."

Then why did you make me resign? That was a question she must never ask; she knew that much.

"In consideration of your past performance, and on my own responsibility, I've chosen to let you keep your insignia and wear it as you depart; I trust your sense of honor not to wear it again."

"No, sir," she said. The bite of sandwich she had taken stuck in her throat. She had not even considered that he might demand their removal. The class ring on her finger—Hal's ring, as he wore hers—suddenly weighed twice as much.

"It's hard for you to believe now, I'm sure, but you will survive this. You have many talents, and you will find a use for them . . ." He took a long swallow of his tea, and actually smiled at her. "Thank you for not making this harder than it had to be. Your resignation was . . . masterful."

The sandwich bite went down, a miserable lump. She wasn't hungry; she couldn't be hungry. She ate the rest of the sandwich out of pure social duty.

"I understand you've arranged transport for noon?" he asked.

"Yes, sir."

"You don't have to say *sir*, Ca—Mistress Vatta."

"I can't help it," Ky said. Tears stung her eyes; she looked away.

"Well, then. I would advise that you go out at 1130, while classes are in session. MacRobert will remain with you until your transport arrives, to deal with any . . . mmm . . . problems that may come up. Since the story broke on the early news, the media have been camped at our gates; it'll be days before that dies down."

For a moment she had been furious—had he thought she'd do something wrong?—but the mention of media steadied her. Of course they would be trying to get in, trying to interview cadets. Of course the daughter of the Vatta family would interest them, even if Mandy hadn't mentioned her, and someone would be bound to have a face-recognition subroutine that would pop out her name.

"And there's another thing." She had to look at him again, had to see the expression of mingled annoyance and pity that was worse than anything he might have said directly. "The Bureau demands—I realize this isn't necessary—a statement that you will consider all this confidential and not communicate with the media."

As if she would. As if—but she took the paper he handed her and scrawled her name on it in a rough parody of her usual careful handwriting.

"You have almost an hour," the Commandant said. "MacRobert will fetch you when it's time." He drained his cup and picked up one of the lemon cookies. "And—if you'll take advice—drink the rest of that tea, and eat those sandwiches. Shock uses up energy." He rose, nodded to her, and went out, shutting the door softly behind him.

To her shame, Ky burst into tears. She snatched the tea towel off the tray and buried her face in it. She could always claim she'd spilled the tea; she wasn't a cadet; she didn't have to tell the strict truth. Five hard sobs, and it was over, for now. She wiped her face, spread the tea towel out again, and set everything back on the tray in perfect order. No—her cup was almost full. She drank the tea. She ate another sandwich. Disgusting body, to want tea and food at such a time.

The silent room eased her, made calm possible. She got up and paced the circuit, looking at the titles again. Then she took down the logbook labeled *Darius II* on the back. Just this once—and what could they do to her if they disapproved?

When MacRobert came for her at 1127, she was deep into the logbook, and calm again.

Outside, the weather had changed, as if her fortune changed it, from early morning's sunshine and puffy clouds to a dank, miserable cold rain with a gusty wind. Her luggage made a pile in the relative safety of the gateway arch; she stood in the shelter of the sentry's alcove, where she could just see the street beyond, and the gaggle of reporters on the far side. She was still in cadet blue; the sentry ignored her, and MacRobert checked off her bags on a list before turning to her.

"They'll be near on time?" he asked.

"I expect so," Ky said. The lump in her throat was growing now; she had to swallow before she could speak.

"Good. We'll have to frustrate the mob over there . . ." He cocked his head. "You're not half-bad, Vatta. Sorry you stepped in it. Don't forget us." His voice seemed to carry some message she couldn't quite understand.

"I won't," she said. How could he even suggest she might forget this? Her skin felt scorched with shame.

"Don't be angrier than you have to be."

"I'm not." She might be later, but now . . . anger was only beginning to seep toward the surface, through the shock and pain.

"Good. You still have friends here, though at the moment there's a necessary distance—" He looked at the clock. 1154. "Excuse me for a few moments. I'll be back at 1200 sharp."

Ky wondered what he was up to, but not for long. The chill dank air, the gusts of wind, all brought back to her the enormity of her fall from grace. She was going to have to go out there, in the cold rain, and pick up those bags and put them in the vehicle in front of everyone in the universe, obviously disgraced and sent away, and be driven home to her parents like any stupid brat who's messed up. Like, for instance, her cousin Stella, who had fallen in love with a musha dealer and given him the family codes. She remembered overhearing some of that, when she was thirteen, and telling herself *she* would never be so stupid, *she* would never disgrace the family the way Stella had.

And now it was on all the news, whatever had actually been said, and it was all her fault.

A huge black car whizzed past the entrance, flags flapping from its front and rear staffs, and she saw the reporters across the way turn, and then rush after it. "The back entrance!" she heard one of them yell. Their support vans squealed into motion, turned quickly across the street, and sped after the black car. She glanced at the clock. 1159. She stepped out of the alcove into the archway and saw a decent middle-aged dark blue car swerving over to stop at the archway. Twelve hundred on the dot. Two men—the driver and escort—got out of the car.

"I'll help with these." MacRobert was back, and already had two of her bags in hand. "Vatta, you get in the car. Jim, get her trunk," he said to the sentry. In moments, Ky was in the backseat, her luggage stowed in the trunk or beside her, and the two men were back in the car.

"Take care, Vatta," MacRobert said. "And remember what I said; you have friends here . . ."

At the last moment, she stripped off the class ring and handed it to him. "You'll know where this should go," she said. She couldn't keep it; she could only hope that MacRobert would get it back to him discreetly, that Hal would understand.

The car moved off, sedately, rejoining the traffic stream, and turning at the first corner; Ky glanced to the right and saw a crowd of news vans partway down that block. What, she wondered, did MacRobert want her to remember? That he was kind as well as brusque? Or how stupid she'd been?

The Vatta employees in the front seat didn't talk on the way to their first stop, the warehouse office at 56 Missalonghi. There, the escort got out and her uncle Stavros climbed into the backseat with her.

"Kylara, my dear . . . are you all right?"

"I'm . . ." She did not want to come apart in front of Uncle Stavros, father of the notorious Stella. "I'm fine." A lie, and they both knew it, but the right thing to say.

"We're going over to the airfield—" That would be the private airfield, of course. "You'll be on a flight to Corleigh; your parents had to run over there to take care of some business a week ago."

Ky put her mind back to work: Corleigh. Tik plantations. Source of both wealth and problems, because the labor force knew all too well what tik extract brought on the interstellar market, and felt they weren't getting enough of the profits. "Pickers or packers?" she asked.

Her uncle nodded approvingly. "Packers. The pickers got a new contract last year, and the packers insist they add more value and need another two percent on top of the five percent increase year before last."

She hadn't seen the sales figures for tik extract since the holiday before last. "So . . . what's the quote running?"

"Thirty-eight two seven—down a hundredth from last year; Devann's come into production, though we judge their product only third-rate. I think the market'll be back up, but we'll see."

Ky knew her uncle had brought this up mostly to distract her, but it did make the journey easier. "What's their production base?"

"Twenty thousand hectares, five thousand in eight-year-olds, five each in seven, six, and four. Rumor has it they lost their entire planting five years ago, and all the surviving trees lost a year's maturity. Soil's good, climate's marginal."

"Labor force?"

"Well, now, that's more of a problem for them than they want to admit, and that's where their quality falls off. They recruited from the immigrant lists, and none of 'em are experienced. Most of the ag-credentialed immigrants are row croppers who know nothing about trees. What I hear from the market is that their pickers are damaging the fruit, and the packers aren't tossing the damaged stuff. It's been a year longer than they planned, after all, getting any income off the place at all, so they're trying to make it up."

Ky glanced out the window as the car swerved; they were nearing the private airfield now, and a truck with the blue and red Vatta Transport insignia had slowed for the turn into the cargo bays. Their car sped on to the passenger entrance, paused at the check station for their driver to flash the scans, then followed the service road past the elegant little charter terminal with its tropical garden and colonnade, for those departing or arriving on chartered flights, and on around past the private terminals to the Vatta Transport complex, all in blue with red trim. Sitting out on the apron was the sleek little twin-engine craft in which Kylara had flown from island to island most of her life.

"You can't pilot yourself today, Ky," her uncle said, as the car slowed. "Under the circumstances—"

Her vision blurred. She knew she wasn't safe to pilot anything, not like this, but—

"It's Gaspard; you remember him." She did; Gaspard Ritnour had been her first flying instructor, though the family wasn't supposed to know that. "Let's get you aboard." Kylara moved quickly from the car to the aircraft. Automatically she put her feet in the right places on the step and wing, and started to slide into the copilot's seat.

"You'd better ride in the passenger compartment," her uncle said.

Ky felt herself flushing. "I won't try to grab the controls," she said.

"It's not that, Ky," her uncle said. "Gaspard—explain it to her; if she's going to ride up front you'll have to take steps. I need to get back—"

Ky buckled in and one of the ground crew slammed the door.

CHAPTER
TWO

Ky said nothing as Gaspard finished preflight; he didn't explain what her uncle had meant. She sat quietly, waiting. One thing she'd learned at the Academy was how to wait without fidgeting. She did not even put on the copilot's headset.

Gaspard murmured into his own voice pickup—contacting traffic control, she assumed. Then he turned to her.

"Put your headset on," he said.

"Why?" Ky asked.

"You're visible up here." It took her a moment to figure out what he meant. Anyone looking in—with a long lens for instance—could see her, whereas back in the passenger compartment the smaller windows had little shades.

"Damn," Ky said, snatching the headset. It wouldn't be enough, she knew. She shrugged out of her uniform jacket and tossed it onto the seat behind; Gaspard pointed behind her. A Vatta crew flight jacket, matching Gaspard's, hung there. She pulled it on quickly, then twisted to see if she could shut the window shades back in the passenger compartment . . . but someone had already done that.

"They'll assume a regular flight crew," Gaspard said. "Unless you're sitting there in cadet blue . . . with insignia . . ." Ky fumbled at her blouse collar; she'd forgotten the collar insignia, which a long lens might be able to catch. They were embroidered; she would have to turn the collar under. She did that while he signaled the ground crew, and let the plane roll forward slowly.

"Better," Gaspard said.

Would the headset obscure enough of her face, though? She swung the voicelink up as far as possible. They were out from between the Vatta hangars, onto the taxiway. A single-engine yellow plane swung onto the taxiway in front of them. Ky looked down at the familiar checklist. If she was to be the copilot . . . this is what she would be doing.

They moved on. As they passed the little terminal parking lot, Gaspard said, "Do something that looks good."

Immediately, Ky pulled up the manual checklist and reached overhead as if going through a final preflight.

"What I love about flying with you, Ky, is that you always react the right way," Gaspard said. Ky looked at him, surprised; the grin he was aiming down the centerline of the taxiway looked genuine. "That couldn't have looked more natural if you'd rehearsed it for days. I spotted a fire truck in the wrong place. Now . . . we're going to be really exposed during takeoff and for the first hour. Since you're already up here, and I entered for two crew just in case, you'll have to stay here." He paused. "I know your uncle said no flying, but someone's got to be traffic watch, and if you can help . . ."

"I can help," Ky said.

"Good. I'll take 'er up, but you stay on the controls with me."

Ky turned up the volume in her headset and heard traffic control give them clearance for takeoff after the little yellow plane. They paused as the yellow plane swung into position; she could see it shudder and then begin its takeoff roll. She checked the boards. This plane had every avionics gadget, and an AI autopilot perfectly capable of handling almost every contingency, but Gaspard preferred to take off and land on manual, to keep his skills current. "And because it's just plain fun," he said now, as he usually did. "There's something atavistic about shoving the throttles forward myself."

She felt the same way, as they turned into position and the power of the engines fought the brakes for a moment before Gaspard released them. She loved it all, from the acceleration down the runway to the moment when they left the ground to the steep climb out over the factory district.

Once they were a half hour offshore, at cruising altitude, Gaspard relaxed and pulled out his hotpak of coffee. "Well, girl, I'm not sure what anthill you kicked—or kicked you—but your father and uncle were certainly upset. Want to tell me about it?"

"I . . . can't. Can't fly and talk about it, anyway."

"Fine. Let me finish this and I'll take it back." He swallowed quickly and relieved Ky at the controls. "Not that I'm pushing you, you understand, but." But he wanted to know. Of course.

"I had to resign from the Academy," Ky said.

He whistled. "Didn't you keep your antifertility implant up to date?"

"Not that! I wouldn't . . . !" She stole a glance at him.

"Sorry," he said. "It's just—what else could make you do it? Your family's not yanking you out for some business reason . . . ?"

"No," Ky said. "I . . . did something stupid. It caused a stink. Such a big stink they wanted me gone."

"You? I can't imagine what big stink you could cause. Now if you were a bonehead like that kid who told a Miznarii priest that he was being treated unfairly and prevented from practicing his religion, and that the service was hostile to Miznarii and had a policy of putting them—how did he say it? first in danger, last in promotion—that is what I'd call a big stink."

Ky's heart sank. "That . . . was my fault."

"Your fault? How? You aren't even . . . oh shit, Ky, you were just helping someone again, weren't you? What'd you do, get him in contact with this Miznarii?"

"Yes." She could hear that her voice was choked with tears.

"Um. I can understand they might be peeved with you—it's headlined in the news—but it's not bad enough to make you resign."

"They think it is."

"They'll wish they hadn't," Gaspard said. "Though it may take them a while. So . . . you're in disgrace, is that it?"

All the misery broke through, and she felt tears burning in her eyes. She couldn't speak.

"Thing is, Ky, disgrace doesn't last forever." She caught the quick movement of his head as he turned to look at her and looked away, out the window, where a blanket of cloud lay between them and the East Shallows.

"It can," Ky said.

"Usually doesn't," Gaspard said. "Whatever stupid things you do, you can do smart ones later."

"Somehow I don't think so," Ky said. "When I try my hardest, that's when I do stupid things."

He looked at her. "It's not my place . . . ," he began.

"Oh, go on, everyone else will lecture me, too."

"I'm not going to lecture you." He looked out the side window, sighed, and engaged the autopilot. "Logged: all boards clear, no traffic reported or scanned. Estimated flight time three hours fifteen minutes."

"We'll be home in time for supper," Ky said. Her throat closed again. It had all happened too fast. She'd awakened as a senior cadet, in the honor squad; she'd eaten breakfast at the head of a table of cadets, in charge of that table, reminding the lowly cads to sit straight on the edge of their chairs and take no sugar in their drinks. She'd eaten that scrap of lunch in the Commandant's library as a disgraced ex-cadet, and tonight she would eat supper in the family dining room, the family disgrace come home to roost.

"You want to talk about it?" Gaspard asked. He was only ten years or so older than she was, she thought. Younger than the Commandant or her father, older than all but one of her brothers.

"You know." Her hands moved as if of themselves. "I tried to help, and it blew up in my face."

"You know this kid well?"

"Mandy? He's—he was—in my diviso. Last year the cad intake officer asked me to take him under my wing. Third-years get handed a cad to baby-sit. Mandy was mine. He had a rough time, being Miznarii, but he did fairly well." The Miznarii considered even implants immoral modifications of the basic human, so those of their children seeking higher education were always at a disadvantage. They attended only those institutions where students had to study without implant assistance, but, as with the Academy, the other students had used them before.

"As well as you did?"

"No, but—" Her voice trailed away. Who would expect a Miznarii from Cobalt Hole to do as well as she had? "Better than expected," she finished.

"So . . . you give the kid a model he can't reach, and he asks you to do him a favor, and then he backstabs you. Think he did this just to cross you?"

She hadn't considered one way or the other. What did Mandy's intention matter? It was betrayal even if not intended.

"I think . . . I think he meant to get the Academy in trouble."

"More than you?"

"Yes." As she thought about it, more than that, even. "I think he wanted to get the whole system in trouble. The War Department, the Academy, the military, maybe even Slotter Key."

"Yeah. And you were collateral damage, maybe."

"Probably." It hurt, even so. She had thought Mandy appreciated what she'd done for him, all the hours spent tutoring and rehearsing.

"He want to sleep with you?"

Ky felt the wave of heat up her neck. "If he did, it would have been unpro—wrong of me—to have noticed."

"If? You honestly don't know?"

She knew, all right. She knew perfectly well why Cad Mandy Rocher had pulled off his overrobe slowly, stretching, before the underclass wrestling matches. She knew he'd wanted her. No word had been spoken. No word need be.

Gaspard nodded as if she'd answered aloud. "So he lusted after you and you repulsed him."

"I didn't repulse him!" Ky said. "I just didn't encourage him." He could stretch all he wanted and it did nothing for her; she had Hal in her mind's eye and there was no comparison.

"Dirty little scum," Gaspard said. Ky glanced at his face; he looked like someone about to be very angry.

"I'm sorry," Ky said.

"Not your fault," Gaspard said. "You're a good girl, Ky; you always have been. Taken advantage of, and thank all the gods you don't believe in it went no farther. You're well out of that."

"I thought you thought I would be a good officer . . ."

"I did. You would have been. But a waste, in a way." He grinned at her. "Never mind. Just think of them all, in their stiff scratchy uniforms, while we're flying down to the sunny isles of delight. Out of that nasty cold—"

"I like the cold," Ky said. She did not want to think of Hal, who might be storming up the stairs to the Commandant's office to find out where she was at this very moment . . .

"That's not what you've said other leaves."

"No, but—all right. Yo ho for the tropics." Her laugh sounded hollow, and he shook his head at her.

"I know it seems like the end of the world to you—that's because you are a good'un and you care. But life goes on, Ky, and you'll get over this. You don't want to hear it but it's true, just like you didn't want to hear that there were things you couldn't do with an airplane . . . but that was also true."

"All right, all right." She stared out at the blanket of cloud. Ahead, it frayed into puffs more and more isolated . . . and as they flew nearer that edge, the blue sea showed below. There to starboard, the distinctive hook shape of Main Gumbo, from this altitude a flat outline of white surf filled in with dark vegetation. She looked sunward . . . the wakes of ships showed clearly as darker ripples against the even pattern. In the passage between Main and Little Gumbo, a tanker surrounded by its attendants. Crawdad, beyond Little Gumbo, was a many-legged dark blot.

An hour later, the dark blue lightened as they neared the Necklace Reefs. From cobalt through every shade of turquoise, as the water grew more shallow, until at last the ragged brown tops of the reefs broke through white surf.

Corleigh showed at last: a dark line that thickened, surrounded by shallower water that looked, from this height, like bands of blue and turquoise, each shade defining a depth. They flew over the main harbor, with its guardian headlands rising sharply from the water; surf broke white on the rocks. Ky counted two cargo ships, the interisland ferry, and a thick cluster of small craft before they were past the harbor and over the warehouses of the harbor district. Beyond those, the neat little town, with its central park, a green square with the spire of the War Memorial glinting in the sun. Corleigh's small commercial airfield had a scatter of small craft parked in a row; Ky knew that the daily Island Air service would be two hours behind them.

Inland, Harbor Valley sloped gently toward the central ridge; Gaspard banked left and Kylara looked down on the vast tik plantations between the coastal cliffs and the higher ridge with its mixed scrub. Not a monoculture: these were old plantations, interplanted with secondary and tertiary crops in a careful balance to maximize both production and resilience.

On the far side of the ridge, she knew, were the newer plantings. She had imagined bringing Hal to meet her family, on graduation leave; he was a mainlander and had never seen the far islands. She would have been explaining it to him, the order of the plantings, the yields of the different ages . . . She pushed that thought back.

Ahead, the island narrowed and the central ridge sloped abruptly down to end in a rumple of lower hills; she could see the outer reef's ruffle of surf beyond them. Taller trees, the sheltering groves of the Vatta household, cloaked the landward side of the hills. Gaspard called the Vatta home field as he eased their plane down, neatly countering the predictable gusts that swept between the twin hills. Ky felt her throat close. She had been able to let her mind drift, while in the air, but soon she would have to face her family.

She stared out the window, noting that the jabla trees were in bloom, pink fluffy puffs among the darker green of the haricond and jupal. The red tile roofs of the house and outbuildings showed among the green, with a sudden flash of light from the big pool. Nearer to the runway were the office buildings, utilitarian cream blocks topped with solar panels, but neat, with a ruffle of red and blue flowers on either side of the main door.

"Give us a hand, Ky," Gaspard said. Ky yanked her attention back to the instruments, and called out items on the checklist as Gaspard made the final approach. Then they were down, and rolling. Ky turned her collar right side out, and reached back for her uniform jacket. She was not going to come home disheveled and disorganized. By the time Gaspard had taxied to the parking line, where old George waited to hook up the tie-downs, she was ready to pass—well, not any official inspection, but any of the staff.

"Good to see you home," George said. "You didn't belong with the likes of them slimes anyway."

Ky knew it would do no good to tell him they weren't slimes. George, veteran of the Second War, loathed mainlanders. He had refused regen treatment for his leg because it would have meant a mainland hospital.

"I'll take your bags," George said now. "Your dad wants to see you right away." He moved stiffly to the luggage compartment.

Ky turned to the office building. No one was coming out to meet her—normal. Were they going to pretend all this was normal? The sea breeze, moist and fragrant, lay its hand on her cheek, and she wanted to yield to it, to be soothed by it, but she was no longer the child who had left here four years ago.

Inside the front door, cooler air swirled around her. She faced a warren of desks and workstations, most occupied by obviously busy people who barely looked up as she entered. On her left, the familiar corridor led to the row of walled offices: her father's, her uncle's, her elder brothers'.

She hesitated a moment outside the door to her father's office, then tapped, and opened the door.

Her father looked up from his desk as she came in. "Kylara, beshi . . . you look like you must feel."

"I'm all right."

"No, you're not. Come here—" He came out from behind his desk and held out his arms. Ky leaned into his embrace. "Shhh, shhhh," he murmured, though she had made no sound. He smelled of the tik plantations he must have walked around that morning, a complex scent she had known forever.

"I didn't know," she said, into his shoulder. "I thought I was helping . . ."

His shoulder twitched. "Do you remember your fifth birthday party?"

How could she ever forget when they kept bringing that up? She had pushed Mina Patel into the wading pool, and Mina had contrived to fall crooked and cut her head on the one place the rim's padding had worn away, because she'd kept her hair bows on, in spite of Ky's advice to take them off or they'd get wet. And it had been for a good cause, because Mina had been tormenting her little sister Asha, who was afraid of the water, and was about to push her, when Ky shoved Mina. Mina had grabbed at Asha when she overbalanced, so they'd both screamed and Ky had been sent inside, at her own birthday party, to sit in glowering misery in her room while her friends ate her birthday cake and her mother—her own mother—made a fuss over Mina Patel.

"You have to learn to think first, Kylara," her father said now, his hands on her shoulders pushing her gently back so he could give her That Look.

"I did think," she said. "At least, I thought it was thinking . . ."

"Well . . . I'm sure you meant well," he said. "Now we have to figure out what to do with you—"

She had thought of that, in the last moments before landing. "I could go to the university and finish a degree," she said. "I have almost enough credits—"

"No," he said firmly. "We can't have that. You can't be here; there's too much publicity."

"I could go to Darien Tech, over on Secci . . ."

"No. It's out of the question. I've already decided—" He paused as someone tapped on the office door. "Who is it?"

"Me." Ky's older brother Sanish opened the door and put his head in. "Are you busy—oh, Ky. You're here."

As if he didn't know. As if they didn't all know. As if he hadn't come to gloat, in a big-brotherish way.

"Come on in, San. I was just telling Kylara what we came up with."

"You were in on this?" Ky asked. She could feel her neck getting hot.

"All I did was look up figures," San said, spreading his hands. "Don't blame me."

"We weren't going to tell you until after supper," her father said. "But since you are here a little early . . . and after all, your mother wants her time with you . . ."

Her heart sank. While she'd been sitting, bored and miserable, in the plane on the flight out, they'd had time to plot out her whole life, probably. Just like when she was thirteen, and they'd decided that a trip in space as an apprentice on a Vatta freighter would get that nonsense about the military out of her head.

"We think it's clever," her father said, with a glance at San that told Ky exactly who he thought was the clever one of the family. Not her, of course. "You'll have a chance to prove yourself, and you'll be well out of the way."

Out of the way. Like a naughty child. She was not going to cry. "Well, what is your marvelous idea?" she asked in a voice that even she could hear sounded sulky.

"We're sending you out to the Rift with a ship going to salvage," her father said. "You'll have a cargo on the way out, sell the ship, then come back commercial. Altogether it should take at least eleven months, and by then things will surely have died down."

Ky glared at her father and older brother. "You'd think I'd blown up a ship," she said.

"Don't be overdramatic, Ky," her father said. "No one's accused you of anything like that. We're trusting you to do family business. It's an honor—"

"No. You're sticking me in a corner. Hiding me—"

"We could do that well enough by giving you a job in inventory control right here at the tik plantations. Be reasonable, Ky."

"But—I'll be gone months and months—maybe years. And it's boring—"

"The heat will be off you by then, and it may not be boring. You'll be heading out into the Borderlands."

"Maybe." Ky glared, but she already knew she would take the job. What other choice did she have? "I guess it's all right."

"Good. You're taking the *Glennys Jones* to Lastway. We'll send you some help. Gary Tobai for loadmaster, Quincy Robin as crew chief."

"Dad, they're *old*."

"They're experienced. You need that. New captains—"

"Captain! You're making me captain?"

"Were you listening? I offered you the ship."

"I thought you meant as shipping agent or something. I don't really know how to captain—"

"You have a license."

"I have a license, yes, but I haven't done it. I haven't worked on a commercial ship since *Tugboat* . . . er, *Turbot*."

"That's why we're sending along someone with experience. You'll do fine, Ky. All you have to do is be guided by Gary and Quince."

All she had to do was listen to her elders by the hour. But a ship—even an old wreck like *Glennys Jones*, and a captain's listing—made up for a lot. "All right . . . thanks, Dad."

"That's better. Now, go over to the house. Your mother's waiting. Oh, and we've scheduled your implant replacement."

She knew better than to suggest a quick comcall instead, but she dreaded what her mother would say.

Sure enough, she had scarcely come through the door when her mother started in. "Kylara, how could you? You were just getting to know that nice Berlioz boy, and now—"

"Mother, I didn't—"

"And look at you! You haven't a bit of makeup on! How can you expect to find a young man if you go around looking like some tough off the docks?"

"Mother, please—"

"And your father says you're going away for months, and I've had no time at all to take you around . . . If you're out of circulation too long, you know, people will forget about you—"

"That's the idea," Ky said. Though if Charley Berlioz forgot about her that was all to the good. Despite her mother's prodding, she had no interest in Charley. It was Hal . . . except now it wasn't, almost certainly.

"Well, it's all very well on the political side, but on the matrimonial side, it's a disaster. They'll go and marry unsuitable girls, rather than you, and Slotter Key is not exactly full of eligible boys."

"Mother, I'm sure that eventually—" At least her mother was still harping on marriage into some civilian family; at least she hadn't caught on about Hal, whom she would not have considered suitable.

"Well, we have to do something about your clothes." Her mother started off down the hall; Ky trailed behind, feeling the same reluctance she had so often before. She knew what spacers wore, and what ship captains wore, and she knew, without waiting for her mother to say so, that those simple outfits were not what her mother had in mind.

"Even if you are in the wilds of the Borderlands," her mother said, opening Ky's closet. Ky could see that someone had already unpacked her luggage and put things away. "Even there, you must be prepared to present yourself properly. Perhaps even especially there."

When her mother was in one of these moods, it was easy to forget she was also a professional engineer of considerable reputation. It was the family background, Ky thought: being the eldest daughter of a socialite—for Grandmother Benton was still making news in the gossip columns with her endless string of admirers.

"Not this. Not this either," her mother said, flinging clothes to one side. "I know you thought you'd spend the rest of your life in uniform, dear, but surely you had more sense than this—" She held out an outfit in rust and green which, Ky had realized only after paying for it, made her look like someone a day away from death.

"Sorry, Mother," she said.

"I don't care what your father says, you simply must get some suitable clothes." She eyed Ky up and down. "You aren't shaped like anyone else in the family, worse luck. I can't just tell you to put some meat on your bones. You have meat; it's just not . . ."

"Mother!"

"Oh, be reasonable, Kylara. You'll be representing the family; you must have clothes and they must fit. I'm not saying you're ugly or misshapen; you're just not . . ." Again her voice trailed away. "Well," she said, after a moment's awkward silence. "Measurements first and then we'll see what we can order. Shops here on Corleigh are useless, but if something can be delivered to the ship before you leave, that will do."

The last thing Ky wanted to do was stand in the middle of the room while her mother ran a clothes scriber over her, but she stood in the middle of the room while her mother ran a clothes scriber over her anyway. Halfway through, with her mother tut-tutting about the way the uniform had concealed what was after all an acceptable shape, it began to be funny. She wasn't ready for it to be funny—for anything to be funny—but a bubble of laughter caught in her throat and she could feel the corners of her mouth turning up. Here she was, back home being measured for clothes yet again, clothes that would, she was sure, turn out to be impractical and uncomfortable.

"What are you laughing at?" her mother asked, from knee level, without looking up. Her mother always knew, without having to see Ky's face, when the ill-timed laugh demon caught her in the throat.

"Nothing," Ky said, sulky again.

"It's not funny," her mother said, scribing her lower legs, her ankles, her feet.

It was, though. Everything else in the universe was horrible, but this one thing was funny.

The dinner chime saved her from unseemly giggles; her mother stood abruptly. "You'll want to get out of that," she said, without specifying what that was. They both knew.

Ky took off the uniform she had been so proud to put on that morning, stepped into the 'fresher briefly, and put on loose slacks, blouse, and overrobe for dinner. She left the remnants of her past on the bed. Someone would take them away, clean them, fold them, put them somewhere . . . She didn't care where.

Dinner on the wide veranda . . . Father, Mother, and Sanish. Ky slid into her usual seat, facing the garden. Candles flickered in the evening air. Someone had gone to the trouble of preparing a festive meal—they had had, she realized, the hours she was in the air to put it together. The haunch of 'lope, boned, stuffed, and rolled, in a pastry crust. The stuffed grape leaves. The "tower of heaven" salad. Once again her body surprised her with its insistence on refueling; she ate ravenously but barely touched the wine.

Her father and San talked of island politics—not the labor dispute, but such things as the proposed new desalinization plant, the possibility of a branch of the central university on the island, the state of the waste recycling facility at Harbor Town. Ky listened as if to a debate on the vid; it all felt unreal. Too many changes too fast.

"We have to have enough time to get her some clothes," her mother said suddenly. Her father and San stopped in the midst of telling each other what an idiot Councilman Kruper was.

"How long?" her father asked.

"I can get clothes offworld," Ky said.

"No," both her parents said. Her father sighed.

"Ky, you're going to be a Vatta captain; you will represent Vatta Transport. You have to start out with something suitable. But Myris"—he turned to his wife—"it has to be quick. Three days."

"Impossible," her mother said. "We don't have a fabricator here; we'll have to go to Harbor Town and that's—"

"Less than an hour by plane. *Glennys* would have left tomorrow, but I put a hold on her. We can't delay; we have delivery commitments."

Delivery commitments were, her father had once said, a natural force. Vatta Transport's default rate on delivery commitments was the lowest in the industry and one reason for their wealth.

"Five," her mother said.

"Four. Absolutely no more. And she doesn't need much. Captain's uniforms, shipboard and port. Not much more than that."

"Kylara, we'll start ordering after dinner," her mother said. "Bond Tailoring will have to do. I'd much rather you used Siegelson & Bray, but they can't possibly do it in less than a week . . ." Her mother glared at her father.

"Four days," her father said. "You have the measurements; you can start without her. Tonight, Ky, we'll go by the clinic and get your implant in—that'll let you sleep on it so you'll be in cycle in the morning. All loaded with the current codes and everything."

She had not had an implant since she left for the Academy—cadets weren't allowed them. She was used to doing without, though she had missed her implant a lot that first year at the Academy. She was not sure she wanted one again. But she needed the extra capacity, with all she had to learn in a hurry. She shrugged. Better an implant insertion than more talk about clothes. "I'm ready," she said.

Insertion went easily; the implant access port still met all the specs, so all she needed was the device itself. She expected the moment of nauseating disorientation, the strange visual auras, the itch in her nose. Before she could access the implant, she had to go through the initialization protocols—the longest part of an insertion—and then the implant unfolded in her mind like a flower, each petal a gateway to another database. The displays flickered past, the communications links—now activated only for the clinic units—let her answer the questions without speaking aloud.

"Checks out," the medic said finally. "Any problems at your end?"

Ky blinked at him. They both knew—because she was sending it—that she was seeing him with a vibrating pink halo, and they also knew this was a transient visual phenomenon common to implant insertions, like the other sensory auras she was having—the smell of freshly ground pepper, the echo effect to all sounds. It would be gone after a good night's sleep, during which time the implant and her biological brain would have some kind of serious discussion without her consciousness around to kibitz. "No problems," Ky said, aloud this time.

"Good. Call me at once if you experience sensory auras tomorrow, or any difficulties with coordination, balance, after one hour from now. My recommendation is that you go to sleep as soon as you can."

"I will," Ky said. Her father took her back to the main house, where she staggered only a couple of times going down the hall to her room. She remembered her first insertion experience very clearly; she had been seven, getting a child's school expansion kit, and she had insisted that her balance wasn't affected, she didn't need to lie down and take a nap . . . all the way to the ground when she fell off the pony. I'm fine, she'd said, lying on the ground and looking up at a pony hazed in a supernatural golden glow, its wings waving gently in the breeze. My pony has wings, she'd said. No one had believed her. She'd woken from that nap with a bruise on her rump and her brothers prancing around the room waving their arms, pretending to be flying ponies.

Enhanced memory was one side effect of implants and their insertion. She pulled off her clothes, put on a gown, turned off the light, and lay down.

She had been sure she wouldn't sleep, but the moment her head hit the pillow, she was out. She woke, remembering no dreams, at first disoriented because sunlight played on the opposite wall from the garden window in her room—and she expected instead the cold dim light of a winter dawn in the capital. Misery hit her again, and she rolled over, burying her face in the pillow. Her career. Her hopes. Her friends. Hal . . . he wouldn't even know what happened. She hadn't actually started crying when something landed with a thump on her back.

"Rise and shine, lazybones," came her brother's voice. "You've got to hit the books."

Ky rolled out of bed, threw the offending roll of towels back at her brother—wet, he must have just come in from swimming—and stalked into the 'fresher with as much dignity as possible. Her implant offered the time, the temperature, the humidity, water temperature of the 'fresher, her own pulse and respiration if she wanted it. She didn't. She ate a hasty breakfast in a corner of the kitchen, and then settled down to the pile of data cubes her father had left for her to read. Everything there was to know about *Glennys Jones*, about the route she was to take, everything she needed to know about the Vatta Transport codes. At intervals her attention drifted to her disgrace, but she yanked it back to the matter at hand. She could not think about it . . . any of it . . . without going to pieces. If she was to be a cargo ship captain, she had better things to do than feel sorry for herself. The implant fed her accessory information whenever she asked. She was deep in the revised space regulations applicable to licensed carriers Class C and below when her father and brother came home for lunch.

"How's it going?" her father asked.

"These are done," Ky said, pointing to that stack. "I'm into space regs. Why on earth did they restrict Class Bs from carrying nutrient components? Seems to me that's what they're ideally suited for."

"Politics," San said. "But I'm not supposed to say that."

Her father gave San a look. "P & L," he said. "They've moved into nutrient component production, over on Chelsea. They transport the stuff very efficiently in purpose-built Class Ds; they're just protecting their investment."

"Closing out competitors, both producers and shippers," San said.

"San."

"They're our competitors; I don't see why we can't be plainspoken at least at home," San said.

"They're also our friends. You might have married the girl—"

"Not me," San said.

Ky watched this interchange with interest. San arguing with her father? That was new.

"Lunch," her father said firmly, leading the way to the veranda. At midday, it was shady, breezy, scented with roses and jasmine. Her mother didn't appear. She often skipped lunch with the family. Ky wasn't hungry—she'd done nothing all morning but read—but she picked at a salad. Her father frowned at her. "You should get out a little, Ky. If you don't eat, your mother will pester me."

"I need to finish these," Ky said.

"Not today. I didn't think you'd be half so far along. Take the afternoon off."

Two hours later, Ky lay stretched on a towel by the pool. An hour's swim had worked out kinks she hadn't realized she had, and now she dozed in the warm shade. Her father had been right. She had needed the break.

"Kylara Vatta, what do you think you're doing?" That voice, harsh as a parrot's cry, nearly sent her rolling into the pool in a defensive maneuver. Aunt Gracie Lane. Aunt Gracie Lane, who disapproved of idleness at any time, and also had strong views on appropriate bathing costume. "Anyone could see you!"

Anyone who was a member of the family, or a guest. Possibly a lascivious gardener peeking over the wall of the pool enclosure, but certainly no one else.

"I'm resting after swimming, Aunt Gracie," Ky said.

"You're lazing about doing nothing useful," Aunt Gracie said. "Get some proper clothes on and get busy. You're supposed to be helping your mother arrange your wardrobe."

Her mother, just coming to the pool behind Aunt Gracie, shrugged.

"Yes, Aunt Gracie," Ky said, scrambling to her knees with the towel clutched to her.

"I would have thought the Academy would teach you some discipline, but clearly . . . I suppose that's why you quit."

Too many things wrong with that to argue. Ky held the towel between her and Aunt Gracie's disapproval, and sidled around, pricking herself on one of the gardenia bushes, to back gingerly toward the house. The moment Aunt Gracie transferred her gaze to something else, she whipped the towel all the way around her and scuttled for the veranda. Some things never changed.

Clad in slacks and shirt, she emerged from her room to hear Aunt Gracie's voice down the hall. "—do something about that girl, Myris, you'll be sorry! I can't believe you and Gerard are actually letting her go off alone, unsupervised—"

Ky thought of running away, sneaking out through her window, but Aunt Gracie would certainly have something to say about that, too. It was going to be a very long four days. Three point three eight, her implant said.

CHAPTER
THREE

Most of the ordering could be done remotely. The next day Ky flew the single-seat herself to Harbor Town where Bond Tailoring's senior fitter checked her mother's measurements and admitted that they'd been correct. Ky picked out ship boots, dock boots, formal and informal shoes for nonbusiness wear. Despite her mother's complaints about her shape, she was close enough to stock measurements that only slight alterations would fit her for most things. The captain's tunic, however, had to be custom-made.

"Still, that cuts a day off our estimate," the fitter said. "Only four items. We'll have them tomorrow evening."

"What time?"

"Oh, you should plan on picking them up the next day," the fitter said. "Just in case."

Ky left the shop with her footwear, stopped by Amerson's for some personal items her mother didn't need to know about. If she was going to be off on her own alone, and not under military discipline, she could choose the lotions and scents *she* preferred, ignoring her mother's ideas of appropriateness. Her crew would just have to put up with it. Then she walked back up the street to catch the shuttle to the airport. She was back home by lunch . . . or rather, back at the home airfield. She stopped by the office to tell her father when the clothes would be ready.

"Gracie's on the warpath about you," her father said.

"I know."

"You might want to do your bookwork here today," he said. He didn't quite twinkle at her, but there was an edge of humor in his voice.

"Thank you," she said. "Where's an empty workstation?"

"San's off checking yield in the young plantations; you can use his office. Don't answer the phone."

Ky dumped her shoes and boots in the corner of San's office, and pulled up more of the data she needed on his station. Facts flowed into her mind: the history of the *Glennys Jones*, details of her last trip through maintenance, background information on the crew, details of the contract. She hardly moved until her father opened the door to tell her it was time for dinner.

"I'm not sure what Gracie's got in mind for you, Kylara, but you probably should come back here tomorrow. Or just go out. You won't have a chance to snorkle or ride again for a long time."

"Would that be all right?" Ky asked.

"You've been working hard. I'm sure you can decide how much more work you need to do. Take the day if you feel like it."

Ky dreaded the thought of dinner, but Aunt Gracie, her mother told her, had retired to her room with a headache. Ky thought about a late swim in the pool, but remembered in time that the guest room had a clear view of the pool, and sound carried over water. Instead, she rummaged in her closet and found her snorkling gear, then linked her implant to the home library's marine database for an instant to download whatever she might need.

Early the next morning, she was down at the shore shortly after dawn, squinting into the light to check the buoys supporting the protective nets that kept out the larger marine predators. How long had it been since she had a day to herself, a day free to do whatever she wanted? She couldn't remember—years, anyway. Every brief vacation from the Academy had been filled with duties—courtesy calls on this or that family member, dinners, parties, required shopping trips. Now the day stretched before her, empty as the beach itself.

Little waves slid meekly up onto the sand, leaving interlocking arcs of wet behind them; squirts of water revealed the hiding places of burrowing clams. Ky struggled into her wet suit, clipped on her safety beacon, put on gloves and flippers, and almost fell on her nose when she started toward the water and caught a flipper in the sand.

Once in the water, she moved slowly out to the first of the broad, knobbly coral heads, where she knew she'd find a flurry of brilliantly colored small fish. Her implant gave her the names. A black-tooth undulated into her view; she turned to face it. It retreated to deeper water, then dove into the sandy bottom, fluffing sand over itself. Her implant marked that location; she would be careful not to step on it.

She had set the timer for two hours; when the implant beeped, she stroked back to shallow water, then stood up. She felt heavier; she always hated coming out of the water once she was in. Her father had used that as a metaphor for growing up, leaving the easy support of a family and carrying her own weight, but she resented his lecture. Unless it meant you could drown in your support system, and this day she simply wanted to enjoy the beauty.

She looked again at the lagoon, and thought about the rest of the day. She could saddle a horse and ride out through the plantation, or . . . she could stay here. She queried her implant. Aunt Gracie was on the move. All the horses were in use. Half-annoyed and half-relieved, Ky waded back into the water and let herself rest on its buoyancy. She wasn't hungry, and the suit had its own water supply system. When she tired of the water, she pulled herself back up to the beach, to the shade under the trees, scooped out a hollow in the sand, and took a nap. She woke to the turquoise and pink sky of evening, and stared a long time at the colors as they deepened before she turned her back on them to head for the house.

"I made this just for you," Aunt Gracie said at breakfast the morning Ky was leaving. She handed over a gaily decorated sack. Ky almost dropped it when she took it; it must weigh, she thought, five or six kilos.

She looked in. There, swathed in bright-colored flowery wrapping paper, were the unmistakable shapes of three of Aunt Gracie's special fruit-spice cakes. Aunt Gracie beamed at her.

"You'll be gone a long time, and I always say that a taste of home is the best thing to cure homesickness . . ."

Aunt Gracie's fruit-spice cakes were, without doubt, the densest mass of flavorless, tooth-breaking pseudofoodstuff in the galaxy. She produced them at intervals, for birthdays and holidays, and the family disposed of them discreetly as soon as she was out of sight. Even a sliver of Aunt Gracie's product left Ky with a day or so of gastric uneasiness.

"Uh . . . thanks," Ky said. She could always leave them under her bed as insect repellent blocks . . . she'd done that with the ones Aunt Gracie had given her each year to take to the Academy.

"I know how rushed it can be, when people leave on a long assignment," Aunt Gracie went on. "So let's just let Jeannine put them in the car for you right this minute . . ."

San made a sound; Ky looked at him, and his lips were folded tight but his eyes danced mischief.

"Thank you," Ky said again. She handed the sack to the maid and resigned herself to dumping Aunt Gracie's creations into some unsuspecting trash container on the way to her command. She was not going to spend five kilos of her personal baggage allowance on inedible crud.

She finished her juice, and made her escape—not without kissing that withered old cheek—to the car, where her father waited to drive her to the airfield.

"If you're planning to dump it somewhere," he said without reference, "don't do it in sight of anyone who might, by any conceivable means, know anyone who knows us. Your aunt Gracie's connections are legendary. The only reason she doesn't know the whole truth about your resignation is that it's a state secret. But she suspects, and she'll worm it out of someone inside another week, I'm sure. I don't want to have to deal with her if she finds out you've tossed her cakes in the trash; it was bad enough when she found out you'd been leaving them under your bed."

"How did she find that out?" Ky asked.

"Bribed the staff, I shouldn't doubt," her father said sourly. "But look at it this way. Anything is a commodity to someone. In a very large universe, your aunt Gracie's cannonballs may be someone else's favorite underwear."

Ky snorted, surprised into a laugh for the first time since her private disaster.

"Courage, Ky," he said, as he stopped the car and leaned over to give her a kiss. "You've got what you need to start a good life. Go."

Gaspard was waiting on the apron. "You look better," he said, as he looked up from checking the oil. "So, what did the family do for you?"

"I'm taking *Glennys Jones* to the scrapyard," Ky said. She took her duffel from old George and slung it into the baggage compartment. "It will keep me out of the public eye." The boring start to a dull, boring career as a truck driver in space, she did not say. She looped the tie-downs around the two bags, and slammed the door shut, latching it carefully.

"And give you a chance to show your talents," Gaspard said. He went on with the preflight check while she looked around, trying to fill her memory with the home she would not see for months, maybe years. Maybe ever again, space being what it was, and life being less certain than she'd thought the last time she left.

"Well . . . assuming I have any." What talents did it take to captain an experienced crew on a boring one-way run? Now if she could figure out a way to avoid scrapping the ship and surprise the family with a great triumph of trading . . .

"Don't fish, Ky; it doesn't become you."

"Right. And we shall hope I don't exercise my talent for leaping in to help . . ."

"At least not until you're a little more experienced," Gaspard said. "Though you could help me, if you would, by agreeing to copilot on the way in. There's some serious weather between us and the mainland." She had seen the satellite images; a cold front nosing under the warm sea air and lifting clouds to towering heights.

"Of course."

"Good, then. Let's be going. That front's going to toss us around some."

Ky climbed into the copilot's seat, and concentrated on her part of the checklist as they finished preflight and started the engines.

The first hour in the air, retracing her recent flight home, was almost pure sightseeing. The colors of the water, changing with depth, with the shadows of clouds . . . the reefs . . . the various islands. Puffy cumulus clouds arrayed in rows along the wind's path, all white and innocent . . . but ahead, a line of taller clouds, their ramparts denser. Ky had no time to brood, as she helped Gaspard ease the plane through the front's turbulence, and only the navigation instruments could have told where they were.

The city lay under dense clouds spitting cold rain, just as it had been when she left. At least here there was little turbulence, and landing offered no problems. Gaspard turned onto the ramp that led to the private terminal, and then again to reach the Vatta hangars.

"Good job, Ky," he said, when he'd handed her down from the wing.

"You'll be fine with old *Glennys*. Shouldn't wonder if you don't start your own private fleet with her or something."

Ky started. Was she that predictable?

"Have to start somewhere, after all," he said cheerfully, and winked. Then he turned back to the mechanic who had come out to greet him.

Her first task, she thought, was getting rid of Aunt Gracie's cakes. She hadn't asked Gaspard to let her toss them out into the sea—Gaspard might be her friend, but he might also be one of Aunt Gracie's spies. At no point in the route from the airfield to the shuttle field was she alone and in reach of a disposal chute. The five kilos dragged at her arm. She had to carry them herself to have the chance to lose them . . . but a woman in a Vatta Transport captain's uniform carrying a bright flower-patterned bag, obviously heavy, would be noticed and remembered. Blast Aunt Gracie!

Vatta captains, she had been told, did not ride commercial shuttles to orbit. At least not here, where Vatta maintained its own small fleet of surface-to-orbit transport. As a captain, she had her own tiny compartment, outfitted as a workstation, with stowage for her duffel in the same compartment. She remembered her first trip alone to the orbital station, when she'd been thirteen and headed for three months as the lowest of apprentices on *Turbot*. She'd been crammed into crew seating with four other family apprentices (each going to a different ship) and fifteen regular crew, and she'd been stiff, as well as scared, by the time they arrived.

This was much better. She spent the time reviewing crew information, committing faces and names to her implant's perfect memory. At the Vatta orbital station, she debarked ahead of the rest, and caught the first tram outbound for the docks. She had given up on Aunt Gracie's cakes for now; she turned them over to the Vatta handler along with the rest of her luggage. It would reappear in her cabin aboard. All she had in hand was the tidy little captain's case, with its datalinks, command wand, and orders. She tried to sneak up on *Glennys* without being spotted, but Vatta security was far too good for that. She had an escort all the way from the Vatta gates to the boarding platform, and when she got there, Gary Tobai left off polishing the Vatta family seal on the rail and turned to her.

"Well, if it isn't the newest captain in Vatta Fleet." He grinned at her, but Ky thought she detected a bite to his tone. "Mouth got you in trouble again, did it?"

"All I said was . . ." Ky shut her mouth and shook her head at him. "If you know that much, you know I didn't do anything wrong."

"Wrong? No. Wrong way to do something right, maybe. I thought you were supposed to be our white hope with the military."

"I thought so, too. So when I found something that needed to be fixed—"

"You jumped in and fixed it. I understand that, but you could have anticipated it would cause trouble."

"I was trying to avoid trouble." Should she even explain how convoluted the right procedures were, and why she'd chosen to work through contacts the family had given her? No. He wanted to condescend, so he would, no matter what she said.

"You were not bred to avoid trouble," Tobai said. "Your family takes it on, shakes it like a dog shaking a rat, and tosses it to one side." His voice softened. "As you did, Captain."

Captain. He had actually called her *Captain.* She pushed aside the rest of what he'd said. "So, now that I have a ship, what can you tell me about her?"

He scowled. "You haven't looked at the listing?"

Ky closed her eyes and recited. *"Glennys Jones,* three hundred meters overall length, 200 meters beam, keel plate laid in Bramley's yards eighty-seven years ago, refitted in '04 and '38, drives replaced in '43 with expanded cruising range, fully loaded to one hundred seventy-nine days, or two hundred fifteen days empty and crewed. She has two main cargo holds, three auxiliary holds, and no autoloading capability. The largest container that will fit through the main cargo hatch is three meters by two point seven meters, and standard access now is three by four, which limits her pretty much to specialty cargo. She can't take loose bulk cargo like grain, another limitation. She's been used to haul perishables, but on her last trip the refrigerating system broke down, and Vatta had to pay the shipper for the goods as well as a penalty for nondelivery, and insurance didn't cover it all. The company's out seven hundred thousand credits. Repair of the refrigeration system would cost another five hundred thousand, so Ships decided to use her for base-supply runs and sell her for scrap when her inspection ran out."

Ky paused for breath. Tobai had been nodding approval, but when she paused he didn't say anything. She went on. "So now she's due for recertification, but she probably wouldn't pass, and they're shipping her off to Lastway. I know all that, all that's in the listing. What I don't know is what her other peculiarities are. Things not in the list. I'm sure you do, because you've probably crawled all over her with a microscanner."

"You're right about that," Tobai said. "I've shipped on her five times in all, but not in the past seven years, so I had to renew my acquaintance with the lady."

"This old—"

"Now don't say that. It never does for the captain to badmouth the ship. Ships are sensitive."

Ships were metal, ceramic, polymer machines; they had brains of a sort, but no feelings. Ky had been told that the first time she came aboard a ship. But however sensitive the ship wasn't, Gary Tobai was, and she wanted him on her side.

"Sorry," she said. "I didn't mean anything by it."

"Better not to say it at all, then," he said. "Now—what you need to know is that we have to load the starboard main hold first, then the port auxiliary, starboard auxiliary, main port, and the third auxiliary, if we use it, last. We need at least a half point more mass to starboard, or she won't stay in trim. That last engine refit did something screwy to the frame, though no one will admit it. There's also a problem with the attitude jets, but all I have is hearsay. Quince could tell you more about that."

"Dad says they've assembled a cargo for us—are you satisfied with it?"

"All done, including crew trading," Tobai said. "How much are you reserving for crew shares?"

"A scrap run, one-way? What's the usual split?"

"I'd recommend the third auxiliary hold. That's 15 percent of the total. Limit it to luxuries, is what I told them. Retain 4 percent for captain's space, and split the remaining 11 percent by seniority."

"I've already bought in for 10 percent; should I donate the 4 percent?"

"No, crew would wonder what was going on if you didn't claim it. We're going to have trouble enough; your father had to pay a surcharge for a one-way trip since they can't make a profit on the way back. Whether you fill it or not, reserve it. Your dad sent over some; he said you wouldn't have time to deal, but I could add a few things . . ."

"Fine." She could put Aunt Gracie's miserable cakes in there and no one would ever know. "If you come across something that would be prime at Lastway, let me know. I'm up to my nose in chores, and we're supposed to push for a quick departure."

He grinned again. "That's what I like to see: captains doing more than sitting in the captain's chair."

When she got to her cabin, she found a stack of packages: presents from her parents, from her brother San, from . . . she stared at the card that had come with a child's kit for a military ship, a Dragon-class cruiser. MacRobert had sent her a present? She ripped open the envelope. In the same precise, blocky letters that had once informed her, in her first winter as a cadet, that she had two demerits for the state of her bunk, he offered best wishes. "If you ever need to let us know about something," the message went on, "remember that dragons breathe fire. I will be most interested in your progress with this model."

That was beyond odd; Ky stared at it a long moment before putting the model kit on the back of her closet shelf, on top of the note. She could not imagine what she would need to tell the space service, besides something rude and anatomically impossible. MacRobert's rumored connection to covert operations ghosted through her mind—but that was cadet gossip, surely? And why would he pick a disgraced exile like her to work with even if it were true? She turned to the other presents.

Her parents had, with their usual practical approach, sent her a sizable letter of credit for Lastway. For clothes, her mother suggested; her father, who signed it last, said "For yourself." Ky measured the amount against the upgrades the ship needed and came up very short. Still, it was a start. San had sent her a polished tik seed; it fit comfortably in the palm of her hand, its glossy surface a rich red-brown. She put it in her pocket, where she could touch it often; the letter of credit she put in the lockdown of her desk.

"Captain?" Someone tapped at her door. "Need a time for castoff, Captain."

She had forgotten that very elementary detail. She was the one who had to say "Cast off at 1400" or whatever she chose. She opened the door to find Riel Amat, her senior pilot, waiting with a databoard. He looked a little older than the picture she had in the crew list.

"We can be ready by 1320, ma'am, or anytime after," he said. "Traffic Control says they're expecting some congestion later, but should be clear until 1500. They're asking for a time."

"Advice?"

"Fourteen thirty would be about right, ma'am, with a little leeway each way . . ."

"Fourteen thirty it is, then, Riel. Thanks. Anything else I need to be doing?"

"There's paperwork on the bridge, sign-offs and stuff. Crew's all aboard, accounting's cleared, they just need your signature."

"I'll be right there."

He nodded and turned away. Kylara took a deep breath, glanced at herself in the mirror . . . the uniform *did* fit well, no doubt about it. Still the whole situation felt unreal. She, Kylara Vatta, was about to go into space as captain of her own—well, her family's—ship. And she didn't even know enough to set a departure time without asking her pilot. What was she thinking? And yet, she was the captain, and she was going. Excitement stirred; for the first time, the thought of her former classmates brought no pain. They would be sitting in class—or studying—and she was on her way into space. It hardly seemed a fit punishment.

Quincy Robin, whose space-fresh skin belied her sixty-plus years of experience, met Ky in the starboard passage as she headed for the bridge. "I heard about you, youngster. Good work."

"Not everyone thinks so," Ky said, hoping for a compliment.

"What did you want, a ship *and* praise?" Quincy said. "They don't give ships to people for doing bad work."

"Even old ones about to go to scrap?"

"Someone has to take them," Quincy said. "She's not so bad. She was a good ship in her time. Did you know she pioneered the Foregone run? I wasn't on her then, but a few years later I served on her when her class was the backbone of the Vatta fleet. Go anywhere, do anything—that was *Glennys* in her youth. And middle age, for that matter. It's a shame she's going to scrap."

"What would she need to pass inspection?"

"Depends on whose inspection. She's safe for this trip, in the hands of people with some sense. Her drives are good enough. Her attitude controls, though, really need to be replaced. The last three adjustments haven't held more than a few months each. For Slotter Key registration, she'd need an upgraded environmental system. The one she's got is safe, but not up to modern standards; the new regulations they passed last year will catch up with her. Her reserve tanks are five hundred liters short. Then her navigation system is out of spec for age. Thing is, it's full of proprietary data and software that would be hard to transfer to a newer one."

"So what would it cost to bring her up?"

Quincy pursed her lips. "You could probably do it for—oh—five to seven million. And out on a frontier world like Lastway, she'll bring ten to eleven as scrap, and some idiot may try to keep her whole and run her even farther out in the Borderlands. I wouldn't, not without some work."

Old Ferrangia Vatta had started with a beat-up tramp cargo ship when the Scattering suddenly pulled away the best ships and left the rest of human-occupied space in disarray. *Miss Molly* still belonged to the family, displayed in the Number One repair slot. Ky, along with her generation of school kids, had clambered through *Miss Molly*'s narrow passages and old-fashioned ladders, and listened to the story of those perilous first voyages.

And now she had a ship of her own . . . bound for scrap or glory. It seemed an easy choice. Easy, tradition said, was also stupid. It wasn't really her ship; it belonged, as its registration stated, to Vatta Transport, not Ky Vatta. Ky settled into the captain's chair on the bridge, inserted her command wand, and started working on the many, many, many forms that captains had to sign off before a ship could be cleared for castoff.

Between these chores, she glanced at the bridge crew. Sheryl Donster, navigator. Seven years with Vatta Transport, formerly on *Agnes Perry*. She was heavyset, light-haired, and staring intently at a screen full of numbers; Ky had no idea what the numbers were. Ky wondered why her father had wasted a navigator's time on a run like this. The routes had all been mapped; she had current data cubes that should send the ship on automatic from one mapped jump point to another. They wouldn't need a navigator unless something went wrong.

Riel Amat, senior pilot and second in command. Eleven years with Vatta Transport, and before that a space service veteran. Lean, dark, clearly an Islander like her. Her implant told her he'd been born on Little Gumbo. Ky wondered what he thought of her, if he knew why she'd left the Academy. His expression gave nothing away.

The least experienced, pilot-junior Lee Quidlin, had only two years deepspace, as pilot-apprentice on *Andrea Salar*, but he'd been born on Slotter Key's main orbital station and had been planetside only during senior school. He had a broad, friendly face under a shock of taffy-colored hair.

All solid, experienced, personnel who could probably make this trip with no captain at all. She would have to prove herself. She would have to make no mistakes. With that thought, she went back to the paperwork.

Undock and castoff went smoothly; Ky had nothing to do but sit in the captain's couch and watch her experienced crew do what they had done so often before. The tug towed them out to regulation distance and stood by while Engineering powered up the main insystem drive and tested the backup. All functioned nominally. *Glennys Jones* set off on course with no fuss and no surprises.

And with no speed. Functional, efficient insystem drive though she had, it produced less than 80 percent of the acceleration of newer systems. It would be days, not hours, before they dared shift into hyper. Before anything disastrous was likely to happen.

During those days, Ky tried to adjust to her new reality. No fixed schedule, no rapid alternation of classes, physical training, study periods. The empty hours seemed endless. Ky read and reread the manuals for every ship system and followed her crew around asking questions until everyone was snappish. They had seemed so levelheaded before the journey; she worried about the possibility of contamination in the environmental system until, on the fourth day, she overheard Tobai explaining to Beeah Chok, engineering second, that it was just new-captain's-disease, and they both laughed. She backed away, went to her cabin, and dosed herself with a soporific.

Ten hours later she awoke clearheaded and cheerful. Even Aunt Gracie's cakes didn't seem an insoluble problem. She could almost believe that someone, somewhere might find them palatable . . . or useful as doorstops or something. She tried not to think about her past, and found that not-thinking easier when surrounded by the worn fabric of old *Glennys* and the routine of a ship in passage. She set herself daily tasks—exercises both physical and mental.

Day by day she learned more about her crew, always uncomfortably aware that they were all older than she was, all more experienced. The youngest, Mehar Mehaar, had still spent several years on ships. How could they respect her, she wondered? How could they believe she was anything but a rich girl, captain only by the grace of wealth? She continued to study, pushing herself to disprove what she was sure they thought. At the end of each ship day, she wrote up her log, though it mostly consisted of one paragraph listing all systems as nominal. If a military life was long periods of boredom punctuated by moments of stark terror—as one of her instructors had said—then civilian life seemed to be long periods of boredom interrupted by moments of dismal reflection.

Only now and again she wondered what her classmates were doing—what had happened to Mandy Rocher? what was Hal thinking? were the critical midterms coming up or just past?—and put it quickly out of mind. That was behind her; now she had a mission—a job, she corrected herself—and she could find some busywork to keep her mind occupied and those moments of reflection few and far between.

One of those mental occupations centered on the ship. Gaspard's words kept picking at her. What if . . . what if she could make enough in trade to buy *Glennys* herself? And fix her up, and get her through an inspection, and own her own ship? Be an independent trader, like her ancestor.

Her father would have a cat. Her father would have a full-grown mountain cat sprouting green-feathered wings and a forked tail. Her orders were very specific. Transport the goods. Sell the ship. Bring the crew home commercial on the profit. She knew if she did that, she would be offered another position—maybe a better ship, maybe not— on another run, and in a few years she could be captain of one of Vatta's showpieces. Her mother would keep looking for suitable husbands; she would in the end marry the scion of some other commercial family—someone from the energy field, perhaps, or even 'lope ranching. Not Hal, of course. Even if they ever met again, even if he still cared for her, he wouldn't risk his career—she wouldn't let him risk his career—marrying a woman who had been expelled from the Academy for a security breach. She would marry someone suitable for a rich commercial family, someone dull. She would leave ships, settle down, have a few children, work in the firm's head office.

That put a chill down her back. The firm's head office, across town from the Academy: plushly carpeted, paneled in solid wood of exquisite grain, with handwoven drapes, custom desks the size of her bed at home, and soft-spoken staff waiting hand and foot on the senior members of the family. As a senior member of the family—she saw herself twenty years on, a formidable matron in a watered-silk business suit, in an office like her uncle's—she would interact with members of government, with the military. She imagined, so vividly that she broke out in a sweat, having to shake hands with one of her classmates—gods grant it wasn't Sumi, who was probably working off a dozen black points for not being satisfied with someone's explanation of where Ky had gone. Gods grant it wasn't Hal. Whoever it was in uniform would know— would know she'd been expelled in disgrace—and in that handshake express either pity or ridicule or . . . something she didn't want to face.

In the dark of her cabin one sleep-shift, she stared at the steady telltales: green, amber, orange, red, blue. If only they would blink, or change their pattern, anything to distract her. But they glowed on, tiny colored eyes in the dark, staring at her . . . she reached out and switched on the bedside lamp.

She was not going to take another soporific. She was not going to worry her crew. She looked around her cabin for something to do and saw MacRobert's present. She hadn't opened the box yet. Model-building had never been her passion, but it was something to fill the hours between—she looked at the chronometer and shuddered—now and breakfast.

Inside the box she found the expected jumble of pieces, and a much-folded paper with directions in four languages. She unfolded it, and found that someone had underlined some of the words in Balsish—yellow—and Visnuan—green. She turned it over. A few underlinings in Franco—orange—and fewer yet in Angla—red. What—oh. MacRobert's storied past in covert ops. It must be some kind of puzzle, a test of her ability or something. She wasn't in the mood for any such test, or any secret pact with the Service. She ignored the underlined words and took out something that looked as if it should be the keel plate spine, and checked its stamped number against the list on the paper. It was the keel plate spine. She laid it aside, and stirred the pieces with her finger, trying to spot the six portal struts that should—on this model—fit into the keel plate spine. She found five, but the sixth eluded her until she noticed the off-color piece she'd assumed was an exterior member because it was cream-colored, not gray.

By breakfast, she had the keel plate spine and the portal struts assembled. The directions didn't explain why one portal strut was cream-colored, so she shrugged and put it in the number one slot. Possibly parts from different but similar sets had been mixed at the factory. Unless it was another part of Mac's test—but she wasn't in school now, and she didn't have to take any stupid test. After breakfast, she borrowed a magnifier and pair of needle-nose pincers from Quincy Robin's engineering shop and spent an hour peeling tiny warning labels off a strip and laying them carefully—right side up for the position of that part when the model was fully assembled—on the pieces that would, in real life, have such warning signs. Even with the magnifier, the Space Service logo was too small to read. By lunch she had all the labels on. She made a quick tour of the ship and went back to work assembling the interior structural members.

She slept that night without medication or early waking. When the lights came on for mainshift, she stared at the model taking shape on her desk and decided to ration herself to one hour a day. She wanted it to last. She toyed with the idea of buying other models, keeping one always in reserve.

Ten days later, when *Glennys* wallowed uneasily into endim translation, Ky watched the strain gauges and wondered how the ship had passed its last inspection. She didn't miss the tension in Quincy's expression. Shipping out as a junior on one of the newer transports, she'd never had to worry about the ship's fabric coming apart, but now . . . Maybe it was her chance at glory, and maybe it was her chance to die. Her crew seemed mostly calm about the noises and the vibration, though Lee had turned the color of bad cheese. Ky hoped she didn't match him.

Once through translation, Quincy shrugged and shook her head. "I didn't expect that much wobble," she said. "Still, it ought to be good for the number of translations we have scheduled, plus a few more."

Glennys settled back to being an old but not unsound ship. The telltales that should be green were all green; the ambers were amber; the few reds—indicating emergency systems on live standby—were red.

Over the next few days she checked in with her crew every few hours, but spent the rest of the time running cost/benefit analyses. She wouldn't actually do it, she told herself. She couldn't do it. It was impossible in every way. But . . . it couldn't possibly hurt to figure out what it would take, just as an exercise. Better than imagining herself in an office in Port, entertaining her classmates in uniform. Better than finishing the model too soon and having nothing to do with her hands.

Pharmaceutical components to Belinta, 31 percent of estimated cargo value. Time-limited, with a penalty for late delivery or nondelivery, and a bonus for—a time so short that *Glennys* couldn't have done it in her youth. No bonus, then. Price prearranged, profit guaranteed and nonnegotiable. That wouldn't do it, though it put them well on the way to the tickets home from Lastway. What then? The bales of fabric scraps—old clothes, actually—for Leonora? The raw zeer nuts, the crates of modular components for Lastway? Her own crate of luxury goods, the hand-blown crystal bowls and vases, the bolts of silk brocade?

The numbers didn't add up. If they were very, very lucky, they might—possibly—make enough to equal what the ship would bring for scrap. They could not possibly make enough to equal that plus the cost of renovations to meet inspection standards.

Ky called up the inspection standards for the third time. Nobody cared if their holds were inconvenient, though some trade stations would charge a premium for space to ships that could not use automated freight handling systems. But the environmental system, drives, navigation and communications systems . . . those had to pass. While there were sections of space in which no one bothered with inspections—or rescuing those whose ships weren't sound—she didn't want to go there.

She doodled on a spare pad. What would it take, really? What was she willing to give up? Or—since she was now in the business of trade and profit—what was she willing to trade?

CHAPTER FOUR

C ustoms at Belinta, their first port of call, should not have been a problem. Ky shifted from one foot to the other, and struggled not to point out that every single item on the delivery manifest—raw materials for pharmaceuticals—had been preordered. The Customs Inspector was an unmodified human, but she had seen a Mobie and a pair of Indas on the way to this office, and she wanted to see what other humods were in the system. Finally the Customs Inspector looked up from the readout and glared at her as if she had sprouted horns.

"The thing is, we see more than enough of you Slotter Key hotshots," he said. "Always trying to convince us our tariffs aren't reasonable—I'll bet you wouldn't like it if we did that."

Ky refrained from pointing out that Belinta couldn't reciprocate whatever injury they felt they suffered; they didn't have the bottoms to haul their own freight anywhere outsystem. Vatta Transport didn't need more enemies.

"We have only approved cargo," she said, in what she hoped was a voice sufficiently pleasant to avoid offense. "Aside from what's in personal stowage, which is all locked down."

The Customs Inspector looked at the list again. "Preordered pharmaceutical precursors—that gives us value-added—and tik extract. All right. What about agricultural machinery?"

"Not on manifest," Ky said promptly, wondering what they had against agricultural machinery. "Is that—do people try to smuggle in ag machinery?"

"No, no. We're looking for it. It was supposed to arrive last year; we hoped you'd have it, since you're from Slotter Key."

"A Vatta ship?" Ky asked. Surely someone would have told her if a Vatta ship had gone missing on this run.

"No. Pavrati. They're the blue-and-white ones, right?"

Pavrati did indeed have blue-and-white colors. They were based on Serinada, not Slotter Key, though they registered their ships in Slotter Key; they dominated the coreward trade. Vatta held an equal share in the outer ranges. "The ship didn't arrive?" Ky asked.

"A Pavrati ship came, but no machinery. They said it had all been diverted."

Sold off, more like. Pavrati Interstellar Shipping was the example held up to young Vatta trainees of how not to operate a shipping line. Rumor had it they survived by running contraband.

"We tried to contact the company—Pavrati headquarters and the shipping agent for the manufacturer—but we haven't heard anything. And we've asked every ship that's come by." The man said, "We've heard nothing." Belinta was a good hundred years behind Slotter Key in development; a missing shipment like this could cause them real trouble.

"I'm sorry," Ky said. "But I don't know anything about it. If it's a Pavrati contract, I doubt the manufacturer would send a replacement by Vatta."

"We told them next available," the man said. "We really need it." He looked at Ky as if she could create agricultural machinery out of thin air right in front of him.

"Who are you calling on this?" she asked.

"I'm not sure. I just know we're looking for it—but the Economic Development Bureau can tell you more. If there's any way, any way at all that we can get something—we've lost a year's production already—"

She opened her mouth to deliver a standard apology—it was not her concern, she had a route to run, a mission to accomplish—but the words wouldn't come. Possibility tickled her ambition. What if this turned into a lucrative contract, lucrative enough to repair the ship? She told herself it was impossible, but she asked the question anyway. "Does the Economic Development Bureau have an office onstation?"

"Oh, no, Captain. You'd have to go planetside. You'd have to have an appointment. You do have a consul here, of course."

Of course. She had orders to visit the Slotter Key legation on every planet, to be polite and charming and give nothing away while gathering any useful information to be passed back to the family. A very boring duty, she'd thought, but an excuse to wear the scarlet-lined formal cape which she liked in spite of herself.

"But you'll try?" the man said.

"I don't know," Ky said. "I'll have to consider what it does to the rest of my schedule. I'll think about it." She was already thinking about it. She was already imagining a fat contract that would give Vatta Transport, Ltd., leverage in this system and herself a ship in which she had owner's shares. A contract whose negotiation would excuse her spending a few more days downside, exploring her first alien world.

Before she left the station, Ky made her reservation at the Captains' Guild—"an acceptable expense chargeable to the company." She also placed a call to the escort service Vatta Transport used—"a captain never prowls about alone; if no senior crew accompanies, a captain will hire an escort from the usual service [list appended.]" Belinta was supposed to be a safe port, but this was her first voyage; she would take no chances. Executive Escort promised to have a suitable individual on call when she arrived. She chose to meet the escort at the Captains' Guild.

On the down shuttle, she leafed through travel brochures she would never use, such as "Beautiful Belinta, Belle of the Hub Worlds." Nobody but the residents would call this sector the Hub Worlds, unless they thought the rest of the wheel had fallen off. Belinta advertised "unparalleled cultural opportunities," "scenic sights," and "marvelous experiences for the value-conscious traveler."

The "cultural opportunities" looked like a group of people in costume singing something; and the "scenic sights" looked like a cliff over an ocean. Ky wondered what kind of brochures Slotter Key handed out to tourists. She wondered if Slotter Key had any tourists.

She turned over some of the others. "Salzon's Singing Sands," far across the planet, looked like piles of gray dirt, but the "Singing Sands Luxury Resort" promised "unparalleled self-indulgence amid the shimmering dunes." "See the Sights of Mystic Valross Valley" showed a mountain valley, with a large red arrow pointing to the Mystic Valley Luxury

Resort perched on a cliff on one side. Mystic Valley's hostelry promised the same unparalleled self-indulgence as well as horseback tours to Spirit Falls. More interesting—at least in the brochures—was the "Sea Isle Reef Extravaganza Tour" with stays in the Sea Isle Luxury Resort promising the now-familiar unparalleled self-indulgence.

The brochures were archaic—plasfilm, with inert illustrations and no linkup codes. Ky put them aside for the next passenger to enjoy as the shuttle landed. Belinta had only one shuttleport, near its capital. She caught the City Center train, using the coupon from the brochure. No humods on the train, a disappointment; aside from the dull clothing, everyone seemed normal. She came out of the grimy, strange-smelling station across a paved street from the Captains' Guild, a dark brick building in a row of other dark brick buildings, with the starred flag of the Captains' Guild waving in a gentle warm breeze over the entrance.

She had been to the Captains' Guild with her father back on Slotter Key, where he—like all the Vatta senior captains—was personally known to all the service personnel. But this was her first time to enter a guildhouse in her own right. She half expected the doorman to ask for her ID, or suggest that she wait in the Visitors' Lounge for her father. She resisted the impulse to flick her dress cape back from her sleeves to reveal the rings, and walked toward the door as if she owned it. The doorman at the Captains' Guild opened the door for her at once, and the on-duty steward met her in the lobby.

"Captain Vatta, a pleasure. Right this way, please." Of course: their implants would have picked up her ID before she arrived. Her overnight bag disappeared with a bellboy up a flight of stairs; the steward led her to the registration desk. "Just to check that everything's in order—" It was. Ky looked automatically at the status board. *Princess Cory*, Captain R. Stennis, Ind., NR, LPoC Vauxsin; *Pir K.*, Captain J. Sing, Ind., R, LPoC Local System; *Glennys Jones*, Captain K. Vatta, Vatta Transport, Ltd., R, LPoC Slotter Key. She made herself quit looking at her own name on the status board—"Captain K. Vatta" right out there in public—and tried to extract from the simple list all the information she could. Two independents, one staying in the guildhouse and one not. *Pir K.* was probably an insystem rig; Ky wondered what she carried and to and from whom.

"Your room, Captain—number six, second floor. You require assistance?"

"No, thanks," Ky said.

"Will you need us to arrange an escort?"

"No, thank you," Ky said. "I have contacted a service already. I'll call them again from my room and let them know I've arrived."

"They should have met you at the 'port," the desk clerk said. "Unless you requested that they not . . ."

"I said here would be fine," Ky said. "But thank you." She ignored the elevator and went up the carpeted stairs to the second floor where a single short cross-hall made it clear that the Captains' Guild on Belinta didn't expect much business. Her room overlooked the street and although it contained all the amenities the Captains' Guild promised its members, it was smaller and plainer than the room her father had shown her back at Slotter Key's Guild residence. Ky turned on the comconsole and uplinked to her ship, giving them her onplanet contact codes. Then she called Executive Escorts, where the same pleasant voice promised to send someone over immediately. She had just unpacked when the desk called to tell her that the escort had arrived.

Back on Slotter Key, Vatta had its own security personnel, wearing company colors; Ky had never dealt with outworld security firms before. The stocky young man in dark green tunic and brown pants looked nothing like the Vatta employees, but his ID patch fit the information she'd downloaded from the escort service. Conor Fadden, senior operative, certified and licensed to carry those firearms deemed appropriate for private hires on Belinta. He had the little bulge in the left temple that indicated an implanted skullphone, and the larger bulges under his tunic that must be his weaponry.

"Mr. Fadden," Ky said, as she came into the lobby. He turned from the desk.

"Captain Vatta? You're not the same Captain Vatta—?"

"No. It's my first run here." The _here_ slipped out, implying more experience than she had, because of the way he'd looked at her. "Your credentials, please." The Captains' Guild staff would have checked already but Gary had impressed on her the need to check everything herself.

"Of course, ma'am," he said, handing over a datapak. Ky ran the hand scanner over it—clean—and then offered hers to his hand scanner. He took his ID pak back and straightened. "Where first, Captain?"

"The Slotter Key legation," Ky said. "If it's close enough, I'd like to walk."

"Easy close enough," he said. "Just across the street and down a ways." He led the way to the door, and then out onto the street. According to the Captain's Guide, escort services could provide a range of services, but the only one authorized on the company account at Belinta was "guide, basic protection."

Ky felt a strange combination of young and important as she walked with her armed escort along the street of a city on a planet she'd never seen before. It smelled different. People dressed in different colors, different styles. Although Belinta was supposed to have "nominal normal" gravity, her feet didn't seem to hit the ground with the same impact as on Slotter Key. Ky tried not to gape at the sights, keeping her eyes firmly on the Slotter Key flag which her escort had pointed out, a short walk away. When they got to the Slotter Key legation, she nodded to the guards at the gate and handed them her ID pak. They nodded back, ran a scanner over it, and opened the gates for her. Her escort paused; the guards checked his ID, and then allowed him into the gatehouse. Ky walked on up to the door; another uniformed guard opened it for her.

Inside, the legation's reception area had tiled floors and cream-colored walls hung with tapestries representing the Six Colonies. Ky handed her ID pak to the desk clerk, a cheerful middle-aged woman, who ran it through a reader and returned it. "Need to see the consul, Captain Vatta?"

"Yes," Ky said. "A matter of trade and profit."

"It's always nice to see a Vatta representative here. A tisane, perhaps? I will inform the consul that you wish to see him."

"Thank you." Ky sat in the comfortable chair the clerk pointed out, and looked through a window into a covered garden filled with Slotter Key natives. Not, of course, a tik tree. She sipped the tisane the clerk brought her.

"A new Vatta on this run?" The consul appeared quickly. He looked like a northerner and had a North-Coast accent. His ID patch provided a name, Parin Inosyeh, and a brief biography. Ky ignored it; her own wiring would store it for her. "Trade and profit, you say?"

Ky nodded. "A Pavrati shipment. Ag machinery that didn't arrive on the last Pavrati ship. Customs say they asked for a next shipment priority. I want to bid on it."

"Does Vatta approve?"

Ky blinked. How could he ask that when the main office was light years away . . . oh. She was Vatta here. So—did Vatta stand behind this venture or was it personal, a captain's gambit? She could commit Vatta to a course of action that would not play out until after she returned shipless, the old hulk sold—or she could work this solo, and—if it came out as she hoped—use the profits to refit the ship. If it didn't, she would be out of luck, but Vatta wouldn't be harmed.

She had not thought that far. She felt stupid that she had not thought that far.

"I have not decided," she said, hoping she sounded more capable than she felt. "There are advantages either way, for me, my family, and Slotter Key. More information would help, and that is why I have come here. I would like to know—" Her mind raced swiftly through the decision matrices, noting blank cells she most wanted filled. "I would like to know Pavrati's trading history here, and where that could be found. The customs employee I spoke to, Inspector-junior Ama Dissi, directed me to the Economic Development Bureau, which he said had tried to find out where the shipment went astray, and obtain a replacement. I need an introduction to that Bureau."

"Indeed. Some of this I can help you with, certainly. Pavrati began yearly contacts here some six years ago, and increased their service to twice yearly two years ago. The initial contact of my predecessor with the Pavrati concerned a customs dispute about interdicted psycho-actives. Recently . . . let me just say that it would be indiscreet of me to complain that Pavrati captains have been a plague to this office for years—always demanding, never asking. So I would not say that. I would say that if Vatta brought trade and profit out of this, it could only help my office perform its duties and possibly improve relations between governments."

Ky wondered how much "incentive" from Vatta had contributed to his attitude, or if Pavrati captains had really been stupid enough to alienate their own government's consul repeatedly. She remembered those entries on the books, something she'd questioned back in what now felt like distant youth. *We don't bribe people, do we?* she'd asked in horror, only to be glared into silence by her father and uncle. It was not a bribe, they'd explained. It was merely a courtesy, too small to do more than suggest that Vatta Transport was a friendly and cooperative entity.

As neutrally as possible, she said, "I was hoping you could inform me of local law and custom in such matters."

"Easily. These people distrust outworld traders as they breathe air. They consider us all cast in the same mold, and blame any of us for all of us. If you were to make good on a promise Pavrati made, they would be very surprised, and probably indecently grateful. As for Pavrati's reaction, they care not. There are no statutes requiring notification of intent."

She thought that over for a long moment, while the consul finished his own tisane. She could commit Vatta . . . she could go independent. She had just made a huge blunder going independent at the Academy, but this was different. Here that boldness protected the family . . . she hoped.

"It's my venture," she said to the consul.

He nodded. "First command, I assume? Yes. You Vatta seem to run to adventures on a first voyage in command."

Did they? No one had told her about that. "I am not looking for adventure," Ky said firmly. "Trade and profit."

"Oh, certainly. Only fools look for adventure. But I daresay your orders didn't mention scooping Pavrati contracts, not that I'm asking."

She didn't know whether to be annoyed or amused at the twinkle in his eye. She went back to the other issue.

"The Customs Inspector mentioned an Economic Development Bureau?"

"Yes. Hidebound, stuffy, and suspicious, like all these people. If they've been stiffed by Pavrati, they won't pay up front, but they're honest enough and if you deliver the goods, they'll pay in good credit. I'll be glad to give you a letter of introduction—they still go in for that kind of formality—to the right office."

"Thank you," Ky said. "That's most helpful."

He shrugged, a very North-Coast shrug. "Anything to relieve the tedium. It's normally months between ships, with nothing much to do in between but listen to their complaints. You can't believe how tedious these people are. Imagine—for amusement, they play some idiotic game with sticks and balls on horses, of all things."

"Polo?" Ky asked.

"Something like that." His eyebrows went up. "You know about it? I hadn't imagined that anywhere on Slotter Key we had anything like that—I've never been on a horse in my life."

North Coast . . . Slotter Key's industrial hub. Considered themselves superior, North Coasters did. The rest of Slotter Key, Ky suspected, felt much as her family did about North Coasters. Necessary folk, but stodgy and proud.

"I've heard of it," Ky said, without mentioning where. "We're expected to know a lot of customs from all sorts of places."

"I suppose," he said. "Well, if you know enough to chat about chuckles"—Ky realized he meant *chukkers*—"you'll get along fine with them, or as fine as any of us can. But look out; they might ask you to get on a horse and play."

"Oh, I think I can stick to trade and profit," Ky said.

"Well, then—you'll have dinner with me, this evening? I'll have a letter for you by then, and I'll call ahead as well to see when you might get an appointment. Where are you staying?"

"At the Captains' Guild," Ky said. "And thank you. What time?"

"Eight local. I'll send the legation driver for you, and put a ping on your alarm."

Outside, the moist air carried all the smells she'd imagined when, as a junior apprentice, she'd been stuck on the ship polishing the floor while the captain and senior crew were onplanet. Here was a whole world she had never seen before; it was hard to believe she was really here, that she had just been talking to a consul, captain to government representative. Her escort joined her at the gate. "Where to?" he asked.

Ky just wanted to walk around, experiencing the strangeness, but that wouldn't do, not on a company account. "There is a harbor here, yes?" Harbors meant shipping, and shipping was her business.

"This way," the escort said, pointing. Ky called up a city map on her implant—he was leading her the right way. It seemed silly to check, but it was protocol. They started off, still on foot. Around her, the native population of Belinta went about its business, dressed very differently from the people on Slotter Key. Most wore some shade of green—gray green, greenish brown, yellowish green, bluish green—with a plaid shawl slung around the hips for the women or shoulders for the men. Their legs were bare from the knee down to sandals with turned-up toes, but they wore long-sleeved tops with snug cuffs. What was that about?

She slowed down, feeling the slight difference in the way her foot hit the ground, noticing the odd quality of the light, and the smells . . . What was that? A gust of wind lifted her cape and the smell grew stronger. Not unpleasant or pleasant, just enticingly different.

The street they were on curved to the right and ended at a tangle of buildings beyond which stretched an undulating surface of dirty yellow water. In the distance, she could see the dark ragged line of another shore. She called up her infovisor: it was an ocean . . . or rather, this was a bay, and the ocean lay off to the right somewhere. The Greater Ocean, on their maps. Ships carried cargo on that water, just as on Slotter Key; she eyed them as she walked along the street that paralleled the docks. Big ones, little ones, in a bewildering variety of designs: high at the prow with low, rounded sterns, high at both ends with a straight low section in the middle . . . she had no idea which design was meant for which service. Would the escort?

"What kinds of cargoes do they carry?" she asked.

"Lot of it's wood," he said. "Over there, it's the mills—behind them, the forest still. Food and fiber, too, from the farmland away east of here. Riverboats come down with ores and such from the mountains."

"What kind of local transport organization?"

"There's the Amalgamated Transport Trust—that's a group of shipping companies, agree on rates and that kind of thing."

She had already looked that up and was again a little surprised at herself for checking up on the escort service.

Across the pavement on the shoreside were tall blank-fronted buildings—obvious warehouses—bearing names and logos which meant, to this world, much what Vatta Transport meant to hers. Tall doors stood open; she toyed with the idea of going in and introducing herself to a manager or two, but the ships were too interesting. She could do that tomorrow if a data search suggested it might be profitable. She came back in time to dress for dinner.

Dinner at the legation was almost as elaborate as the fanciest dinners at home. The consul had invited several government officials to dine with them; Ky was very glad she'd worn one of the formal outfits her mother had insisted on.

"You're very young, aren't you, to captain an interstellar ship?" asked the wife of someone in the Waterways Commission. The implant, loaded with information the consul provided, handed her the names: Cateros, Sylis and Max.

"Fairly young, yes," Ky said.

"I wouldn't let *my* daughter go out there, so dangerous, don't you agree, Max?" The woman laid a hand on her husband's sleeve; he turned abruptly.

"What? Sanna? Ridiculous." He smiled briefly at Ky. "Not at all the same, Captain Vatta. You have been trained to this life for most of yours, no doubt." He didn't wait for her answer before going on. "And what do you think of our homeworld, Captain? We're still in the early stages of development, but already the waterways form a fine transportation network."

"It's lovely," Ky said. "I haven't seen much of it yet."

"But you did see the harbor today. Quite roomy. As development proceeds, we'll need all that space."

"If it doesn't silt up," said someone down the table. Ky queried her infochip: Samfer Wellin, Minister of Agriculture.

"It won't silt up," Minister Cateros said. "My engineers assure me that the scour of the Big Yellow will continue to keep it cleaned out." He glared down the table and the Minister of Agriculture subsided, then opened another topic.

"Captain Vatta, I understand you're going to be talking to the EDs about importing some machinery for us . . ."

Clearly Belinta was not a world given to keeping secrets. Ky just managed not to glance at the Slotter Key consul. Had he been the source, or was it the talkative customs official? "I was told up on your station that equipment you'd ordered had not been delivered, and was urgently needed," she said.

"That's true. Was supposed to come last year and didn't. We need it badly; we're points below projections on production because of it—"

"That's not your department, Wellin. Your job is getting the most out of what we've already got." Minister Cateros seemed to puff up like a bullfrog. Ky looked down at her plate. She didn't need a teaching tape to know that the men were rivals, and that Cateros thought he outranked Wellin.

"I can't plow fields with polo ponies," Wellin said. He stabbed a slice of roast as if it were Cateros. "If we'd imported heavy stock as originally ordered—"

"They'd be stuck in the muck up there," Cateros said. "You just have to get the job done, Wellin . . ."

"Do you play polo?" Cateros' wife asked Ky with a desperate smile.

The men stopped and stared at her.

Ky shook her head. "No. I do ride, but I've never played polo. Not formally anyway."

"Not formally? What does that mean?" Cateros sounded grumpy still.

"Oh, my brothers and I had read about the game, so we sneaked some brooms out of the pantry, and tried it."

"You grew up on a planet?" asked Wellin's wife. "There was room for horses?"

"Oh yes," Ky said. She wondered if the woman thought all spacer crews grew up on ships. "Slotter Key has plenty of room . . . where I live, many people ride." Always be ready to talk about any neutral topic, her father had said. You never know what it might be, but be ready.

"You should come to a match while you're here," Cateros said. "You can use our box."

"Thank you," Ky said. "I don't know how much time I'll have."

"There's a match day after tomorrow on the City grounds. If you don't have an appointment."

"Thank you," Ky said again.

"I'll see you have my number," Cateros said. He looked at the ornate timepiece on the wall. "Good heavens, it's late. We're due at Erol's wedding rehearsal, Sylis. We must go—you will excuse us," he said to the consul. They both stood, as did Sylis, looking confused. The others all stood, until Cateros and his wife had left. Then, in a straggle, the other Belintans excused themselves, leaving Ky facing the consul across a cluttered table.

"That went well," the consul said.

"Really?" Ky said. "They seemed angry to me."

"They hate each other, but I got them to come and sit through most of a meal together. Captain Vatta, if you can possibly stand it, please go watch that polo match. I'm sorry to say that I simply can't make head or tail of it, but you have a clue. Perhaps that will loosen Cateros up a little, and be a chink in their armor."

"I can try," Ky said. She could, she supposed, watch a polo game and make polite conversation.

"Good. I have transmitted a letter for you to the Economic Development Bureau, and here's a hard copy for you to take tomorrow. Your appointment with the Assistant Minister for Procurement is at eight local time: that's midmorning to these people. He's supposedly going to arrange additional appointments for you. Let me know if he doesn't."

Garsin Renfro, the Assistant Minister for Procurement, was a tall, thin man with the long face Ky had begun to think of as Belinta-normal. "Can you really get us that machinery?" he asked.

"I don't know yet," Ky said. "But very likely."

"How long would it take?"

"Where had you found it before?"

This led to a long explanation of the process, starting with bid requests sent out to a dozen manufacturers and proceeding at glacial pace through every detail of what had happened. Ky kept wanting to interrupt, but made herself listen. Her father had always said no one could tell which detail would make trade and profit . . . but she was fairly sure none of these would.

"So . . . you were happy with the quality of the bid samples from FarmPower and Pioneer Agriculture Supply, and FarmPower had a closer outlet?"

"That's right. Actually five suppliers met the quality standards. But

FarmPower gave us the best overall deal, and they charged shipping only from Sabine. We ordered shipping by fastest scheduled carrier, and that was Pavrati; they come in every sixty days." He looked at her as if she might object; Ky smiled.

"That's understandable, if you had an urgent need."

"We did—we do." He shifted in his chair. "I won't—I can't—burden you with all that's involved, but this delay has cost us . . ."

"Of course," Ky murmured. "Now—your government's contract with Pavrati. Was it exclusive?"

"No. The Board isn't authorized to make such deals. But they were the next, on the schedule. I spoke to the Pavrati captain myself; he assured me they could pick up the machinery on their way outbound, from Sabine, and just store it until they came back. We'd hoped to have it sooner—that another ship could pick it up on the way in—but he said no, they stop at Sabine after Belinta, not before. But he would be back in about one hundred twenty days, he said, and that was well within our parameters."

"So when he came back . . ."

"He didn't come back," the man said sourly. "The next Pavrati ship wasn't the right one, and we knew that. We didn't even ask. Then no Pavrati ship came for another one hundred twenty days, twice as long as usual. We'd queried, of course, but they had no explanation. When that one arrived, it didn't have our machinery, or any explanation. It wasn't the same ship, or the same captain, and he knew nothing about our shipment. We'd asked FarmPower in Sabine if the goods had been picked up, and they'd assured us they had. So at least the captain hadn't spent our credit on fancy clothes." For a moment the man's gaze rested on Ky's formal captain's cloak, as if it were encrusted with precious gems.

"That must have been very confusing," Ky said.

"Confusing and infuriating. FarmPower claimed they'd delivered our goods to the ship we specified, and they had no further responsibility. Pavrati, when we finally got a reply from them, said that taking goods aboard outbound and carrying them on the long legs of the circuit would result in storage charges in addition to shipping charges, whereas we had prepaid only base shipping from Sabine to Belinta. They tried to charge us for the balance right then and there, said it should have been prepaid. And besides, they said, the ship had never arrived at its next stop and was listed missing."

"Insurance?" Ky asked.

He glared at her as if she had just insulted him. "Insurance! Do you have any idea what insurance charges are for a cargo like that? We're a young colony; we don't have money to throw around. Of course we had some insurance. But not full value. The insurance company won't settle until we can give a cause for nondelivery, and for that we need a statement from Pavrati. They say they won't sign it until we pay what we owe for storage, and we aren't going to pay for storage and shipping of goods that never arrived."

"I see," Ky said. "And you want someone to bring a new order?" She had never been to Sabine; she wasn't entirely sure what the standard routing was, whether Vatta had regular service there.

"Yes," the man said. "But we aren't paying first this time—it's pay on delivery."

"Our policy," Ky said, "requires at least a deposit on account. You're asking me to change my schedule—"

"We're not going to be cheated again!" the man said. "You Slotter Key pirates—"

Ky put up her hand. "A moment. Vatta Transport, Ltd., are not pirates; we are licensed, bonded transporters."

"It's all the same," the man said. "Take our money, and for nothing—"

"Has anything consigned to Vatta ever failed to reach its destination here?"

"No. Not yet."

"Then—" *Don't blame us because you didn't have sense enough to hire us* was hardly tactful. "Not all firms are alike," Ky said instead. "Vatta Transport is sorry that you have not been served well by another firm, and that this incident has damaged the image of Slotter Key businesses."

"I suppose it's not actually your fault," the man said. "But we're so far out—"

Which wasn't Ky's fault. Was this the time to push for a mutually agreeable solution?

"What do you think happened to the Pavrati ship?" the man asked.

"I don't know," Ky said. "They could have had a drive failure—"

"Drive failure! You mean—that happens?"

"Yes," Ky said. "Usually going into or coming out of FTL space. Any little bit of debris in the jump lane can cause that much damage—it's why we only travel to places with a decent traffic control crew. Or they might have collided with something bigger—" Leaving a dangerous smear of debris on the mapped routes. "Piracy you mentioned—they could have been intercepted somewhere—"

"But surely Pavrati would have told us about any of that—"

"No," Ky said. "In the first place, they may not know what it is yet, and in the second place they won't want it known, lest someone else profit by the knowledge."

"Seems ridiculous," the man said. "They should at least tell our insurance company . . ."

"If they know, yes. But when a ship disappears . . . space is big and ships are small."

"Ships really do disappear . . . they're not lying about that?"

"Ships can," Ky said. Across her mind ran the list of Vatta Transport, Ltd.'s disappearances. They had a good record, the result of prudence, hard work, and another dollop of prudence on top. The spaceways, her father had said when she first mentioned the Academy, offer risk enough.

"Well, then . . ." His voice firmed. "Your consul tells me you have the authority to decide if you want this contract. As I said, we aren't going to pay in advance this time. What are your rates?"

"We have no consignments for Sabine," Ky said. "Nothing we can sell there." She had tried to find something in the cargo for Lastway that would sell on Sabine, but nothing fit. "And you have no consignments, either, do you?"

"No. We've never had exports to Sabine."

"Well, then. That means it's a dry run over, and a paying cargo back. If we're not getting an advance, that means a surcharge for the extra distance—"

He scowled.

"Think about it," Ky said. "You want us to go out of our way, without profit on one leg; if we know we're going somewhere, we carry cargo there, and that means we only need to charge each shipper for the distance their cargo actually travels. Now, have you asked for bidders again, or are you planning to buy from FarmPower?"

"Well . . . no."

"Well, then," Ky said. "Let me suggest this . . ."

The haggling continued for hours, with breaks for refreshments, but in the end she had what she thought was an acceptable deal. She had missed the polo match, but she didn't much care.

CHAPTER
FIVE

The closer she came to the station, the more reluctant she felt to tell her crew, her experienced baby-sitting crew, about her bright idea and the contract she'd signed. What would they think? Would they insist on telling her father? She was the captain. She had to approve all communications. Would that stop them?

Gary Tobai met her at dockside. "How'd it go?"

"I need to talk to you," Ky said. "You and Quincy, anyway."

"Trouble?"

"No. My office, when you can."

"Now works for me," he said, dashing her hope that she could have a few minutes to think up how to say it. "I'll get someone on dock watch, and call Quincy—ten minutes?"

"Fine," Ky said. She went quickly to her quarters and tried to organize her thoughts. Quincy and Gary appeared long before she felt ready.

"So . . . what is it?" Quincy asked as she came in. The tone said "What have you done now, youngster, and how hard is it going to be to fix it?"

"We have a contract," Ky said.

"A contract. You mean—another contract? You do remember the assignment is to take this ship to Lastway and scrap her . . ."

"Yes, I remember. But trade and profit is trade and profit. Belinta was our only time-defined delivery. The goods for Leonora and Lastway are all spec. This is a profit run."

Quincy's mouth tightened. "How much?" Gary asked. "And what do we have to do to get it?"

Ky explained about the Pavrati failure to deliver a prepaid order, and the Economic Development Bureau's urgent desire for agricultural machinery before their attempt to open the Hamil Valley to farm settlements failed.

"And the profit," she said, ignoring the twitch in Gary's cheek, "is enough—with the profit we can reasonably expect from the sale of our Lastway trade goods—to do a refit at some reasonable yard, enough to bring her up to spec." Or almost.

"Hmmmm." Quincy looked down. Ky couldn't read her expression.

"Payment or profit?" Gary asked.

"Profit," Ky said. She tensed, knowing the next question.

"So how much is the advance?"

"Well . . . actually . . . they'll pay on delivery. They paid Pavrati in advance, and the manufacturer in advance, and they don't trust us."

"So . . . you're talking a spec run, and . . . do we have to pay for the merchandise?"

"Yes," Ky said. "But it's hard goods; if they don't cough up, we can sell it somewhere else. And we get a residual, the rights to any insurance settlement."

Quincy let out a stifled sound and buried her face in her hands.

"What?" Ky said. "It's not that bad an idea . . ."

Quincy looked up; tears rolled down her face, and her shoulders shook. She was laughing, Ky realized, laughing so hard she couldn't speak.

Gary, when she glanced at him, was grinning. "Ky, Ky, Ky. We wondered how long it would take."

"How long what would take?"

"You. So prim, so proper, so very earnest—" He chuckled, and shook his head. "I knew it wouldn't last. It never does."

Ky felt her neck going hot. They were treating her like a child, and—

"You're so Vatta, is what he means," Quincy said, through the laughter she was trying to control. "Trade and profit, right? If there's an angle—and then it is your first ship." She shook her head, still laughing.

"The thing is," Gary said, "there was no way you were going to take this ship off to scrap if you could help it. I'll bet you that you'd been wondering if you could possibly earn enough for a refit before you ever got aboard."

"Not . . . exactly," Ky said. They were both grinning now, not sarcastic grins, but genuine glee. "You knew," she said. "You knew all along . . . did my father know?" Gaspard must have known, she realized. He must have assumed that any Vatta would find a way to save a ship from scrap.

"He knows you," Quincy said. "I don't suppose he knew about the Pavrati nondelivery, no, but he knew you."

"I think Ted got it," Gary said to Quincy.

"Depends on how we set the time," Quincy said. "From the time she made the contract, or from telling us?"

"Now what are you talking about? Ted got what?" Ky asked.

"The ship's pool," Quincy said. "Actually we had two, one for you taking a contract, and one for you figuring out a different way to make a profit."

"I don't know whether to laugh or cry," Ky said. She had not even imagined a ship's pool on her performance. "You were all sure I'd try to save the ship?"

"Did anyone pick no?" Gary asked Quincy.

"I don't think so," Quincy said. "I'd have to look at all the entries so far."

"Just what did you expect me to come up with?"

"Who could guess?" Quincy said with a shrug. "First-run captains have done all sorts of things. There've even been a few who followed exactly the line they'd been given, but most of those end up working for someone else. Now—let's take a look at this contract you signed. Spec, and we have to buy the goods up front?"

"Yes."

"Could be worse," Gary said. "You've got a letter of credit from the family, I suppose?"

"Yes," Ky said. "It's on Crown & Spears at Lastway, but that should be negotiable elsewhere, but we also have the payment on delivery for the cargo we brought in. That's actually Vatta Transport, money, though. I'd rather not use it."

"Quite right," Gary said.

"So, I thought Sabine Prime," Ky said. "The Economic Development Bureau has given me the specs for what they want. Sabine has several manufacturers of the kind of equipment they want, plus used-equipment dealers."

"Is that where they ordered it from in the first place?"

"Yes. From FarmPower. But they'd take equivalent stock from another manufacturer, or used, in order to get something here quickly, they said. And that's in the contract." Ky pointed out the relevant paragraph.

"And how much do you know about farm machinery?" Quincy asked.

"Me?" Ky said. "Nothing. But there are books, and it's two months to Sabine." Quincy and Gary both rolled their eyes. "What? You don't think I can learn?"

"Mitt may know," Gary said. "But let me see that—we may have a load problem."

"I checked the hold layouts," Ky said.

"Yeah, but . . . some of these brutes will have to be disassembled, and then—we have to shift the Lastway cargo around. We aren't fully loaded, but we'll need easier access in these tight spaces . . ."

"Store some of it here," Quincy said. "They aren't paying in advance, so they can store our stuff free."

"It's worth trying," Gary said.

Somewhat to Ky's surprise, the Bureau of Economic Development was willing to put Ky's Lastway cargo into storage for no fee, as security against their timely return. Ky had Gary check out the sealed storage facility; to her it looked like any other sealed storage facility. They had no special requirements, so she wasn't nearly as concerned about temperature, pressure, and so on as about pilferage.

"The locks and seals are good quality," he reported. "If something goes missing, it'll be because someone used the main hatch and the key for it."

"What do we do if they do?" she asked.

"We have their ag machinery, and we keep their ag machinery until they return our cargo."

This was getting more complicated by the minute. Ky extracted Aunt Gracie's fruitcakes from the rest of the cargo—maybe she could unload them on Sabine, and they fit into one of the lockers in her cabin—and signed off on the stowage contract.

Glennys Jones eased away from Belinta Station under her own power—Belinta's single tug service being occupied with an insystem carrier—and Ky tried not to fret. Ted Barash, Mitt's assistant in Environmental, had indeed won the pool, and used it to treat everyone to a meal just before they left. Ky tucked a mint she'd saved from the dessert tray into her mouth and went back to her calculations. Two months to Sabine. Say a week to locate the machinery, a week to do the paperwork, some days to load—to be safe another week—and then two months back to Belinta, and a week to unload, process the paper, reload with their Lastway cargo. Five months, all told, by which time the family would expect to hear that she was in Lastway, though Lastway would still be four months away.

She would have to let them know sometime, she told herself. But when? Not now, when they might tell her to stop, or send someone to help her fix her mistakes. Maybe once she had the cargo loaded at Sabine Prime? Or when she was back here and they'd be expecting word anyway?

The imagined message appeared in her mental vision, expressed in perky tones unlike her own: *Hi Dad, all is well, I'm on Belinta with a load of tractors and we made a lot of money and don't have to go to Lastway after all. Your loving daughter . . .*

No. Definitely not. *Slight delay, don't worry* wasn't much better.

She forced her mind away from the wording of a message she didn't have to send for several months, at least, and called up the ship's reference library. Farm machinery. She knew what they used in the tik plantations back home; she had even been sentenced to a fortnight of hard labor—as she'd called it, bootlessly, at the time—driving one of the harvesters.

The Belinta Economic Development Bureau wanted ag machinery to convert thick forest into productive farmland. As a colony world with limited repair and manufacturing facilities, they wanted machines designed specifically for such use—very rugged, low maintenance, easily repaired. They were willing to trade off the advantages of multipurpose machines for the increased life-span of a dedicated single-purpose machine.

What they'd really wanted—what they had intended to have—were draft animals, horses and oxen, self-replicating, self-repairing, long-lived, but they'd been overruled by the aristos among them. Instead of draft animals, they had polo ponies—all owned by the rich, who weren't about to let them pull a cart, let alone a plow. The machine equivalents were faster, if they worked, but right now they had nothing but small tillers people had planned to use in their gardens. Hardly suitable for serious farm work.

So—tractors to pull various field equipment. Multigang plows, harrows, planters, harvesters. Rugged trucks to haul their produce on rough roads. Ky thought they were making a mistake not to include road-building machinery in this order, but they were the customer.

She compared the specs the EDB had given her to the information in the database, and found nothing that the EDB hadn't told her. All these things were fairly standard, and should be easy to find. The database also had the current market value of the equipment, in the currency of several systems. Unless Sabine Prime's prices were over the top, she should have enough for the cargo.

It was going to work. She shut down the library link and allowed herself to relax. She'd been through it again and again, on her own and with Gary and Quincy. It was a good plan, and it had no obvious holes in it.

So why this nagging cold chill that ran up and down her spine? She told herself it was just the leftover loss of self-confidence from that mess with Mandy Rocher. Naturally she would distrust her own judgment for a while. But this had nothing to do with Mandy or Miznarii politics. This was just straight-up trade and profit, something she'd known about since childhood. Simple, straightforward, easy. It was all going to work.

Endim transition felt even rougher with no cargo aboard; Ky would have crossed her toes for luck if she could.

"We really do need to get that tuned," Quincy said, when the vibrations settled down. "It's degrading faster than I thought it would, to be honest. There's a pretty good shipyard on Sabine that could do us an interim fix, probably wouldn't take more than three or four days."

"And how much money?" Ky asked.

"We'd have to ask."

"We don't have much," Ky said. "We can't draw on the company accounts for this—the ship's not authorized for repairs. And we're using my letter of credit to cover expenses." Maybe she should have been bolder about taking the Belinta delivery payment herself instead of depositing it to Vatta Transport, Ltd.

"I know," Quincy said. "I thought she had at least ten more transitions in her, but that last one wrenched something. If she's that rough coming back out, we'll have to get it fixed. If not—I suppose we could risk the trip back to Belinta, but I'd rather get something done. I've only got the three engineers, you know."

"There's nothing we can do now?" Ky asked, already knowing there wasn't.

Quincy shook her head. "Sealed unit. It either works right or it starts degrading. I'll tear down the supports, try rebalancing before we shift back, but I don't think it's the supports. I think it's the unit itself."

Fine. A rotten little sealed unit the size of a large suitcase could mess up her whole plan. To keep herself from hovering behind Quincy's shoulder during the rebalancing, she took out the ship model and forced herself to work on it. Even if it did remind her of what she'd lost, it was better than driving her crew insane. She kept up her exercise periods, using one of the now-empty holds. In a way, she found it reassuring that she did not need the rigid schedule of the Academy, the shouting of instructors, to make herself exercise. But then, she reminded herself, lack of initiative had never been her problem.

She was back on the bridge for the down transition; she could not help noticing how many of the crew found it necessary to be there as well. She nodded to Riel, who gave the slightest shrug before touching the controls.

Down transition brought them out where they should be—whatever was giving *Glennys* the problem didn't seem to affect navigation, at least—but that was all the good news. The ship trembled, creaked, even groaned as vibration stressed her structual members. Ky clenched her teeth to keep from crying out along with her ship. It felt like hours, but only a few minutes passed on the ship's chronometer. Finally it steadied. Several new status lights came up red.

"Mandatory repairs," Quincy said. "We have to replace that sealed unit."

Ky didn't argue. She could still feel a faint tremor in the ship's fabric. She certainly didn't want to take this ship back through endim transition again without a repair. Instead, she began downloading Sabine local information. Sabine's manufacturers, drawing on a wealth of raw materials in their system, produced solid, basic agriculture, mining, and construction equipment for many of the colony worlds in this sector. Their advance sales information systems offered everything Ky needed to plan the stowage of their intended cargo. Sabine also offered a variety of ship services, from consumables to complete refitting.

She and her crew pored over the information. If she spent all her letter of credit on agricultural equipment, she would have very little left for repairs. If she didn't, she'd short the order from Belinta. Surely they'd understand if she had to repair the ship . . . surely a couple of tractors short wouldn't upset them.

But it would. She knew in her bones that they were really as dour, as inflexible, as unforgiving, as they'd seemed. They'd accept a fait accompli, but they'd hold it against her—and worse, against Vatta and Slotter Key—forever. She had to find some way of doing it all—fulfilling their order, repairing the ship, getting back to Belinta . . . There was always credit, though the interest would cut into the profits . . .

"Welcome to FarmPower," the interactive salesprof announced. The voice was cheerful. "We are here to serve your agricultural needs. Please select one of the following options. If you have items on order and wish to check their manufacturing status, please speak now . . . If you have items on order and have received notice of shipping, and wish to check their shipping status, please speak now . . . If you wish to place an order for new items, please speak now . . . If you . . ."

"I need to speak to a sales representative," Ky said. Sometimes these things could be interrupted.

" . . . need to register a complaint, please speak now. Have your invoice number ready . . ." The voice paused, and something that Ky knew was meant to be music tinkled uneasily in the middle distance. She had no invoice number, because she hadn't placed an order yet. The salesprof paid no attention to her interruptions, and she finally gave up. She had to go planetside anyway; she'd contact FarmPower from there.

Sabine Prime smelled very different from Belinta; Ky sneezed as something acrid got up her nose as soon as she cleared Customs. She saw no humods at all in the passages, and only about half the people had the telltale bulge of implants. This time her security escort—a tall, thin man named Seward Humphries and clad in the charcoal brown livery of his employer—met her at the shuttle station, and guided her to a bubbletube. He seemed alert and competent, but radiated an unwillingness to chat with clients. Ky didn't mind; she had plenty to think about as they neared the capital city. Sabine City—commonly called Sabine or even Prime—had sprawled across a river; the far side appeared to be more industrial, judging by the stacks and cooling towers.

The Captains' Guild here was much larger than that on Belinta; the status board listed dozens of ships. Ky checked in, sent her luggage up to her room, and went directly to the Slotter Key embassy. It was only a few blocks away; she chose to walk, her escort silent beside her. Sabine's citizens favored bright colors—a relief after Belinta—and some of them carried a small, round, bright-colored object in one hand. Ky had no idea what it was, but the shapes were the same even though the colors varied. Ornate glazed tile designs livened the fronts of the buildings, with exuberant decorative arches over doors and windows. Ground vehicles varied from large mass-transit cars—some red, some green—to tiny three-wheeled confections in various pastels, which unfolded to reveal a single seat inside. And the noise—after Belinta's relative silence, the busy chatter of Sabine's city crowds almost deafened her. She and her escort, she thought, must be the only two walking together who were not talking loud enough to be heard a block away.

The Slotter Key embassy was hardly larger than Belinta's small legation—or so she thought, until she noticed the bustling staff and realized that it must also occupy the adjoining buildings.

"Captain Vatta," said the desk clerk. "So nice to see you." He was heavily tattooed and freckled around the tattoos. "We're always glad to see Vatta people here. What can we do for you?"

"Trade and profit," Ky said. "I'm on a contract run from Belinta, picking up agricultural machinery. Do you have performance files on repair yards?"

"Repair yards? For ag machinery?"

"No, for ships. I'm wondering whether to have a minor problem fixed here or wait until I get back to Belinta." She was reluctant to reveal just how big the problem was.

"Oh, you'd want to do that here," the desk clerk said. "Sabine has superb repair yards, and yes, we do have performance stats as reported by Slotter Key citizens who've used them. Would you like that now, or popped to your ship?"

"Both, please," Ky said. "My engineer has the stats from Belinta for comparison, but I suspect you're right."

"Just a moment," the clerk said, and blinked, accessing the legation's internal database. "There," he said. "Anything else?"

"Reputable sources of used farm machinery," Ky said. "I already have contact with FarmPower, but they're not selling used equipment anymore, they say."

"No. They dropped their used equipment sales two years ago. Higher profit margin in new, and they'd just unloaded almost all their stock to the Chigwellin Combine anyway. Chigwellin got the contract for a twin-world system about eight jumps away, and they bought up just about all the used farm equipment anyone here had."

"So . . . no one has used?"

"No one you'd want to buy from, Captain Vatta. FarmPower and the other manufacturers all quit taking old machinery in trade after that, and put the money into new manufacturing capacity. Our local agricultural unions sometimes have used machinery, but it's low quality."

"I see." What she saw was the start of a problem she hoped wasn't as big as it looked. If she was stuck buying new equipment at top price . . . but had no ship to get it back to Belinta . . . she might as well not buy it. On the other hand, fixing the ship—assuming she could—would leave her with no cargo to take to Belinta.

"Thank you," she said, after a pause, and the clerk nodded.

"You'll want to pay respects to the consul," the clerk said. "He takes courtesy calls at 1600 local time on the second and fifth day of the local week . . . that's tomorrow, which around here they call Umpord. Shall I put you down?"

"Yes, thanks," Ky said.

"And here is a hardcopy of another file I loaded for you, local regulations and current warnings pertaining specifically to Slotter Key citizens. I call your attention to the Foreigners' Curfew, underlined in red: they are serious about that, and you will require a local citizen escort to be abroad after curfew. You have an escort, I presume?"

"Yes," Ky said.

"A licensed escort service suffices; if you choose to be out with an unlicensed escort after curfew, be sure he or she has his or her citizenship card. It is most inconvenient when our staff is asked to intervene in cases of curfew-related arrests and detentions. And things are rather tense just now." The clerk, formerly so friendly, now seemed severe.

"I understand," Ky said. "I have a licensed escort, and no intention of wandering about without one."

"Good. And the most important local taboo, on page eighteen, is underlined in green. Never, under any circumstances, sneeze without using a sprayer immediately afterward."

Ky had had no inclination to sneeze, but now her nose tickled. "But doesn't that spread infection?"

"It's symbolic. Don't ask me, I think it's stupid, but you'd better buy a sprayer. The cheap ones are actually considered in better taste."

Ky rubbed her nose. "So . . . anything else?"

"No, I've put you down for the call tomorrow; the consul will expect to take tea with you. Allow a half hour, though it will probably be less; it depends on how many show up. Dress is afternoon business; your captain's uniform is fine."

"Thanks," Ky said. She collected her escort outside the embassy, and called up a list of other ag machinery suppliers. None listed prices lower than FarmPower's, but since a few listed no prices at all she put in queries.

"Where would I find a . . . er . . . sprayer?" she asked her escort.

"In general merchandising emporiums," he answered. "There's a shopping arcade just a few blocks away . . ."

"Fine," Ky said. "That's where I need to go . . ."

The shopping arcade, floored in tesselated stone laid out in floral patterns, had fascinating little shops on either side, and one large store with several doors. Her escort led her to the farthest, and then to a sales rack whose shelves were covered with items Ky would not have recognized as sprayers. She did recognize them as the rounded objects so many pedestrians carried. Pink, green, blue, yellow . . . painted with what must be intended as flowers . . . but how did they work?

"I don't understand," Ky said.

"The incense bead goes in here"—he pointed—"and the igniter is there, and you squeeze this—" *This* was an accordion pleated arrangement that Ky had not realized could flex. "These are all expanded to show the design," he said. "But they compress to fit in a pocket."

"Incense bead?" Ky said. "Igniter?"

"For the aroma," he said. "If I might recommend—a neutral scent, like rainwater, is most appropriate for professional visitors. There are presumptions made about, for instance, honey musk or spiced fruit, no matter what your intentions."

"So where are the incense beads?" Ky asked. He pointed out little packets of tiny round beads in various colors. Ky found "falling rain," and then picked out the least garish of the sprayers—green with blue flowers. She paid cash for them, and then had her escort explain how to insert the incense bead, and how to compress and then operate the sprayer. He didn't smile, but she could sense his approval. Stupid tourist does something right, for once.

When she queried her insert, she found a list of prices from other suppliers . . . none better than FarmPower. Drat. She had to hope now that either FarmPower or a repair yard would extend credit, based on her family name. She had better check again with her crew on the extent of necessary repairs.

Back at the Captains' Guild, she called up to the orbital station. Quincy burst out laughing when Ky showed her the sprayer and explained its use.

"That's the silliest thing I ever saw," she said.

"I know. But what I need now is your best assessment of what repairs we absolutely have to make, and what we can defer. Nobody's selling used ag equipment, and nobody's prices—that I'd trust anyway—are lower than FarmPower's."

"The sealed unit, of course. But Ky, we can't tell about the rest of it until we tear down the whole drive sequence. Depending on how much damage it did as it degraded, we could have cavitation in the main chambers. And once we start tearing it down, we're committed to fixing whatever it is . . ."

"Yeah. I know. Well, tomorrow I have a courtesy call to pay on the consul—he only takes courtesy calls two days a week—and in the meantime I'll see what I can do about arranging financing. There's no way my cash on hand will pay for both the equipment and the repairs. We'll have to find a cooperative soul who will trust our honest faces."

"I wouldn't count on that," Quincy said.

"I'm not," Ky said. "It's wishful thinking. But something has to work."

"Captain's problem," Quincy said. "Mine is diagnosing something without looking at it. But just for your planning—the going rate for a new sealed unit here is fifty thousand credits, installed."

Something was going to have to give somewhere. Ky forced herself to eat a solid, stodgy meal in the solid stodgy dining room of the Captains' Guild, and hoped none of the other captains could see past her face to her fears. No one spoke to her but the waiter. She signed the tab and went back to her room to wrestle with information available on the public 'net and the intractable number of zeros on her letter of credit.

FarmPower, in the tail end of its recorded sales pitch, mentioned its credit terms. Sheer robbery, but she didn't have to worry about the interest rate because ". . . we do not extend credit offplanet;

this includes consignment carriers. Please make arrangements with the financial institution of your choice. FarmPower apologizes for any inconvenience . . ."

So she would have to pay cash for the ag equipment. Fine. Then she could find a lender for the ship repairs. Lots of people borrowed to pay for ship repairs . . .

By morning, she had a list of the equipment she needed, and signed on to FarmPower's interactive sales site again. The total brought a whistle of dismay. Prices were up 3.8 percent from what Belinta had paid—not surprisingly, but still. She was going to have to find a lender for that, too, or have no down payment for the ship repairs.

The list of financial institutions willing to do business with a first-trip independent captain, even one named Vatta, was short and not sweet. Over half were lending companies whose own ratings didn't make her cut. Her name and letter of credit got her an interview with the Loan Department at Crown & Spears, but their rates were . . . high.

"I have the signed contract with Belinta's Bureau of Economic Development," she said, tipping the fac to the loan officer's implant.

"That's good," the loan officer said. She was an older woman with silver hair pulled back into a braid. "That means we can almost certainly approve the loan. It does not, of course, change the interest rate."

Ky's implant calculated the total cost, including transfer fees, and compared it to the profit margin she'd originally loaded. Ouch.

"And I should warn you," the woman said, "that the way events are proceeding between Sabine Prime and Sabine Secundus, you would be wise to procure any necessary funds soon. Interest rates will be rising, I'm quite sure."

From her earliest training, she knew that anyone pressuring for a quick deal had other priorities than the customer's welfare. But when she queried the implant's newsfeed, she found that the woman was right: Sabine Secundus and Sabine Prime had long been at loggerheads over some obscure religious matter, and it looked like the conflict might erupt in violence any moment. The market, though volatile, looked to be headed up, in anticipation of hostilities that would require increased manufacture of war goods.

Great. So she was short of money with a ship needing repair and a contract, and she might be in the middle of a war as well. How many other rules of safe trading could she break? She thought for a few moments; the woman didn't rush her. If she could get the cargo up to the ship, then trouble on the surface couldn't prevent her from getting it . . . and the ship repair facilities were in space, where again a surface war wouldn't affect them. True, Secundus had supporters on the mining world, Tertius, but her implant indicated no ability by either Prime or Secundus to sustain a war in space.

She would rather have locked in ship repair first, but in the event . . .

She arranged the loan as quickly as she could, for as much of the purchase price as she could. From the bank, she was able to contact Farm-Power and arrange transport of the machinery to orbit—at least "freight on board" in the price meant that delivery was covered, though not transfer to her ship. From the bank's secure com booth, she let Tobai know what was coming, and when, and briefly explained the political and economic problems involved.

"And yes, I know, we still have to get the ship repaired, but at least we won't have the cargo impounded."

"See your point," was all he said. "When is delivery?"

"Tomorrow or the next day, depending on cargo shuttle availability. They say it'll take four shuttles, and their estimated load time here is six hours per. They're starting to move the cargo to the shuttle port now, though—or anyway, they said within four hours. I'll keep on it."

"Fine, you do that. If we're in a hurry, we may need to hire some temp labor, for loading . . ."

"We can't," Ky said. "At least—we shouldn't."

She looked at the time when she came out of the booth. Close enough to her courtesy call on the consul. The morning's calls had all taken longer than she hoped. Her implant reported that she could get by without returning to the Captains' Guild for a trip through the 'fresher. A simple tuning of pores . . . her skin tingled, briefly, and for a moment she smelled a sharp herbal scent she couldn't name, then it vanished.

Someone sneezed, across the walkway, and instantly yanked a screaming yellow sprayer from his pocket and sprayed something that smelled like melons. Ky tried not to stare. Other pedestrians ignored him, Ky noticed.

"Captain Vatta—" That was her escort, who until now had been as quiet as a robot servant.

"Yes?"

"I am receiving information relevant to your safety. It is my considered advice that we proceed immediately to the embassy."

"What's going on?" Ky asked.

"I—would rather not speculate," he said. "My concern is your safety, and I am sure your officials will explain if there is need."

If the loan department at the bank was worried, and her escort was worried, perhaps she herself should be worried.

"That's where I was going anyway," she said. "It's only a short distance; do you think it's still safe to go on foot?"

"At present, yes," he said.

"Good," Ky said. "Let's go, then."

CHAPTER
SIX

By the time she reached the embassy, she knew something was going on. The streets were oddly quieter; though people were talking, they had lowered their voices. Pedestrians would occasionally stop short—listening to their implants, probably—and then stride on, looking tense. Ky wondered if any of them were reservists being called to active duty. Her escort ducked into the guard's kiosk; Ky went on into the building.

"Ah, Captain Vatta," the desk clerk said. "Have you heard the news?"

"That Secundus and Prime are unhappy with one another, yes," Ky said.

"There's been a demonstration at Majel Dis, in Secundus," the clerk said. "We just heard . . . four deaths confirmed, many injured."

Ky could think of nothing to say.

"The consul would not commit the discourtesy of failing to greet you, Captain, but he is rather busy and would appreciate it if your visit could be . . . brief."

"Of course," Ky said.

"We will be updating our citizens with whatever information we have, of course," the clerk said. "We recommend that you authorize an override to your implant, so that we can send to you directly whether your skullphone is on or not."

"That's fine," Ky said. She thumbprinted the form he held out.

"Now," the clerk said. "Let me show you to the reception room."

The reception room, a parlor overlooking a small garden planted with native Slotter Key flowers, was centered with a large table, laden with refreshments. The consul greeted Ky warmly, as if nothing were going on, and led her to a pair of chairs near the window.

"Captain Vatta, so pleased to see you. I'm Doss Verdin, senior consul. Does this mean that Vatta Transport is setting up more frequent regular service here?"

"Not to my knowledge, sir; I am on a contract run from Belinta."

"Ah. Belinta. We have had complaints from that quarter."

"They blame Slotter Key for the Pavrati not delivering their ag machinery," Ky said.

"I know," he said, pinching his nose. "They said so many times. I tried to explain that Slotter Key and Pavrati Shipping were not the same entity, that we had no control over Pavrati, and so on. I understand you're here on the same errand from Belinta?"

"Yes. Perhaps Vatta can redeem Slotter Key . . ."

"I hope so," he said. "You're aware of the political problems we have here now?"

"I just heard," Ky said. It didn't sound particularly bad yet.

"I was wondering, Captain, if perhaps you could do us a favor."

"Of course, if I can," Ky said.

"We have four Slotter Key citizens on the beach at present. One of them caught chahoki fever; he and the others were quarantined, and their ship left without them. They've been here almost six months; their visas are running out, and although I might get an extension, this is not the best time to ask for one. I wonder if you need any extra crew, or if you'd be willing to take them as supercargo until you can drop them someplace they're likelier to find work . . . ?"

"We're not a large ship," Ky said slowly. But spacers helped stranded spacers, unless stranded for the wrong reasons . . . and Tobai had said they could use help . . .

"We don't have funds to pay their passage," the consul said. "But we can pay their way up to orbit, and we could offer a small sum toward supplies for them." He looked grim. "Sabine Prime has a history of impressing foreigners without high status into their military—I can't stand by and see these people conscripted, and yet I can't keep them in the embassy."

"What are their records like?" Ky asked.

"Ordinary," the consul said. Ky's implant lit, and she looked over the files he'd just sent her. Experienced, licensed in their specialties, no black marks from their last two employers—all that their traveling records held.

"I can do it," Ky said. "But I'm ashamed to admit I'll need that honorarium for extra supplies. Belinta demanded that I purchase the cargo, and we had a bit of trouble on the way so we also need some repairs. Supplies for another four people are just out of range."

"We can stretch to that," the consul said. "And thank you. They will thank you as well. Shall I send them up, or do you want to meet them?"

"I want to meet them," Ky said. She was not going to foist onto her loyal, experienced crew some strangers she hadn't even met. "Are they here?"

"Yes. We'll just have a cup of tea and—" His face went blank. Then he shook his head. "I'm sorry, Captain, but it's urgent and I must respond. I'll have them sent in. Take as long as you like chatting, but I would recommend you have Zar arrange their shuttle tickets and your honorarium as soon as possible. Things are getting nasty over on Secundus." He left the room, and a few minutes later the clerk—Zar?—ushered in three men and a woman, all in spacer clothes. They looked at Ky and the woman gave a tentative smile.

"Captain Vatta? Of Vatta Transport?"

"Yes, I'm Captain Vatta . . . you're Specialist Lucin Caliran Li, environmental, right?"

"Yes, Captain. Thirteen years experience. We were hoping—wondering—if maybe—"

"The consul explained you were all stranded thanks to chahoki fever—your ship left you behind."

"That's right."

"And you need a ride somewhere—I said I'd meet you and we'd see."

"Thank you, Captain. Left us high and dry, they did, and only the minimum in our drop account, too. We tried to get work, both shipside and downside, truly we did . . ."

"I believe you." The record the embassy had kept showed that; the consul clearly thought they were honest and diligent. They had even taken over work in the embassy garden, to the chagrin of the former gardener. "It's a small ship," Ky said. "We're headed to Belinta with a load of agricultural machinery. After that Leonora, and after that Last-way. But at either Belinta or Leonora you might be able to find another berth. I can't pay you—"

"That's fine, Captain. Just to get away from Sabine, that's enough." Li turned to the others. "This is Specialist Seth Garlan, also environmental, Technician Paro Hospedin, drives maintenance, and Specialist Caleb Skeldon, cargo."

Ky knew that already from the files the consul had given her, and was interested that Li introduced them in strict order of seniority and the others said nothing as she did so.

"Well, let's just chat a little. Specialist Garlan, you have seven years ship service, is that right?"

"Actually twelve, Captain, but only seven in environmental; I was hoping to make pilot, but turned out to have an immune problem with the pilot implants. Legacy of a childhood bout of tick fever, they thought. My family had a farm up on the North Coast." He grimaced. "And yes, I was the one who got sick here."

"Well, you're out of quarantine now," Ky said. She knew vaguely that tick fever was a problem on Slotter Key's North Coast, but otherwise nothing about it and it wasn't relevant at the moment anyway. "How about you?" she said, turning to Technician Hospedin.

"My training's from Pearce Institute," he said. "I have an A-class certificate in drives, for both insystem and FTL drives; six years onboard experience. My last requal exam was eighteen months ago, just before signing on *Apple Blossom Song*, the ship that left us here. Most of my shipboard experience has been with Plackman-Moreson 8800 insystem drives, and the Rollings series G FTLs, but I did my onboard apprenticeship in an old R-class freighter with PM-42s for insystem and a II-C FTL." His voice had the pedantic rhythms Ky associated with drives specialists.

"Our FTL's a Rollings F-230," she said. "It's needing replacement of the sealed unit, and possibly more."

His face sharpened. "If the sealed unit goes bad in a Series F," he said, "you're looking at cavitation damage in the main chamber as well. The back-buffer wasn't nearly as good in that series . . ."

That was what Quincy was afraid of, she knew. "We're looking into it," she said. She glanced at the last man, who spoke up without waiting for her to ask.

"Caleb Skeldon, Captain. Cargo specialist. Mostly I've been in charge of refrigerated holds, and I have only three years onboard experience, eight months of that on *Apple Blossom Song*. Before that I worked for a downside shipping firm, warehouse inventory and maintenance."

All very straightforward, as were they all. Ky saw nothing in their faces or demeanor that rang warning bells. She ignored the fact that Skeldon looked to be about her own age, and had chiseled features, wavy blond hair, and a dimple. Aside from the light hair, he could have been Hal's brother. That was irrelevant. She was an officer, after all, and his looks meant nothing to her. What mattered was that these four were Slotter Key citizens in a jam . . . The little voice in her head that said *Here you go again, leaping to rescue* could surely be ignored this time. She was doing a good deed, that was all. And at the request of the consul. No one could disapprove of that.

"Well," she said, sitting back. "Let me tell you about me and my ship, and then if you want to come with us, we'll talk to that clerk about arranging your transport up." They nodded; Skeldon opened his mouth as if to speak, but subsided at a glare from Li. "I'm one of the Vatta family," she said, "but I'm here on a private contract, not a family contract. The ship's old, but until the problem on the trip here from Belinta, she seemed sound. And we're having that repaired." She hoped. "Our contract calls for us to deliver a cargo of agricultural machinery to Belinta; we'll leave as soon as the cargo's loaded and repairs are finished. It's a several-week trip. Our crew capacity is twenty, and our environmental system could handle twice that number easily. At the moment, we have ten crew aboard. Any questions?"

Li spoke for them all. "When may we go up, Captain?"

"Let me ask that clerk," Ky said.

Zar must have been listening in, because he had all the preliminaries taken care of. "This afternoon's shuttle is all booked, Captain, but I have them listed on tomorrow morning's, on the embassy account."

"Good," Ky said.

"And I can cut you a check for their share of mess expense from here to Belinta, also on the embassy account. Standard government reimbursement. I'd suggest you purchase supplies quickly; the situation's getting nastier by the minute."

"Right," Ky said. "Can they stay in the embassy until the shuttle leaves?"

Zar nodded. "It would be advisable. They've been in transient housing—you have anything back there? If so, I'll send a uniformed runner for it."

"We didn't want to leave anything, the way things were," Li said. "Our duffel's with us."

"Good," Zar said. "I'm afraid the accommodations aren't great— you'll have to share space with the embassy's guard detachment, and we've cancelled all leave and liberty. Captain, if you'll come this way— and Li, I'll send someone to take you to the guard quarters shortly."

"Thank you, Captain Vatta," Li said. "We hoped—and of course Vatta . . ."

"Come on, Captain," Zar said.

"We'll have them escorted to the shuttle station tomorrow," Zar said when they got into the next room. "Shouldn't be any trouble, I hope. It's a big help, your taking them off our hands like this. We really don't have room here to shelter them; we've got a half-dozen merchant families, resident here for years, who are coming in tomorrow for the duration, plus the children of a dozen more, and we're going to be crowded. We're setting up dormitories upstairs . . ." He shook his head. "But that's not your affair. Let's see about that check—wait, here's the schedule of standard payments. If you need to file a protest . . ."

Ky's implant compared the cost of standard rations from a chandler at the orbital station to the reimbursement.

"No, that's fine," she said. "Do you have a comset I can use to contact my ship and let them know what's coming?"

"Of course, Captain Vatta. Secure set, right over here—" A cabinet in the corner of the room. While Zar began the surprisingly lengthy process of transferring embassy funds to her account, she contacted Riel Amat on board ship, and explained the situation, sending along the personnel files, and told him to go on and order supplies.

"Are you sure about this, Captain?" Amat asked. "Four strangers? And with a war starting?"

"The embassy vouched for them; it was an official request. They were stranded because of a quarantine matter—their ship wouldn't wait. And now they're subject to conscription, the consul said. Gary said we'd need help reconfiguring those machines to get into our holds. The embassy's paying their mess expenses—"

"But no passage fee?"

"No. And yes, I know we need the money. But they're our people, Riel."

"I hope so," he said. His lips were tight. She wondered if he thought he should be in command.

"Besides, Dad always said the government reimbursement schedules were generous. There'll be a little left over after you order the supplies."

"I hope that, too. All right—I'll place the order right away. Four additional. When are you coming back up?"

"When I arrange financing for the repairs. Let me speak to Quincy—" Riel cut Quincy into the circuit, and Ky spoke to her. "What's your estimate now, anyway?"

"I can tell you more in another twenty-four hours. Teardown's slow on this old girl. Last people who put 'er together meant her to stay that way. Listen, Captain, if there's war brewing you'd best come back up here—it may be time to contact Vatta headquarters and arrange repairs through them. I know this wasn't your assigned mission, but—"

She could just imagine her father's reaction. "I'll see what I can do here," she said. "You don't have the full specs on the repair yet anyway. I'll be careful." She signed off before either could say more, and came out of the booth. Zar handed her a hardcopy of the transfer; her implant agreed that the money was in the ship's account. Maybe this was a sign that things would now go right.

"I'm sorry, Captain Vatta, but it's against our policy to extend credit to independent captains for major repairs." The Helmsward Yard had seemed the perfect combination of quality and value for their repairs. Until she said she needed to arrange financing.

"But I'm not an independent—I'm part of Vatta Transport, Ltd."

"But your application states that you are incurring this risk as an individual . . ." The finance officer looked at her from under bushy gray brows. "Are you representing Vatta Transport, Ltd., or yourself?" It was clear he wasn't entirely sure of her identity at this point.

Ky tried not to glare. "I am Kylara Vatta; my father is CFO of Vatta Ltd. But this particular venture is my idea—"

"In other words, you are applying as an individual, and it is as an individual that I must reluctantly refuse your application," the finance officer said. "I have no doubt that you have your own reasons for doing this, but we simply do not extend credit to individuals."

"But my family—"

"Is not in the contract, Captain. No, I'm sorry, we simply cannot do it. Good day."

It was not a good day. It had not been a good day since Quincy had called down to report that the misbehaving drive had cavitation scars "you could put a fist into." Now it was more than squeezing out the fifty thousand credits for the sealed unit; this was going to take big money. It had become even less of a good day when the Captains' Guild inquired delicately just how long Captain Vatta meant to stay and when Captain Vatta would like to settle her bill and with what. Ky reminded the desk clerk that Vatta Transport, Ltd.'s account was, in all stations, classified 5A, and thus had no limit, and found that the concern arose because she was not on the list sent to them yearly of expected Vatta arrivals. They agreed to retract their request when she was able to prove who she was, but the argument frayed her patience. It was clear from the streets that the threat of war had frayed everyone's patience.

And now this. She walked out of the office with as much grace as she could muster and wondered what now. Her escort fell in beside her without a word. He had already suggested that she stay in the Captains' Guild or return to her ship—for her own safety—and she had already refused. She had a contract . . . She now had the merchandise to fulfill that contract, but . . . she didn't have enough money to repair the ship. She could get the merchandise—but then she couldn't get it back to Belinta. Or she could get the ship repaired enough to make it back, without the merchandise.

It was like those logic problems in children's activity cubes, where a problem seemed impossible unless you looked at it in a very different way.

Ship or merchandise? Impossible, which meant it had to be the wrong question. She could not—would not—renege on her deal with the Belinta Economic Development Bureau. That would foul the family name even though she had taken on the contract as an individual. Vatta would come through; Vatta had to come through. So there had to be some way to get the merchandise and the repair; she just hadn't thought of it yet.

The obvious thing was to call home—tell Vatta Transport, Ltd., what the problem was. They would bail her out; she knew that. But it would be, if not a black mark, a gray one. She had not followed the plan laid out for her, and even if Gary and Quincy had made it clear no one really expected her to take the ship tamely to Lastway, her decisions had led to a problem. A problem involving cash flow, which was . . . embarrassing. She hadn't overspent an allowance since she was nine and bought all that candy for visiting cousins.

She really wanted to find a better way. There wasn't a better way. If she didn't want to renege on the contract and she didn't want to risk spreading herself and her crew in a fine dust somewhere in deepspace, she had to have more money and no one, on the brink of a war, was going to lend it to an independent.

Back at the Captains' Guild she ignored the desk staff and went up to her room. Best get it over with. She set up the room's secure comdesk for an intersystem call and waited for the access light to go green. While she waited—on these smaller worlds, it could take a few minutes— she kicked off her shoes and hung her dress cape in the closet. The room seemed stuffy after the crisp air outside, but the windows didn't open. Shrugging, she sat on the end of the bed and massaged her feet, with one eye on the comdesk. The little voice in her head ran through all the things her father might say and the tone of voice he might use, and she carried on a long imaginary conversation defending her actions so far.

The light was still red. Had she set up the call wrong? She reached out for the hardcopy sheet of directions to check that just as the local system rang. It shouldn't do that. No local call should come in while the comdesk was set up for intersystem access, even if it was on standby. She picked up the handset anyway.

"Yes?"

"Captain Vatta, our board shows that you are attempting to place an intersystem call . . ." The voice on the other end did not identify itself.

"Yes, I am," she said. "Who is this?"

"We require an additional credit deposit for intersystem calls," the voice said. "Please make arrangements with the desk staff—"

"My credit here is 5A," Ky said, trying for icy. "That is supposed to cover all services . . ."

"We have no prior record of your account," the voice said. "Vatta Transport, Ltd., has a 5A account, but you—"

"We went over this already," Ky said. "I am Kylara Vatta; my father is Gerard Vatta, CFO of Vatta Transport. You've already verified my identification . . ."

"But you are here as an independent," the voice said. "We have received information from Helmsward Yard to that effect . . . I'm afraid we cannot consider your account covered by Vatta Transport, Ltd.'s credit rating. We will expect you to settle your account another way. And in the meantime . . ."

Rage brought her up off the bed, almost to tiptoe; she clamped her jaw on the words she wanted to say, starting with whatever sneak at Helmsward Yard had called the Captains' Guild and continuing with the ancestry, present attributes, and probable postlife destination of the person on the line.

"How unfortunate," she managed at last, in a flat voice. "Since I was in the process of calling home to instruct my father that I would need more funds to secure an investment opportunity. However, I don't need *your* equipment to make that call. Excuse me." She signed off the comdesk, jammed her feet into her shoes, and reached for her cape. She could use the embassy link to the ship, and the ship had its own intersystem link capacity if the consul didn't feel like trusting her for an intersystem call.

As she stalked past the front desk, the clerk tried to catch her eye; she ignored him and nodded to her escort. "We're going to the embassy, then back here," she told him. In the lobby, several captains were gathered around a vidscreen; she saw a swaying mass and smoke rising above it.

Away from the Captains' Guild, anger drained away as she walked. They were pinheads, and they would regret being pinheads someday, but right now she had to contact her father and arrange a funds transfer. It didn't matter if she was embarrassed at having to ask. All that really mattered was getting herself and her ship and crew to a safe place. Already things were worse on the street; her escort looked worried as they were jostled by hurrying pedestrians.

"Captain, we should take transport on the way back," he said, as they neared the embassy.

"Agreed," Ky said. She had never been in a war, though she'd heard stories, but she could feel the mood of the street.

The guards at the embassy entrance checked her ID carefully, then let her through; a different desk clerk checked them again.

"You were here yesterday," he said, after consulting a log.

"Yes. But today I need to make an intersystem call to my family, back on Slotter Key."

"I'm sorry, Captain, but we're sending out only diplomatic signals now."

"I suppose I'll have to go up to the station and link in via my ship then," Ky said.

"The Captains' Guild has a secure uplink," he said.

"But the Captains' Guild is being sticky about my credit," she said, wondering if the embassy could help.

"About Vatta credit?" he asked, brows raised.

"Yes. Even though I'm the CFO's daughter and fly the Vatta flag, because I'm on an independent contract they're acting as if Vatta won't cover the bill. I don't suppose you can get it across to them?"

"Oh, dear," he said. "This is not a good time, Captain; Secundus has threatened to blockade Prime. My advice to you is to get yourself up to your ship and out in space as fast as you can. Call from there, if you have the time—"

Ky felt cold all over. If the planet were blockaded . . .

Her implant pinged her. Tobai reporting that the ag machinery had arrived, and the four strays. That was something. But she could not be stuck down here while her ship, cargo, and crew were up there and needed her.

"We could get you onto a diplomatic shuttle to the station," he said, interrupting her thoughts.

"Thank you," she said. "When—"

"It leaves in a little less than two hours," he said. "The next would be tomorrow morning. I know all the commercial shuttles are full. Rats and sinking ships, et cetera."

"Which bay?" Ky asked.

"Twelve. You'll need your IDs; I'll put your name on the list—" He did so as she watched. "Transport from here to the 'port takes at least forty minutes."

"I have to pick up my duffel at the Captains' Guild . . ."

"Best hurry," he said.

Ky's escort had caught a short-haul transport; it took them fifteen minutes to get back to the Captains' Guild. Ky hurried upstairs, stuffed her things into the duffel, checked her account, retrieved the signed agreement from last night about her credit, and went back downstairs. Before the desk manager could open his mouth, she spoke.

"I am checking out. I have your signed agreement from yesterday that you will charge the Vatta Transport account; here is the authorization code again, and the account number. I want a receipt."

"But—"

"Now," Ky said. She had no idea what, besides frustration, was in her voice, but he backed up a step.

"Yes, Captain Vatta." He glanced at the data sheets she'd laid before him, and printed out a hardcopy of the receipt, *Charged to Vatta Transport, Ltd.* on the last line. "I'll need your signature . . ."

Ky scrawled *Kylara Vatta, Captain, Vatta Transport, Ltd.* on the yellow copy and handed it back.

"Have a good trip," he said as she turned away. In the lobby, the same cluster of captains was still watching the vidscreen, now showing someone with a strange hat talking at the camera.

Her escort had another transport waiting. "You don't have to come," Ky said.

"I do," he said. "I'm not letting you go alone, not in this. It's my duty."

"Very well. Let's go."

Traffic to the shuttle port was slow and heavy, but they arrived in time. Ky signed off the escort's time card at the entrance to Bay Twelve, and slung her duffel over her shoulder. The guards at the gates were thorough with their ID check—as she expected—but she made it onto the shuttle in plenty of time to find a seat and belt in. Like the Vatta private shuttle, the diplomatic shuttle had separate compartments for VIPs and the ravening hordes. Unlike the Vatta shuttles, captains of ships did not count as VIPs, and Ky found herself wedged into a narrow seat between two other Slotter Key citizens who had decided to leave.

"It's ridiculous," grumbled the man on her left. "If the government had just opened the Tertius mines to investment—"

"It has nothing to do with Tertius," said the man on her right. "That's just a side issue; the real problem is Secundus' perception that Prime is misrepresenting them to the universe as a backward, violent society—"

"Well, they are—," said the other man.

"They're pioneers. Pioneers have to be tough to survive."

"They don't have to have a habit of blowing up their neighbors. That's hardly a survival trait."

Ky felt like the net in a tennis match. "Excuse me," she said. "I just got here two days ago, and I have no idea what's going on." That wasn't, strictly speaking, true, but she hoped it would slow down the high-speed volleys.

They both looked at her as if they had not realized there was a human in the seat between them.

"Oh!" said the one on the right. His eyes focused on her uniform. "Uh . . . you're a merchanter captain? Uh . . . Vatta Transport?"

"Yes," Ky said. "Picking up a load of ag machinery."

"Oh, ag machinery," said the one on her left with a tone that suggested it might be something else. "Well . . . did you visit Secundus?"

"No," Ky said. "FarmPower's here on Prime."

"Yes, of course. Of course. Secundus . . . you heard me say they are pioneers . . ."

"What made it come to a head now is that the Prime government decided not to open the Tertius mines to investment, but to keep them as a government monopoly. To prevent destabilizing overexploitation, as they put it. Actually, to keep control of the richest mineral deposits in this system and funnel the output to Prime's industrial backbone—FarmPower among them—and ensure that Secundus keeps buying its . . . er . . . ag machinery from Prime's suppliers."

"And meanwhile," the other man said, "Prime's telling everyone that Secundus is backward and not worth trading with—bunch of ignorant roughs who shoot visitors in the street for no reason."

"It has happened, Harmy," the first man said.

"No more often than on Prime," the other man said. "The case they always cite," he said to Ky, "was a university student—one of a group—who went to Secundus on break. They went to get drunk and disorderly far from home, if you ask me. Anyway, the young man not only got drunk and disorderly, he pulled a young woman down from a wagon, ripped her clothes half off, and was about to rape her when she shot him. It would have been less trouble overall if she'd killed him, but she shot for deterrence instead, so he was able to come home and tell everyone what unreasonable people there were on Secundus."

"If they had proper law enforcement," the first man said, "it would never have happened; a policeman would have stopped him the moment he grabbed her off the wagon."

"Yes, but there was a reason she shot him. It wasn't 'senseless.' And there are streets in Prime's cities where you need a team of escorts, not just one."

"Criminal elements are everywhere."

"Including in First Families and government bureaus."

Ky interrupted, sensing another long volley about to begin. "So—Secundus is a pioneer society? How do they think they'll do in a war against Prime?"

The men stopped, looked at each other, and her, and said simultaneously, "I don't think I should comment on that." In eerie synchrony, they opened their workcases and began staring at the little screens.

Ky sat back, thinking, and wondered if either of the men would start a conversation again. She wondered all the way to the orbital station, and they didn't.

Back aboard her ship, she found her crew hard at work breaking down the ag machinery into components that would fit the odd-sized holds. She nodded at Gary Tobai, and headed for the bridge and its comdesk.

CHAPTER
SEVEN

No one was sitting at the comdesk board when she got there; with the captain onstation and on the way to the ship, that made sense. They were all busy trying to get the ship loaded.

Ky sat down and inserted her command wand, then entered the string of codes for intersystem ansible access. Whatever had a hair up the rear of the Captains' Guild wouldn't affect access from the ship; by law and treaty, all ships were guaranteed such access. While she waited for the connection, she flicked on the nearspace advisory channel.

"—an emergency like this," she heard. "Unprecedented, we simply have no idea what will happen now . . ."

That did not sound good. Ky queried her implant, realizing that it had been more silent than usual since she'd entered the diplomatic shuttle. She'd assumed the shuttle had security masks in place, but that shouldn't have been a problem on the orbital station. The implant fizzed the way it did when it needed an adjustment, then produced a warning symbol, followed by what was obviously an official announcement.

Due to conditions beyond our control, public access to channels is restricted until further notice. We apologize for any inconvenience. Stay tuned for more

information as it becomes available. Thank you . . . Due to conditions be-
yond our control . . .

Ky damped the implant and looked at the display on the comdesk.
The intersystem access telltale still glowed red, and as she watched it
began to blink. After a long moment, it went dark.

"No one ever thought anything like this could happen," someone on
the nearspace advisory channel was saying. "Attack on intersystem ansibles is just . . . just unthinkable."

Not really. Ky remembered one of the lectures in Strategic Analysis,
in which a discussion of the consequences of successful interdiction of
intersystem communication had delved into the reasons someone might
do it and the consequences thereof, economic, political, and military. It
had happened—far away, and decades past, and those responsible were
no longer alive—but it had happened. So some people had thought
of it, and presumably also whoever had—her mind came back from
that moment of shocklike drift. No ansible meant no message to Vatta
Transport, Ltd., and thus no funds, and thus . . . no repairs for getting
her ship safely out of this system before whoever had taken out the ansible decided to attack the orbital station.

A variety of epithets ran through her mind as she felt the goose
bumps rise on her skin. This was not a training simulation, a classroom
exercise. She was sitting on an unspaceworthy ship at a space station
orbiting a world at war, and one side or the other had just demonstrated
the ability to mount an attack in space, at the same time neatly cut-
ting off this system from real-time communication with the rest of the
universe.

She called up the station display of ship status. The good news was
that the display still worked, and purported to be up-to-date. The bad
news . . . ships were already signing up for departure queues, and one—
Susie G—had just executed an unapproved emergency disconnect. She
didn't bother to put her name in the queue; *Glennys Jones* wasn't going
anywhere without her drive repair. She tried for a video access, and to
her surprise was able to see a typical newcaster talking away in front of
an image of explosion. She turned up the sound on that.

"—No one is believed to have survived the explosion of either ansible
platform; the death toll is estimated to be at least seven hundred fifty
and could be several times that. InterStellar Communications local office has no comment at this time—" ISC, the monopoly which controlled both communications and financial ansibles across hundreds of

systems, would make someone wish they hadn't done it . . . They had fought some succesful limited wars to keep local governments from taking over ansible linkages. That response would come far too late to help her, Ky knew. "—Sabine system is now cut off from regular communication with the rest of the universe," the announcer said. "No word yet that anyone has claimed responsibility, but Sabine Prime's Solar Royal has accused Secundus rebels."

At least they had already loaded the supplies for the trip back to Belinta. Ky suspected that prices were going to skyrocket in the next few hours.

She heard someone running along the passage to the bridge; Gary Tobai and Riel Amat burst in. "Ky—Captain—you're here! You know what's happened?"

"Some idiot blew the ansibles, yes," Ky said. "And no, our transfer didn't come through. It must've happened while I was in transit. We're stuck here on a vulnerable station with a malfunctioning drive. At least we have food, right?"

"Right, Captain. Supplies all loaded. But the drives—"

"I know. And I can't call home—I could have, if the stupid Captains' Guild hadn't refused my credit rating, but they did, and eight hours makes a difference." Eight hours ago, when the ansible was still working, when those people were still alive . . . Ky pushed that thought away. "So—what do we have, if anything?"

"Insystem's still fine, so far as I know. But the deepspace is gone—not just the sealed part, but there's cavitation damage in the linkage—"

"I know," Ky said.

"And if we try to use it, there's no telling where we might end up."

"I understand," Ky said. "But if the insystem drive is okay, we could get away from this station, which I do not doubt is going to be attacked . . ."

Amat frowned. "It's a long way to anywhere else . . . where would we go?"

"I don't know. Yet. How are we doing on cargo loading, Gary?"

"It's coming. Sixty-five percent at the moment. We'd left open space for drives access for repairs—if we block that up—"

Then a repair crew, if she could find one, and if they would extend credit, wouldn't be able to get at the drives. But the ship without drives was nothing but a target. But the ship without cargo was useless . . .

Too many variables, too many conflicting priorities.

"How about the four I sent up?" Ky said. "Are they any use?"

"Oh, yes. Good workers, all of them. If we just had the drive in order—"

"Understood." Ky tried to make her brain work faster. It had to work faster; she had to find a solution to this. And the logical thing to do was try to find a repair yard. "I'm going to see what I can do about the drive problem. I'll switch our contract to Vatta Limited, and see if that shakes 'em loose, though with war breaking out and the ansibles gone, who knows? See if that drives tech thinks he can install parts if I can just get the parts. We could stand off somewhere on insystem drive, and install the stuff ourselves, maybe." And if he left her alone for a few minutes, she might be able to think clearly.

She called up the station directory and found the orbital offices of six firms with orbital yards. Helmsward Yard, Ltd., Sabine Systems, and Artco Yards all had a Superior rating, but Helmsward had already turned her down for financing. She doubted they would reconsider her application if she now claimed to be operating under Vatta's umbrella. In fact, in light of the ansible attack, they might think she was trying to misrepresent herself if she changed her story. When she checked the status of the others, *Artco* had relisted itself Unavailable. She called Sabine Systems, and a nervous-sounding voice on the other end said their chief engineer would have to get back to her.

That left Colley & Co. and Bartlin Brothers, rated Acceptable in the guide, and RealValue Repairs, unrated. She tried Bartlin Brothers; no one answered. Colley & Co.'s com was answered by a man who was both out of breath and annoyed. "Are you kidding?" he said, when she started to say her ship needed repairs, and then he hung up.

Gravity, her father had said, ensures that stuff rolls downhill until it hits bottom, and some psychic gravity was definitely at work here. RealValue Repairs sounded like the kind of place only the desperate approached. The kind of place where they removed parts from the previous repair job, cleaned and polished them, put them in fresh containers, and sold them as new. Where they had more experience in faking and cheating than actually repairing.

But what choice did she have?

Quincy's call from the drives bay gave her an excuse not to call them. "If you can get us a sealed unit and about ten meters of good-quality liner, we might get this done ourselves," she said. "It'll take us longer than a proper yard, but it's doable."

The first good news. Things got bad until they started getting better . . .

"I'll see what I can do," Ky said. Maybe RealValue would sell the parts. Quincy should be able to tell if the sealed unit was really sealed, and there had to be some kind of function test she could apply, short of going into FTL flight . . . and liner, that was a visual test. She knew how to do that herself. And maybe there were other suppliers . . . She queried her implant.

The comboard flashed red and a message came up on the screen: ALL SHIP TO STATION COMMUNICATIONS SUSPENDED EXCEPT TRAFFIC CONTROL TO SPACECRAFT. Great. Just great. Now she would have to leave the ship to get any more supplies.

No. She would send someone. She was the captain; she was responsible for them all. She would not leave the ship now, of all times. She called Quincy again.

"I need you to go onstation and find us that sealed unit," she said. "They've cut off ship to station communication, except for official contacts. I can't even get a list of suppliers, but I do have one contact name from before: RealValue Repairs. I don't want to leave the ship myself—"

"Quite right," Quincy said. "And I shouldn't either. I'll send one of the junior engineering crew. You do know RealValue has a bad rep."

"I suspected it; they're unlisted. But all the others have shut up business—I can't get through. We can sit here with nothing, or try to get permission to leave the station and go crawling off on insystem— which means we'd have to crawl back in a few weeks—or we find someone to sell us the sealed unit and some liner material. And RealValue is the only name I have."

"I have a couple others, not repair places but suppliers," Quincy said. "I'll send Beeah. You'll need to give him the financing options."

The financing options, which consisted primarily of begging someone to trust that Ky was really Vatta Transport, Ltd.

"Of course," Ky said. "Send him up and I'll give him the works." Since the station/ship commercial channels weren't working, Ky printed out a hardcopy of her master's license, her ID, and a statement on the Vatta Transport, Ltd., letterhead which authorized Beeah Chok, engineering second, to make binding legal contracts contingent on her signature.

Beeah showed up on the bridge in a crisp-jacketed Vatta Transport uniform completely unlike his usual working coverall. "Quincy said I had to look official, Captain," he said. "With trouble on the docks, I don't want to get taken in for something. Quincy gave me the shopping list—what else do I need?"

"This," Ky said. "Vatta Transport, Ltd., authorization to purchase, my authorization . . . and don't worry about getting the best price. Pick up whatever news you can, and make it snappy. Someone's going to close down this station soon, one way or the other . . ."

"Attack a station?" Beeah said, his eyebrows going up.

"Someone attacked ansibles," Ky said. "I expect an attack here; I would have broken us loose already if we had a working FTL drive."

"Right," Beeah said.

"Check the dockside intercom on your way off our patch," Ky said. "If anything happens, I want to be sure we have that much linkage."

"Will do," Beeah said.

She watched him on the monitors as he went; at dockside, he picked up the microphone and spoke.

"You hear me, Captain?"

"Loud and clear, Beeah. What can you see from there?"

"Not much. A lot of empty dockside. Looks like they may've closed the big hatches between here and Y-Zone, with just the personnel locks between. That may be why the ship-to-station ordinary linkages are down. That was all optics, probably. See you later, Captain."

Ky watched him go, chewing her lip. It wasn't safe. Nothing was safe, right now. ISC would have noticed immediately when their ansibles went down; they would respond, but who knew how long that would take? She and the *Glennys Jones* and all her crew could disappear into this war, and nobody would ever know what had happened. Her family would wonder . . .

But they would know, she realized in the next instant. Vatta Transport, Ltd., used the same ISC ansibles as anyone else; Vatta ships had a regular schedule through Sabine. The Sabine ansible would be monitored by someone at Vatta's home offices, and they might even know already she was here, if that monitoring included a list of ships currently at Sabine's orbital station.

She hoped it didn't. She hoped very much her father didn't know that she was a long way from where she was supposed to be, in a developing war zone, and out of ansible contact.

The board meeting opened on time, for a wonder. The media ruckus downstairs had almost delayed the arrival of Ky's father, but he had time for a half cup of coffee before strolling, elaborately casual, down to the boardroom with his brother.

"Any news?" Stavros asked.

"Not yet," Gerard Vatta, Ky's father, said. "We shouldn't hear anything now until the first stop." He raked his hand through his thinning hair. He didn't need to say more; Stavros knew the plan.

"It's a shame," Stavros said. "She was doing so well."

"Yes. And thanks again, by the way, for being available for a pickup."

"Of course."

"And don't think I don't know you're biting your tongue not to mention Stella."

"Much as I love Stella, I'm not having to bite my tongue, Gerry. She and Ky are nothing alike. Stella is eighty-seven percent feeling. We should've tweaked that in the embryo, but you know how it is . . ."

"I do indeed. Thanks anyway, and for handling the press so far." Gerard clapped his brother on the shoulder, and let him enter the boardroom first. Almost everyone there was family but, even in the family, etiquette demanded that the CEO enter before the CFO.

"How much is all this going to cost us?" one of the nonfamily asked. Stavros paused, on his way to his chair, and glanced at the man, and then at Gerard.

"No reason it should cost us anything," Gerard said. "People aren't going to give their cargo shipments to someone else because my daughter blundered with another military cadet."

"But our military support contracts?"

"I have been assured that they are not in jeopardy. Ky wasn't pilfering from cargo locks, after all; she just fell for a pitiful story from a handsome lad, as girls have done for thousands of years. The military understand that. Now if we tried to send classified cargo by a ship she commanded right now, they might raise their brows. But we aren't, so there's no problem."

"All that publicity—"

"Is focused on a possible love affair . . . It will die down."

"But if your daughter talks to the press—"

Gerard cocked his head at the man. "Jas, do you really think we haven't thought of all that in the past five days? I assure you, Kylara is not about to talk to any press, and they are unlikely to locate her." It was bad luck to claim an absolute, but by now she should be well out of reach of any Slotter Key news agency. Even within the company, only a few knew which Vatta was aboard the *Glennys Jones*.

Eventually, the news agencies figured that out, too, and the press of eager reporters at the Vatta offices dwindled, finally disappearing after juicier game. Gerard no longer saw even mid-news "updates" on the mess. He congratulated himself—by the time Ky got back, the whole thing would have died down completely.

When the arrival report came from Belinta, he breathed a sigh of relief. Just as planned, nothing had happened. That wouldn't last, if he knew his daughter, but she had weathered the first voyage. Gary Tobai's report suggested she had done all the predictable things, and made the right adjustments. After all, what did Vatta really need with a military connection in the family? They were all basically traders, not warriors. Ky was cut out to be a trader captain, and now she was on the right path.

A few days later, the next message from Gary brought a grin to his face, and he called Stavros' office.

"Well, she took the bait," Stavros said.

"Vatta to the core," Gerard said. "I take it you got the tightbeam from Quincy or Gary."

"Both. You can practically hear their gleeful cackling."

"What kind of scheme has she cooked up? They didn't send me the details."

"I'll send it to you, but it's classic trader. A bit risky financially—she's agreed to go on spec, buy the cargo, and trust the buyer to pay up on delivery. On the other hand, the customer's a government bureau, the parameters of acceptable cargo are clearly defined, and the Slotter Key consul told her they were good for it. The profit from this will cover some of the repairs . . . If she scraps that ship, I'll be very surprised."

"I hope we gave her a big enough letter of credit," Gerard said.

"It never hurts to have to scrimp a bit," Stavros said. "Remember our first venture?"

"Of course . . ." It had been wilder than this, and they'd nearly lost the ship, playing tag with a planetary militia they hadn't known about, but it had, in the end, paid for the repairs on *Matilda C.*

"She'll do fine. The ship's sound enough for that much, anyway. If something major doesn't go wrong—and if it does, I'm sure she'll have the sense to get in contact."

"I hope so."

"And if she doesn't, the others will."

"I wonder when she'll break out the fruitcake," Gerard said. Theirs hadn't been fruitcake by Auntie Grace, but sausage by Uncle Evers. Hard as a rock—they'd actually bashed one would-be sneak thief with it—and deemed inedible by all but the starving.

"I'd like a picture when she does," Stavros said. "She really hates that stuff."

"It is vile," Gerard said. He shook his head. "The things we do to our younglings."

Time passed. Gerard tried not to fret. Ky would be making a sensible, reasonable passage to Sabine, which was the closest source of ag equipment. Or she had chosen another place, for a good reason. She would not report in when she arrived, because she would not want to tell headquarters she was playing a lone game. He remembered what that felt like—going out of bounds for the first time, being alone—with a ship full of crew—where no one in the family knew the location. Heady excitement, stomach-churning responsibility. And he'd had Stavros along.

She had good crew along. He knew that. They would take care of her, and she was not an idiot anyway. She might make a profit or not, but she would be fine. He would not, absolutely not, spy on her via the Sabine ansible. He could of course ask someone to get the list of ships in system, but that was . . . not fair. You gave the young ones rope to see how far they could swing . . . You did not hover, or it wasn't a real test. They needed to know later that they really had been out there on their own.

"Gerry, have you seen this?" That was Stavros, leaning on the doorframe, waving a printout of something.

"Probably not," Gerard said. "Though I'm not sure what it is . . ."

"News bulletin from Sabine system," Stavros said.

Gerard's heart stopped; his vision blurred. "Ky—"

"Gerry! No! I'm sorry—there's nothing—but there's political trouble. I'm wondering if we should break cover and order her out."

Vision came back, red-hazed, and Gerard drew a shuddering breath. "She's . . . not . . . ?"

"No. But Prime and Secundus are moving toward war this time, apparently. It's a slice off the WarWatch page, and they're pretty solid . . ."

He knew that. But now he had to know more.

"Who's on watch?" he asked.

"I already checked. The ship's there, at the station. Captain Vatta is planetside, has been several days. She'll be at the Captains' Guild, no doubt. I haven't made a call yet, but I was wondering . . ."

"Let's see." Gerard could focus his eyes now, and he scanned the news item quickly. Probability high, with an analysis of forces on both sides sufficient to worry about. "Secundus is crazy," he said. "If this is all they've got."

"They've got those shipkillers," Stavros pointed out. "And speculation that at least four of them could take out an orbital station."

"Um. What's the projected timeline . . . Yes, I think we should get her out of there. How can we . . . oh, I know. Ky knows we have an ansible watch, and a news item like this would be reason to check and see if any Vatta ships are in the area. If we send it to the Captains' Guild for 'Any Vatta Transport, Ltd., captain' she won't know we know where she is."

"Good. I'll do it, general alert. We need to put out the word to our regular route captains as well." Stavros got the blank look common to those accessing multiple implant links at once, and then smiled. "Done. We should have acknowledgment in a few hours. It'll be interesting to see what she does."

Less than an hour later, Gerard's implant shrilled at him the news that the Sabine system ansibles were out, presumed destroyed. He stared out his office window at the evening, the city lights beginning to twinkle through the dusk. Without thinking about it, he found himself staring far across the city to the Academy, visible only as a gap in the regular lines of light. If that miserable lying little fox of a Miznarii had caused his daughter to end up dead in a war . . . He shook himself. That was no way to think, not now.

"Gerry." Stavros had come to his door. "Are you all right?"

Gerard tried to laugh; it came out a croak. "I'm . . . not," he said. "If Ky—"

"She's not Stella," Stavros said, coming into the office. "Stella wouldn't make it. Ky—I'd bet on Ky. She's smart, she's got some military training, enough to recognize the signs—"

"What if they blew the station at the same time as the ansibles?" Gerard said.

"She was on the planet, she'll be fine," Stavros said.

"No . . ." Gerard worked through it as he spoke. "If she sees trouble coming, she'll go back to her ship. She'll try to get it away. But there wasn't time—we had that report the ship was docked only a few hours ago." He could not help but picture the station exploding, the ships docked there flung wide, losing atmosphere through the docking tubes, other explosions, Ky's body flung into space, her last agonized breath a cry for help that never came.

"And maybe she's fine," Stavros said. "We can't know until ISC gets ansibles up and running, so the best we can do is stay sane until she shows up wondering why we worried. Say she did go back to the ship.

She knows trouble's coming; she buttons the ship up; she asks permission to undock; she breaks away if she has to. She's smart, Gerry. She'll survive."

She's not your daughter, Gerard wanted to say, but this was his brother, who had already been remarkably forbearing. And it was all the comfort he had, or was going to get, until the ansibles were back up.

"We'd better not tell the others," Gerard said.

"You're right about that," Stavros said. He sighed. "It was easier in the olden times, when our ancestors believed there were magical beings in the sky who could intervene. Our modern religions are fine for destressing from the everyday, but it would be nice to have a real lightning-throwing god to pray to about now."

Gerard laughed, and his laugh was almost normal.

After Beeah left, Ky tried to think what to do next. What if someone attacked the station while they were docked—would the station have any warning? Would they share such warnings with the ships? Her mind worked through possibilities with excruciating slowness, though she noticed that the chronometer was clicking over slowly, too. Station attacked, station blown, decompression—

Of course. Right now the ship shared atmosphere with the station, part of their allotment of station resources as covered by the daily dock charges. Station air, station water. But that meant if the station lost atmosphere, so would they.

So the first thing was to button up. It would take longer for Beeah to get back aboard, and cargo to load, but she could worry about that later.

She called down to drives, where Quincy was presumably still working with her subordinates to plan the quick replacement of the sealed unit.

"Yes, Captain?" Quincy didn't sound scared. Ky hoped she herself didn't.

"Just in case, I want to button the ship up. Beeah's off ship, but the dockside intercom works; we checked it."

"Good thinking, Captain," Quincy said. "I should have thought of that. I'll be right up to give you a hand."

In the next few minutes, system by system, they shut off all the connections to the stations but the communication lines and the docking grapples. Air, water, cargo bay hatches . . . all sealed. Ky watched the shipboard systems come online, one by one, looking for signs of anything wrong. All the telltales stayed green as they should. Their reserve water tanks were full, their growth chambers properly stocked and balanced.

Suddenly the comdesk lit: incoming call from the stationmaster, with visual. A stocky man in uniform glared from the screen. "*Glennys Jones*: report status to Stationmaster."

"Captain Vatta, *Glennys Jones*, status docked."

"Our sensors indicate you've closed hatches and withdrawn from station circulation: explain."

"Concern for safety," Ky said. "If there's an attack on this station—"

"You have data suggesting an attack on this station?"

"The ansibles were attacked," Ky said. "Someone has the capacity and willingness to attack space targets. This is a big one. If the station loses air, I don't want to lose mine."

"Oh. Well, we understand you have a crewman on the station, is that correct?"

"Yes, it is. Beeah Chok, engineering second; he's on an errand for me."

"What kind of errand?"

"We need some equipment," Ky said. "I sent him to purchase it."

"He should return to your ship. Station Security will inform him." The signal clicked off. Ky stared at the blank, silent screen.

"This isn't good," Amat said, coming onto the bridge and settling in the pilot's seat.

"I know that," Ky said. She glanced at him; his face was set. "You were in the space force, Riel—any advice?"

"Not a lot of options here, Captain. Glad you came back up when you did."

"Maybe Beeah will have good news for us," Ky said. She didn't believe it, but she could hope.

"An embargo on all ship components," Ky said. "Why?"

"To prevent our giving aid and comfort to the enemy," Beeah said. Station Security had delivered him to dockside hours after that last contact from the Stationmaster's office. He leaned against the bulkhead and took another bite of sandwich; he'd arrived rumpled and hungry. "They don't want us taking a sealed unit to Secundus."

"I don't want to take a sealed unit to Secundus," Ky said. "I want to put it into my own ship so I can take tractors to Belinta."

"That's another problem," Beeah said.

"What, tractors?"

"Yes, Captain. You see, they aren't convinced that what we have are tractors for Belinta. They think 'agricultural equipment' is just a cover for weapons and things for the rebels."

"Why would they think that?" Ky said. "We have a contract with Belinta . . . I told everyone that and it's the truth. FarmPower has the manifests of what they sent, as well. I can prove—"

"Captain, don't glare at me. I know that. But they're in a panic. Nobody thought Secundus had the weapons to hit the ansible platforms. What they say is that you were using your own money, and borrowed money; if you really were hired by Belinta, why wasn't Belinta's name on the funds transfer? And they know our holds weren't large enough to take the equipment without dismantling it. FarmPower told them so, and apparently someone at FarmPower suspects we sold the farm machinery and bought weapons with it."

"From whom?" Ky said. She felt like someone caught in a bad play. "I haven't dealt with anyone but FarmPower, the bank, and the embassy—except for buying that stupid sprayer."

"I didn't say they were rational. They're scared, Captain, and they're determined not to let us have any ship components."

"Great."

"And they would appreciate it, they said, if you would pay all docking fees up to date immediately and on a daily basis hereafter."

Ky tried to think of a suitable epithet but nothing seemed strong enough for the situation. "Why don't they just insist on coming aboard and inspecting the machinery for themselves?" she asked.

"They probably would, but they're afraid we might have it booby-trapped. They figure if they hang onto us, we can't deliver it, and if we blow up with them, it serves us right."

"So why didn't they come to me directly?"

"Well . . ." Beeah looked at the deck, and Ky wished she had a scanner to read the inside of his head. She'd never seen him blush before. "It's . . . they think if they open a link, you'll do something. It would let you set off something, they said."

"Oh, for—" She still could not think of the right comment for that kind of boneheaded stupidity. A worse thought occurred. "So if the station does blow up, they'll probably blame me—and maybe Vatta Transport—even if we had nothing to do with it!"

"I guess they might," Beeah said. It was clear he hadn't thought of that. She watched his expression change as he took it in. "Captain . . . what are you going to do?"

She hadn't a clue. But captains weren't supposed to say that. Instead, she said, "Go down and send Quincy up, please." When he'd left the bridge, she called Gary to the bridge as well. Surely a combined hundred and fifty years of experience ought to be worth something.

"What's up?" Quincy asked. "Beeah said he couldn't get the equipment—"

"No, and there's worse. Wait until Gary gets here."

Gary came in a moment later, out of breath. "Damned multigang disk cultivators anyway. Stupid things will not stack well, even half-covered in sticky tape. What is it, Captain?"

Ky outlined their situation. "I won't say it couldn't be worse," she said. "Because it always can. But I wanted your comments on this . . ."

"Not advice?" Gary said, rubbing his head.

"I'll hear it if you have it," Ky said.

"It's a right mess," Quincy said. "Like you said, if some saboteur blows the station, we'll likely be blamed for it and we won't be there to defend ourselves. Vatta, too, you're right. Slotter Key, even. And we'll be blamed for not making the delivery to Belinta, as well. And we can't go anywhere," Quincy said, looking worried. "Insystem drive, fine, it's working, but it's slow and there's nowhere in this system we can go. We need that sealed unit."

"Even if we had it, we'd have a big problem," Gary said. "If we undock without authorization, they may consider that proof of bad intent and attack us. I don't see what we can do but stay here . . ."

"Are we completely spaceworthy for insystem travel?" Ky asked.

"Yes, but it's no good to us . . ."

Ky held up her hand, and Quincy stopped. "It's like this," Ky said. "So far I've been reacting to things—I suppose you could consider the Belinta deal initiative, but it practically fell on me out of a tree. Here on Sabine, I've been pushed by circumstances. If I just follow along doing the obvious thing, it's going to get us killed. I realized that while Beeah was talking. If we're going to get out of this, we have to act. Reaction may kill us, but inaction certainly will."

Amat shifted in his seat; Ky glanced at him and found him looking at her with peculiar intensity.

"What?"

"Nothing, Captain. You're making sense. Go on."

"What are you planning?" Quincy asked.

"I don't have a complete plan," Ky admitted. "But the longer we stay here with our ship locked to the biggest remaining target in local space, the more likely we are to be hit. So the first thing is, we undock, with polite apologies to the station. Prep us for undock and insystem travel."

Quincy blinked, then nodded. "Right, Captain. But how are you going to contact the station, when they're blocking contact?"

"They'll have receivers tuned for broadcast, I'm sure. Get us ready, that's all. How long?"

Quincy glanced at the bridge status boards, then at Gary. "Your cargo all locked down?"

"Cargo secure," Gary said. Ky could not tell from his expression what he felt about her orders.

"Fifteen minutes, then. They'll detect it in eight, Captain."

"Right." Ky set an alarm for eight minutes and the other two left the bridge faster than they'd come. Time to address the rest of the crew. She cleared her throat, and thumbed the intercom.

"Crew—this is Captain Vatta—" Her voice was steady, but it still felt odd to call herself Captain Vatta. "We are preparing for emergency undock. All sections report green status. Expect emergency undock in less than fifteen minutes. Warning count will be given starting two minutes before undock. Off-duty crew bunk down; this may be rough."

She heard footsteps in the passage, the rest of the bridge crew hurrying to their stations.

"What happened, Captain?" Lee Quidlen slid into his seat, snatching at the restraints with a practiced hand, and logged in.

"There's a war starting," she said. "You know about the ansibles being attacked. The station suspects that we might be bad guys, and won't let us have the replacement sealed unit. Which leaves us a choice between sitting here like a target, or moving off and hoping no one blows us up . . ."

Sheryl's hair was wet and her skin glistened; she must have been in the shower. But she was in her seat in moments, calling up the ship's navigation functions. "Got any idea where to go?"

"Away from here or anyplace else someone would want to blow up," Ky said. "But close enough we can get back if it turns out we have a chance to refit. We have to get repairs somewhere, but I'm sure ISC will be doing something about the ansible damage—"

"Mmmph. So we just go out and try to find some nondescript system real estate for the duration?"

"Lacking FTL drive or weaponry, yes."

"Sounds good to me." Sheryl turned to her controls.

"Lee, you take the undock; I'll monitor drives and balance," Riel said. Lee grunted acknowledgment. Ky glanced at the chronometer. Eleven minutes. Something hissed; she looked up and saw the bridge hatch sliding shut; then pressure pulsed at her ears; seals testing. The hatch slid open again.

"Cargo green," came Gary Tobai's voice. Then, more softly, "Suggestion, Captain?"

"Go ahead."

"Suits? Have 'em out?"

Of course. "Captain to crew," Ky said. "Suit up as duties allow, stay on ship atmosphere for now." Her own suit, in its sealed pouch, was under the captain's seat. She pulled it out, shook it loose of the pouch, then realized she was still in shore uniform.

"I have to change," she said to the back of Lee's head. "Two minutes."

He nodded and she dashed to her cabin, blessing the daily routine of the Academy. Skinning out of shore clothes, a quick trip to the toilet, into formfitting shipsuit, into the pressure suit, back to the bridge.

Slow. Two minutes, five seconds. Nine minutes to go.

"Environmental green," said Mitt Gossin from his control station. Ky acknowledged that, sank into her seat, and the safety harness slid out to enclose her in its protective webbing.

"Crew quarters green."

"Seals green." Now *Glennys Jones* was as safe from harm as it could be; it would take real weaponry to breach the hull, and anything that size would harm the station. It might even survive a hit on the station, depending on how close and how big. Still, it was attached to the target and not able to maneuver on its own.

Brrrp. The alarm. Eight minutes.

"Insystem drive initiation." Quincy, sounding bored, which meant not bored at all. Nothing happened at first but a light blinking on the main board. Then the undertone, felt more than heard, of the insystem drive spinning up. The light flickered, then steadied: successful drive initiation. The station would detect that; what they would do about it remained unclear.

"Umbilicals disengaged." Clicks, thunks, hisses, as *Glennys Jones*' attachments went from "sealed" to "retracted."

"Emergency disconnect boosters enabled." Soundless, this: merely an electrical signal to the safety interlocks that prevented accidental discharge.

Two minutes now. Ky reminded herself to breathe. Surely the stationmaster would make contact. They didn't need the cable links; they had broadcast . . . and what would she say?

"Pilot's board green," Lee said. "Emergency disconnect on your mark, Captain."

"Captain to crew, take stations for emergency undock maneuver, and report" Ky said. She watched the lights blink on, section by section reporting them secure.

At sixty-seven seconds the comdesk lit up. "Stationmaster to *Glennys Jones*. What do you think you're doing?"

"Stationmaster, this is Captain Vatta commanding *Glennys Jones* . . . We are preparing to undock." That was obvious. She watched the chronometer's numbers tick over.

"You don't have permission. You don't have clearance. There are other vessels in the vicinity . . ."

"Then I suggest you provide information on their whereabouts and courses via Traffic Control, and restore communication with this vessel."

"You will stay where you are; you will cease and desist any attempt to undock; you will shut down your drive—"

"We are going to undock," Ky said. "It's not safe to stay here, and you've cut us off from critical data."

"If you continue, we will consider that proof of hostile intent—your weapons—"

"I register formal complaint, under Article 389.4 of the Intersteller Commercial Code," Ky said. Invoking that article meant that automatic recording of her message would go into the most secure storage on the station, unalterable by the station staff. She wished she'd thought of it sooner. "Vatta Transport, Ltd., cargo ship *Glennys Jones*, outbound from Sabine Prime, with a cargo of agricultural equipment purchased from FarmPower, invoice number 893547699, on contract with Belinta Economic Development Bureau. This ship was refused access to critical ship components for repair on the grounds that it was in clandestine relationship with Sabine Secundus. This ship has just been accused by the stationmaster of carrying illicit weaponry. No prior inquiry was made, no investigation was pursued, and no official of the station contacted the captain to ascertain the truth. Now the stationmaster has stated that this ship's undocking will be interpreted as a hostile act. This is in violation of the Commercial Code; Vatta Transport, Ltd., requests a formal inquiry into this matter at the earliest possible date. I formally deny the charges that have been made."

"You Slotter Key types are all pirates," snarled the stationmaster. That, too, would go into the sealed record, and ought to make for an interesting hearing in a few years, whenever the circuit court got to it.

Ky glanced over at Lee and held up her hands, folding down one finger at a time. At the last, he touched the controls for emergency disconnect boosters and *Glennys Jones* popped out of her docking slot like soap out of a wet hand. As they cleared the station's hull, the scans came alive. They weren't the only ones who'd left in a hurry. At least three shuttles were nuzzling the shuttle bays, and two more hung at a little distance, one of them fairly close to *Glennys Jones*. Larger ships were pulling Gs to get away. Ky said nothing; pilots didn't need distractions in crowded space. She widened scan. The radiation signatures of the ansible explosions made two very bright flares on her scan, with the red icons that meant "Danger." And something else.

"That does it, Vatta," said someone from the station. "You'll never dock here again."

"That's the truth," Ky said, cold prickles racing each other up her spine. "You've got more problems than me . . . Check your deep scan." Warships, two of them. Not with the Sabine Prime star-and-mountain icon, either. Sabine didn't have much of a space navy anyway; they patrolled system space for pirates with stubby maneuverable little ships that mounted only a pair of ship-to-ship missiles. The ships on scan were much larger, and probably much better armed. They might be ISC come to find out what happened to their ansibles, but even ISC couldn't get someone here that fast. Probably. Which meant they were most likely someone very nasty indeed. She glanced at Lee, who was clearly still concentrating on nearby traffic.

Silence, anyway, from the station; that light disappeared from the board.

"Riel," Ky said. "We have a problem."

"Naw . . . Lee can clear that shuttle easily, doesn't even need insystem . . ."

"Deep scan. Warships. Get us away from the station, Riel. I'll look for cover. Sheryl, you concentrate on avoiding collisions."

She had the nav charts up on her board now and tried to think like a cadet with a tac problem in class, and not a cargo captain in an unarmed ship in a war zone. What did the enemy know, and what did she know? The warships had no downjump haze around their icons; they had been in the system—she checked the backtrace—four hours. Jumped in at low relative vee above the ecliptic. Two small jumps to place them where they were, in the classic "attack and blockade a planet" configuration. They would have had time to locate and identify all the ships at the station, which meant that just putting a planet between them and *Glennys Jones* wouldn't accomplish anything.

The thing was . . . it wasn't a tactical problem in class, it was real life. And she was a captain, with all a captain's responsibilities . . . just not the kind of ship she'd ever thought of having. No weapons.

Commercial-grade shielding only. A cloud of "if only" hovered over her: if only she'd just done the expected thing . . . if only she'd had the ship repaired at Belinta before coming here . . . if only she'd called home before the ansibles were blown . . .

No time for that. Riel, after one startled glance at the deep scan, reached over and switched the insystem drive from standby to engage.

"Lee, I'll take over now. I can't push the old lady up fast," he said to Ky. "She'll gut-choke on us. I'll have to ease into it."

"Do what you can," Ky said. Had those warships blown the ansibles? Her scan data weren't good enough to backtrack the ships' movements, but it was a reasonable guess. The station should be able to figure it out, if that did any good. Whose warships were they? Not Prime's, and not Slotter Key's . . . and anyone else probably wasn't a friend.

She had the comdesk open wide, ready to pick up anyone's transmission . . . Something squealed, and a spike ran up the visual display.

"What was that?" Lee asked.

"Batch-pod," Ky said. Military used them, to send messages out of a system with no ansible. Their endim transition produced a characteristic squeal and blip. So someone—probably the warships—had sent information to someone outside the system. More warships? Invaders? Not pirates; pirates didn't have this kind of resource base. At least not near Slotter Key. Someone hired by Secundus, was the most likely answer. So—who were they talking to, with a batch-pod?

She should have read up more on Sabine's history and political setup. Hadn't she heard the stories? Hadn't she grown up knowing that a trader captain must know what was going on, or else?

And now she was here and it wasn't a story.

Glennys Jones, easing up to her insystem cruising velocity at the modest acceleration her aging frame would endure, moved far more slowly than Ky wanted, opening distance from the station. Ky called up the supplementary military/mercenary database, searching for the icons the warships projected. There it was. Mackensee Military Assistance Corporation. The listing described it as "a consultancy service," but farther in Ky found a paragraph describing "additional services which may extend to the provision of personnel and matériel when employer resources are insufficient to the accomplishment of specific goals outlined in the contract . . ."

Mercenaries indeed. It was heartening to notice that the mercenaries stated as policy that they did not take contracts involving "actions defined as piracy under the Interstellar Uniform Commercial Code" but less heartening to note the exceptions from that code permitted "in time of war or insurrection." Those exceptions permitted civilian ships to be boarded and inspected, though no personnel were supposed to be harmed and no cargo taken . . . though again with exceptions. "Except in cases where the civilian ships are deemed to be carrying matériel of military significance . . ."

Matériel of military significance could be anything from medicine to weapons . . .

But probably not tractors, disk cultivators, spring-tooth harrows, harvesting combines, Ky hoped.

Reading further: the listing ended with a pious statement of belief in a deity Ky had never heard of, and the advice to potential customers to consider carefully whether they really had anything worth fighting over. "War is not a game," the last paragraph read. "War is nasty, dirty, brutal; we hope that potential customers will find a way other than war to solve their problems. But if conflict is inevitable, then the least destructive approach is that which leads to a quick, decisive conclusion. In that case, our expertise may be of service."

As a Saphiric Cyclan trained in logic, Ky found this disclaimer both dishonest and funny. She could just imagine the up-rolled eyes and folded hands . . . with a third invisible hand held out for the payoff.

She hoped that some of the listing was correct, though, because if these mercenaries really didn't want trouble with all the commercial shipping concerns, they might well leave a Vatta ship alone. In that case . . . why had they blown the ansibles? Surely they would know that would bring the ISC after them?

Unless . . . someone else had blown the ansibles? Someone who detected their approach and wanted to send an alarm message—but then, why not just send it, via ansible? Someone—perhaps their employers—who had the bright idea to interdict ansible communication in the simplest way.

If Secundus had hired mercenaries to advise them or fight for them . . .

"Attention all ships . . ." Her comdesk informed her that this was a recorded message, origin one of the warships. "All ships in Sabine system. For your own safety, it is imperative that you reply on receipt of this message, using standard UCC channel seventeen, with the following information: ship name, ship registry, ship owner, ship captain. In that order. This is Colonel John Calvin Tessan, Mackensee Military Assistance Corporation, in command of the Mackensee Engineer Battalion and Expeditionary Force."

The message repeated, clearly a recorded loop, and Ky stared across at Riel.

"What're you going to do, Captain?" he asked. She noticed, with a clarity that bothered her, that he looked scared.

"What I'm told," she said. "We have two very large warships insystem, and more possibly coming in. They could bat us into pieces without even trying. I don't want them to try." She set the com to channel seventeen, checked the setting once more, and transmitted, without comment, _Glennys Jones_, Slotter Key, Vatta Transport Limited, K. Vatta.

A lightlag later, her board lit again and an unrecorded voice came out. "Vatta Transport ship _Glennys Jones_ continue on present course; do not change course without direction." The voice waited for no answer; the light went off.

"Are we going to hit anything?" Ky asked. Sheryl shook her head. "No, Captain. We could do this for several days—maybe longer, I'll have to look—as long as nobody runs into us."

"Then we'll just keep on keeping on," Ky said. For the time being, _Glennys Jones_ had been dismissed as too little to matter, a nonproblem. She watched on deepscan, aware that other ships would have received that message at different times, thanks to their different distance from the warships. If they obeyed, they also would get orders—the same orders? Maybe, maybe not. At any rate, some of those ships would not get the first message for another hour or so, during which time nothing exciting should happen—she hoped.

But in any event, time to address her crew. Ky took a deep breath, then another, and yawned once to open her throat. Never sound scared, never sound worried: that had been the advice of their second-year rhetoric instructor. Always prepare what you have to say. Have a point to make, and make it. Don't ramble, don't waffle.

"I'm going to let the others know what's going on," she said to the bridge crew. They nodded. She turned the ship's intercom back on. "This is the captain," she said. "Here's the situation. There are two warships insystem, mercenaries. I don't know who hired them, but probably Secundus. They've asked all civilian ships to identify themselves; we have done so. We have been told to stay on our present course, which is what we're doing. According to what I found in the database, their stated policy is not to confiscate commercial ships or their nonmilitary cargoes, or harm their crews." Explaining the exceptions to this policy would only alarm them, Ky thought, so she didn't.

Civilian ships, small merchanters, did not have the clear rank structure Ky had been taught in the Academy. It had bothered her, the first few days, and then she had grown used to it. Now that lack bothered her again. She wanted to leave the bridge and walk around the ship, speaking reassuringly to her crew the way she was supposed to. But she had no exec to leave in charge even for a few minutes, and from the expression on Riel's face, he wasn't up to it.

"Section firsts, to the bridge, please," Ky said.

Gary Tobin arrived first, then Quincy, then Mitt. They all looked worried; Ky did her best to project calm confidence.

"Here's what I think happened," she said. "Secundus hired some mercenaries. They call themselves the Mackensee Military Assistance Corporation, and the communication I got listed an Engineer Battalion and Expeditionary Force. The onboard database doesn't have much, but I remember from the Academy that many mercenary units provide technical assistance and training as well as weaponry and troops. They often call their training cadres engineers, whether or not they do any engineering."

"So this would be both instructors and soldiers, you think?"

"I think so, yes. Secundus managed to come up with the down payment—these people don't come fight on spec—but didn't have enough to finance more than a short stay. That's why they needed to have the ansibles out."

"But is this company . . . reliable?" Quincy asked.

"I don't have enough data. At the Academy, they taught us about the history of mercenary forces in space, and those that had once operated in our own system, and the theoretical limits of mercenary activity, but they didn't tell us which currently active units abided by which conventions, if any, with regard to civilian spacecraft." Ky paused for a sip of water. "We weren't expected to be on civilian spacecraft."

"So what do we do now?" Gary asked.

"What they tell us," Ky said. "We have no weapons and only moderate shielding—nothing that can stand a hit from their kind of weapons. If we're lucky, they'll decide we're no threat, not worth impounding, and after some delay the ansibles will be back up and we can get through to Vatta, let them know we're all right—and by the way, send money because we need some repairs."

"And if we're unlucky?"

"They impound the cargo. Or they impound the cargo and the crew. Or, worst case, they use us for target practice. But since we can't do anything about it right now, our job is to keep the ship operating as smoothly as possible." She paused; no one said anything. Always give your people something to do, she'd been taught. "Mitt, I want an analysis of environmental right down to the eighth place: we have four additional crew on board, what does that do to our cruising range? Every factor you can think of—atmosphere, water, nutrition—everything. What will attempted repairs do to that analysis? Heat output, higher respiratory rate of exchange, whatever. Quincy, I need to know everything—everything—about the repairs we need. Nothing's too trivial. Gary, since the load's secured at this point, I'd like you to do a personnel survey. The crew records tell me what people's listed expertise is, but I never heard of a spacer yet who didn't have at least one unlisted specialty known to a friend. Find it all out, and route it to my desk. If we have someone who used to cobble together ansibles out of paper clips and moly wire, or counterfeit some currency, I want to know it."

"You have an idea, Captain?" Quincy asked. Ky could hear the tension in her voice. She felt queasy. Quincy was her senior by decades; Quincy had the experience she needed; she did not want Quincy to be worried.

"Of course she has an idea," Gary said with just a bit too much emphasis. "She's the captain."

Ky winced inwardly. She was the captain who had landed them in this mess. They were still looking at her expectantly, as if the idea they assumed she had would emerge in glowing letters on her forehead. So . . . she had best be the captain who got them out of this mess. If she could. "I have several ideas," she said. Never mind that they ranged from useless to gruesome at the moment. "I need more data about our capabilities, before I can be sure how to use them."

"Makes sense," Mitt said. "I'll get to it then. And an estimate of range under different management, as well. Whether it would do any good to conserve food supplies, things like that."

"Exactly what I need, Mitt," Ky said. "Good thinking." She smiled at him; and he smiled back. The other two blinked, then managed their own smiles.

"I've got some data now, from the repair planning before we left the station," Quincy said. "Do you want it now, or when I have the whole thing—?"

"When you have it all," Ky said. "In case something you found before changes in the light of the new situation."

"Oh—yeah—it probably will," Quincy said. Her next smile was more natural. "I should've thought of that. I must be getting old, Captain."

"Old age and treachery," Ky said. "Not a bad combination."

"I'm on it, Captain," Gary said when she glanced at him. "If anyone has a hidden talent, I'll find it."

"Good," she said to them all. "Now—we also need to be sure we're fresh and ready to deal with whatever happens. How long have you been up, ship's time?"

They looked blank for a moment. "But you need the data now," Quincy said, without answering the question.

"Probably not for hours," Ky said. "They're talking to the other ships—look at the plots. I need you all rested, fed, alert, and the same for the rest of the crew. We pulled out in a hurry, but now we need to get on a schedule that keeps us fit." Dock schedule put the whole crew on the same shift except for the standing watch. On insystem drive, they needed rotating shifts. "Quincy, Gary—make up your section schedules, then go off; Mitt and Lee will have to stay up another six, then work into the rotation. Clear?"

"Yes, Captain."

"And eat something hot," Ky said. Hunger and fear went hand in hand.

"Yes, Captain."

"I'll be around the ship for a while, then I'm turning in, too. It was an interesting day on Sabine before I got to the station . . ." And what was it in local Sabine time, she wondered. She didn't feel tired yet, but she knew she was. And tired captains made mistakes.

They could not afford any of her mistakes.

CHAPTER
NINE

When the others left the bridge, Riel was still hunched stiffly over the pilot's command board. Ky levered herself out of the captain's seat, surprised at how stiff she was herself, and went across to him.

"Yes, Captain," he said without looking up.

"Any navigation hazards in the next six hours?"

"Not at present, Captain. But if those warships jump in on us—"

"They know our course, and we're doing what they told us to do. If they want to blow us away, they can, but they should be pursuing more reasonable tactical goals. Meanwhile, I need you rested for whatever happens later. Let Lee take over and you go get some sleep."

"Captain, I was just coming on when we left—I was swing-shift watch—"

Ky felt annoyed with herself—she should have known that. Too much had happened too fast but that wasn't any excuse.

"All right then . . . but consider that you're first pilot, and we may need you worse later. At least consider going off at half watch."

"All right." He sat back for the first time, stretched his arms, and turned to look at her. "I never was in anything like this before, you know. I was in space force, yeah, but—that was in a military ship, and anyway we didn't see any action."

"Most people don't," Ky said, quickly replacing the thought *Neither was I* which would not be reassuring. "I'm just following doctrine . . ." Academy doctrine, taught in class—classes where instructors sometimes reminded cadets that theory wasn't everything, that real wars had blown old theories into fragments before. And doctrine from the point of view of combatants, people who would have the big guns."

"I'm glad we have you," Lee said. "At least you have some military experience." He glanced at Riel, an apologetic look meant to soften that near accusation. Riel didn't react.

Ky felt as if someone had dropped a spaceship on her shoulders in normal G . . . which indeed someone had. She just managed not to say *It wasn't real military experience; education isn't experience*, another truth best left unsaid at the moment. Lee trusted her; that trust was good for him, and for his performance, which led to good for the ship and the rest of the crew.

It still felt like too much.

Except that below the pressure of that trust, below the worry, the concern that would become gut-churning anxiety if she let it, was something else. Something that led directly back to the Academy, to her first days there, to the string of cadet honors she'd earned, to the ambition she'd had to be not just an officer but a good officer, not just a ship commander, but a good—even an outstanding—ship commander.

Becoming captain of *Glennys Jones* had reawakened it to some degree, but the complexity of the business end—getting a contract, dealing with manufacturers and finance officers and so on—had blurred it, almost hidden it. Now it sprang up again, that little bright flame that had driven her to apply to the Academy in the first place. Danger ignited it—ignited her—the way nothing else could do.

Deep in her heart, she too was glad the *Glennys Jones* had her as captain. Despite her inexperience, she was convinced that no one else could commit any more deeply to her ship's welfare. She would get them through this. She would save her ship. She would save her crew.

And somehow, despite all obstacles, she would deliver those blasted tractors and harrows and combines to Belinta.

She came back from that moment of euphoric dazzle to find Lee still looking at her as if he expected her to say something.

"We'll do," she said to him. "We'll do." She walked back to the command chair, trying to think what next, and realized that she was still in a pressure suit. So were they all. Pressure suits would not help them if the warships fired on them, and were uncomfortable and less efficient . . . She smiled back at Lee, who was still looking her way. "Time to get out of these things," she said. She turned to the intercom. "Captain to crew—return pressure suits to storage, with routine maintenance checks." Then to Lee, "If Riel's sitting the desk, you're the one to go rest. I'm going to be moving around the ship, Riel; I'm in contact if you need me."

"Fine, Captain." His voice now sounded relaxed; he was unsealing his suit.

She hoped she was right. At some level she knew she was. She went to her cabin, pulled off the pressure suit, and hung it in its locker, properly connected to its recharge connectors. All the readouts were normal, as they should be.

Now for a walk-through. Down the passage to the galley, where she found the new crew fixing meals for the rest of the ship. They wore their suits, but they had the sleeve cuffs undone, the gloves tabbed back; she could tell they'd already been at work here when she ordered suits stowed.

"What's for dinner?" Ky asked, as if it were any ordinary day.

"Captain!" That was Li, but they had all stiffened when she spoke. "Sorry, Captain, we just—"

"You're busy, I know that. What are you giving us?"

"Er . . . quick and hot, Quincy said, so we're using the fresh stuff and making a crunchy sorga"—a Slotter Key favorite, fresh vegetables chopped into a spicy sauce—"with chicken slivers and rice. Nothing fancy."

"Sounds good," Ky said.

"Ten minutes, Captain," Li said.

"Want to thank you again for taking us out of Sabine," Skeldon said. His expression, a mix of gratitude and admiration, made Ky uneasy.

"Skeldon," Li said; he reddened and said no more. Li went on, "We are grateful, Captain Vatta. We didn't know how bad it was going to get, of course, but to get not only a ride out, but with Vatta . . ."

What did she think Vatta could do for her, when they had no communications and no FTL drive? Why was Vatta that special to her?

"We'll do," Ky said again, as she had to Lee, and again it seemed to be the right thing to say.

She left the good smells and warmth of the galley and headed for the environmental workspace. There she found Mitt and Ted, out of their pressure suits, both busy with handcomps running simulations.

"Dinner in ten minutes," Ky said as she came in.

"The sim's coming along," Mitt said. "Luckily we'd recharged everything when we came in. We were running light-crewed, so four extra isn't putting any strain on the main cycles at all. But I don't know how many days we can squeeze out of it yet."

"Well, don't forget to eat," Ky said. "Whatever we'd save by not eating today isn't worth it. Tomorrow we can starve if we have to, but those perishables won't do us any good anywhere but inside us."

Ted laughed, and even Mitt grinned at her. "All right. But I should eat here."

"No," Ky said. "You shouldn't. The new ones have put some effort into this, and we're all going to eat together like civilized folk, even if it is cramped. Your sim will run without you."

"It might finish—"

"And so you'll see it after supper, when you can't interfere with dessert."

"Dessert!" He looked shocked. "They aren't wasting essential supplies on dessert, are they?"

"I have no idea," Ky said. "But surely one dessert won't unbalance everything? And if you think it does, we can always pull out my Aunt Grace's fruitcake."

"No, we should save that for emergencies," Mitt said.

If this wasn't an emergency, what was? Ky didn't want to think of the emergency that would require them to survive on three of Aunt Gracie Lane's fruitcakes.

"Less than ten minutes, now," she said.

From environmental to engineering was a short walk and a single climb. Quincy and her juniors, also out of pressure suits, were poring over diagrams, schematics, holograms; a display board was covered with their lists.

"Dinner in seven minutes, troops," Ky said, and then wondered where she'd gotten the "troops" from. But they looked up at her with such confidence that her heart turned over. "In the crew rec area," she said, to forestall the same protest about leaving the area that she saw in Quincy's eyes.

"It leaves sections uncovered," Quincy said.

"You're all linked in," Ky said. "As I am. And seconds from active control boards. We eat together." She glanced at the chronometer. "Less than seven minutes, and it smelled good. At least one of our newbies can cook."

"All right," Quincy said, with a quick shake of her head. "We'll be there."

Gary Tobai and his cargo crew didn't argue at all, but headed for the crew rec area—by then it was five minutes to dinner, if the newbies had their timing right. And if they didn't, a minute or two wouldn't matter.

Ky followed the cargo crew up the passage, then went on as they peeled off into the loos. She went back through the galley, where the smell was even better than before.

"They're starting to gather," she said. "We'll eat in the rec area. There's just room. I'll be back in a minute or two."

Forward to her cabin—a quick touch to her hair again—and then to the bridge.

"Riel, you're linked, right?"

"Of course, Captain."

"Well, then—come to dinner. We can race each other to the bridge if we need to, but we all need to see one another's faces right now."

"But leaving the bridge—"

"The log's running, Riel. If something goes wrong, it's my neck and not yours. It's not a suggestion."

"Yes, Captain."

"And get the rest of the way out of that suit," Ky said. "You might as well be comfortable for dinner."

A line from an ancient text, many thousands of years old, came to her; they had studied Old World military history one term. The Spartans, the night before the Persians attacked the pass, had eaten well.

"Yes, Captain." He stood up, stripped off the pressure suit, and put it away, meticulously checking every readout and connection. Ky didn't hurry him; she used the time to check her implant's linkage to every compartment for the fiftieth time, and look again at the longscan display. The warships had moved, of course—they would not sit there to be targets in case Sabine Prime had weapons they didn't know about. A sprinkling of Prime's little cutters lit up the screen in no particular formation that Ky could recognize; most were coasting. The afterglow of the ansible explosions had changed shape and color as the debris spread and cooled.

"Ready, Captain," Riel said finally. Ky queried their mutual linkage—live and clear.

"Fine, then," Ky said, and led the way off the bridge. That was unorthodox; that was, if anyone complained, illegal. Someone was supposed to be on the bridge at all times. Linkages could fail. But the most important linkage was human, heart-to-heart, and for that they needed one another. Ky stopped by her cabin just long enough to pick up the little candlepair her mother had insisted on including. Supposedly it had been patterned after one from Old World, a pair of candleholders in a single-footed stand.

The rec area tables had been shoved together, and someone had found or improvised an actual tablecloth and set the rather uneven-looking table with *Glennys Jones'* best china—the familiar red-and-blue-lined Vatta pattern, with a little red sailing vessel in the center and the ship's name underneath. Ky set the candlepair in the center. Of course no one lit open flames on a ship, but the safelights set on medium flicker were lovely enough.

Her crew crowded around the tables. Those who had found seats stood up; Ky looked at each face, and tried to think of something to say. Before the silence became too awkward, she said, "We can't let it get cold; it smells too good," and sat down. There was a surprised chuckle, and the others also sat.

"What are we going to do about—," began Beeah Chok, through a mouthful of sorga.

Ky held up her hand. "No business at dinner. Not this dinner anyway. Our new crewmembers have cooked us a good one, and I want to enjoy it. So when they've had a chance to eat a little, we can get to know them better."

"Seth has a wicked sense of humor," Mitt said. "I can tell you that much."

Ky nodded, and worked her way through the excellent sorga—realizing that she had completely missed whatever meal should have preceded it, in her dash to get off the planet and then off the station. The others ate more slowly, and the talk picked up around her.

Seth was explaining that his sense of humor had come from his grandfather Jandrai, not his grandfather Garlan. Lucin Li countered with a story about her grandfather Li, a custom knifemaker.

"Chanhodri Li?" asked Gary Tobai.

"Yes," Lucin said. "You've heard of him?"

"I have one of his knives. Fine piece of work. Inherited it from my dad, who got it from your grandfather. Small universe, eh?"

"May I see it?" Lucin asked.

"The knife? Sure." Gary fished in his pocket and brought it out. Ky looked at it—a small black-handled folding knife. It looked smoothed by time, well-cared for, but nothing unusual.

Lucin peered at it. "Ah . . . this was in his second series of blades. See—this little mark here? He wasn't entirely satisfied with the first series—exchanged them for these when he found the owners. Did your father show you the second blade? It doesn't look as if you'd used it in a long time."

"Second blade . . . ," Gary said. "There's no second blade . . . is there?"

"Kind of a trick," Lucin said. She did something Ky couldn't see and another blade slid sideways out of the handle. "Grandfather was trapped in a collapsed building once—big sea storm, over on Westering. In the debris he couldn't get his big folding knife out of his pocket—he couldn't get his arm to move back enough to pull it out. He had a small screwdriver, and finally made a hole in his pocket so he could push the knife out forward, bit by bit. When he started making knives after that, he always had what he called the escape blade. Lot of people never noticed it."

"Isn't that . . . illegal?" Gary asked.

"Some places, yes. That's why it wasn't ever advertised, and why it's not metallic. He didn't think the laws should prevent someone saving his life. And a screwdriver, he said, was a damn poor way to cut through heavy cloth. Here—" She handed it back to Gary. "Feel this ridge? Run your thumb along it the way you want the blade to go."

Gary ran the little black blade in and out several times. "Huh. I sure didn't know that was there. My dad . . . well, this came to me after his accident, so if he knew, he never had a chance to tell me."

Ky, feeling much better now that she'd eaten, joined the conversation. "So . . . what about you, Paro? Where are you from, what's your family like?"

Paro Hospedin grinned. "Westerling family, like Lucin's. Shellfish farming, back in colonial days. Then shellfish processing, but we were bought out by Gramlin fifty years or so ago. Our side of the family moved into transportation—nothing to scare Vatta Transport, mostly ground routes from Westerling back east. I caught the spaceship bug early on, wanted to work on the ships themselves, see new worlds, all that. My father said I had to get an education first, and pushed me into the technical end."

"Good for him," Quincy said. "It's easier to get it in one lump than piecemeal, while you're working."

"Agreed. I wasn't sure I wanted drives, but he said I had a good mind for it, and there'd always be ships that needed me."

"As long as someone has a general background, too," Quincy said. Beeah and Mehar rolled their eyes. Quincy scowled at them. "It's important," she said. "You young people always want to specialize in the high-paying fields, but if you don't have the background, you're out of luck if the ship's expert in the blogowitz generator gets a knock on the head and you have to deal with it."

"What's a blogowitz generator?" asked Caleb Skeldon.

"She made it up," Mehar said. "It's imaginary, what she calls a teaching tool."

Caleb still looked confused. Beeah patted him on the shoulder. "Never mind, Cal, this is an old engineering argument. Probably as old as engineering. They have it in medicine, too."

"Just trying to understand the ship," Cal said, applying himself to his rice and chicken.

"It's fine, Cal. They can confuse me sometimes," Ky said. That wasn't strictly true, but Cal looked like someone who needed a kind word right then. He wasn't just handsome; he had the lost-puppy look that made her want to protect him. Danger signals pinged in Ky's head.

"So, Cal, tell us about yourself." From the look on Mehar's face, she had the same impulse as Ky and it was safer for her. Ky mentally detached herself from the lost puppy and handed him over.

"Eastbay City," Cal said. "My family's nothing special, just ordinary working folks. Ma works in the hospital, fluids tech, and my dad's an accountant . . . that's how I got into inventory control, through accounting. Accounting was boring. Inventory control, at least there's something going on. I always wanted to go into space anyway. I guess it was playing *Harmon the Hero* games when I was a kid. I know there's not really any Evil Overlord, but . . ." He chuckled and pushed his rice around.

"I used to play that," Seth said. "Customized my copy so Harmon had my face and whoever I was mad at that week was the Evil Overlord. Got caught at school once playing it in class, and of course it was Professor Jesperson, and of course it was his face as Evil Overlord."

"What did he do?" Ky asked.

"Laughed. It was worse than getting angry. I felt like an idiot." Seth shook his head. "Then the headmaster came in and asked what was going on, and Professor Jesperson erased the set and said he'd just found an illicit game-player and erased it. I never did completely understand that man, but once I didn't have the game-player, I managed to get top marks in that class."

"My best friend and I modified our desk paks so we could chat in class," Mehar said. "Nobody thought it was possible, so they didn't check them out every time. We'd have gotten away with it all term if another class hadn't used our room . . . Two kids started fiddling with the controls and, of course, they couldn't keep a secret when they found out."

Everyone had finished eating now. They all seemed relaxed, as she'd hoped. Ky caught Lucin Li's eye. "Better clear up now," she said. "I'll get out of your way . . ."

"Yes, Captain," Lucin said. The others all rose, some stacking plates and others picking up the serving dishes. Ky picked up the candlepair and switched it off.

"With the captain's permission," Riel said, "I'd really like to get back to the bridge."

"Certainly," Ky said. "We stretched the regs; we don't want them to snap."

He grinned, as she'd hoped, and headed upship to the bridge.

"Now," she said to her section firsts. "About that schedule . . ."

"It's all ready, Captain," Gary said.

"And I have the preliminary environmental report," Mitt said.

"Good. Anything critical I need to see right away? I'm overtime myself; I'm turning in for six hours unless someone needs me."

"No," Mitt said. "Like I said before dinner, we're in good shape. I have a couple of alternative models, but everything's stable. Report's on file."

"Same here," Gary said.

"Good," Ky said. "We'll all think clearer after some sleep."

Back in her cabin, Ky stripped off her clothes—not *too* stinky—and put them into the 'fresher while she took a full shower. She ran through the calming exercises of Saphiric Cyclans as she dried her hair, laid out a fresh uniform, and fell into bed only to remember that she hadn't written a log entry since she got aboard.

There was, of course, the recorded log, and Lee would have written up a pilot's log, but tradition and training said a captain never slept without updating the log in actual writing.

At least she could do that wrapped in a soft robe and not in a uniform. Ky pulled out the logbook—still so new, most of its pages empty—and her stylus. She piled pillows behind her and started on the day's events.

When she'd finished a terse report, she looked at it a long moment before closing the logbook. If . . . if something happened, and that logbook were the only surviving evidence, would a reader understand it? Would he see choices she had not seen, better courses of action?

She could see nothing but one bad option after another.

She slipped the logbook and stylus into its drawer, and then turned out the light. Maybe a good night's sleep would give her the wits to find a way out of this.

She woke up to the sounds of a ship on insystem drive, nothing more nor less. The ship was alive—air moving through the vents, liquids moving through pipes—she heard a distant gulp that she knew from experience was the galley drain. She stretched, feeling the mild stiffness of muscles held too tense the day before. But rested. She sat up, looked at the chronometer, and muttered a soft oath. She should have known they'd let her sleep too long. Into uniform, teeth clean, hair brushed smooth.

She came out into the passage feeling wide-awake and hungry again. In the galley, Cal Skeldon was wiping up the sink; she nodded to him as she checked her implant. Riel was off-duty; Lee was sitting the board. Alertly—he noticed the tick at his implant and answered at once.

"Nothing new, Captain."

"Can I fix you something, Captain?" Cal asked. That ingratiating smile again; Ky shook her head.

"I'll just get some cereal," she said. Before she could reach for a bowl, he had handed her one, along with a packet of breakfast grains.

"Thanks," she said, turning away to open the cooler. She found a packet of berries and added them to the bowl, then took out the cream jug. He was still there, clearly ready to do anything she asked. She poured the cream onto the berries and grains, and handed him the cream jug.

"I have to get to the bridge," she said.

"Of course, Captain," he said, eyes bright. She would have a talk with Mehar, she decided; this had gone far enough. She took her breakfast up to the bridge. Lee looked up.

"Were you ever planning to wake Sleeping Beauty?" Ky asked. "Or were you waiting for a prince?"

"Gary and Quincy said to let you have at least eight hours," Lee said. "Was that wrong?"

"No. I just didn't plan to sleep that long." Ky sat down in the captain's seat and turned on the intercom. "Captain's on the bridge. Section firsts, if you're finished with that assignment, come on up." She took a spoonful of berries and cream and grain. "Where are we, Lee? Anything to worry about?"

"No, Captain." The plot came up on Ky's desk. "We're not going to hit anything in this system. Not anything mapped, anyway. The warships have moved in on Sabine Prime; there's been an engagement of some kind with Prime's space force, such as it is. They haven't blown the station yet, though we're far enough out it could have happened and we wouldn't have heard."

"Any sign of ISC?"

"No downjump markers that I can detect. If they've come in, they've come in with something small, distant, and careful. I wouldn't know yet if they just arrived across the system, of course."

Scan-lag was such a pain. It was possible to link ansibles to scan and get an almost-instantaneous scan of an entire system, but that took the ansibles off-line for other uses. Aside from that, they were limited to lightspeed or less. Ky finished her berries and grain, setting the bowl aside just as Gary, Mitt, and Quincy appeared.

"I hope you're all as rested as I am," Ky said. "What have you got for me? Mitt, you first."

"Current consumption, we're good for eighty-seven days. Gary spent all the government letter of credit on supplies, is why it looks so good. Our system's designed for straight recycling of atmosphere and water; there's no design capability for onboard food generation."

"We could modify some of the equipment," Quincy put in. "But we don't have seed stock. We'd have to figure out a way to purify and prepare the basic cultures."

"I can't really recommend that," Mitt said. "Unless it's that or starvation."

"We'll hope it's not," Ky said. "You, Quincy?"

"Well, the ship's in pretty good shape, aside from the problems we knew about already. Nothing's leaking. Nothing's coming apart under this acceleration. On the other hand, we have to consider insystem drive fuel consumption. Since we can't jump out of this system with no FTL drive, we need to be able to get back where we came from in order to get that replacement sealed unit."

"Fuel consumption so far?"

"Seven percent. I know that doesn't seem like a lot, but it all depends how long this goes on."

"Gary?"

"Load's all secure. I've been collecting the skills list, like you asked me to. Hand-painting flat-pics seems like a useless sort of thing to mention, but—"

"We don't know what might be useful," Ky said. "Let me see here . . . flower painting, yes. Surf fishing with rod and reel. Once achieved a perfect score in Bzzx—what is that?"

"A gameplayer classic. The one where you shoot little biting things that try to eat your garden plants."

"Mmm . . . and designing and hand-sewing festival costumes." She couldn't think of anything more boring, herself. And that was Mitt, of all people. "Pistol-bow competition? What's that?"

"That's—you know what a crossbow is, right?"

"Ancient weapon, now used in sports. Sure, my brothers had one. They never would let me play with it, and it disappeared about the time Hanar moved out. He used to shoot fish with it, and sometimes rabbits."

"Pistol bows are much smaller. I asked Mehar about it; she says they even proposed them to Vatta main office as a shipboard security weapon. They won't penetrate hulls or bulkheads, and they don't have any combustibles, so they're legal on most stations. She says they look scary to dockside thieves and they had much less trouble on *Palatine* when the outside watch carried them."

"That makes sense. So we have a pistol-bow expert—how many pistol bows do we have?" For a moment she imagined the glorious defense of the ship, her crew with pistol bows against—real riot-control weapons that could rip holes in the ship. Not a good idea.

"Only the two Mehar has—her own personal practice and competition bows."

Just as well, then. She wouldn't be tempted. Still, if Mehar could hit something with a pistol bow, she might be good with other weapons. If they happened to find any. She went on with the list. Two who could knit, and one who could crochet. One who could blow glass. Five cross-trained in another ship discipline than that on their primary papers.

Nothing that immediately sparked an idea for how to get out of this mess. Nobody claimed to know how to fashion an ansible out of yarn and some extra carrots, which is what they had most of.

"Well," she said when she came to the end of the list and found her three section firsts looking at her as if they expected she'd come up with a complete answer. "That's all very interesting, but I think the next step is to see if the Mackensee folks want to talk to us. I'd like to quit using fuel to go somewhere we don't want to go, for instance. We're well out of their way, unless they plan to blow up Sabine Prime itself."

"Do you think they'll answer?" asked Gary. "If they're busy fighting—"

"Won't know until we try," Ky said. "If they're too busy they won't answer, or they'll tell us to be quiet. I'm going to suggest that we need to reserve fuel for maneuvering. Chances are they don't know we've got this much left."

CHAPTER
TEN

Even though she had made the decision, Ky hesitated before trying to contact the mercenaries. They would be busy, probably in the middle of a fight . . . If she were their commander, how would she react to the interruption from a silly little civilian cargo ship?

It would depend, really. It probably wouldn't be the first time that a civilian ship asked for further orders or wanted to change the ones it had been given. That must happen several times an operation. So there must be someone monitoring that channel, expecting ships to call in and complain or beg. What happened next would depend on the mercenaries' protocol for handling such calls, and on her approach to them.

"Was there any com activity on channel seventeen?" she asked Lee.

"I logged some very faint," Lee said. "It wasn't for us, all we got was outwash."

So the others were contacting the mercenaries. And by their plots, they weren't being blown away instantly. That was something, but was it enough? Ky would have given a lot to ask the advice of experienced spacers, preferably military. Despite the air of distaste which had colored Commander Staller's comments on mercenaries during their military law course, he had considered mercenaries true military organizations. He would know—any of them might know—what to expect in this situation.

Their expertise lay impossibly far away, in time and space; she had no connection there anymore, even if the ansibles hadn't been out . . . but she did, she remembered.

The card that had come with the ship model from MacRobert . . . what was it he'd written? "If you ever need to let us know about something, remember that dragons breathe fire."

But she wasn't a dragon, and *Glennys Jones* wasn't a dragon-class cruiser. Of course . . . Mac knew that. Mac knew . . . and somehow he'd given her a way to get their attention. Now she regretted the resentment that had kept her from plugging away at the mystery hidden in the instructions . . . some kind of recognition code, probably, if only she understood it. Not advanced communication devices; she was sure that the model wasn't a compact ansible, for instance . . . but why?

Why was she sure? Would she know a compact military-grade ansible if she had one in her hands?

"Captain—" Lee was pointing to the comdesk when Ky shook herself out of her thoughts. A light had come on: incoming message.

"Captain Vatta, *Glennys Jones*," she said.

"*Glennys Jones*, this is the Mackensee Military Assistance Corporation ship *Victor*. Does your ship have active gravity controls?"

"Yes," Ky said, through a throat gone suddenly tight and dry. "Confirm active gravity controls."

A long wait . . . minutes crawled past, each seeming years long, before a reply came through. Unboosted communication, then:

"*Glennys Jones* cease boost, repeat, cease boost. Transmit cargo manifest, personnel manifest, vessel's operational status on this channel within one standard hour. Crew personal effects need not be enumerated but all weapons must be listed. Personnel manifest to include full name, state of origin, current citizenship, age, sex, occupation. Operational status to include systems status. Prepare for inspection. Acknowledge."

"They're going to *board* us?" Lee said; he sounded scared. Ky was glad someone else had voiced that fear.

"Maybe . . . maybe not." Easier to be calm when she had someone else to be calm for. "They might just do an external inspection." Unlikely but it was a chance.

"What can we do?" Lee asked. His voice was still tense, pitched higher than usual.

"Right now, what we're told," Ky said. "Cut the boost—we wanted to do that anyway. We can't fight, we can't run, and it won't do us any good to argue." She thumbed the transmitter. "*Glennys Jones* acknowledges: cut boost to zero accel, cargo and crew manifest, and ship operational status to be transmitted this channel within one hour."

No immediate answer, of course. She looked at longscan again. There—one of the warships' icons appeared next to one of the larger merchanters.

"Gary, I need the cargo manifest and an annotated crew list, including our four newbies—and check if anyone has anything a military boarding team might consider a weapon."

"A good team could consider a pillow a weapon," Gary said. He sounded more grumpy than scared, but his expression was worried.

"Be serious. The kind of thing they'll be upset about if we don't declare it. Firearms, knives, that kind of thing." Vatta Transport, like Slotter Key generally, had a relaxed attitude toward personal weapons. Crew were not supposed to take weapons off the ship onto foreign soil—which included orbital stations—but they could have anything on board which fit into their personal space.

"Ten minutes," Gary said. Ky turned to Quincy.

"You heard them. I need whatever they will consider relevant operational status."

"Right. Fifteen minutes. I need to be sure I list all the warts."

The lists, when completed, came to Ky. She looked them over . . . a sad little list it seemed now. A crew of seeming nonentities, all from Slotter Key, with a boring utilitarian cargo, on a ship that could serve as a textbook example of antiquated, inefficient, and scrapworthy. "Weapons" included Mehar's two pistol bows, twenty-three personal knives—mostly small folding pocketknives like Gary's—and nine kitchen knives, from paring to chopping. Ky wondered about that—the mercenaries hadn't said to include kitchen cutlery in the list but the big butcher knife would certainly kill someone.

She sent the lists off in good time, and turned on the intercom.

"We've received communication from Mackensee," she told the crew. "As some of you already know, we've cut acceleration on their orders, and sent off cargo and crew manifest. They said prepare for inspection, so I expect that when they get around to it, they'll come out here and look us over. They may board the ship to check our actual cargo against the manifest. Keep in mind that they have the guns and we don't—we will comply with their orders until further notice."

She wondered if she should have included the last three words.

"If any of you have any personal weapons which you failed to tell your section head about, do it immediately. I can think of few things that would anger a military commander more than finding concealed weapons."

An hour later, she got her answer from the mercenaries: "Folding knives under six centimeters in length are of no concern, nor is kitchen cutlery. You will receive specific instructions for inspection."

Riel had relieved Lee, and they had all eaten a sketchy meal, when the icon of a Mackensee warship appeared only a few hundred kilometers away. Near-scan bleeped a mass-proximity warning as the comdesk lit again. Ky nodded to Riel, who damped the warning siren.

"*Glennys Jones*, acknowledge."

"*Glennys Jones*," Ky said, dry-mouthed again; her heart raced in her chest. "This is Captain Vatta."

"This is Mackensee ship *Victor*. We will be doing an exterior inspection prior to boarding. Lock down your controls; we don't want accidents."

Ky nodded to Riel, who pulled the safety cover over the controls and latched it.

"Controls locked," she said.

"Describe your personnel vacuum lock."

"It's an emergency escape lock that provides access to an escape passage leading from the stern to crew quarters. Capacity is four." Ky added the schematics to her voice message and heard a grunt from the other end.

"How old is this tub, anyway? That design's ancient."

"Keel laid eighty-seven years ago, refits in '04 and '38, last drive replacement in '43."

"What's your normal personnel access?"

"The dockside forward, but it only opens to equal pressure within a few millibars."

"All right. Here's what you're going to do. We do our exterior inspection. Meantime, get your crew assembled—do you even have a space big enough?"

"Crew rec, just barely."

"Fine. Get them in there except for bridge watch; you can have one com tech—do you have a com tech?"

"Not separately, no, sir."

"Well, someone to handle communications, and your pilot on

watch. They're to sit quiet, hands off the controls, and wait. The rest of the crew, unlock personnel lockers for inspection, unlock all hatches, drawers, everything. Put all personal weapons except small pocket knives in the galley—you do have a galley, right? You listed kitchen cutlery—"

"We have a galley, yes."

"Lay out all the weapons in the galley. Unlock, but leave closed, the food storage units. Now—your cargo holds are aired up or vacuum?"

"Aired up," Ky said.

"Are your cargo loading hatches vacuum capable?"

"Only one of them," Ky said. "And they're small, compared to modern ships."

"Umm . . . our exterior scans are showing that. And you claim your FTL drive is nonfunctional. About time to scrap that old crock."

Not now, she hoped. Not right this moment with them inside of it.

"Now for you—I am speaking to Captain K. Vatta, right?"

"Yes," Ky said. Cold sweat ran down her backbone.

"You will proceed alone down the escape passage to the lock. You will not wear protective gear. You will tab in on the hardwire ship com, and wait for the signal from the boarding party; the code IDing our boarding party will be *blackfish*. You will operate the lock for our boarding personnel. Following their entrance, you will obey the orders of their commanding officer. If you disobey, your ship is toast. Got that?"

"Yes," Ky said. "Operate the exterior lock for your boarding party, alone, not in pressure suit."

"Good. You have approximately twenty minutes to prepare for inspection." The connection went dead. Ky sat back, and took a long breath. Always breathe, her Academy instructors had said. What they hadn't said was what to do after that breath, when you were stuck in a ship with no options.

She took another breath, and addressed the crew again, repeating the instructions she'd been given. She could feel the same fear seeping along the corridor, out of the bulkheads, that she herself felt. Who could she get to sit the comdesk in her absence? Who was the most levelheaded? Quincy? Gary? Mitt? They were the most experienced, but she needed them to keep their sections steady. Certainly not one of the newcomers, whose steadiness she didn't know.

She called Quincy separately. "I need a calm person to sit the comdesk," she said. "I'm supposed to wait near the emergency lock to cycle the boarding party in."

"Not alone!"

"Yes, alone. That was specified. Just find me a com-watch person, Quincy. We're going to try to get through this without casualties." If it was possible. If they didn't plan to blow the ship after taking off everything of value. She turned to Riel. "You're officially second in command, Riel. I'm leaving you on the bridge; use your best judgment if something happens to me—"

"I don't know—" All the faint condescension he'd shown her until now—experienced crew to the unqualified neo—had disappeared. "I never expected—"

"None of us did," Ky said. "Suck it up, Riel; this isn't a game. You're on deck." She couldn't believe she was the one talking to him like this. She was younger, less experienced . . .

His face changed. "You're not scared . . ." It was not quite a question.

Ky shook her head. "Scared or not scared isn't the issue. You know that. It's doing the job. You're trained; you've got the experience; you'll do it. And after all, the most likely thing to happen is that they look us over and decide we're insignificant."

"What if they're grabbing people—hostages or recruits or whatever?"

Ky spread her hands. "I can't stop them, Riel. But I don't expect they will, not on a campaign." She should think of something for him to do, something to occupy his mind, but nothing occurred to her and she couldn't take the time. "You'll do fine," she said as she left the bridge.

She stopped by her cabin to use the toilet and straighten her hair. If she was going to meet these mercenaries, she was not going to look like a rat pulled out of a drain. She made sure that her stowage compartments were unlocked, and then moved quickly through the ship, past crew who were coming to the rec area, and made her own check of locks as quickly as she could. No time to inspect contents, but at least she could see for herself that lockers had been unlocked.

The hatch to the emergency escape passage, never locked, opened away from her. The passage lights came on as she entered, and began pulsing in sequence—intended to guide escapees in the right direction, but annoying now. She didn't have time to worry about overriding the automatics. Ahead, the small bay just inside the vacuum lock glowed with warm colors from the amber and red outlining the lock's inner hatch. Ky plugged the cord of the wall-hung exterior com unit to her earbug and waited. She had ample time to review the instructions for manual operation of the lock which were shown in print and illustration both on the bulkhead next to the comunit, and to look at the empty cubicle of the lock itself, shown on the monitor from the vidcam inside.

The voice, when it came, was far too loud. *"GLENNYS JONES.* BLACK-FISH. BLACKFISH. OPEN UP."

"Captain Vatta here. Initating outer hatch opening." She pushed the buttons; servos whined and a vibration shivered under her. Aside from inspections, the vacuum lock was never opened and it resisted, finally coming loose with a *smuck* of pressure seal. A vidcam went blurry as the pressure loss caused momentary condensation, then cleared again. Armored figures moved into the lock interior; behind them something thin and glistening stretched into the dark. Ky stared at the monitor. Dark armor, streaked with thin lines of metallic paint in a spare, abstract pattern, hung with bulges that must be equipment. Very obvious weapons—

"Close outer lock," came the command in her headset.

"Closing outer lock," Ky said. The outer lock closed slowly, hesitated. One of the figures reached back, grabbed the inside push bar, and yanked; the hatch thunked shut. "Pressuring up," Ky said. Air hissed into the lock; when pressure equalized, inner hatch controls were enabled. "Opening inner lock," Ky said.

The hatch opened into the lock; Ky stepped back against the bulkhead to let the invaders out.

The first in line faced her, and kept a weapon pointed at her. Ky stood still, hoping they couldn't detect her pounding heart—but they probably could, if those suits had the capability of Slotter Key's combat suits. The second pulled the inner lock shut, then moved a short way down the passage.

"You're Captain Vatta?" The voice came through her earbug; she didn't know if the speaker was in the suit or still outside.

"Yes," Ky said.

"Kind of . . . young, aren't you? Are they robbing cradles these days?"

"First voyage," Ky said. She was not going to rise to that bait. "It was supposed to be a milk run."

"Lucky you," the voice said. "I suppose we should be glad you had the sense not to play hero. Tell me, is your entire crew straight out of infant school, or is there someone aboard with a gray hair or two?"

Ky refrained from saying that they had the crew list. "Most of them are older than I am," she said.

"Caretakers?"

"Something like that." She thought of making the comparison with senior NCOs and young officers, but thought better of it.

"You don't get upset easily, do you?" the voice asked. She wasn't sure what the right answer to that one was.

"I try not to," Ky said, with a slight emphasis on the "try."

A faint grunt answered her, then, "Well, suppose you cycle another round in, then."

Ky worked the controls; the outer lock opened more easily this time, with less noise, and the next two entered. When she had completed the sequence and two more armored figures crowded the little space, the voice spoke again.

"Unplug from the phone—I'm switching to external speakers. We'll handle the lock from here. Start back up the passage. We're right behind you; don't try anything."

She could think of nothing to try. She led the mercenaries up through the escape passage, trying to move calmly, trying not to think about those dangerous figures behind her, their weapons pointed at her. After all, if they'd wanted to shoot her, they could have done that right away. And if they'd wanted to blow the ship, they could have done that, too. Whatever it was they wanted, so far it included keeping her alive and the ship in one piece.

Gerard Vatta, pacing his office, waited through the clicks and buzzes, the bleeps and clicks, that involved an intersystem call. He could imagine all too clearly the distances a signal must travel to InterStellar Communications headquarters: the light-years from Slotter Key's system to the relay at Beckwith's Star, more light-years from Beckwith's Star to Nexus II, and from Nexus II to Nexus I. More light-years than his age.

Finally the open line . . . but now he had to convince layers of underlings, whose jobs depended on keeping the officers of ISC insulated from people like him, that this time they should instead let his call go through. He had one in: Vatta Transport had been a steady supporter of ISC over the years, when other long-haul shippers had argued for laws restricting ISC's monopoly. Lewis Parmina, now only three slots away from the CEO-ship, and rumored to be the chosen successor to the current CEO—had been a Vatta guest more than once at Corleigh.

He kept his voice pleasant and firm, pushing down the impulse to scream at Parmina's personal assistant, who—when he finally got through to her—wanted him to call back the next day at three P.M. local time. He repeated again that the matter was urgent, and the setup time for an intersystem call made it impossible to be that precise.

"Oh—you are calling from outsystem, then?"

He had explained that more than once at every level. "Yes, I am," he said. "This call originates in Slotter Key, approximately one hundred eighty-seven light-years away, through two intermediate relays."

"Oh. Well, I'll see if Mr. Parmina can speak with you. He is a very busy man."

It seemed a year but was, by the chronometer on the wall, less than ninety seconds before Parmina spoke. He had the strong nasal accent of his homeworld, but he was not that hard to understand.

"Gerard Vatta—it's been too long, Gerard, since I was out your way. What can InterStellar do for you?"

"You've lost ansibles at Sabine Prime," Gerard said. He knew he should respond with some pleasantry, but it was the middle of the night here in Slotter Key's capital city, and he was grumpy with exhaustion. "My daughter's there—"

"With the Slotter Key space force? What are they doing in Sabine?"

Clearly Parmina had kept up with the Vatta family, at least enough to know that Ky should, by now, have been a commissioned space force officer.

"No, as a Vatta Transport captain. The military thing didn't work out—"

"I'm sorry," Parmina said. "But your delightful daughter—so spontaneous as a child—not really the military sort, was she?"

"No." Somehow it was worse that someone outside the family would have predicted Ky's failure. He pushed that aside. "But the thing is—something bad must be happening in Sabine system. We don't have any ships in the area. Ky's in there with an old tub that was on its last legs—she was taking it on its last voyage, to salvage—" Never mind that she wasn't supposed to be in Sabine anyway. That was family business. "And I was wondering—"

"I understand your concern," Parmina said. "As a father, if that were my daughter, I'd be frantic." His voice cooled. "I hope you'll understand that I cannot comment at all on what ISC thinks about this, what course of action, if any, the company might choose to take. Encryption is all very well, but—"

"I know that," Gerard said. "I don't expect that." He'd had hopes he knew were irrational. He had more sense than to mention them. "What

I wanted to ask was—in the event that ISC finds out something about—well, about Ky—is it possible you could let me know? I know it's probably against policy but . . . well . . ."

Parmina's voice was warm again. "Gerry—right now I can assure you that we have no information on anything in Sabine system; all we know is what you know: the ansibles went down in a catastrophic way. In the event that we reestablish communication, our first priority has to be restoring service—but yes, if we happen to find out anything about your daughter, I will do my best to see that it's routed to you. It's irregular, but you've been a longtime supporter, and I know how I'd feel if it were my daughter . . ."

"Thanks," Gerard said. "I owe you. And how is Denise doing at Solvena?"

"She's making good grades, finally, but she's changed her major three times in the last two years. If I understand their transcript system, the courses she'd passed might qualify her for assistant gerbil trainer in a zoo . . . Why is it, Gerry, that daughters invariably go after something either impractical or unsuited to their character? All my sons went straight into business, but Denise . . . it's like she has a magnetic repulsion to anything that would do her some good."

This begged for a similarly condescending comment about Ky, but Gerard could not make himself tell about Ky's expulsion, not while she was in danger—if she was even still alive. "Daughters!" he said instead, in a tone he hoped sufficed. "You're right about them."

"I'll do what I can, Gerry," Parmina said, in a tone that signaled the end of the conversation. "But I can't promise anything, you understand that."

"I do, and thanks again. I appreciate your willingness to even listen to me."

"Always," Parmina said. "And the next time I'm out your way, I'll be sure and stop by."

The line closed to the standby buzz. Gerard turned off his desk unit and turned to face the window. Out there, the city lights, like stars . . . and somewhere his daughter. In here, the darkness and the waiting.

"I hate waiting," he said aloud; the sound of his voice startled him, and he forced a chuckle. Time to go back to his city apartment and try to sleep. Tomorrow he was supposed to fly back to Corleigh and host the annual estate picnic. He wanted to commandeer the fastest courier ship Vatta had, and go find out if Ky was all right.

*   *   *

The ISC repair ship *Cosmos*, routinely assigned responsibility for ansible maintenance in Sector Five—twenty-three systems of which Sabine was one—had received the company's current upload on military security. Every military organization known to be operating in Sector Five, with its current—or believed to be current—location and mission. ISC agents stationed on ansible platforms reported daily on military activity— among other things—which enabled repair ships like *Cosmos* to know what they might be getting into when they came to repair an ansible that went offline.

Jed Sinclair, senior analyst aboard the *Cosmos*, looked over the updates. Three such organizations had relevant notations and had not shown up on any ansible listing since the Sabine ansibles went out. Barkley's Best, a fairly new organization, had taken its entire fleet and personnel into jumpspace from Matlock seventeen days before the Sabine ansibles went out. They were three mapped jump points from Sabine, though military vessels often used odd, indirect routes. Mackensee Military Assistance Corporation had dispatched two cruisers from its home base on Knifecroft; they jumped out of their system eight days before the Sabine ansibles went out. Gruin Colonies, Inc., had sent three ships out eleven days before the Sabine ansibles went out.

Jed thought about that. Gruin could almost certainly be taken off the list. Gruin used its security forces to put down riots and rebellion in its colonies; it had never—so far—attacked anyone else. Barkley's and Mackensee were both straight-up mercenary forces, for hire to anyone. Worst case, they were both at Sabine.

He didn't believe worst case. ISC's tap on the financial ansible, which gave him information on funds transfers into and out of the system, suggested that Secundus didn't have the resources to hire two different mercenary companies.

So, which was it and what difference did it make? He was pondering when new data popped up on his screen. Barkley's had shown up on the Timodea ansible, apparently involved in the dispute over owner- ship of some uninhabitable but mineral-rich minor worlds.

Mackensee. They had a profile, and that profile . . . did not include blow- ing up ansibles. Interesting. ISC had fought some bloody engagements to convince everyone—planetary governments, system unions, space militias and mercenaries—that ansibles were not target opportunities.

They had an unwritten but generally known policy that allowed combatants to fight over control of communications without actually damaging the ansibles or their platforms, with ISC committing to cooperation with the victor. Mackensee had acted correctly—from ISC's point of view—in other wars it had fought. In fact, Mackensee had an "acceptable" rating on a scale where there were only two values and a large, wide, deadly line between them.

So what was its problem here? Who had forgotten the hard lesson taught last time? Who wanted to be down-rated, with all the consequences of that change? Had Mackensee blown the ansibles, or had someone else done it, to downgrade Mackensee or simply to get ISC attention?

And most important, what would happen if *Cosmos* jumped into the system and started working on replacement ansibles?

Jed forwarded his conclusions to the *Cosmos* captain and back to headquarters. Then he downloaded all the data ISC had on the Sabine system and started looking for a sneaky way in.

Master Sergeant Cally Ray Pitt, twenty-eight-year Mackensee veteran and fire team leader for the boarding party assigned to *Glennys Jones*, had loaded the trader's crew stats into her implant. As always, the most dangerous time came first, when they had to depend on a civilian ship captain to be smart and steady. Most were. A few weren't, a few panicked right at the moment of boarding and tried something stupid, and although Mackensee personnel were willing to blow away difficult neutral civilians, it was bad for business. So she always hoped that civilians would behave like good little civs, not get in the way, follow orders.

Glennys Jones, on exterior inspection, looked like the old tub she was . . . an antiquated and inefficient design, decked out in the colors of a famous and very respectable trading firm. Cally had seen Vatta ships before, rotund well-kept ships with neatly uniformed crew guarding the docking access. Not as good as military, by a light-year or so, but certainly a quality organization, as civ organizations went. So why were Vatta keeping this old scow, and why was it captained by a Vatta family member?

A very very young Vatta family member, in fact.

She watched the young Vatta captain carefully. The crew stats had told her age—which she'd assumed was a mistake until she saw the woman's face. A young face, a young person's racing but steady heartbeat, a young person's lung capacity—her suit picked up the woman's vital signs easily, as it would have detected the residual effects of longevity treatment. The woman was actually that young, and a captain of a seriously deficient little ship.

And not nearly scared enough. What did she know, that she wasn't panicking? She should be terrified by the proximity of large, threatening, armed and armored soldiers, faceless—Cally knew the woman couldn't see through the visor. She was scared, but she wasn't panicked.

Cally tried to push her, teasing her about her age. The woman didn't budge, emotionally. That said something. Few young civs had that kind of emotional discipline.

"Cally—talk to me—what's happening?" That was Sid, back on *Victor*. They'd have a recorder running; she had the little eyeblink on her helmet; they'd see what she saw and hear what she heard. But Sid wanted her analysis as well, at least when nothing was—thankfully—happening.

"The captain's young and there's something—she's not reacting like I expected."

"Trouble?"

"None yet. She's done everything I told her to, but—I dunno."

"Bad feeling?"

"Not really. Just don't understand something about her."

"Go on, then. We're on the ticker."

They were on the ticker indeed. Some idiot—possibly their employers and possibly someone else—had blown both ansibles in this system, and ISC would be crawling all over this place sometime soon. Nobody wanted trouble with ISC. Gods grant they didn't blame Mackensee . . .

They really, truly needed to let ISC know they hadn't done it. They really, truly needed to know who had long-range missiles like that and the will to use them and how many were left. Meanwhile, she was stuck in the narrow emergency evacuation passage of a ship older than her own grandmother, real time, following a captain who looked like a schoolgirl in Mama's uniform, and if there was anything on this ship worth confiscating, she'd be very much surprised. With a schoolgirl captain, a girl whose every expression, every movement, communicated habitual honesty, if they said they had a holdful of tractors and cultivators and combines, they probably had exactly that.

She did not believe, however, that their FTL drive's sealed unit was really totally blown. Not unless this fresh-faced schoolgirl was the family disgrace, and they'd sent her off in a derelict hoping it would come apart somewhere in jumpspace and rid them of a problem. She shook her head mentally—shaking her head inside the suit would create problems she didn't want—at the memory of that face. First off, Vatta Transport didn't have that kind of reputation. She'd shared drinks with some Vatta crew when they were on the same station, nothing going on. Vatta would fire incompetents, sure. Any company would. Vatta kids who weren't good on ships were put to work onplanet. That was typical, too. They weren't going to risk their profit margin by letting the bad eggs handle ships. But Vatta took care of its own. They wouldn't send a whole crew off to die, just to rid themselves of a disgrace.

Besides—how could a nice girl like that be the family black sheep? Cally had long experience of family disgraces male and female; at least two thirds of the applicants for Mackensee were family disgraces. Sex, intoxicant addiction, dishonesty, theft, legal problems . . . This Vatta girl didn't fit the profile. What it looked like, given the crew profile, was exactly what the girl had said. Supposed to be a milk run—new captain, experienced crew, see how she does, get all the new-captain jitters out of her, meanwhile not wasting an experienced captain's time taking this wreck to the junkyard. Next time out she'd have a real ship, probably do a good job with it, for a civ.

Her bad luck at war caught up with her. But—given no problems— she'd be out of this in a month or so, heart whole and unscarred. Mackensee had no quarrel with Vatta Transport. Mackensee wanted no quarrel with Vatta Transport. Mackensee wanted no quarrel with anyone, just a straight contract and good credit.

And if there were problems, she would die, that nice girl, that daughter of the family with the experienced crew and the old tub of a ship. Cally thought of her own daughters, all but one safely far away on a world at peace, with steady jobs, and that one safely dead, victim of random violence while Cally'd been off on a mission.

There was always that possibility, for parents and for children, and Cally was mindful of it, as someone who had survived the years from recruit to master sergeant must be.

CHAPTER
ELEVEN

Ahead of her, the captain's trim back moved through the escape access hatch into the ship's regular passage—blessedly wider—and then toward the rec area where the crew had been told to assemble.

"Tell 'em to sit down on the deck, hands on knees," Cally said.

The Vatta captain's voice didn't shake as she gave the order, even though her biostats were still showing elevated P & R—pulse and respiration. As Cally came into the rec room, the suit's chemsniffer picked up aromatics it labeled fear—a lot of them, from a lot of people. She was doing a quick count, coming up one short, when the captain said, "Where's Skeldon?"

Cally's suit picked up the name, displayed a visual and a note from the crew manifest. Caleb Skeldon, age twenty-four Standard, sex male, height 197 cm, handsome as a storycube hero . . . definitely possible trouble. The suit labeled him threat.

"He was here a second ago," an older man said. Gary Tobai, the suit matched face to crew manifest. Age seventy-four, sex male, loadmaster, expression worried, no chemscent of aggression. Not a threat. "I turned around, when you said sit down—he was right behind me . . ."

The captain's chemscent shifted from fear to anger; the suit's analysis shifted her icon from no threat to possible threat. "Blast it all—what's he think he's doing." She raised her voice. "Skeldon—get back in here and sit down."

No answer. Cally boosted the suit's sensors. Down the passage, to port—in some compartment—breath sounds and something rasping on cloth. It would be below the captain's hearing, but that didn't mean she didn't know. She could have set this up. Or it could be a young idiot.

The rest of her team was aboard, eight of them in all. Gil back at the lock, just in case. "Jeff, cover these. Mitch, Grady, Sheila, come with me." Then, to the captain, "You're going to lead us to the bridge, Captain, and I suggest you convince your crewman to surrender himself."

The captain called again. No answer. From the way the others had obeyed her, it wasn't that she was slack.

"Go on," Cally said. The captain edged past the close-packed sitters to the passage beyond; Cally followed, weapon ready. "How long has Skeldon been on your crew?" she asked.

"A few days," the captain said. Annoyance edged her voice. "Four Slotter Key spacers were stranded; the embassy asked us to get them out. He's the youngest." And the dumbest, was in the tone of voice.

That made sense. New crew, not yet used to this captain, and the right age to think he should be a hero. Though if the captain had tried to plan an ambush, he was the sort she'd use.

"He have a weapon?" Cally asked the captain.

"Not that he declared," the captain said. "But then he didn't tell me he wasn't going to follow orders, either." The tone was bitter. The back of her neck had reddened; she was a hot-reactor then. Flushed up when she got angry suddenly.

Cally's suit picked up the sound of footsteps intended to be soundless. Whoever that was—Skeldon, for a bet—was in a compartment to port; when she boosted the IR sensitivity, she could see the hot footprints going in the hatch ahead of them, none coming back out.

"What's the next compartment portside—on the left?" she asked. The suit didn't show any hesitation, any telltales of recognition or readiness, in the captain's posture or movement.

"My cabin," the captain said. "Bridge is just ahead, on the right."

"Stop," Cally said. The captain stopped, and did not turn around. Another surprise. Most civs did automatically turn to face the person they were talking with. "Where could Skeldon go from where he was? Without our seeing him?"

"The galley, my cabin, the bridge. There's a maintenance passage, that next hatch on the left, it's the fast way aft past crew quarters to the hold control nexus."

"And where do you think he went?"

"Maintenance passage would be my guess," the captain said. "If he's scared, trying to hide. The holds are aired up; he might try to get in there and hide. If he went to the bridge, Quincy'd send him back, but I can check—Quincy—did Skeldon come onto the bridge?"

"No, Captain. Is everything all right?" That voice came from a speaker mounted high on the bulkhead, but Cally's suit also picked up the voice itself, coming from the open hatch to the bridge up forward.

"No. He skedaddled from the rec area, and the boarding party wants him back."

"Can we turn the bridge monitors back on?" asked the voice from the bridge. "We could find—"

"No live scan," Cally said. Live scan could give information as well as receive it. "What about your cabin?" she asked the captain.

This time the captain did turn around. "My cabin—why would he? It's off-limits to crew anyway, and there's no place to hide in there—it's a dead end."

All Cally's experience told her the captain wasn't lying. But the hot footprints went into the captain's cabin. Protocol was, the ship's captain led the way everywhere they went at first, and took the first shot if things went wrong. Protocol kept them alive—had kept *her* alive for twenty-eight years and she didn't plan to die until enjoying a long and luxurious retirement. This captain didn't deserve what was going to happen, but life wasn't about what people deserved.

"Well, then," she said. "Let's go check out your cabin. Need to see your logbook. We'll deal with your crewman next." In the team communication channel, she said, "He's in the captain's cabin; she may not know it. We'll take 'em down as protocol; she's mine. Grady, he's yours." Protocol didn't require killing her; Cally would make that decision as the action unfolded.

The captain still had that slightly furrowed brow—not the dramatic furrows that meant acting, fake confusion, but the slight wrinkle of real thought. The flush of annoyance had faded—typical of the type, quick anger and quick recovery. She turned and went on up the passage, Cally right behind her, stepping on those hot footprints like she couldn't see them—which she couldn't, if she didn't have IR boost implanted somewhere. Grady moved up beside Cally. As the captain slowed to turn into her cabin, Grady took a long step past her. The captain hesitated, glancing that way.

"Go on," Cally said.

The captain shrugged, and stepped into her cabin; her head swung to the left as something caught her eye. If she'd known, she would have looked straight or to the other side—Cally had just time for that thought before the wild-eyed young hero leaped forward, shoving the captain aside and aiming a ridiculous little punk pistol at Cally. The round clicked on the field of her helmet even as Grady blew him down with a riot needler. The captain, unprepared for the shove, had stumbled and fallen sideways into the path of the damped round, which still had enough force to do damage; her arm was bleeding. Cally's swing at the captain connected too late; the suit's augmented strength gave it the force to fling the captain across the cabin into a locker. The captain made one short cry and then lay still.

From down the passage, loud voices. Of course. "Jeff, keep 'em quiet, keep 'em there. Skeldon attacked with a firearm—I don't think they knew he had it. He's dead. Captain's injured, we'll render first aid. Sheila, secure the bridge crew." First thing, keep order. Next thing, did they have one deader or two?

Her suit said the captain had P & R, BP dropping. Cally called up the med subroutines, and moved across the bloody deck—that carpet was going to be harder to clean than proper tiles—to the captain's unmoving crumpled form. Experience helped. The small-caliber, low-velocity penetration of the damped pistol round in the arm—first-aid stuff, painful but not dangerous, need some rehab, nothing too difficult. IR scan showed heat already in an ankle, probably a sprain, trivial. Head or spinal cord injury was the worst possibility; she'd meant to knock the captain out of the way as gently as possible, but her crewman's shove had created movement sums that flung her too fast, the wrong way. And she needed her helmet off to find out more. The way she was lying, it could be a broken neck, but the young sometimes had very flexible necks. Best not to move her. Best to call a real medic.

"Pitt to *Victor*."

"What's up, Pitt?"

"Need a medic, possible C-spine injury, not ours. Captain of this tub."

"Just finish her, why don't you? We're in a bind; we don't have time to play nursemaid to civs."

Because she was young and maybe dumb but not bad, Cally thought.

Because she'd been straight-up about the whole thing, and if all the nineteen hells were coming down on Mackensee, a good deed might make the difference to whatever gods watched over mercenaries. Vatta Transport was, after all, Vatta Transport and this had to be family.

"My call," she said, which was true. "Send me a medic." And to her team, "The captain's injured; I've called for a medical team. I'll talk to the rest of the crew. We'll want to clean up this mess." The mess that had been a handsome blond youngster who thought for some reason a punk pistol, a spacer's bar special, would stand up to military-grade armor and weaponry. He'd probably had a crush on the captain or something; he'd wanted to show off; he'd wanted to protect her. And because of him she was lying there with a hole in her arm and maybe gorked as well.

Cally had her own opinion of young men, having trained a goodly number. Young women could be just as stupid, but unless children were involved they rarely indulged in gratuitous heroics. Gratuitous back-biting was another thing.

She clambered up from that first examination, and thought at the motionless form, "Live, damn it."

The faces that turned to hers in the crew rec space were all pale; the most senior looked at least ten years older than he had before. Cally undogged her faceplate and ran it back. Let them see a human face—they needed that right now, even though those nearest seemed fixated on her boots and legs. Probably the blood. With the faceplate open, she could smell it.

"I'm Sergeant Pitt," she said. "Your crewman Skeldon tried to ambush us; he's dead. Your captain is alive, but injured; I've called in a medical team."

"How bad is she hurt?" asked the old man. Tobai, she reminded herself. "Can't I go see her?"

"We don't know yet," Cally said. "She's unconscious, and my training is not to move unconscious victi—patients. Tell me about the medical facilities on this ship."

"Well, we have a medbox for minor emergencies . . ." One medbox. *Victor* had thirty, a double-row down one side of surgery.

"No regen tanks? No trauma suite?"

"Er . . . no. We don't—we didn't—ever need them." He swallowed, licked his lips. "Please—let me go see her . . ."

"Known her long?" Cally asked.

"Since she was little," Tobai said. "First time she came aboard ship, with her dad, I was a second-shift cargo handler. Not on this ship, o' course. She was maybe hip high on him then, trailing her older brother."

"Good kid?" Cally asked. "Quiet type? Did everything right?" She figured yes, from the contained, controlled emotions the captain had shown.

"Ky?" That got a momentary grin out of him. "I wouldn't say that, exactly, not the quiet part. Good, yes, but no sugar baby. Honest—sometimes too honest. That's why—" His mouth snapped shut abruptly, as if he'd almost said something he meant not to.

"I want the medics to see her first," Cally said, returning to his question. "Best not move her. Best wait a bit. Someone's with her, monitoring vital signs. Just you sit tight."

He nodded, mouth clamped on something he didn't want her to know. And what could that be?

She sent Jeff to check the galley, where—as per orders—the weapons the crew had listed were laid out on the table. He popped the video to her helmet display. Two pistol bows . . . she hadn't seen pistol bows in a long time . . . some knives, including the obvious kitchen cutlery. All that was by the book. The crew lockers were by the book—no hidden weapons, and only the personal effects you'd expect from experienced crew on a ship they didn't expect to be on that long. Spare ship suits, a properly primed good quality pressure suit for each, shore clothes, entertainment cubes and disks and viewers and players. Someone was studying for a higher rating in spacedrives and had the study cubes; someone else had yarn and needles and a half-completed sweater. Little keepsakes, not worth much—they'd have the good stuff back home, somewhere in Vatta Transport storage if they had no permanent residence.

None of the crew were trouble but the one who'd died. That made sense.

"Here's what you're going to do," she said, as Gil reported the medics were coming through the lock. "You know your captain's hurt—you know our medics are coming to work on her. As long as you do what you're told, she'll be fine. Cross us up, and she'll die. Clear?"

They all nodded, looking solemn and worried, just as they should.

"Go back to your compartments and lie down on your bunks. If we need you to do something, you'll be told. In fact—who's on galley duty?" She knew that civ cargo ships rotated that, if they were too small to have a permanent crew.

"I am," came a small voice to one side. Small dark-haired woman. Mehar Mehaar, engineering fifth. Someone raised a hand. Mitt Gossin, environmental section first. So they mixed sections on galley duty . . . interesting. Many ships rotated it by sections. And she wanted the section firsts available.

"Mehar," she said; the woman startled to find that Cally knew her name. "Mr. Gossin, you're a section first—you need to stay loose. Mehar, they'll be sending over ration packs for the boarding party and medics, if the medics stay that long. All you have to do is heat them up. Jeff's secured your weapons for the time being; you won't need the kitchen knives. The rest of you, go to your bunks and lie down. We'll keep you informed."

They clambered up awkwardly and moved to the side just as the medics came through with their equipment. Cally had already pointed them to the captain's cabin; they'd had time to replay the vid of the engagement. They didn't need her crowding that small space. When they'd passed, she went on forward to the bridge.

There she found two more worried faces. "Is she all right?" asked the old woman sitting the comdesk. Quincy Robin, chief of engineering, almost as old as the ship.

"She's alive," Cally said. "The medics are with her now."

"What happened?"

Cally explained briefly. Quincy's color had come back during that, and now she snorted. "Idiot boys!"

Cally agreed with her but wasn't going into that. "Understand you're head of engineering."

"Yes."

"You reported no functional FTL drive. How did this ship get here with no functional FTL drive?"

"It failed us coming in," Quincy said. "I swear I thought it had ten more jumps in it, at least, when we left Slotter Key. But there was a little wobble coming into Belinta, and then it was worse leaving Belinta, and the downjump to Sabine—well, the sealed unit went haywire, and we've got cavitation damage downstream . . . ."

"Um." So much for using this ship as a courier, which was what the Old Man had hoped for. *Victor* carried spare sealed units, but nothing that would fit on this tub.

"We were trying to arrange repairs at the station when you blew the ansibles—" Quincy glared at her. Cally realized that the old woman wasn't scared. Was that good or not?

"What makes you think we blew the ansibles?" she asked.

"You have the big guns," Quincy retorted. "Nobody else would blow ansibles."

Civ thinking. People who have the weapons would use them, never mind why.

"We didn't blow the ansibles," Cally said. No reason not to tell them that. No reason not to start setting the record straight. "We don't want trouble with ISC."

"Then who did?"

"Don't know. Not us, that's all I know. So, your FTL's out. What about your other systems?"

"Fine so far." The old woman was still angry. Not scared a bit—well, the old were like that, if they weren't scared of everything.

Ky woke slowly, as from deep sleep. It didn't feel right. What didn't feel right, she wasn't sure at first. A smell . . . not the smell of her cabin. Astringent, even medical. She opened her eyes. Above her, too close, was a shiny curved surface; when she tried to move, her arms bumped into something firm and unyielding.

The curved surface lifted away from her face. Now she could see more—and nothing reassuring. Too far away, now, the overhead with rows of lights; too big, the compartment in which she lay enclosed in something uncomfortably like a coffin. *Medbox,* her mind told her.

She struggled to put facts together in a string that made sense. Medbox meant injury . . . She had been injured? When? Where? And this place she was in . . . what was it? Where? A face hung over her; she had never seen it before, that she was sure of, if nothing else.

Its expression was serious. The mouth opened.

"Do you know your name?"

Name. What you call yourself, that is your name. Ky fumbled around in a brain that felt like a basket of wool puffs, until a sharp angular fact prodded her inquiry. Name. Your name from him meant my name to me . . . My name is . . . "Kylara Vatta," she said.

"Ah. And do you know where you are?"

She looked around as far as she could see over the rim of the medbox. For some reason it seemed more like a ship than a hospital onplanet. "I'm in a medbox," she said. "On a ship? I don't know for sure."

"Do you know the date?"

She had no idea. The whole concept of *date* seemed slippery. "No . . ."

"No matter," the man said. The knowledge that he was a man and not a woman had slid into her mind without her thinking about it. "What's the last thing you remember?"

She didn't remember anything, but she pushed at the gray fuzzballs. Past the screen of her mind ran the equations for calculating oxygen output from a Class III environmental system per square meter of reactive surface—so she recited that, and then the ones for calculating drift on downjump.

"Think of a person," the man said.

She tried, but couldn't remember anyone to think of—person meant someone like her, like the man leaning over the medbox. Suddenly a cascade of faces appeared on the screen. Her father, her mother, her brother, her uncle, Cousin Stella, Aunt Gracie Lane, Gaspard, the Commandant, Mandy Rocher . . .

"Ah . . . ," the man said.

The faces combined in scenes, in actions. Then a white streak blanked out everything for an instant, as if lightning had fired inside her head, and she was abruptly completely awake, oriented, rememoried, and very, very frightened.

She knew what that was. That was a memory module insertion. Someone had her memories on a mod, and they'd just reloaded her brain.

Which meant her brain had been . . . at least stuck in off and at worst completely gorked.

And she knew why.

"That *idiot!*" she said, meaning Skeldon.

"It was a stupid thing to do," the man agreed. "I gather you didn't know about it."

"No, I didn't know about it." Residual fear made her cranky. "I told them—"

"We know that much—it was on your recorder. What I'm asking is, did you know he had that crush on you?"

"No," Ky said. Then, less willingly, "Not exactly. I knew he was too grateful that we took them aboard, but I thought he'd go for Mehar in the end."

"The end wasn't long enough," the man said. "Here's the situation: you were knocked cold and got a bullet in the arm. The bullet was no problem; the stray needle we took out of your ankle was no problem either. But the head injury was bad enough that we did a pattern extraction and replacement once we'd stopped the bleeding and controlled swelling."

"You're . . . the mercenaries. Mackensee Military Assistance Corporation?"

"Yes. And you're aboard the *Victor*, our command ship for this operation, because your ship lacked the right medical facilities."

"My people?" Ky asked, trying to sit up. The medbox restraints held her back.

"They're all right so far," the man said. "Now—before you exit the medbox—I need to do some final tests of function. Just lie quietly and answer my questions."

She couldn't do anything else . . . The medbox restraints held her and even if she got her arms loose, she didn't know how to unlatch a medbox from inside.

"I'm projecting a visual chart above you, and what do you see on line ten?"

Ky read off the symbols. After that came a color vision test, and a test of depth perception, and then pictures of her crew, to see if facial recognition was working. It was.

Finally he unlatched the box, removed the restraints, and helped her sit up. For a moment, she felt dizzy and nauseated, but it passed, and she was simply there, inside a warship's surgery, sitting on the opened case of a medbox in a row of medboxes, wearing a pale blue shift with MMAC PROPERTY stamped on it. Across the wide compartment was another row of medboxes, six with their status lights on, and down the middle a row of operating tables, shrouded in the hoods that kept them sterile until needed.

"It's—as big as a hospital," Ky said. She had not really thought about how much medical treatment a mercenary force might need. For that matter, she hadn't seen this part of a Slotter Key warship, either.

His lips twitched. "War isn't a pretty business. We have thirty medboxes, ten operating sets, five regen tanks—and that's active. We have the stored capacity for field hospitals as well. Now—ready to stand up?"

Ky pushed off the edge of the medbox. Her knees felt rubbery, but she was able to stand.

"Immobilization does that—nothing we've come up with prevents at least temporary weakness. Now—I'm sure you've got your own medical personnel back home; I'm giving you a cube with details of the treatment you received here, some of which they may want if you need other treatment within the next standard year. Slotter Key does use standard calendar units, doesn't it?"

"Yes," Ky said. She focused on the "back home." If they were giving her medical reports for the doctors back home, surely that meant they weren't intending to kill her . . .

"Your arm and ankle responded well to the regen tank treatments; you should however do fifteen minutes a day of rehab exercise—the details are on the cube—to regain strength at the maximum rate. Your C-spine injury may cause you some difficulty as you get older; I would advise you to consult your medical personnel about a regen treatment when your neural recovery is complete. We've got it stabilized, but I wouldn't be surprised if there were a little soft-tissue damage which we couldn't regen because of the primary brain injury."

"C-spine injury?" Ky said.

"Yes. Luckily, Sergeant Pitt knew enough not to move you until the medics got there. But it's perfectly stable now."

Ky resisted the sudden urge to put her hands up and feel around her neck. It didn't hurt—nothing hurt, really, but the knowledge that she'd been knocked silly and taken off the ship like a bundle of rags . . . she, the captain, who was supposed to ensure the safety of her ship and her people.

"When can I get back to my ship?" she asked.

"I don't know—after the major talks to you, probably. It's up to command, not to me. You're fit for duty, as is. Well, once you get clothes on. I'm afraid your uniform is . . . pretty much gone. Just a moment." He walked to the far side of the compartment; Ky leaned against the medbox she'd come out of and wondered about the six others with lights on. That was easier than wondering what she was going to do now.

The man came back with a neatly folded bundle; for the first time she noticed what must be a nametag stenciled on his tunic. Dubois.

"Your ship's sent over a clean uniform. You'll want to change, and any moment now you're going to want to use the toilet."

She did, she realized.

"Right through there: you can also shower, if you like, though the medbox does a sonic clean every four hours. When you're dressed, come out and you'll be escorted to the major's office."

He did not tell her not to try to escape. She could figure that out for herself, and clearly he knew it. Ky took the bundle and retreated through the door marked STAFF ONLY. Inside she found three shower cubicles, deep sinks, and a row of toilets. Sonic cleaning or no, she wanted a shower and shampoo, and the brisk water washed away another layer of confusion.

When she combed her hair at the mirror above the sinks, she could see nothing of what had happened. Her arm had a puckery scar that looked old, well-healed, but no soreness, even when she raised it high overhead. Her ankle's scar was smaller, hardly visible. Her hair seemed shorter. She put on her uniform—the alternate one her mother had insisted she buy; it was annoying even now that her mother had been right—thankful that whoever had sent it had included underwear. When she'd pulled on the soft-soled ship boots, she felt much more like herself.

"I meant to tell you," the medic said, "we don't extend regen to cosmetic results, but that scar on your arm will respond to about two hours of regen, if you ever want to get rid of it."

"It's fine," Ky said. "Thank you." She was annoyed with herself that she hadn't thanked him before.

"Quite all right. It was orders, after all."

"Thank you anyway," Ky said firmly. She was in the right about this, at least. "Clearly you—and others in this place—saved my life."

"You're welcome," he said, shrugging as if the thanks made him uncomfortable. "Corporal Conas will take you to see the major," the man said.

Corporal Conas was waiting, armed. Ky wondered what they thought she could do, that they needed to give her an armed escort, but she walked forward when he gestured.

The major—Harris, his name was—sat behind a desk in a tiny office so bare and tidy that Ky wondered if it was a real working office, or just a place chosen to interview hapless civilians. He did not smile but introduced himself.

"Captain Vatta, we have a problem."

She knew she had a problem, but not any problem they shared.

"What is that, sir?" The sir came out automatically.

"You're aware that someone blew the system ansibles . . ."

Someone implied that it wasn't the mercenaries . . . "Yes . . . ," Ky said.

"We didn't do it. We don't blow ansibles; we don't want trouble with the ISC any more than anyone else does. Overcharging monopolistic pirates they may be, but what they do is essential, and what they do to people who bother their ansibles is . . . exorbitant." He paused.

"I see," Ky said.

"Naturally, everyone thinks we did it," the major went on. "Warships appear; the ansible platforms blow. Obvious. I'm sure by now the ISC has figured out where we are, and is thinking the same obvious thing. The only party who won't believe we did it is the party who actually did it, and so far no one has claimed responsibility. It would be far handier if the mercenaries were to blame."

"I see," Ky said again. She did, in a way. She had wondered about that; she *remembered* wondering about that. Why would mercenaries, who depended on ansible communications as much as anyone else, risk the serious and permanent annoyance of the ISC? Control of ansibles was one thing; destruction entirely another.

"We have, besides the operation we were hired to perform, several other tasks now facing us: we need to clear ourselves with the ISC before they come barreling in here and blow us up on spec, and we need to house hostages safely in the meantime, lest we incur judgment for their fates as well. We had hoped to use your ship, the smallest, as a courier to the ISC, but I understand that you have no FTL capability."

"Right," Ky said. "And we also have a commitment to deliver agricultural machinery, now in our holds, to Belinta."

"Neither of which is possible without an FTL drive, isn't that correct?"

"That is correct, yes, sir." Ky took a deep breath. "Major Harris, if I may ask, would it be possible to obtain a sealed unit from the repair yards on Sabine Prime's orbital station?"

"Not now or in the immediate future," Major Harris said. He did not explain why, and Ky was reluctant to ask. He cocked an eyebrow at her. "You are not acting like most civilian captains, Captain Vatta—most of them try to bluster and scold and command me to do what they want."

"It's my first voyage, Major," she said.

"Um. I suspect it's more than that. What are you, Slotter Key space service operating undercover?"

Ky felt her eyes widen. "Me? No, sir."

"You're very free with your *sirs*, Captain Vatta. I don't mind it, but it's . . . reminiscent of a discipline I'd expect to know better than you. Master Sergeant Pitt remarked on your demeanor as well."

"Sergeant Pitt?"

"She's the one who broke your neck, and then called the medics. Not your average civ, she said about you. More like an officer candidate." He looked at Ky a long moment. "You have something to say, Captain Vatta?"

"Not really, no." She left the *sir* off with an effort. "You have an extracted pattern from me and I don't doubt there was some interrogation while I was in the medbox."

"And that, too, is not something I would expect a young and inexperienced civ trader to know." He leaned back, hands behind his head. "Look here, Captain Vatta. It is not our practice to harm neutral civilians, which you clearly are. But we have a proposition for you—a proposition that could work to your advantage later. I am not going to offer that possibility to someone who won't come straight with me."

Ky thought about it. It was only her embarrassment, after all; there was no strategic value in his knowing that she had been kicked out of the Academy. "All right," she said. "I was kicked out of the Slotter Key space academy in my last year."

"I see." It was his turn for that noncommital comment. When she said nothing more, he said, "Why?" after waiting a few moments.

"I trusted someone—a junior cadet—and tried to help him out. He lied to me. He just wanted to make trouble for the government, and my 'help' gave him that opportunity. It embarrassed the admiral, and . . ." She spread her hands. "I was the handy sacrifice."

"That's two young men you've trusted unwisely," the major said. "If I were you, I'd stop doing that."

Mild as the rebuke was, Ky felt her face going hot. It wasn't fair; she hadn't "trusted" Skeldon. She struggled with her emotions. The major went on.

"Just a bit of advice I'd give any young officer. Everyone makes mistakes. But not the same ones over and over."

"I don't even *like* them," Ky muttered. The major grinned.

"Young men in general, or these young men?"

"These—but they seem so . . . so helpless, sometimes."

Major Harris laughed aloud, and Ky glared at him. "Sorry," he said. "But the first thing mercenaries lose is the rescue fantasy thing. My advice is, the next time you see someone you think you need to rescue, walk quickly away on the far side of the street." Then he sobered. "But that's not important—it's your life and not mine, even if it did nearly get you killed and did actually end your military career. What I have to propose now affects both of us."

CHAPTER
TWELVE

Ky felt the rise in tension. "And what is that?" she asked.

He looked at her a moment, and then nodded. "All right. We had hoped to use your ship as a courier to the ISC, but since you have no FTL drive, we can't. However, we need a place to stash some neutral civilians who might otherwise give us problems. Your ship is more than adequate for that task. The only problem is that some of them are older than you, and—at least in their own estimation—rank higher. We would prefer to have civilians under civilian command—saves us work, and prevents certain kinds of problems—but that will depend on you. We would, essentially, like to hire Vatta Transport to transport—temporarily and in this system—some passengers. For that service, we are prepared to pay standard per diem for an expected duration of that transport." He glanced down at his desk display. "If our calculations are correct, that would come to something in the neighborhood of two hundred fifty thousand credits."

Two hundred fifty thousand credits. That would repay the loan on Sabine Prime and finance the repairs to the FTL drive as well . . .

She tried not to smile. "You do realize we have limited quarters for additional personnel," she said. "How many were you anticipating?"

"Your environmental system will handle a total of seventy, isn't that correct?"

"Seventy! Yes, though that's right at redline. Fifty-five's the rated limit. But we don't have the space—"

"You have cargo holds—aired up, I'm informed. We'd supply some amenities—pallets and blankets—"

"My cargo holds are stuffed full of cargo," Ky said. "On contract to the Economic Development Bureau on Belinta."

"They'd have to be emptied—or at least enough to accommodate fifty additional passengers. With your present crew that keeps you under the redline."

"Just barely," Ky said. "And we can't just dump cargo—we have a contract. You understand contracts—" She could not believe she was arguing with a man who had her completely at his mercy, but Vatta stubbornness held her spine stiff.

"Indeed we do undertand contracts, Captain Vatta—it is in pursuit of our own contract obligations that we find ourselves in need of your ship. For which we are willing to pay reasonable fees. Do you understand necessity?"

She did. "Yes," she said, admitting it. "But that cargo—"

"It's your customer's money," Major Harris said. "Surely there's insurance?"

"Actually, no," Ky said. "They had an earlier shipment which was lost—by another carrier. Their insurance is not willing to pay on that, because the cargo completely disappeared. They hired me to bring them another, but insisted it be on spec."

"So—it's your money in your holds?"

"Yes."

He stared at his desk display, lips folded under. When he looked up, Ky thought she saw the ghost of a smile in the crinkles by his eyes. "All right, Captain, here's our best offer. We'll have people help you net your cargo, and put a homer tag on it, so you can pick it up later. In fact, we'll help you load it later. *And* we'll pay the full per diem for those passengers. If you command. Otherwise, we'll have to put a military crew aboard, intern your crew, and you—we'd just keep you here—until this is over, and where will your cargo be then?"

Trade and profit . . . "Very well," Ky said. "I accept your offer."

Now he did smile. "Captain Vatta, I predict you are destined to have an interesting life. We'll have that contract ready in hardcopy in a minute or so, and then, if you're ready, we'll return you to your ship."

"I'm ready," she said.

"And thank you for not asking more details of our operation," he said as he stood up. "It shows uncommon . . . discretion."

"I'm trying to learn, Major," Ky said, as demurely as she could.

He shook his head at her. "Slotter Key should have hung the other fellow out to dry, not you, Captain. They don't know what they're missing. Though your commanders might have had ulcers . . ." He reached out his hand and Ky shook it. "Now, let's get over to Legal and get that contract signed and sealed, shall we?"

The ship's legal offices consisted of a warren of little rooms and one large conference room with a big table. Here Ky and the major waited—she noticed that one armed guard still trailed them, but stayed outside the door here—until another officer came in.

"I hate these subordinate contracts," he said as he came through the door. "Always a mess, always so many exclusionary clauses . . ."

"Senior Lieutenant Mason, this is Captain Vatta," Major Harris said.

"Captain Vatta," the man said, extending a damp hand to be shaken. "Now, I understand you're from Slotter Key?"

"Yes, that's right."

"Signatories to the TriSystem revision of the Interstellar Uniform Commercial Code?"

"Yes," Ky said.

"Well, that simplifies things. Now—do you want to read this yourself or shall I explain it?"

"I'll read it," Ky said.

"Since you have no legal representation, I am bound to assist you in understanding anything that might be unclear—"

"Thank you," Ky said, reaching for the sheaf of hardcopies. He released them with seeming reluctance, and she opened the folder. Familiar terms stared back at her. *Consignor, consignee,* liability for this and that . . . she read through, carefully, mindful of lessons learned in the family, that it's the clause you skip over that destroys your profit when you don't fulfill it. When she looked up, she said, "I don't see anything about immunity in case of untoward circumstances not resulting from the negligence of Vatta Transport."

"They'll be on your ship, under your control," the lawyer said. "What else—"

"Natural causes," Ky said. "And it's a war zone; I'm not going to have Vatta Transport held liable for stray shots, or capture by the other side."

The lawyer gave the major a long look, and then said, "All right . . .

we'll change it. Won't take a moment," and reached for the papers. Ky handed back the one involving carrier liability and held onto the others. He glowered, but walked out with the one sheet.

"Lawyers," Major Harris said. "They always try something—of course, that's why we pay them."

"True," Ky said. "Our company legal staff's the same."

"They taught you well," Major Harris said. "Though we don't intend to have any accidents and blow you away . . ."

"Good," Ky said. They sat in almost-companionable silence until the lawyer came back, with a new page fourteen that included the missing clause. Ky read it, inserted it, and nodded. "All right—I'm ready to sign."

Major Harris signed for the Mackensee Military Assistance Corporation, and she signed for Vatta Transport, Ltd. The lawyer signed a line that specified the contract had been prepared in accordance with the Trisystem Universal Commercial Code. Then Major Harris stood up. "Let's get you back to your ship," he said. "Your passengers will start arriving in about six hours. I'm sending a working party and nets to help with your cargo."

The trip back to *Glennys Jones* went swiftly. Ky and the members of the working party all wore pressure suits—there was still no way aboard except the little escape vacuum lock—and she sat webbed to the bulkhead in the back of one of the warship's assault shuttles, lurching to and fro with the abrupt changes of acceleration required by a rapid transit.

Ky went first through the lock, with two others, and on the inside a guard in armor waved her on up the passage. She drew a long breath; her ship still smelled like her ship, like home. She came out of the passage to find another guard, this one not in armor. This was a lean woman with close-cropped gray hair and PITT stenciled on her uniform. "You can take your pressure suit off here," the guard said. Ky stripped out of the suit, and the guard's eyes widened. "Captain Vatta—you look great."

"Excuse me?"

"Sorry—you probably don't remember. I'm Master Sergeant Pitt, and I'm the one who knocked you down harder than I meant to."

"That's all right," Ky said. "And by the way, thanks for calling in the medics." She suspected that for all the fine phrases in the Mackensee advertising, standard operating procedure would have been to finish her off.

Pitt shook her head. "Right thing to do. Anyway, they said you were coming back today; I'm glad to see you looking so well."

"How are my crew?" Ky asked.

"Fine. They've all been very sensible, and very worried about you."

"We now have a contract with Mackensee," Ky said. She pulled her copy out of her uniform jacket. "Have they told you?"

"Yup. We're to help unload as many cargo holds as you say we need to, net and beacon the cargo, and then help you through loading passengers. It's your ship, Captain. You tell us what we need to do, and we'll do it. For my sins, I'm your liaison."

"Right, then. First thing, I want to let the crew know I'm back, and functional. Next, we'll get Mitt's assessment of the environmental system, and Gary's assessment of cargo—he'll know the easiest and fastest way to unload stuff."

"They're waiting in the rec area," Pitt said, nodding forward. "I'll just stay here and organize the working party. They'll need to stay in pressure suits."

Ky went forward to the rec area. Her crew were scattered around the tables, consuming some meal—she realized she was not oriented to ship's time and didn't know which it was—and talking quietly. No guard stood over them. That much was good. She wondered what to say, but then Quincy looked up and saw her.

"Ky—Captain! How are you?"

"Fine," Ky said. "I don't have an implant, though. What I do have is a contract."

"A contract!" Quincy looked almost angry. "We thought you were dying—"

"Luckily not, though it was apparently a near thing. I've got my medical record with me, if anyone's that curious. I'd just as soon not look—what they told me was scary enough."

"But—what do you mean by a contract?"

"Mackensee has hired Vatta Transport to care for some neutral civilian passengers while we're stuck here in this system. I know"—Ky held up her hand to forestall objections— "I know we don't have cabin space or comfortable facilities. I know all that. We're going to net our cargo and put it out with a beacon, to pick up later, and bed passengers in the cargo holds. Mitt, first thing, is our environmental system holding nominal in all ways?"

"Yes, Captain."

"Good, because we'll be stressing it. They're sending us fifty, and they'll be here in about five hours. Gary, what's the easiest hold to unload that will hold fifty people for some days—room for pallets and some exercise space?"

"Standard configuration . . . not stacking bunks, just pallets? And we don't have that many pallets—"

"They're coming, too. Wait—I'll get Master Sergeant Pitt." Pitt would know how much space to calculate, she was sure. Pitt did, and in minutes Gary had figured out the simplest way to unload cargo and take on passengers.

That was the last quick and simple action of a day that had started in sick bay and showed no signs of ending. The holds' pumps sucked out the air, leaving them ready for opening the cargo hatches to vacuum. Then the unloading began, with Gary Tobai handing out labels to stick on each part of the load, and on each netful. When they had the holds empty, the nets stuffed with equipment, they had only an hour to prepare the holds for their passengers.

Close the big hatches, release the air in the tanks . . . airing up was one thing, but warming up quite another. The mercenaries' work crew, laying out bedrolls on the decking, positioning the portable toilets, showers, sinks, left puffs of breath smoke behind them. No time to hook up the plumbing, though all the equipment was positioned where it would be most convenient to the ship's existing lines. At least water wouldn't be a problem, with their existing stores and recycling.

"If you don't mind my asking, Captain," Master Sergeant Pitt said, "have you ever been in charge of a refugee situation?"

"No," Ky said. Master Sergeant Pitt reminded her a lot of MacRobert, back at the Academy. "You have suggestions?"

"Yes, Captain, if you don't mind—"

"Not at all," Ky said. "Pretend I'm the greenest young officer you ever saw—what would you try to get me to do, without actually telling me?"

Pitt grinned. "It's not my place to say, you know."

"No, it's your place to hint, insinuate, and invisibly lead." Ky decided to come clean. "I don't know if they told you, Master Sergeant Pitt, but I'm a flunk out from the Slotter Key space academy, and if I'd paid closer attention to Master Sergeant MacRobert's hints, I wouldn't have trusted the wrong person and been kicked out."

"Ah—MacRobert is the fellow who gave you that warship kit?"

"Yes," Ky said. She didn't like thinking of strangers in her cabin going through her things, but of course they had, and no use being angry about it now.

"That explains a lot," Pitt said. "All right, then, Captain, here's what you need to do." She listed actions, some of which Ky had already thought of—assigning teams for shift work to keep the place tidy, prepare meals, etc.—and some of which she hadn't, like placing guards on the galley and crew storage. "Thing is," Pitt said, "they're going to be angry, and bored, and some of them—the captains of the other civ ships—are going to think they should be running this, not a baby-faced kid like you. You have to convince them otherwise. And you have to not let any pretty boy like that Skeldon get past your guard."

Was everyone going to assume that she had trusted Skeldon too much? Probably. Probably Gary or Quincy had told Pitt about her fifth birthday party, too. And no time to brood about it now, or about the description of her as "baby-faced kid."

"I don't have an implant now," she said to Pitt. "So I'd appreciate it if you'd send that list to Quincy. She's the closest I've got to a master sergeant of my own."

"They couldn't save your implant? Sorry."

"And they recommended I not have a new one fitted for six months, until any remaining neuro reshaping is definitely stable. But I didn't have one in the Academy, so it's not as bad as if I had depended on it for the last four years."

"That's good." Pitt paused, then went on. "I could give you recommendations, based on my observations and reports I've gotten from buddies working with your future passengers, of who's good for what."

"Thanks. Any info you have I'll take." And do with what she would, but she figured Pitt understood that.

Then the passengers began to arrive. Unfortunately, to keep the cargo holds aired up meant that all the incoming passengers had to cycle through the escape vacuum lock and then be shunted down the maintenance passage and into the area prepared for them. The passengers, Ky was told, comprised the senior ship's officers from all the civilian ships interdicted in the system: captains, first and second officers, communications personnel, and engineering firsts. The passenger ship *Empress Rose*, of the famous Imperial Spaceways, would serve the mercenaries as a courier—a choice that meant her passengers would be delayed as little as possible—but her captain would be interned on *Glennys Jones*.

All the passengers had been informed of the situation, and the mercenaries seemed confident that they would be reasonably cooperative, but Ky had her doubts. She didn't intend to show any of them.

Instead, she wore her dress uniform, with cape, and stood at the turn from the escape passage to the maintenance passage, greeting each person who came aboard. Without an implant assist, she had no way to know which was which, so it was a spare "Good day, welcome aboard, that way please . . ." greeting, but it was a greeting, and she could tell from the expressions that her captain's rings and cape had an effect.

When the passengers were aboard, the work party carried in the rations taken from the civilian ships. These stuffed the little galley and its storage, and filled half the rec area as well. She hoped it would be enough. Ten days, fifty additional people, three meals a day . . . one hundred fifty additional meals to prepare, in a galley meant for a crew of less than twenty.

But they were alive, unharmed, and with any luck would survive this and even be paid.

"Time to go," Pitt said finally. "We've unloaded all your supplies; your passengers are secured in the cargo holds. Someone should come behind us to secure the hatch."

"Right," Ky said. "Gary, if you'll see to the hatch."

"And thanks, Captain, for being sensible about this."

Ky grinned. "Thanks for not killing me." She watched the mercenary walk away, already fitting the helmet on her pressure suit. What would it have been like, to have someone like Pitt at her side year after year? For a moment, she allowed herself a last moment of grief for the lost opportunities . . . but the opportunities now before her were exciting enough.

She went forward to the bridge, where Riel was in the pilot's chair as if he hadn't moved since she left.

"I hope you've rotated shifts," she said.

"Yes, Captain. Glad to have you back."

"I'm glad to be back. And for our next adventure, let's get through the next ten days or so with no such excitement, shall we?"

"I certainly hope so," he said.

She sat in the command seat and flicked on the circuits. With the earbug in, she could access data almost as quickly as with the implant. A fast check of ship systems for herself—and *Glennys Jones* was fine, except for the FTL drive. Video from the cargo holds, where her passengers were standing around in clumps, showed talking and gesturing. When she listened in on the audio, most of the talk was angry. That wasn't good.

She turned on the intercom. "This is Captain Vatta. Once again, welcome aboard the *Glennys Jones*."

A tall man with silvery hair, in a captain's uniform, turned around, glared at the nearest vid pickup and approached it. "I demand that you come down here and straighten this mess out. What did they mean, you had a contract with them?"

Thanks to the earbug's link to the personnel files, she knew this was Captain Kristoffson of the *Empress Rose*.

"Captain Kristoffson, I will be speaking to you and the other captains shortly. As you must realize, we have a great deal of work to do to make this ship as comfortable and efficient as possible in the next few hours. Bear with us, please, as we get this done. We should have a meal for you all in about three hours—"

"This is outrageous! This is nothing but a cargo hold! It's not even warm. You can't seriously expect us to sleep on the cargo deck in these"—he glared around—"these disgusting bedroll things. I demand a stateroom. Captains of respectable ships do not sleep on the floor . . ."

Ky's first impulse to share her cabin with the more senior captains had been quashed by Pitt's advice, but it would not have survived this.

"Excuse me, Captain Kristoffson, but this is not the time to make complaints. I will consider your complaints later. At the moment, I need you and the other captains to organize the work parties needed to finish making your holds comfortable. I'm sure your personnel would be more comfortable commanded by familiar officers, so I've arranged a rota which permits shipmates to work together."

"Work parties! Passengers don't work, Vatta—of course, you don't know about passenger ships—" Her temper rose at the contempt in his voice. She glanced at Riel, who made a rude gesture.

"I'm sure you're aware that this is not a normal passenger service," Ky said. "Things are difficult for us all . . ."

"Not for you, apparently," he said. "You can loll in whatever passes for luxury on this tub—not that I expect it's much—"

"Enough," Ky said, in a voice borrowed from the Commandant. Somewhat to her surprise, it worked—Kristoffson blinked and looked stunned. "I have just returned from having surgery on the mercenary flagship—I was nearly killed when my ship was boarded, and I don't see any scars on you, sir. Don't push your luck."

His mouth had dropped open; now it shut with a snap. "I—I—they didn't say that—"

"No reason for them to. I'm lucky to be alive and so are you. Let's keep it that way."

"But I still think—"

"Captain, as you must realize, this ship is not large enough to give everyone the quarters they deserve, and it would be unfair to play favorites. The working crew will stay in the crew quarters, and the passengers will stay where they're put. Is that clear?"

"Yes . . ." His eyes narrowed. "But I still intend to file a complaint. It must break some law for a neutral civilian to sign a contract with a mercenary company."

"Actually, no," Ky said. "Most cargo firms sign transport contracts with mercenaries all the time. Section 234.6, Universal Commercial Code. If you were combatants or war matériel, that would be Section 234.7." She thought of pointing out that he might well have had mercenary officers as passengers when they were on leave or undercover assignment, and thought better of it. Instead she went on, "I realize this has all been a grave inconvenience for you, but we're all going to have to make the best of it." She waited a moment for that to sink in, and then repeated. "Captains, please organize your ship's personnel into working parties. We have been given basic information about the qualifications of passengers; in addition to the work parties dealing with food, sanitation, and maintenance, we may be requesting specific personnel to assist in ship systems areas where the very small existing crew is overloaded."

Other captains visible in the pickup nodded, but Kristoffson still looked uncooperative. Too bad, Ky thought. She kept the video and audio monitors on, but cut off the intercom to the holds. Instead she called the galley.

"How's the meal prep going?" she asked.

"We figured out how to keep all the frozen stuff that doesn't fit in the freezer," Gary said. He sounded tired; he probably had been up for three shifts running. "We turned the heat off in number three and put it in there. Quincy's trying to cobble up a cooler for the perishables that won't fit into storage, and the cooks are using up whatever won't fit in either."

"Good," Ky said. "Questions?"

"Do we try to keep the food sources separate, and feed the different ships' crews stuff off their own ships?"

"No—too complicated," Ky said. "I don't even know if they brought proportional amounts off the various ships."

"There's gold-eye raspberries off *Empress Rose* . . . I've never even tasted one . . ."

"Enough for everyone?"

"For one meal."

"Serve 'em up," Ky said. "If that captain brought 'em for his own special meals, he can just suffer through sharing."

"Trouble?"

"He'd like to be," Ky said. "He's used to being in charge and he thinks being stuck in the cargo hold of a freighter is the worst that can happen."

"You be careful," Gary said, his brow furrowed. "We don't have that fancy medical team to fix you up if anything goes wrong again."

"I know," Ky said. She rubbed her neck, which was beginning to hurt. It was probably just tension.

A few minutes later, Beeah brought trays up to the bridge: her tray had a large bowl of gold-eye raspberries, a jug of cream, and some sugar, as well as a hearty sandwich of thin-sliced meats and cheeses. "Gary said you sounded like you needed to eat. Riel, here's yours, too."

"I probably do," Ky said. "I think my last meal was . . . I don't even know."

"The others will be ready on time, Gary says, but how are we going to get them down to the passengers?"

"That's what the work parties are for," Ky said, through a mouthful of sandwich. "What is this stuff, anyway? Tastes expensive."

"From *Balknas Brighteyes*—they had trays of already-sliced meats in one of the coolers, so we thought better to eat them now. All kinds of stuff I didn't even recognize, but tasty."

"Mmm. Soon as I finish this, I'll go down and meet with the captains, explain the rota I've been working on." Ky gulped down another bite. "I'd better take someone with me, in case that idiot Kristoffson tries anything."

"The *Rose's* captain? What's he done?"

"Acted like a spoiled brat at summer camp," Riel answered around his own bite of sandwich. "All huffy and demanding and complaining."

"Thinks I've done something wrong by taking a contract with the mercenaries," Ky said. "Dad always said passenger carriers were snooty. So I'll just take someone along . . . Mehar and her pistol bow, I think."

The nine captains looked unhappy but said nothing at first as Ky handed out the work party rota. "Right now, only the toilets interface with our environmental system," she said. "We need to get the showers and the sinks hooked up as well. I know your senior engineers are with you—so we'll need to get their help to work with my engineering first, Quincy Robin. I understand your schedules were all synched with ours two days ago, is that right?"

They nodded.

"Good," she said. "That means the meal we're about to have is second-shift main meal, and—"

"I expect that you will reserve rations from the *Empress Rose* for *Empress Rose* personnel," Kristoffson said. The other captains gave him a look.

"That isn't possible," Ky said. "We have limited storage space for perishables. Although we've allocated additional cargo space for frozen rations, we've combined all the rest in order of use."

"But our rations are gourmet quality!" Kristoffson said.

"You were planning to feast on fancy stuff and champagne while the rest of us ate sardines and crackers?" That was Captain Lucas, of the Balknas Line cargo ship *Balknas Brighteyes*. "I hate to disappoint you, but the rations we sent aboard were not so bad that we need your red ripe strawberries or whatever it was."

"Gold-eye raspberries," muttered Kristoffson, now red in the face.

Lucas shrugged. "Good enough, but I prefer summerberries from Winterfast, lightly dusted with cinnamon."

The two men were both looking puffy about the neck, and Ky could have laughed.

"Actually I prefer to find out what Captain Vatta needs from us to make this as comfortable as possible," said another man—Captain Paison, she saw from the list. A good ten centimeters shorter than Captain Kristoffson, stocky, dark hair graying at the temples, and enough weathering on his skin to show that he didn't spend all his time aboard ship. His ship, the *Marie*, was about the size of most Vatta transports. "If we haggle too long over kitchen affairs, Captain Vatta—who actually has a ship to command—might just decide to go back to work and ignore us." He winked at Ky.

"But it's—," Kristoffson started. Paison held up his hand and Kristoffson was quiet.

"Captain Vatta, my two engineering staff are at your disposal. Perhaps after eating? I'm sure you'd like to get all the plumbing hooked up as soon as possible."

"Yes, I would," Ky said. "You'll all be more comfortable when you have shower facilities and somewhere to wash up your things. As you know, this is a small ship, and this many personnel aboard puts us at the limit of our environmental system. Unfortunately, this means we must ration water use, especially in the first few shifts, to be sure that nothing unbalances the tanks."

"But there are shower units," another captain said.

"Yes, and I assure you I will be as generous as possible with the water allowance. The calculations our engineering staff made support a maximum of three fairly short showers per hour, which works out to one per twenty-four-hour day per person. However, for the first day, as the system adjusts to more throughput, I'm asking you to hold that to one shower per hour down here. My crew is also restricting use."

"What about cooking and eating?" Paison asked.

"We'll be flash-cleaning cooking and eating utensils, to conserve water and pressure on the environmental system," Ky said. "Since we're not under boost, we've trailed a Peterton line and that will provide enough extra power to cover it."

"We were told to bring tableware," Kristoffson said. "We were not told it had to be flash-proof."

Ky was ready to let Kristoffson eat off the deck with his fingers, but she held onto her temper. "I'm sure your company can make a claim against Mackensee for whatever damage is done to your tableware, Captain Kristoffson. My main concern is that everyone on this ship have sufficient food, water, and air to survive until this is over."

The others nodded, as if they agreed this made sense. Kristoffson looked around for support and found none.

"Now," Ky said. "The meal's almost ready, in the galley, but we need people to carry it down here. I've assigned that duty first to *Marie* . . . so, Captain Paison, could you assemble your work team, please? I'll take them back to the galley with me."

He nodded.

"The rest of you, please speak to your engineering personnel and let them know that after the meal they'll be assisting Quincy Robin in hooking up the rest of the plumbing."

CHAPTER
THIRTEEN

Paison's work party, like Paison himself, seemed sensible and willing; they and Ky's crew managed to get all fifty meals to the passengers in one trip. Predictably, Kristoffson was furious that the golden-eye raspberries were being shared with everyone. Lucas wasn't thrilled with the discovery that his ship's expensive deli cuts were being shared, but it was clear he didn't want to look like Kristoffson, so he claimed he'd told Ky that, of course, all his ship's rations should be shared.

Finally they were all eating, and Ky had time to chat with Quincy about the plumbing work to be done. Quincy and her engineering crew, with the help of the environmental techs, had been working on the backside plumbing, from the environmental system to stubs with a separate set of cutoff controls.

"Thing is," Quincy said, "If they ever forgot and all showered and flushed and washed clothes or whatever at the same time, it definitely could overload the system. We could just hook up one shower, one toilet and one tub, but that would be really inconvenient. What I thought was, we could have it set up so that only two showers could go at once, one in each hold, with a timer on so they couldn't just stand there for an hour."

"I know one who probably would," Ky said, thinking of Kristoffson. "Good thinking, Quincy."

"We could also do a max water flow for the whole system, but that would mean drops in water pressure in every outlet when anyone used anything. So I decided against it. Mitt's added another two units of culture, so he says in twenty-four to thirty-six hours we should be able to maintain maximum throughput."

"How's it going to work when they leave?" Ky asked. "No—sorry—I should ask Mitt that."

"Already done," Quincy said, grinning. "Twenty-four to thirty-six-hours to cycle down, and then we're back on normal usage."

"So how do you want to organize the work crews?"

"I'll supervise one, and Beeah can supervise the other. Very basic stuff, just sticking pipes and seals together and then connecting them through the bulkhead to the stubs we have. Shouldn't be more than two hours' work, max."

"Sounds good to me," Ky said. "I'm going to my cabin for a bit—"

"Er . . . Captain, I'm sorry, but your cabin isn't . . . exactly what it was. Are you sure you want to do that?"

"Oh." In the flurry of activity, she had managed to forget about Skeldon's attack. "I still have things I need in there . . ."

"Well—if you need to switch cabins, we section firsts can move into yours and you can have number two."

"I'll be fine," Ky said. She hoped she was right. Now that she thought about it, she really didn't want to go back in there. But she had to.

"I'll come with you," Quincy said.

"You don't have to do that," Ky said. "I'll have to get over it someday." She stood up. "In fact, someday is now." She headed down the passage with a wave; Quincy trailed her.

Her cabin, the hatch neatly closed. What would she find inside? She didn't know. She took a deep breath and opened the hatch. At first glance it looked just the same. She had a moment of dizziness, a visceral memory of being shoved, of pain, of falling. She stood still, waiting for it to pass. Next she saw the state of the deck carpeting. Paler and darker blotches, the palest near the hatch . . . It looked as if someone had splashed bleach all over it and then stirred with a mop. Cabinets on the bulkheads looked streaky rather than smooth blue-gray.

"They used something their ship sent over," Quincy said. She had come up behind Ky. "Supposedly, there's no chance of contamination now, and no toxic residue."

"Good," Ky said. "But it's a good thing we aren't trying to sell this ship as a yacht or anything."

"So . . . we're back to selling the ship for scrap?"

"Right now we're back to staying alive as long as possible," Ky said. "Let's not complicate matters."

"Yes, our situation is so simple," Quincy said. Ky looked at her.

"You must be feeling better; you're back to being ironic."

"Ky . . . we're just so happy to see you alive and . . . and well."

"Me, too," Ky said. She thought about telling Quincy that she'd had a memory mod download, but decided against it. "I did remember to tell you that my implant's nonfunctional, didn't I? In fact, they took it out."

"Yes, but I thought those things were supposed to be indestructible," Quincy said.

"Unless someone takes them apart," Ky said. "Which apparently they had to do for some reason, such as—I would guess—making sure I was who I said I was."

"Does that compromise anything we care about?"

"Possibly, but there's nothing I can do about it now, not until I can notify Vatta home office. Luckily, I had only the most basic package: this ship, this voyage, the first-level contact codes, standard contract format, that kind of thing. No company strategy, no other trade routes or conditions."

"Good, then. I'll leave you—it's about time to get those working parties working."

"Call if you need backup," Ky said. Quincy waved, and Ky was left to look around her cabin alone. She opened and closed the cabinets and drawers—yes, clearly they'd been searched, but most things seemed to be in place, even Aunt Gracie Lane's fruitcakes, their flowered paper messily taped down. She didn't see the ship model, but the box was there, and it rattled. Probably the model had been broken; she didn't feel like looking at it right then. Her logbook was still in the desk drawer; she ruffled the pages. None were missing.

She checked out her private facilities—clean, ready to go—and plugged into the ship's system to check on shower availability. Only one shower was in use; she stripped and showered quickly, then changed into an informal jumpsuit while running her uniform through the 'fresher. She yawned, shook her head, and then realized she had been up and working for two full shifts. She called the bridge, to let Lee know that she would be going to bed.

Bed, however, did not bring sleep, tired as she was. She lay first on one side and then on the other . . . Her head felt strange, without the implant. She'd gotten used to that at the Academy; she knew she would get used to it again, but . . . it still felt strange. She had no real traumatic memory of the fight, because she'd been knocked out so fast, but she had all too clear a memory of Skeldon's face before she fell, distorted with fear and desperation. What had he thought he was doing? Why had he been so stupid?

And was she really such a sucker for handsome young men who acted stupid or helpless? Or . . . for anyone she deemed in need of rescue? No. But people thought she was.

It was not a soothing thought. Mandy Rocher, Caleb Skeldon . . . all the way back to various children she'd protected from siblings, parents, classmates. In the silence of her cabin, she could remember every person who had given her advice on the subject . . . but most of the time, they'd assumed her motive even when that hadn't been the motive at all.

Yes, she'd pushed Mina Patel to protect Mina's little sister. But she had gotten in a scrap with her older brother Han because he'd boobytrapped her sports locker, not because he was picking on the gardener's son. It had been merely happenstance that when she attacked him, he'd been shoving Kery around . . . yet the adults had assumed she was trying to protect Kery. She hadn't argued with them, not at that age. Maybe she should have, but her cut lip had hurt too much to talk and she'd been glad to eat ice cream and keep quiet.

She had not trusted Cal Skeldon; she had not been attracted to Cal Skeldon; she had done nothing to him or with him that any reasonable captain would not have done. No special favors, no melting glances, nothing. He'd done what he'd done for reasons of his own, and it was unfair to blame it on her.

Mandy was different. She had trusted him—at least, to be telling the truth when he said he needed a chaplain. But he had been a duty assigned, not someone she had chosen for herself. She'd been told to help him. Clearly he thought he was good-looking and attractive, but she hadn't found him so. She'd helped him because it was her duty. Yet in the end, it all became her fault, and the image of softhearted, softheaded Ky Vatta had another layer painted on.

Why did people keep making this mistake? What was she doing that gave the impression of a gullible idiot?

Major Harris' advice to run the other way when she felt someone's need assumed the same motivation. Anyway, that might work for mercenaries, but she wasn't a mercenary. She had taken in the four Slotter Key spacers because that's what good ship captains did when their embassy asked them for help. Standard procedure, not a quirk of hers. She wished she'd been clearheaded enough to tell him so at the time.

But what if he was right? What if the others were right? What if her motives weren't what she thought they were, and she actually attracted the lost puppies of humanity, setting herself up for trouble? Instead of the practical, problem-solving, energetic young woman she saw in the mirror, could she really be a dreamy, fog-minded fool?

She drifted from self-examination into sleep without realizing it. She woke to the intercom; a glance at the chronometer told her she'd been in bed, nominally asleep, for only four hours.

"Captain's here," she said to whatever emergency had arisen.

"We have a message from the *Victor*." It was Lee's voice. "They're advising that they will be out of contact for at least one standard day, maybe more."

"Did they say why? Ask for a reply?"

"No to both. But I thought you should know. In case you have anything you want to tell them."

She wanted to tell them to hurry back safely, relieve her of her passengers, and deliver payment. That was not a message they wanted to hear, she was sure. "Right. Thanks. Just send 'received,' and log it."

"Yes, Captain." The intercom clicked off. This time Ky lay awake wondering what was actually keeping the mercenaries out of contact. Were they going into action? Had another ship come into the system? And what, if anything, could she do about it?

She rolled over and went to sleep, waking at the shift-turn signal.

The ISC ship *Cosmos* released a stealth drone, programmed to make a low-vee downshift into Sabine's system and report via a tiny onboard ansible. One-channel ansibles, tuned to the repair ship, could not be detected by other ships unless they knew the code.

The jump itself required only a few hours, and the ansible's return signal related information about the system, with the scan delay of its passive scans. The low-vee downshift meant minimal scan blur, but ensured that information about the inner system would not be obtained for some hours. Its location was a solid seven light-hours from Sabine Prime.

But in eighteen hours, the drone had transmitted the ID beacon signal of every ship in Sabine system, including that of the *Glennys Jones*.

That report reached the desk of Lewis Parmina at the ISC home office within another ten hours, and he found it when he came in to work at seven A.M. local time. He looked at it, and wondered whether to contact Vatta now or later. The report said nothing about the safety of Gerard's daughter, only that the ship was transmitting its ID from a location far from Sabine Prime. No other communication related to it had been received. The existence of the ship did not mean the existence of the captain.

But he himself would have wanted to know even that much. He clipped out the location data, and sent a brief note: "*Glennys Jones* is still in the Sabine system, no longer docked at the Sabine Prime orbital station. We have no information about personnel at this time."

Gerard Vatta had set up his office system to ping his implant at any contact from ISC; his implant woke him at three A.M. local time, when he was, for reasons he never understood, dreaming about dancing fish. He signed off the ping, and heard the message in the impersonal voice of the office AI.

So the ship was there, and whole, its beacon still transmitting its identity. But Ky—? He didn't know. He also didn't know if he should tell the family yet. The secret had been hard to keep, but it would be harder to listen to them all wondering about her, when he had no more news.

He rolled out of bed cautiously, not waking his wife, who had not slept well lately. He'd been aware of that, wondered if she had dreams of Ky, and had not asked. She still did not know . . . He wandered out to the kitchen. He didn't want coffee; he didn't want tea. He wanted Ky home safe. He looked in the cooler twice before making himself pour a glass of juice and drink it. From there to his office, and onto the secure line to Stavros . . . no. Better to look at the newsfeed.

The newsfeed, full of the details of the latest dispute about the export tariffs, did not help either his mood or his insomnia. He tried sports, and arts, and finally admitted that it was now almost dawn and he might as well get up properly. He entered the master bath from the hall side, and stood under the shower a long time, eyes squeezed shut against the spray, trying not to think.

He came out of the shower into the bedroom only to find his wife sitting up in bed looking at him.

"Don't try to tell me there's nothing," she said. She had pulled the flower-patterned wrapper around her shoulders; she must have been sitting up for some time. "It's Ky, isn't it? I looked all over the newsfeed yesterday and couldn't find anything about Belinta or Leonora or Lastway. So—what is it? What's happened to her?"

He scrubbed at his head with the towel, trying to think of some way to divert her, but he knew it wasn't going to work. Once on the trail, she wasn't easily distracted.

"Ky's in Sabine system," he said. "She took a contract from Belinta, and went to Sabine."

"The Sabine ansibles," she said. Even in the dim light of the bedside lamp, he could see that she had paled, her eyes suddenly darker against her skin.

"Yes. We don't know what's happening. I called in every favor I could with ISC—you remember Lewis Parmina; he's probably going to be their next CEO—and I just got a message from him. They have a drone probe in the system, and the *Glennys Jones* is still transmitting—still there, still whole. But nothing about Ky."

"I've had dreams all the past week," she said. "But this morning when I woke up, I felt better."

"We have to hope," he said, not sure he could.

"At least she has the right things to wear," she said. And then, scowling, "I know you'll think that's trivial, but it's not. The right things to wear just might make the difference."

"I hope so," Gerard said. "I sincerely hope so."

"When are you telling the others?"

"Stavvi knows. He was there when we first got the word, and we already knew she was in Sabine system. The com watch at headquarters . . . but that's it."

"And now?"

"I think we should wait," he said.

"I think we shouldn't," she said. "Not everyone—just the family—but they should know."

"A secret shared is no secret," he said. "I don't want the media to get hold of this, not after the Academy mess."

"Yes . . . I see your point, Gerard. All right. What can I do?"

"Nothing more than I can. Wait. Pray. At least the ship is there in one piece. Was there, when the drone reported . . ."

"Is there," she said very firmly. "It is there. And for all Ky's blunders, she's had the habit of surviving."

Ship's morning brought a rash of complaints from Kristoffson that conditions were intolerable and he would hold Vatta Transport responsible for a laundry list of deficiencies. Ky looked up relevant portions of the Interstellar Universal Commercial Code to reassure herself that she was not making the company liable for vast damages and then reminded him that in time of war, which this was, passengers were obliged to co-operate fully with ship's officers.

"I am cooperating," he said. "You are simply being unreasonable in your demands."

She was tempted to ask if he thought he could do it better, but he certainly did think that, and she wasn't going to give him the opening. Her job wouldn't be easier if he thought she could be manipulated that way.

"You will have ample opportunity to make a formal complaint later," Ky said. "In the meantime, you will simply have to accept the reality of the situation."

He clicked off and managed to make that mechanical sound into something snippy. Ky shook her head at Lee, who was back in the pilot's chair. "He's trouble," Lee said. "I'm glad you're not one of the temperish Vattas."

"I am," Ky said. "But four years at the Academy taught me to handle it."

"How are you feeling?" Lee asked.

"Better than I could have expected," Ky said. "From what the medic said . . ."

"You looked dead," Lee said. "We were all scared. Those horrible people—"

"It was Skeldon," Ky said. "If that idiot hadn't tried to be a hero, Master Sergeant Pitt wouldn't have hit me."

"But there was no reason to hit *you* . . . You hadn't done anything."

"Protocols," Ky said. "Just typical military; I don't blame her." Now that she thought about it, though, she was being remarkably calm about it. Had they tweaked her memories? Her personality?

"You're more forgiving than I would be," Lee said.

"It's not forgiving, it's understanding," Ky said. "They figure that the captain is the key to the ship, and responsible for everything that happens. That's in the law, too. If you suddenly went crazy and I didn't manage it, it would be my fault."

"So—if they blamed you for Skeldon, why didn't they kill you, too?"

"I'm not sure," Ky said. "But I'm happy about it, and I'm not going to annoy them."

"This thing with the passengers . . . is it really a contract or did they just dump them on us?"

"It's a contract. Strange, but a contract. A good one, too." No reason to tell him about the clause she had insisted on adding. "I hadn't realized that mercenary companies are . . . just a business, really. The contract for haulage looked just like the ones we use for regular cargo, only specifying passengers."

"But why us? They have the other ships they've interned."

"I don't know. If I were guessing, it's that they have a use for the other ships, or that they wanted all these individuals away from their own ships for some reason."

"Will we make anything from it?"

"If they pay—and their credit rating is excellent—it will more than cover the cost of the sealed unit and installation. Assuming there's anyplace to get a sealed unit and someone to install it. I asked about that, and they said, 'Not now' in the tone that means 'Don't bother us.' But surely, when ISC replaces the ansibles, we'll be able to communicate with home, and with Belinta . . ."

Gary Tobai came onto the bridge. "Belinta's going to be furious," he said without preamble. He looked older in some way.

"I know," Ky said. "But there's nothing we can do about it. We can't fight warships. We can't jump out. We can't call and explain. They undoubtedly know the Sabine ansibles are out, and should grasp that whatever's happened is a genuine emergency. What we can do is survive the next few days—and hopefully it will only be a few days—get rid of our little friends, pick up our cargo, go back to Sabine, and fix the FTL drive. That shouldn't take long if the repair yards are still there. At least we know they have the size unit we need, and there can't be that many ships needing that size."

"Probably not. I just hope they're honest."

"As honest as they can be, was my assessment," Ky said. "And I was on their ship and met one of their officers. We do have the contract, in writing."

"Ten days . . . what can they hope to accomplish in ten days? You can't win wars in ten days. You can only lose them that fast." Gary still looked worried.

"Which means the other side won them," Ky said. She shrugged away speculation about the war. "My concern is the passengers' security. With Kristoffson being such a pain, and the way they outnumber us . . ."

"We keep them locked in," Gary said.

"We can't keep them locked in all the time," Ky pointed out. "We have to feed them, and we have only one galley. It's my fault; I didn't think to ask the mercs for a field kitchen."

"I suppose you're right. Are they all like Kristoffson?"

"No, not at all. He's the worst, and I think he's got a small group that he's inciting to difficulty. But the others aren't nearly as bad. There's one, Paison, who's quite sensible. I'm thinking of talking to him, seeing if he'll monitor the situation for me."

"One of us should do that," Gary said.

"Why? I think it's captain-to-captain stuff myself."

"Well . . . you're the captain. Still. Just don't get yourself nearly killed again."

"Not planning to," Ky said. Unfortunately, her background gave her no insight into the management of fifty unwilling passengers in a cargo ship only roughly converted to hauling them.

She wondered if anything in the Commandant's private library would have helped . . . If she'd picked out the right logbook, would she now know exactly what to do?

Probably not.

The rest of mainshift passed with little difficulty—work teams came up to the galley with clean dishes, warmed meals, took them back, washed the dishes. Captain Paison, she noticed on the monitors, was leading his crewmen and some others in calisthenics. Better than sitting around being bored. Mitt watched the environmental system closely, monitoring every slight change in values, since it was functioning near its design limits. The first surge changes had all settled down at the new equilibrium points, but he wasn't taking any chances. Quincy, with nothing much to do since the insystem drive was shut down, came into the bridge several times to discuss the needed repairs.

After a second check around her own crew, Ky decided to interview the other captains one at a time, leaving the difficult Kristoffson for last. Paison, who had been so helpful already, she put first and asked him to come to the galley.

*   *   *

"Captain Paison," Ky said. He smiled at her.

"Captain Vatta—how are things?"

"Fine so far," Ky said. "All systems nominal at this time. And you and your crew?"

"We're fine. I appreciate how difficult this is for you, Captain—all these passengers in your ship, and your cargo out there in vacuum. Tell me, is this your first voyage?"

"As Captain, yes, it is." Never mind that it was only her second voyage overall. "Not exactly going the way it's supposed to."

"You seem to be handling the stress well, though. I confess I'm impressed with your calm."

"Panic never helps," Ky said, grinning. "And I have a very good, very experienced crew."

"Ah. But not experienced at this, I suspect."

"No. Just good." Ky paused, then went on. "Captain Paison, I realize you may not want to answer this, but—what is your impression of Captain Kristoffson?"

"Jake? Known him for years. A hothead . . . not a bad guy but definitely a hothead. He is so proud of being the *Rose*'s captain—and he's acting like a total idiot right now, which you know already."

"My concern is that he might convince others that they should . . ." Ky tried to think of the right word.

"Do something stupid? Mutiny of the passengers or something?" Captain Paison laughed, a friendly laugh and not a scornful one. His eyes twinkled. "I doubt it. Jake might want them to, but I don't think they're that panicky, and he's not really that brave. As long as the gravity stays put, and the air, and so on."

"No reason it shouldn't," Ky said. She hadn't really thought of mutiny, just constant complaints and harrassment, but now that Paison said the word, her stomach tightened.

He cocked his head at her. "Do you want me to keep an eye on him for you? I can understand your concern—you and your crew are outnumbered by a large margin—and if it would ease your mind I could keep a weather eye out."

"Would you?" Ky asked, relieved that he'd suggested it himself. If he knew Captain Kristoffson that well, she hated to ask him to spy on the man.

"Sure. I truly don't think Jake's going to do more than whine and moan and demand special treatment—he was livid about those golden-eye raspberries, but I think you did exactly the right thing—still, you don't need anything else to worry about."

Paison clearly understood her various dilemmas. She was tempted to ask his advice about some of her other problems, but she knew she should keep a decent separation between herself and her passengers. She only hoped she hadn't overstepped it already.

"Thanks," she said. "This is not one of the situations they teach you about in—" She cut that off. She wasn't sure why she didn't want the passengers to know about her Academy training; she was only sure she didn't.

Back on the bridge, she found Quincy, who had taken over as third-shift watch officer, hunched over a complicated-looking readout. "How's the cargo doing?" she asked.

"Fine," Quincy said. "Just hanging out there the way it should. I still think we should have tethered it, just in case, but as long as nobody turns the drive on we shouldn't have a problem."

"Nobody's going to turn the drive on. Anything else?"

"Engineering's fine, except for that FTL drive. I'm a little concerned about the fact that we have five senior and three junior engineers aboard—if they wanted to mess us up, they could. I've made sure we have someone on watch each shift, looking for intrusions."

"I think Kristoffson is our one bad apple," Ky said. Ship sabotage was something else she hadn't thought of. "And Paison's going to keep an eye on him."

"You asked him to?" Quincy raised an eyebrow.

"No, he volunteered. Says he's known Kristoffson for years, thinks he's just a blowhard, but he'll let me know if it gets serious."

"And you're sure Paison is trustworthy?" Quincy sounded doubtful.

"I certainly hope so," Ky said. Her stomach twinged again. If he wasn't, her record for trusting the untrustworthy would have another notch. "How are you getting along with the new crew? How upset are they about Skeldon?"

"They're fine, Captain. They're upset, of course, but he never did really fit in with them . . . The ship that left them behind had a crew of twelve hundred or some such. None of them had met Skeldon before that shore leave anyway—it was a random drawing, who went when. And the military cleaned up his body and your quarters, so they didn't have to see—" Quincy's face tightened and her voice trailed off.

"You did, didn't you?"

"Yeah." Quincy shook her head, looking away. "It wasn't pretty . . ."

"No." Ky had been shown vids of postbattle cleanup at the Academy, and she could imagine the mess. The stains left by the cleaning methods showed how extensive the mess had been. She forced that thought aside. Already Skeldon's face was blurring in her memory. "Well, I'd better do another interview."

Captain Lucas, with no Kristoffson to spark his hostility, seemed a pleasant enough officer. Pepper-and-salt hair pulled back into a short thick braid, dark eyes difficult to read. His Insinyon accent had mellowed to a pleasant brogue, and he professed himself satisfied that Vatta Transport was doing the best it could for its passengers.

"Of course that fool of a passenger captain, that Kris—whatever"— Lucas waved his hand—"that sort always think they deserve special treatment. All he does is complain. But I am happy to cooperate. Though forgive me for mentioning it, but you seem rather young for a captain— unless of course you're a humod variant I'm unfamiliar with . . ."

That was fishing. Ky smiled at him. "I first went to space as crew at thirteen," she said. "Age and experience are independent variables."

He laughed, a quick bark and slow chuckle. "Well said, Captain Vatta. I hope you will be able to keep us informed, as the mercenaries inform you, of the progress of their plans. Despite all else, the sooner I'm back on my own ship, heading out on my own route, the happier I will be."

"True for all of us, Captain Lucas," Ky said. "I appreciate your cooperation at this difficult time."

Captain Opunts of *Bradon's Hope* seemed quiet and contained after Paison and Lucas; he had no questions, he said. He made no complaints. No suggestions. Nothing . . . Ky tried repeatedly to get him to open up, but he deflected all her questions and comments with a perfect shield of calm unconcern. It was like talking to a block of polished stone. He was sure everything would be all right in the end; he said that several times. She watched him head back down the corridor and hoped very much he was right.

Aspergia's Captain Jemin, by contrast, had a wild bush of bright red hair and conveyed suppressed energy. He was talking fast before he even got to the seat Ky pointed out to him. "This is such an unusual situation—unprecedented in my experience and I daresay in yours. I can hardly wait for the ansibles to get back up so I can check that out. Whatever the mercs said, they must have blown them—who else could? Although, there was that case, was it eight standards ago? The one at Hall's Landing? Just agricultural chemicals, didn't they say? And your cargo was something agricultural, wasn't it?" He had a high, slightly breathy voice and spoke in a rapid monotone that conveyed urgency in every phrase. Bright gray eyes, an almost fixed stare.

"Tractors," Ky said. She spoke slowly, deliberately, trying to calm the man. "Implements, not chemicals." Were the man's pupils a normal size, or was he on something? She didn't know; she didn't like having to consider that.

"Well, but we have to do something, don't we? I mean, we're all civilians, traders . . . There's no reason for them to intern our ships, is there? Can't you just run us up to jump and get us out of this system, someplace we can file a complaint?"

"The mercenaries have two warships," Ky said. "This ship has no weapons . . . trying to outrun them would be a very bad idea." He didn't need to know their FTL drive was inoperable.

"Oh. Well, I can see that. Yes. All right, then, I suppose we're just stuck here for ten days. Of course, I don't mean to cause you any trouble, Captain Vatta, but really—that Kristoffson person—he's constantly talking, whining, complaining. It gets on my nerves . . ."

Jemin was getting on *her* nerves. "I'm sure it's a difficult time for all of you—for all of us, actually," Ky said, striving for an even tone, as if soothing a nervous animal. "Captain Kristoffson is probably concerned about his passengers."

Jemin laughed harshly. "That's not what he's talking about. He's talking about sleeping on the floor, and having no private room, and how the rest of us are so uncultured . . . and anyway there's nothing to do . . ."

"I'm sorry," Ky said. "Though there's always Captain Paison's calisthenics group."

"Oh, him," Jemin said. "He's so . . . so hearty. I was just wondering if you had any entertainment cubes . . . something relaxing, maybe? I have my portable reader, but they rushed us so to leave the ship that I left behind my collection of cubes . . ."

Jemin needed relaxing, that was obvious, but she didn't think her collection of technical data cubes relating to this ship and Slotter Key commercial law were what Jemin had in mind.

"Sorry," Ky said. "I will ask my crew what they have, when we have time." She pushed back from the table and stood; Jemin clambered up slowly.

"I just wanted to say . . . this is really very inconvenient," Jemin said, and then shambled away down the passage.

Ky agreed completely. *Inconvenient* barely covered it. And now she had Kristoffson, an interview she could predict would be unpleasant.

Sure enough, he came in haughty and annoyed, and left in the same mood. In between, he managed to complain about everything. The food, the water, the limitation of showers, the lack of privacy, the lack of entertainment, the attitudes and behavior of the other passengers, on and on. Ky listened until he ran down.

"It's a difficult situation for all of us . . . ," she began.

"You can't pretend it's as bad for you," Kristoffson said. "You at least have your own cabin—I suppose even on this tub the captain has some privacy . . ." He thumped the table with his fist. "It's outrageous, that's what it is. Ten days! What if the mercs just run off and leave us to the untender mercies of the ISC?"

"Why would they do that?" Ky asked.

"Because they don't want to be held responsible for blowing the ansibles," Kristoffson said promptly. "Look—if they go—you have to get us out of here—"

"It's much safer to do as we're told," Ky said. "They have weapons; we don't."

"Oh, this is ridiculous!" Kristoffson said, throwing up his hands. He stamped back to the passenger hold without saying more, but Ky could almost see the unspoken words hovering over his angry head.

CHAPTER
FOURTEEN

Several days passed without incident: Kristoffson made no more complaints, though he glowered at Ky when she made her daily visit to the cargo holds to meet with the assembled captains. She wondered if Paison had spoken to him, or if he had decided for himself that complaining didn't work. Paison always smiled pleasantly, as did Lucas; Opunts remained a polite but remote enigma; Jemin now drooped in dramatic boredom. Their various crewpersons stayed politely back while she was there, not interfering. The environmental system continued to hold within its design limits.

Still she felt uneasy. If excessive trust had been her problem, now was the hour for suspicion. On the third day, she spoke to her senior crew.

"One thing—you all have implants, right?"

"Yes, why?"

"You know I don't, anymore—the head injury was bad enough they had to extract mine and use it for a reconstruction matrix." That sounded marginally better than "memory download." "So I'm limited in interface with ship systems to the earbug, and I can't sleep with it in."

"So you want us to be especially vigilant while you're asleep?" Beeah said.

"Not just that. If Captain Paison is wrong, and Kristoffson isn't just a blowhard, he has not only his engineering section head and number two, but his communications officer and a junior com tech. If he's sneaky, he might think of suborning the internal communications so our sensors don't actually tell us what's really going on. My implant had special circuits for that—do yours?"

"Not mine . . ." Quincy looked thoughtful.

"Mine either," Gary said. "It must have been an override thing for captains only."

"I was afraid of that," Ky said. "And we don't have a dedicated com tech aboard. What about our newest crew? Are any of them specialists in internal systems?"

"I'm afraid not," Quincy said.

Ky rubbed her head with both hands. "As I see it, we have two real weak spots. First, someone might steal the command wand: I *am* sleeping with that, and our passengers are locked in. So I don't expect that. Second, someone could reprogram the system to answer a different code. This ship doesn't have some of the internal security features of larger ones; configuring it for a last voyage with a small crew left us vulnerable to a situation no one anticipated."

"Nor could have," Quincy said. "You can't be faulted for that, Captain."

"I'm not feeling guilty, Quince, just concerned. How do we ensure that no one can tinker with the system and take it over? We've got them physically separated . . . but almost all of them have implants and I don't know how theirs operate, what their limits are."

"Mmmph. I didn't think of their implants being able to function with this ship."

"Neither did I until I watched Paison direct his work party without saying a word aloud. I knew they had the implants—the bulge is visible—but the possibility of their being active here slipped by me."

"Manual check of all systems, then. As continuous as we can make it . . . which isn't very, Captain. I have only my five, plus me. Hospedin can help monitor drives, but I wouldn't think he could do general engineering . . ."

"Right."

"Couldn't you put the internal system on voice recognition control, at least as a requirement for changing parameters?"

"I could, but then if something happens to me—and it already has—you're in trouble. Besides, if they are up to something, how hard would it be for them to get a voice pattern off me? They may already have one." Ky shook her head. "No, we need a better way to check the integrity of the system. If you think of anything let me know. Otherwise, keep very close watch. I don't actually expect trouble this shift—if Kristoffson does something, I think it'll be in the next day or so, not now. But I don't want to be caught off guard."

If only they had weapons, real weapons. She asked Mehar to show her how to shoot the pistol bow. "We'll start the easy way," Mehar said, piling pillows behind her practice target. "I used to shoot down in the cargo hold, but this will do. Here—"

It was absurdly easy; Mehar loaded the four-bolt reserve with the color-tipped practice bolts, put a bolt in the groove and pulled back the cocking lever before she handed it to Ky. "Point and click," Mehar said. Ky pulled the trigger and the little bow went *thip* very quietly and across the compartment a bolt stood out of the target. Ky pulled the lever again, and shot again. That bolt buried itself in one of the pillows.

"No recoil," Ky said. "I compensated for something that wasn't there."

"Again," Mehar said. "Be sure the prod's horizontal."

Ky shot again, and again, and when she had shot all five bolts, she looked at the pattern. Nothing to be proud of, at that distance, but four of the bolts were in the target. Mehar pulled them out.

"I always load in the same color sequence," Mehar said. "That way I can easily tell which one went where."

"What's the maximum range on this thing?" Ky asked.

"Depends if you want to puncture something or just kiss it. And of course what gravity you're working in. For target shooting, twenty meters is about the limit. Outdoors, you can treat it like artillery—point it up in the air—and get somewhat more distance, but no accuracy. Pistol bows don't have a lot of draw weight, so they can't give much velocity."

"What I want to do is look dangerous," Ky said. She hoped looking dangerous would be enough. She had reloaded, and now aimed and fired again, as fast as she could throw the cocking lever. "How was that?"

"Pretty good. I might be a hair faster but not much. The best you can hope for with this one is a shot every couple of seconds. You can see why they aren't military weapons for anything but very specialized uses. Slow rate of fire and lousy penetration." Mehar grinned as Ky loaded and shot again. "You have a knack for this, Captain."

"Target practice with pistols," Ky said. "This is more sensitive to tilt, though."

"Yes. At short ranges there's more loft than with most firearms— that's due to the slower speed of the bolt—so if you tilt it, it really goes off to the side. Some of us use an offset grip to help out on that, because the natural thing is to hold the hand slightly tilted. The long crossbows are easier to keep level because of the longer stock."

Ky looked at the weapon in her hand. "They just don't look very dangerous," Ky said. "And what we need is the appearance of danger, more than the danger itself."

"I dunno," Mehar said. "A lot of people associate these with spy stories, where they're usually carried by the bad guys and the bolts are always tipped with something poisonous or corrosive." She pulled out another pack of bolts. "And these can kill, at close range. I use the marker-tips for shipboard practice, but I have the competition bolts with me."

Ky looked at the short, stout bolts and touched the conical steel tips. "Sharp enough. What will it go through?"

"Not military armor, of course. I've never tried it on law-enforcement vests, so I don't know—rumor says it depends on whether they use the kind that sense impact velocity or not. But it goes right through clothes. And of course skin."

"Wish it looked nastier," Ky said. "My feeling is, these are too slow and we have too few of them to fight off an actual mutiny, but if we can startle or cow the instigators—"

"Well, I do have a pack of broadpoints." Mehar dug deeper into her kit. "Here." She handed over the pack of bolts tipped with what looked to Ky like archaeological exhibits—jagged, many-pointed.

"These look dangerous, all right," Ky said. She touched the points lightly. "Did you ever *use* those, Mehar?"

"Used to do a little pot-hunting back home." Mehar shook her head. "Thing is, Captain, none of this has the stopping power of firearms, but pain has a stopping power of its own. Less, when someone's really engaged in a fight, but if they're still standing there making threats . . ."

"I hope we don't have to use them."

Nonetheless, she practiced until—down the longest length of a passage afforded—she could group the five marker bolts in the innermost ring of the target. It would have been fun to have something like this back on Corleigh when she was a kid, instead of the toy longbows that invariably got caught in the undergrowth of the tik plantations where she and her brothers had played. She could have sneaked up on them, left colored dots on their jackets.

She pulled her mind back to the present. This was not a game. If she had to use the weapon, it would be for real. She hoped the presence of the mercenary ships—that obvious threat—would keep her passengers from trying anything.

Ky glared at the scan screens. For tactical situations, she'd been taught, the basic scans were almost useless because of long and varying scan delays. *Glennys Jones* didn't mount any of the equipment that would have let her keep track of where the warships were in anything approaching real time, nor did the ship have the advanced AI to integrate all the data and present a combined plot. It was reasonably good at noticing when things changed, and excellent in the things any cargo ship needed, such as micromillimeter accuracy when docking.

How, she wondered, had the early space travelers ever managed to get from one planet to another in the same system?

Sometime ago—she wasn't even sure how long—one of the warships had been near Secundus and now (if her antiquated system had identified it correctly) it was near Prime. The other one was a long way away from either.

"I'll bet it *was* an ISC probe," she heard Lee say. He and Zelda had been arguing over the temporary appearance of something small and distant, which Ky herself would ordinarily have considered a system glitch. She had seen it only on the recording, where it looked too small to be any kind of ship.

On the fourth day, she had another message from the mercenaries.

"Captain Vatta, we're leaving the system for a few days. The situation is complex; we need to communicate with the ISC about the ansible destruction. We expect to be back in ample time to pick up the passengers on day ten—"

"Leaving—" Ky's stomach clenched. She had trusted them . . . she had depended on them, on the threat of their weaponry.

"Yes. Just continue as you are; we will inform Vatta Transport and your passengers' parent companies of your safety via ISC contacts once we're in a system with functional ansibles. You're not having any problems, are you? Everyone behaving? Environmental system coping?"

"So far." Should she tell them about her concerns? Or would that be seen as immature, weak, panicky?

"Good. We expect to be back in just a few days, as I said . . ."

A faint hissing interrupted; she knew what that meant. The warships were outbound fast, possibly already microjumping toward safe long-jump parameters. And expectations, in deep space travel, still outran performance . . . they might be back, or they might not, if they—and she—were unlucky.

Still . . . they were in a relatively safe situation. If the mercs did not return, she could get her ship back to Sabine Prime, or close enough for Sabine's emergency service ships to come remove the passengers.

So . . . why did she feel as if someone had just poured a jug of ice water down her spine?

Less than an hour later, Captain Lucas called her from the passengers' quarters. "We want to talk to you," he said. "All us captains."

The ice-water trickle turned to a torrent. "What's the problem?" she asked.

"We know the mercs have left. Now's our chance to get back to our ships, get on our way. You can take us back . . ."

"No," Ky said.

"You didn't know they'd left?"

"I knew," she said. "They're coming back."

"I doubt it," Lucas said. "They've probably stripped the cargo off our ships and made off with it, damned pirates that they are."

"They're coming back," Ky said. She wished she was entirely sure.

"You don't know that!" Kristoffson interrupted. "You can't possibly be sure! You have an obligation to take care of us—moral and legal, under the Code. They aren't here; they don't have a gun pointed at you; you have no excuse for holding us against our will."

That might be true, technically, but Ky was not going to give in to Kristoffson. "You're passengers in a time of war," she said. "It's your duty—"

"Oh, stuff some figs!" Lucas said. In the corner of the screen, Paison's mouth quirked. "It's not a war if one of the armies runs away . . ."

"And just how did you know the mercenaries had left?" Ky asked.

They looked at each other first, then back at the vid pickup. "It's our . . . er . . . implants," said Jemin. He was not the one Ky expected to answer. Kristoffson glared at him, but Jemin didn't wilt. "We could pick up signals . . ."

If they could pick up scan signals, or communications signals, on their implants . . . they might be able to contact ships without her knowledge. Ky shivered, and hoped it hadn't shown.

"I can't get you out of the system," she said firmly. "Our FTL drive isn't working. As for returning you to your ships, I don't have enough fuel for the insystem drive to do that." She did have enough to get them to Prime, but that did not fulfill her contract. Nor was Prime safe.

Their voices clashed: disbelief, anger, determination to override her. Ky tapped the mike, and they quieted. "Believe it or not, as you choose," she said. "But the fact is, I'm not jumping you out of this system because I can't. And I'm not wasting what insystem fuel I have running around trying to take you all back to your ships. We're just going to ride this out for the next five or six days until the mercs come back."

"You're scared," Kristoffson said. His voice dripped scorn. "You're just too young, and too scared, to understand that this is our one opportunity . . . Whatever happens now, Vatta, it's your fault."

The vid clicked off, from their end. Ky stared at the blank screen thoughtfully, then called Gary Tobai and explained the situation. "I don't know the range and capabilities of their implants," she said finally. "But we must—somehow—secure the ship's control systems."

"Right," he said. He sounded tired and grim both. "Quincy's got all the engineering personnel on six-on, six-off; we're doing our best, but— you know, from inside those cargo holds, they don't have far to go to access the linkages with hardware, and that doesn't even address wireless attacks from their implants."

"Yeah, I know. Do your best—and I know you already are." Ky signed off, yawning. She'd had little enough sleep herself, in the past several days, and now she would get less. She should take a nap now, because whatever the other captains thought they would do, they probably wouldn't do it yet . . . she hoped.

That nap turned into several hours of deep sleep, from which she awoke to a faint vibration . . . the insystem drive. She surged out of her bed, yanking on her uniform, even as the alarm sounded in her cabin.

"Captain!"

"I'm awake—coming—" In the passage, Li and Garlan, both looking scared, stared at her. "Get Hospedin," Ky snapped. "Drive's on. I want it off."

On the bridge, Riel and Sheryl were busy at their boards. "Drive just came on, Captain," Riel said over his shoulder. "Full boost. I can't get it off."

"And I can't get anywhere with the nav board," Sheryl said.

"I told Li to get Hospedin," Ky said. "He's a drives man; maybe he can get it off."

"What do you think—"

"They got control somehow," Ky said. "Got into the ship's systems—probably one of the places Gary and Quincy were worried about." And if they had control of the drives and navigation controls, they also could unlock the cargo holds . . . they could be anywhere on the ship. She flicked on the monitors that should show the holds. One was blank, not even flickering; the other showed a hold mostly empty, with a clot of bodies crowding the hatch to the maintenance passage.

"Mehar," Ky said into the intercom. "To the bridge on the double. Bring the stuff. Off-duty crew, to the bridge." How had she been stupid enough not to keep one of the pistol bows in her cabin? Was it the injury or something else, that she kept missing things?

"Here, Captain . . ." Mehar, breathless, held out the bow Ky had practiced with and kept the other. Ky looked; Mehar had already loaded the magazine with the broadpoints.

"They're in the maintenance passage," Ky said. "I can't see anything in the monitor for number two. But they've got the hatch open from number one. I'm sure they're headed for the bridge . . . Ah, Quincy. There's not much chance—" Any, actually, but it was worth trying. "—that we can reach the mercenaries now, but send a message—let someone know we've got a problem. Everyone else, defend the bridge. They can't come at you all at once."

She had to go. She had to get down the passage before they got to the branch, where they could split up and come at her from more than one direction. "Garlan, Beeah—come with Mehar and me." Down past the galley, locking the galley hatch after Garlan and Beeah had acquired cutlery, closing and locking the rec area's secondary hatch.

She heard them before she saw them, thanks to the curvature of the passage. Shuffling feet, muttering voices. Her heart pounded; she could feel the surge of excitement through her body as she had before hand-to-hand competitions at the Academy.

And there they were. Five meters away, maybe four . . . she expected Kristoffson, and he was there . . . behind Paison and Paison's mate, who had a prisoner . . . a hostage.

Gary Tobai, his arms twisted behind him, the mate's arm around Gary's neck with a small but wicked knife laid to it.

Surprise stopped her so fast that Garlan bumped into her from behind. *Paison?* He grinned at her surprise, clearly delighted.

"It's time to let more experienced officers take over," he said in the same pleasant baritone, reasonable and smooth as chocolate custard.

"You . . ." Ky heard herself say. She clamped her jaw once more.

He shook his head. "You're too young, my dear. Too easy . . . Jake and I knew exactly how to handle you. He can't do fatherly . . ." Kristoffson grumbled something, and Paison shrugged. "Doesn't matter. We have control of the drives, of the navigation settings, your communications . . ."

She was aware of everything . . . the shine of their eyeballs, the sound of their breathing, the slight increased warmth from so many bodies jammed so close into the passage, the smell of their excitement. Paison, Paison's mate, Kristoffson . . . not the other captains . . . no, there was Opunts, toward the back, looking just as expressionless as ever. Her gaze came back to those in front, and for the first time she met Gary Tobai's eyes . . . gray, slightly faded . . . his expression strained. His mouth moved . . .

"Let him go," Ky said.

"Hand us your captain's wands," Paison said. "Then we'll see. You're just bluffing—you don't have the experience to handle this."

Paison's mate had Gary for a shield. Paison's mate had a knife to Gary's throat, Gary's own little black folding knife.

Back at the Academy, they'd all seen the famous list of standard things not to do in a crisis, taken from entertainment vids in which the plot depended on both hero and villain doing something stupid. Going out alone in the dark on a sudden hunch . . . walking into the dark alley instead of waiting for backup . . . dropping his weapon because his sidekick/sweetheart/child/parent was held by the bad guys who threatened the death of the hostage.

It had seemed so obvious then, when "sucks to be you" meant the screen death of an actor, the death of a character in a book. So obvious that the sidekick who said "Go on!" or "Run!" or "Never mind me!" was also a hero, and the Hero with the capital H should acknowledge that and blow the bad guys away even if his friend/lover/child/parent died. Not waste the sacrifice.

It was a lot less obvious when the face staring into hers was one she'd known for years, and very well since the start of this voyage. The man who was supposed to be taking care of her, the man she respected and . . . yes . . . loved. She had the pistol bow, yes, but . . . she wasn't a storycube hero, she wasn't even a soldier. She was just . . .

"Don't do it, Ky," Gary said. "Don't let them get the ship—" The mate's arm tightened; she could see Gary struggling for breath.

"Oh, my soul," Paison said, "what thriller do you think you're playing in, old man?" He rolled his eyes.

Ky pulled the trigger at that instant of inattention; the saw-edged bolt buried itself in his throat. Paison jerked in reaction, then slumped; a burst of glee hot as lightning shot through her head. She saw the mate's arm move, a red spurt from Gary's neck. She yanked the cocking lever as the next bolt came up, frantic to get a shot off, to save Gary. The mate lunged; her shot missed his face; her next bounced off his chest as he dropped Gary and rushed her, knife extended. Ky twisted, recocked and shot again, at an awkward angle . . . he was only an arm's reach away. The broadpoint sliced his throat from side to side, and bloody air whooshed out, spraying her. He slumped into the bulkhead, twitching. Ky pulled the cocking lever again. Only two bolts left . . .

"Don't move!" Ky yelled at the rest of the mutineers, and indeed they seemed frozen, eyes wide and mouths open in shock. Paison was dead or dying; she didn't care about that, but Gary . . . his blood ran over the deck; the smell turned her stomach.

"You murderer!" Kristoffson found his voice. "Come on, all of you— get her!" He stepped forward, fists clenched. Ky pulled the trigger as she heard a twang of another string from behind her; her bolt and Mehar's both caught Kristoffson, one in the neck and one in the chest. He coughed blood and collapsed, gargling. Again that jolt of glee.

"Put your hands on your heads," Ky said. To her own surprise, her voice didn't tremble; it sounded flat and menacing to her own ears. Slowly the others moved to obey. "Sit down where you are, and don't move." They sat. They looked frightened; she could sense that the urge to rush her had vanished.

"Aren't you going to do something for them?" someone asked from near the back.

"They're dead," Ky said. She was sure Paison was, less sure of the others, but without advanced trauma care they would certainly die. "You are alive, and you will stay that way if you do exactly what you're told. Mehar—"

"Yes, Captain."

"Cover them." Mehar had her own bow; Ky reloaded and handed the bow back; someone took it from her hand. She moved forward, hoping against hope that Gary Tobai had survived. He lay mostly on his back, on top of Paison, his neck twisted and blood flowing from under it.

Under her hand, his pulse wavered; he was breathing, but barely. She had no idea what to do. "Gary . . . can you hear me?"

His eyelids fluttered, his gray lips twitched: no more.

"Is he alive?" asked one of the mutineers. "I was a medic—"

"You!" Ky glared at him. "You're the reason he's dying."

"But maybe we can save him—"

"As if I'd trust you." But who else did she have? Nobody who really knew trauma care at this level. She didn't even know a safe way to move him to the medbox. She glared at the man again, savagely pleased that he paled a little. "All right. You come here—no one else move."

"Sandoval, *Empress Rose,* chief steward," the man said, scrambling forward on hands and knees. "All stewards have basic first-response skills; chief stewards are all certified in advanced precare. Let me—" His hand reached out, checked Gary's pulse, his fingers next to Ky's. He shook his head. "I don't think—" He turned Gary's head slightly, exposing a gaping wound. Even as they watched, the flow of blood slackened; under Ky's fingers, the pulse stilled. A last feeble movement of air warmed Ky's hand.

"He's gone," Ky said. The steward nodded.

"I'm sorry. Without a trauma team, even a medbox can't help."

A vast, empty space opened in Ky's head; she had never seen someone she knew die before; she had no way to identify what she felt, only that it was completely different from what she felt about Paison and his mate.

And she had no time. "Get back with the others," she said to the steward. She would deal with her feelings later. Now she had a ship to save. She pushed herself to her feet.

With Paison, his mate, and Kristoffson dead, the others seemed meeker. Ky didn't trust that; she wasn't in the mood to trust anyone about anything. But she didn't have dozens of separate cells to isolate them in, or the means to create such, or the crew to take care of the prisoners' basic needs. What threat would prevent another attempt to take over her ship?

Decompression would. The fact that it would certainly kill the innocent as well as the guilty didn't bother her at the moment.

"Here's the situation," Ky began, rocking from heel to toe in front of the assembled passengers. "None of us asked for this; it was forced on all of us. We should have been allies. You chose instead to consider me and my crew as your enemies; those of you who didn't back this mutiny at least did nothing to stop it. In the process you killed a dear friend of mine. A man who had worked hard to convert the cargo holds into something more comfortable for you." She paused, and they said nothing. Wise of them.

"I don't trust you anymore," Ky said. "Under the law, we're in deepspace and you know what that means. I'm the captain and you tried to mutiny. I could kill you all and though your employers might grumble, they know they wouldn't have a case in court."

"They said it'd be easy." That was a stocky man in the front row. One of the *Empress Rose* crew again.

"Oh, really?" That was all Ky could think of to say.

"Yes." The man glanced back over his shoulder then looked again at her. "Said we outnumbered the crew, and the only hope of survival was to take over from you, 'cause you were too young and inexperienced and just sitting out here with the drive off nobody'd ever find us again. We'd end up starving and you were too stupid to know it and too scared of the mercs to do anything even if you did know."

"And you believed that," Ky said.

"Well . . . yes. There's more of us. You'd be scared, he said."

Ky bit down on her temper. "And what do you think now?"

"Didn't work, did it? You just killed 'em in cold blood."

"Not cold blood," Ky said. "Paison and the rest of you were attacking me, my crew, my ship. But yes, I killed them, and I will kill anyone who tries the same thing again. Do you believe me?"

"Yes," he said, and heads nodded.

"Good," Ky said. "Keep believing it, because the first time you act like you don't, I'll space the lot of you. I intend to keep my crew, my ship, and myself alive and if that takes killing all of you, I won't hesitate."

Some looked scared; some looked glum; none looked defiant.

"Now—keeping your hands on your heads, back on your feet, and walk, do not run, back to the cargo compartments. When you get there, you will sit down in rows facing the bulkheads." They had to be able to search those compartments, undo whatever taps the mutineers had put into the ship's own system. She turned to her crew. "Beeah, you, Mehar, Hospedin, and Ted take them there. I'm going to get someone to clean up this mess—" She pointed at the bodies.

She stood there as the crowd shuffled away, as Mehar, Beeah, and the others stepped carefully past and herded the mutineers back to their space. Her knees sagged; she couldn't even lean on the bulkheads, spattered as they were with blood still wet, and the smell . . . She staggered back up the passage and made it as far as the galley before she threw up. *Killer.* She felt shamed and sick and horribly excited all at once.

"Ky?" That was Quincy. "What's happened—I can't find Gary—"

"Gary's—" Ky bent over the sink again, trying to rid herself of the guilt.

"Is he hurt?"

"He's dead, Quincy." Ky gulped a mouthful of water, washed her mouth out. "They had him—" Her vision blurred, and she braced herself against the counter. "Sorry . . . we have organic debris . . . need to get it cleaned up. Don't send Alene." Bad enough for the rest of them, but Alene worked with Gary—had worked with Gary—every day.

"I'll . . . get to work," Quincy said.

Ky washed her face and looked down at her uniform. Blood, some still glistening. She could feel it drying on her face. She would have to change. She had work to do . . . she had a ship to run. She had no time to spend on sorting out feelings.

As if from a distance, she heard MacRobert's voice, back when she was a cadet. "Just do it."

All right. She straightened, shook her head, pushed her hair back. Just do it. No excuses, no apologies . . . she went back out to the passage where the stench met her before she came in sight of the mess. Two of the crew, Lee and Seth, were standing with buckets and mops, looking sick. The bodies hadn't been moved.

"What are we going to do with 'em?" Lee asked, gesturing.

A good question. She wasn't about to put those bodies in with food in the cooler and freezer, but they couldn't be left here.

"Space 'em," she said. "We don't have storage. I'll document identity, and then we'll put 'em in the escape hatch and open it." The thought of kneeling beside them with the recorder, documenting prints and ID implants and so on sickened her, but it had to be done. She deserved to do it, after that surge of glee.

"All of them?" Lee asked, looking at Gary's body.

"No," Ky said, shaking herself out of that. "Of course not Gary . . . we'll find room in the freezer for him. But the others. Get a small dolly from Alene, but don't let her come up here and see this. When you've dumped them, ask Mitt what he wants to use to clean the mess. I've got to get it off me—" She paused. No, better do the ID first, while she was still dirty. She went back to the galley, washed her hands and face, put on gloves from beneath the sink, and looked up the protocols for "Death in Transit, Accidental, Victim, Certifying identity of" in the Code, which was the closest category she could find.

Then, when she had the information safely coded, she helped push the dolly down the corridor, helped pile the three bodies in the emergency access against the outside, pushed the controls to open the outer lock.

She felt better when the corpses were safely out in space, where they could do her no harm. Slightly better. She had Mitt shut off the showers to the passengers so that she could shower long enough to get really clean and run her uniform through the 'fresher. And still the shock, the grief she had no time to deal with hovered somewhere in the near distance, waiting to pounce when her attention wavered.

She would not let it waver.

CHAPTER
FIFTEEN

ackensee Military Assistance Corporation had shifted to a more familiar civilian style of corporate organization; clients seemed reassured to find out that MMAC had a business-suited CEO and CFO instead of a commander in uniform. So did the many civilian employees who kept MMAC's central office working smoothly. Its city offices, two floors of the Sugareen Tower West, reflected the profitability of the business, from the polished marble paneling to the hand-woven Ismarin rugs and the leather-upholstered furniture. Pictures on the wall of the reception area were originals, exotic game animals and wilderness scenes, suggesting adventure without hinting at violence. All scenes of soldiers in uniform, or combat machinery, were elsewhere in the private offices of executives or in the conference rooms.

The current CEO, despite his elegant suiting, had been one of the four field commanders until five years before, when Old John Mackensee himself picked him for what they called "taking point with the clients." Three years at a regional support headquarters, with TDY to the city offices, where the civvie staff got used to the quiet, almost cherubic redhead. A year as understudy to Stammie Virsh, who was as craggy as a storycube general.

And now Arlen Becker had the watch, and one of his operations had disappeared when the Sabine ansibles went down. Old John had been on the horn within an hour; Old John missed nothing.

"I don't have to tell you we didn't do it," he'd said.

"Tessan has a good record," Old John had said. "But ISC is going to be all over us when they figure out who's there."

"We could volunteer that," Arlen said.

"Breach of confidentiality," Old John said.

So Arlen sat on it, carrying on the day-to-day work of the corporation, which kept him busy even when there wasn't a crisis. MMAC owned more than military matériel, and employed more than mercs. He was expecting the call that finally came from ISC, though not the rank of the individual who showed up in person in his outer office, demanding to see him.

"She says she's a special adviser to the chairman of the ISC board," his secretary murmured into his implant.

"What do we have to clear?" Arlen asked.

"You have that regional sales conference." Boring, and he was just there to put pressure on the vice presidents.

"I won't go—they can gossip among themselves. What else?"

The list flashed on the implant visual. Nothing that couldn't be shifted a few hours . . .

"Send her in." Arlen glanced around his office—immaculate as always— and set the perimeter safeties. ISC was rumored to employ assassins, but only as a last resort. He didn't think they'd try one for a first contact, but no reason to be stupidly complacent.

ISC's special adviser to the chairman was a short, dark-haired woman with a silver streak over the crown of her head. She wore a slightly crinkled dusty rose linen dress, shoes he recognized as stylish and expensive, and carried an old-fashioned ladies' briefcase in tooled and beaded leather, a pattern of cabbage roses in soft pinks against maroon leather. Rings glittered on her hands; her earrings looked like natural emeralds; they matched her eyes. Her glance around his office missed nothing, he was sure.

He came around his desk, and she offered her hand; he shook it. Small, but firm and cool. She had the calluses of someone who had used a small firearm on a regular basis for a long time.

"Perhaps you'd like to sit here?" he asked, waving her to the cluster of chairs and low couch near a coffee table.

"First, I'd like a straight answer to one question," she said, not moving. It was absurd; she barely came up to his chest, and yet he had the feeling that he was the schoolboy and she was the teacher.

"Certainly," he said, inclining his head.

"Were you hired to blow up the communications and financial ansibles in Sabine system?"

"No," Arlen said. "No one asked us to, and if they had we would not have taken the contract."

"Did you blow them up by accident?"

"To my knowledge, we did not blow them up at all," Arlen said. "And that's two questions."

"So it is," she said, and moved to the seating area. She chose the seat Arlen would have chosen in her position, and set her briefcase on the low table. As she reached for the clasps, she said, "Why don't you sit down, General? This is going to take a while."

He was almost amused at her effrontery; he sat down anyway, and said, "I'm not a general anymore, you know."

"Oh, but you are," she said. She opened the briefcase flat; one side held a compact portable miniansible; the other a rack of data cubes. "Generals don't quit being generals when they put on business suits. You commanded the third in the Wallensee affair, the Jerai border war, and the defense of Caris. Quite able as field commander though I have to wonder why you didn't make use of your amphibious capabilities on Jerai . . . On paper it looks like you could have flanked the enemy . . ."

He could feel his neck getting hot; this would not do. In his mildest voice, he said, "Are you a military historian, ma'am?"

"Good heavens, no. A military analyst. Quite different function. No one in their right mind would let me near students."

Despite himself, he was intrigued. "You know my background, ma'am—what's yours?"

"Backwater world, nasty little cultural conflict. My side won or I wouldn't be here."

"You . . . were involved?"

"Community defense," she said. Her eyes twinkled suddenly; her smile was wickedly pleased. "Come now, General, you didn't think ISC would send someone to talk to you who *wasn't* a combat veteran, did you?"

"You?" He could not get past the fact that she was a plump little middle-aged woman in a crinkled linen dress and fashionable shoes. A pink dress, for the gods' sake.

Her brows rose. "I'm sorry, General, to upset your stereotypes of military women, but on my homeworld, we're all short and if we aren't starved we put meat on our bones. True, I was only in the local militia for three years, but I can assure you I have been shot at and returned fire. My boss felt you deserved to have someone listen to you who understood your problems."

"I . . . see." He shook his head slightly. "I'm sorry—I just—"

"You come from a world where the average height is almost twenty centimeters taller than the average on my world," she said briskly. "I understand that. Now—I am recording—" She did not ask permission, he noted, and he doubted that the office's security systems were interfering with the recorder. "You say that you weren't hired to blow the ansibles, and you have no information suggesting that your force blew them—is that correct?"

"Yes," he said.

"Excellent. Care to tell me why you didn't inform ISC of that at once when you heard the ansibles were blown, and you knew you had a force insystem?"

"Client confidentiality," he said.

"Right," she said. "So—when did you find out?"

"The . . . relay ship, outside the system, reported losing contact. That was"—he queried his implant—"Thirteen forty-two hours, UTC, on Central 346. The relay ship was on a two-hour schedule, though. We heard from other sources that the actual time of ansible loss was . . ."

"Twelve oh-two hours. Yes. You have documentation of the relay ship's notification?"

"Yes, but—"

"We may need to see it later. Now—this was not a full-scale operation, is that right?"

"Right. Advisory, with a five thousand man support team."

"John Calvin Tessan your onsite commander?"

"Er . . . yes." How did she know that?

"Your organization, and your field commanders, all have acceptable ratings with ISC," she said. "And I presume you wish to keep that rating . . ."

"Yes, of course."

"We're going to have to ask you to post a bond, I'm afraid," she said in a tone that carried no regret whatsoever. "Even though you have an acceptable rating, even though we have no evidence yet that your personnel were responsible, they are onsite with weapons capable of taking out two ansibles."

"A bond?"

"It's an unusual situation, you see." She paused, rubbed the tip of one carefully polished pink fingernail along the edge of her briefcase. "It's been six years since anyone last intentionally destroyed an ISC ansible. Political group on Neumann's, you may recall. We dealt with them."

ISC had invaded the system—as they had invaded systems before where someone destroyed their ansibles—and that political group no longer existed.

"Although we had considered the possibility we now face, in previous adverse events the military force at hand was the one which intentionally destroyed ansibles. That's a simple situation. If in fact Mackensee is not responsible here, either by accident or design, as you have stated, then we are faced with something we had considered in theory but not faced in practice. Policy, written in advance of experience, requires that we obtain a bond from you, to be returned upon proof that your personnel were not responsible."

"What kind of bond?" Arlen asked warily.

"The usual. Monetary, or a lien on equipment." She smiled, the kind of feral smile that Arlen knew very well from his own people. "Not quite ruinous, but serious."

"What kind of proof of our noninvolvement will you require, and who will adjudicate this?"

"It is not the practice of the ISC to seek or submit to the judgment of civil courts, as I believe you already know," she said. "We will determine that involvement or noninvolvement on the basis of evidence collected by our own personnel. On the other hand, since we are apolitical except with respect to the communications business, we have no motive for finding one way or the other."

"You're apolitical," Arlen said, spreading his hands on his knees. "I find that hard to believe."

"It's quite true," she said. "We do not care who is the government anywhere; we are not concerned with the crime rate, the state of the planetary environment, or any of the other things which motivate other corporations to interfere in local politics. Thus we need no lobbyists, no political backing. We have one focus: maintaining our interstellar monopoly. No one else can do what we do, and even if they could, we wouldn't let them." She ticked off these points with those delicate pink fingertips.

"But surely—"

She shook her head before he could get that thought out. "We haven't diversified. That is our strength, that others would find weakness. We do one thing well—superbly, in fact—and we protect our market. Since that market is not limited to any one planet, it is in no government's interest to interfere. Some of them are too stupid to realize that, but we educate them." She smiled again.

"All right, you're apolitical. And you want us to post a bond. With whom?"

"You have a choice, since Mackensee hasn't had a prior incident with us. We will discount the amount if you choose to place it with us, or you may choose the full amount placed in escrow at Simmons & Teague."

"And the amount?"

"Twenty million, which I believe is in the range of your contract amount with Secundus."

How the devil did she know that? Curiosity almost swamped outrage.

"There's another thing," she said. "There's a civilian ship captain in the Sabine system of some interest to us."

"Oh?" Curiosity gained ground; outrage subsided. If ISC wanted something, he might have wiggle room on the bond issue.

"I understand from your literature and your history that you do not usually interfere much with neutral shipping, but clearly this operation has not been ordinary. If you could explain what procedures are likely to have been followed, and the likelihood of this individual being unharmed, it would be much appreciated."

By whom? he wondered. Did the CEO of ISC have an errant grandchild on the scene or something? "Who is it?" he asked.

"Vatta Transport, Ltd., out of Slotter Key. Their chief financial officer's daughter was on her first voyage as commander, and was reported in Sabine system just before the ansibles went down. Any information you receive or could provide—"

Vatta Transport, Ltd. He didn't have to look that name up. Vatta had a star rating with their offplanet suppliers. They weren't the cheapest, but they were reliable: their on-time delivery rate was above 97 percent.

"I don't know anything now," he said, spreading his hands again. "We've heard nothing since the ansibles went down. But I can say that our policy is always to disrupt neutral shipping as little as possible. Of course we recognize Vatta Transport as a legitimate shipping company and would have no reason to cause harm." If a young, inexperienced captain hadn't done something stupid, that is. He hoped very much that Mackensee hadn't killed off the daughter of the CFO of a company they needed, but he knew it was possible. "With the ansibles being blown, the onsite commander might have chosen to check out every ship in the system—board them, choose one for a courier, and intern the others." He hoped the Vatta ship had been chosen for courier, in which case it would show up in a few days, in range of an ansible, and they'd have some hard data.

"If you hear—"

"I will let you know. Should I contact you and Vatta, or just you?"

"Either is fine. Now, about that bond . . ."

From her tone, no wiggle room there at all. And whatever profit they'd thought they'd have out of their employer, posting that large a bond would knock it back to a bad idea and a contract they should never have signed. That *he* should never have signed. "I have to get Sig to sign off on this, you know," he said. "Let me just contact him . . ." Though of course he would agree. No one could afford to have the ISC as an enemy.

Undoing the damage the mutineers had done proved more difficult than Ky had hoped. She dared not trust any of the passengers to help. Some of them might still want to mutiny, no matter what they said. She had no specialist with expertise in reconfirming an AI's original command set.

"It's an old system, though," Beeah Chok said.

"Don't I know it." Ky stared at the panel she'd just pulled. "But that doesn't make it better."

"It might. Do you have the system manual anywhere but in the system?"

"I had one in my implant." If the mercenaries had returned it . . . but they hadn't. "And there may be one in the command console." Ky clambered up. "I suppose you want me to look."

"Yes, Captain. It's just possible that the system could be taken down and restarted, if we had the manual."

Ky felt a chill stab of terror. "Nobody takes down ships' AI while they're operational, Beeah. That'd take down life support as well."

"Not necessarily." Beeah laid a diagram on Ky's desk; she tried to make sense of its many interlaced lines. Finally she shook her head.

"I can't see it, Beeah. If you're absolutely sure that you can do it without taking down life support—"

"Well . . . eighty-five percent sure."

"Not enough percents. What if you can't get it back up? We don't have suits for all those people, and the suit air supply's limited anyway."

Beeah muttered something she couldn't hear, but thought she understood.

"They're our—my—responsibility, like it or not. I'll space them in a heartbeat if they endanger the ship or crew again, Beeah, but I'm not going to risk them on a chance like this."

"Well . . . that's all we have, Captain. We can attack the control sections one at a time, but it'll take time. A lot of time; we may be out of fuel before we can shut the drive off."

"It's a chance we have to take," Ky said. "Protect the environmental system above all." She fought back a yawn. They were all exhausted, emotionally and physically, pushing themselves.

She could just sit there and let them drift farther and farther away from their expected location until they starved, or she could do something—anything—to fix the situation. Dumping the passengers still appealed, as a way of easing her frustration, but she knew she wouldn't do that. What were the options, with both the drive and the ship beacon out of order, with ship systems responding only erratically to her crew's instructions? She called a crew meeting.

"Here's what's happening," she told her crew. "We haven't yet regained control of the drive, so we're still accelerating to someplace we don't want to be. The ship's ID beacon seems to be nonfunctioning as well. So not only can we not get back, but no one can find us without very good active longscan. And the only people in the system with very good active longscan are somewhere else. The good news is that the environmental system is still working, so we have air to breathe and water to drink. The food supply, though, at our present rate of usage, will run out in five days. Rationing can do something about that, but not enough to give us a lot of leeway, and we have no idea when someone may find us. Our own scan is still working, but it's not that great, as you all know. It's very likely that ISC or someone else will come into the system before we starve, but they won't know we're here if our beacon isn't up. So beacon repair has to be a priority."

"I don't know anything about beacons," Quincy said. "They're another sealed system; users aren't supposed to tinker with them."

"Well, Paison did, and unless we can figure out how to undo what he did, we're about as visible as coal dust at midnight."

"There are two com engineers among the passengers," Beeah said.

"I hope we don't have to trust them," Ky said. "Because so far the passengers have been nothing but trouble." They knew that, but she needed to say it.

"Why did he disable the beacon, anyway?" Quincy asked. "That's what I don't understand."

"To hide us from the mercs," Riel said. "He wanted to get away, right?"

"But he'd been told they were already headed outsystem," Ky said. "He must've had some other reason."

"It doesn't matter why he did it," Quincy said. "What matters is we can't undo it."

"We haven't undone it _yet_," Ky said. "I'm going to talk to the passengers, and tell them why they're not getting lunch. Mitt, figure out what you need to do to cope with stretching our survival time . . . with less outside caloric input."

"They're going to complain."

Ky's patience snapped. "If they complain, I will space them. Damn it, without them we could last another twenty days, easy." She turned to Alene, who had scarcely spoken since Gary died. "What's the minimum for survival? We'll need to cut ourselves down a third, probably, but we'll cut them to the minimum. And then tell me what that gains us."

While Alene worked on that, Ky went to talk to the passengers. On the intercom; she wasn't risking anything this time.

"You need to know what the situation is," she said. "Paison disabled the insystem drive controls, so we have not been able to gain control of the drive and retrace our course. Paison also disabled the ID beacon, so the ship is now invisible to most scans. Your . . . leader"—she allowed the anger she felt to seep into her tone—"ensured that you, as well as we, would go hurtling off to the far reaches of the system and that no rescue vessel was likely to find us. My crew are attempting to fix that, but as most of you know ID beacons are sealed systems not intended to be manipulated by the user. Unlike Paison and his assistant, my crew has no experience in such illegal activities. That means that our original supply of foodstuffs will not suffice us even if a rescue ship were to show up, so I am instituting survival rules now. My crew goes on reduced rations; you go on minimal rations. I will still try to get you all out of this alive, but believe me that at this point, if any one of you fails to cooperate fully, or attempts to contravene my orders, that person will be spaced. No excuses. Now, Captains Lucas and Opunts, you will come to the number one cargo personnel lock, where my crew will pass you through to confer with me."

She didn't wait to hear their reaction but went back to the galley, where Alene was working on the rations.

"Forty seven of them, thirteen of us. That's sixty. But the rations loaded were for sixty-five, so we have sixty-five times five which is three hundred twenty-five day-rations providing a minimum of two thousand four hundred kcal per day, which is seven hundred eighty thousand kcal total . . . How long do you estimate we'll have to live off this, Captain?"

Damned if I know was the real answer, but not a useful one. "At least ten days . . . twenty if we can eke it out that far."

Alene fiddled with the handcomp. "Well, at ten days that's thirteen hundred kcal per day, which is just above basal metabolism. People will lose a little weight, but not much. Twenty is six hundred fifty kcal per day, which is seriously low. Crew won't be able to work well like that. Now if you put thirteen people at one thousand two hundred, as low as you'd want to go and expect alertness to stay up, that's fifteen thousand six hundred per day, and forty-seven people at six hundred, that could give us seventeen days. Crew efficiency shouldn't drop much, but the passengers will be just barely making it."

"We'll try that," Ky said. "Is there going to be any problem with water? Does changing the diet that much affect recycling efficiency or anything?"

Alene shook her head. "No . . . water's not the limiting factor, nor is air. Just food."

"There's one more thing," Ky said. "I'll donate my great-aunt's fruitcakes. Three of 'em, each an easy two kilos. I don't know what their caloric value is, but you can chew on a piece for a long, long time."

"Some people like fruitcake," Alene said, brightening. Apparently she was one of those people.

"Those people can eat it," Ky said. "And I'll bet they never had my aunt's fruitcake."

Scan was empty. Ky would have been glad to see any ship but none appeared. Her stomach growled and she growled back at it. So far nothing they'd done to the ship's beacon made it work; they were still receding from Sabine Prime as a ghost ship. On anyone else's scan they would show up only as an object in motion. The thought occurred then that some other ship might also be moving out here with no beacon. That was not comforting; it was too easy to run into what you didn't know existed. Day after day . . . she had never been hungry that long in her life, and it was worse for her passengers. The only good thing about being that hungry was that she couldn't sleep . . . because sleep brought the nightmares: Gary's eyes staring into hers the moment before he died, the smell of blood and death, the terror . . .

Icons appeared on the screen all at once: six ships, all identified as ISC. Ky tried to estimate range, but this far out from Prime she had no ranging model. An hour later, another four ships appeared on scan; she had no way to tell if they were an actual hour behind the first group, or had entered the system a light-hour farther from her. These also carried an ISC icon.

"Well, our rescue is here, if we can get their attention," Ky said. She looked around at the bridge crew, who looked like she felt. Nobody cheered. "They may or may not know about us, but either way it would be helpful to be able to talk to them. We have got to figure out a way to generate a signal out of this system."

"We need a real com tech," Beeah said.

"We have real com techs among our passengers, but can we trust them?" Quincy asked.

"Offer them a real meal," Beeah said. "Even a piece of fruitcake." He hadn't liked the fruitcake either. Alene kept insisting it wasn't so bad, but they had cut up only two of them.

Ky mimed gagging. "That might make them sabotage it. Still, it's in their interest to cooperate. The sooner we're found, the sooner we can feed everyone." She hoped that was true. "I suppose I'd better go talk to them."

"Not alone," Quincy said. "You can't go in there alone."

"No, I know that," Ky said. "Mehar, Beeah, you'll come with me. Bring the pistol bows. Look fierce." They looked more grumpy than fierce; she hoped that would suffice.

The captives, seated on the deck, looked pale and miserable. She hated herself for that, but at least they were all—except Paison, Kristoffson, and Paison's mate—alive. "Here's the situation," Ky said. "ISC just dropped a fleet into the system. They can't come help us, however, because Paison and his little clique disabled our beacon and we haven't been able to fix it. That puts our chance of rescue pretty low; on active scan we'll show up as a dead ship unless someone comes in really close, and they probably have other priorities. It could be weeks before they find us, if they do, and the rations run out in another few days. So if one of you has the expertise to fix the beacon, this would be a good time to tell me, and do that job honestly."

Silence. They stared back at her as if she'd spoken to them in an alien language. "We really are running out of rations—you're not just punishing us?" That was a short, balding man toward the back of the group.

Ky shook her head. "No. Why would I do that? You weren't all in on it anyway, and making you hungry wouldn't be the way to make you friendly. Paison and company did us all a bad turn. I don't know what his plan was—"

A hand went up. "I do."

Ky felt a prickle down her backbone. "And you are—?"

"I was his number-two com officer. You killed the number one. I wasn't supposed to be in on it but—he knew all about the ansible attacks. He wasn't about to wait around here until ISC showed up . . ."

"Where did he think he could go in a ship like this with no FTL drive?" Ky asked.

The man looked even paler; his skin glistened in the lights as those around him turned to look at him. "I—I don't think I should say."

"You'd better say, Corson, or we'll break your stupid neck," growled the man next to him. "If you get us killed—"

"And *you* are?" Ky said.

"Hemphurst, first officer off *Balknas Brighteyes*. Idiots have caused enough trouble. Corson, you cooperate or else."

Corson was clearly scared of the big man, but still scared of something else.

"Paison'll—or his group'll—get me if I tell."

"They aren't here and I am," Hemphurst growled. "I don't want to die of starvation because you're scared they'll come after you . . . If you're already dead, what difference does it make?"

Corson looked around nervously.

"What, you think some of 'em are here?" Hemphurst asked.

"I—I don't know," Corson said. "I don't think so, but—there's still people from our crew and the *Empress*. What if one of them—"

"Well, you know I'm here," Hemphurst said. "And I meant it—you help us get out of this, or I will kill you and then we'll have one more ration . . ."

"All right . . ." Corson looked down, then up. "I don't know all of it. But I do know the *Marie* wasn't the only ship Paison had insystem. Why the mercs didn't find the other, I don't know—it must've been stealthed somehow. But anyway—Paison was regional boss for the Barrenta gang. Posed as an ordinary trader, had a respectable history as cover. He had some kind of deal with the government here; the only people he was afraid of were ISC. He knew about the ansible attack: who did it, and why. And the *Empress Rose* was in on it, too. Kristoffson was one of 'em—nobody ever suspected anything of a passenger liner from a line like that. And he was going to rendezvous with his other ship, change the beacon on this one, put an FTL drive in it, and . . ."

"Kill us all," Hemphurst finished. "He was a damned pirate, in other words."

"Kind of," Corson said.

"Which means you're a pirate—"

"No! No, I'm not. I just—I found out something when I was on *Empress*, and they grabbed me and threatened me and then stuck me on *Marie*. There wasn't anything I could do. They watched me all the time—I was just like a prisoner—"

"So what do you know about beacons?" Ky said, interrupting what promised to become a verbal game between Corson and Hemphurst. "Do you know how to fix them?"

"I—don't know," Corson said. "I know some things to try."

"Then you had better come try them," Ky said. "Hemphurst is not the only one willing to kill you if you don't cooperate." She met Hemphurst's gaze; he nodded at her. "And as for the rest of you—anyone else have any expertise in this area?"

"Com Tech Sawvert, *Aspergia*," said a woman on the far side. "I don't know what's been done to the beacon, but I have done beacon maintenance. I might be able to help."

"Good. You, too, then."

Corson and Sawvert made an odd pair, Ky thought, as she escorted them back through the maintenance passages with Mehar and Beeah close behind them. Corson so clearly nervous about retaliation from Paison's people, and Sawvert, despite the effects of hunger, eager to get to work. At the access hatch, Ky stopped them. "Here—before you go to work, have some lunch." It was only a sandwich apiece and a thin slice of fruitcake.

"Thanks, Captain," Sawvert said. Corson nodded; half his sandwich was already in his mouth.

"If we can make contact and get an ETA for help, I'll know whether I can treat everyone," Ky said. "Engineer Chok and Environmental Tech Mehaar will keep an eye on you."

CHAPTER
SIXTEEN

Gerard Vatta's implant bleeped insistently. "Excuse me a moment," he said to the midweek meeting he was chairing.

"Gerry, it's Lewis Parmina at ISC."

His stomach went into free fall. "Yes?"

"Gerry, our people went insystem at Sabine about seven hours ago. And your daughter's ship is not there anymore."

"Not there?" He turned away from the table, from the faces that were searching his own for meaning.

"No," Parmina said. He went on, speaking rapidly. "The story we got from the mercs who came out, and from other civ ships, is that they interned captains and officers on your ship; your daughter was . . . was fine then. They made a contract with her; we've forwarded a copy they showed us to your offices."

Gerard noted but didn't comment on that slight hesitation. *Alive* would have done; *fine* could be defined variably. *Contract*—he motioned to one of the assistants hovering around the main table, scribbled *New contract, Mackensee & Vatta, just in, bring it.* The assistant stepped back with the glazed expression that meant he was querying by implant.

"Apparently they disabled the FTL drive or it wasn't working or something," Parmina went on. "So the ship was expected to be insystem on a particular ballistic course. Its beacon was working; they'd loaded additional rations and supplies and so on to cope with the additional passengers. We found the cargo—"

"Cargo?"

"The cargo your ship had been carrying, ag equipment. It was put outside the ship, netted, separately beaconed, with a copy of the relevant contract, because the cargo holds were converted to hold the passengers."

What the dickens was Ky doing carrying ag equipment, anyway? She'd set off with a cargo of mixed trade goods. One corner of his mind quickly put together a first stop at Belinta, a relatively young colony, and Sabine, known for its ag equipment in this region. He turned back to the table, waved, mouthed *Later* and left the room, heading for his office.

The rest of his mind stayed with Parmina, absorbing every word, every nuance of tone and expression.

"The contract states she had picked it up on consignment for the Belinta Economic Development Bureau. It was found on the course the mercs told us to check, right where the ship should have been. And the ship wasn't there. There were old traces of drive usage—apparently she turned on the insystem drive sometime after the mercs departed the system, but without a beacon trace, none of the scans in the system picked it up. We have no idea where she went, or why the beacon didn't show on anyone's scan."

"That can't be good," Gerard murmured.

"No . . . Gerry, I'm sorry. I really hate having to tell you this. If it were my daughter . . ."

"Don't apologize," Gerard said. "I can't thank you enough for telling me this much. A drive signature—at least that's not an explosion. I don't know what it means, but . . . there's a chance."

"We'll keep looking," Parmina said. "The primary mission has to be restoring ansible communication and ensuring the security of our people and equipment, but then—"

"Do you have an estimate on that?" Gerard asked.

"We'll have a skeleton system up, for nonpublic and emergency communications, within another couple of days. Very limited bandwidth. Rebuilding the platforms for full commercial usage will take much longer.

How long we won't know until we examine the wreckage and find out if any of the power units are usable. And we need to find out how it was done—how they destroyed them."

"But you're in communication with your people there now?"

"Spike ansible—yes, but we can't give anyone else access to that. I have put Ky's name in a priority-one bin, though, Gerry. We've also made it clear to Mackensee that your daughter's welfare is very important to us. If anyone there hears from her—or via any of our ansibles— our security personnel have been directed to pass it straight up to me. You'll have the news as soon as I do."

"Thanks, Lew," Gerard said. "I know you have a lot more on your mind than one little trading ship—"

"The whole Sabine situation is nonstandard enough that I'd be glad of some good neutral input," Parmina said. "The mercs are upset, the Sabine government is upset, no one's claiming responsibility for the ansible attack, and now that ship disappearing . . . It's not just a simple bit of sabotage anymore. I have my own reasons for wanting to find that ship, as well as our friendship."

Something in Parmina's voice left a cold spot, even colder than the rest in Gerard's gut. "You aren't thinking . . . that Ky was involved . . . ?"

"No, no, of course not. I don't think she blew the ansibles. For one thing, there's good scan data from before the attack to show that she was docked at Prime's orbital station. She did undock without permission after the ansibles were hit, but other ships did that, too—the orbital station was the next logical target. But ships don't just disappear like that, Gerry. You and I both know that ship beacons are sealed systems intended to work unless completely vaporized, and vaporized ships don't have a drive path signature. Something weird was going on, with her ship as well as the whole system."

Gerard could think of nothing to say. She had been there, alive after the time when he had feared she was dead. She had been alive until a few days ago, for sure. Now . . . maybe she was alive, even though the disappearance of her ship—or the malfunction of her ship's beacon— suggested something very serious had gone wrong.

"Thank you," he said again, just for something to say.

"I'll let you know as soon as we hear anything else. As for general business, I'd say it would be safe to schedule deliveries and pickups within seven to ten days. We won't have public systems back up by then, but surveillance will be full-on. Got to go, Gerry; we're up to our armpits in alligators." The line went blank.

"So is she all right?" Stavros was in the doorway.

"I don't know," Gerard said. His voice sounded disgustingly normal, he thought. Inside he felt shaky as jelly, but his voice didn't waver. "That was Lew Parmina at ISC. They're in the system; they have eye-witness and other records that show she was there, and she was alive and well up to the point where the mercs left the system. She was just coasting along, ballistic, full of passengers, with her cargo netted out-side, and then—the beacon went off, there's insystem drive residue, and she's nowhere to be found."

"That doesn't make sense," Stavros said, frowning. "If she was being pursued she might wish the beacon were off, but—I don't have a clue how to turn one off and I doubt she did. And why didn't she jump out of that mess? She's got a perfectly good FTL drive—"

"Apparently not," Gerard said. "I'm not clear on when it was disabled, or by whom, but apparently all she's got is insystem drive. What she does have is contracts. One with Belinta, to deliver ag equipment—"

"Which explains why she was on Sabine, instead of almost to Last-way," Stavros put in.

"Yes. The other is with the mercs, for carrying the passengers they assigned her, the officers of the other ships they interned temporarily. We have a copy of that, via the Mackensee Military Assistance Corpora-tion and the ISC; I haven't looked at it yet." He checked the latest de-liveries, and found it. "Here we are. Standard passenger rates for ten days' passage on an assigned course which is the same as that which the mercs gave the ISC, and on which the cargo was found."

"Binding on the firm, then?" Stavros asked.

Gerard winced. If Vatta Transport took over those contracts, it would be an admission that Ky was dead. And yet, their reputation rested on prompt, complete service.

"We can't do anything about the passengers," he said. "Not until the ship shows up. But we can reassure Belinta that they will get their cargo, though it may be somewhat delayed."

"Send someone to pick it up in space or reorder?"

"Let's look at the routings . . . wait a second—" He had come to the last part of Mackensee's message to ISC about the ship and its captain. "They say she no longer has a Vatta implant—what can that mean?"

Stavros shook his head. "How would they know, unless—" He looked at Gerry. "They removed it themselves. She must have been their prisoner."

He would not faint. He would not panic. It would do no good, and she was—she had been—alive, and might still need him. "Routings," he said, in a voice that sounded nothing like his own.

Together, they called up the present positions and routings of all the Vatta ships within two jumps of Sabine system. Nothing that would work easily, nothing that wouldn't break other commitments. *Katrine Lamont* was closest.

"We'll do it," Stavros said. "I'll get in touch with Furman—he knows her, I think. Wasn't he captain when she was on that apprentice trip?"

"I think so," Gerard said. He looked at the schedules. "If I ship today on a fast courier, I can send her a replacement implant, and that stack of mail waiting for her; Furman can pick that up at—where's he going to be? Delian II? Tight, but he can wait for it. We'd still want to confirm that Sabine's stable before we send him in."

"There's a piece missing," Sawvert said. The beacon's capsule lay open, its components spread on the deck.

"He must have taken it," Corson said. "Paison must have taken it out so he could put it in later."

"Or destroyed it," Ky said. "We know he destroyed part of the in-system drive control linkage."

"It's small," Sawvert said. "He could just stick it in his pocket—it's about like this"—she pointed at another piece, a slender cylinder about a finger long—"a number five inducer."

"You're sure it's missing . . ."

"Yes, Captain, I'm sure."

"And I am, too," Corson said. "Everything else looks fine—there's no sign of anything wrong but the missing part."

Something about the shape tickled Ky's memory. She had seen that shape before, but not in the beacon . . . she'd never looked inside the beacon case. Where had it been . . . ?

"Did you . . . er . . . search the bodies after you . . . shot them?" Sawvert asked.

"No." She had had other priorities, like getting the ship back under control and the rest of the hostages safely locked into the cargo holds again.

"It might be still . . . in his clothes . . ." Corson looked sick at this suggestion. Ky felt the same way.

"There's a problem," she said. "We don't have the bodies."

"You—spaced them?"

"I had cargo holds full of you folks, some of you hostile, and a ship to get under control, and no spare space anywhere," Ky said, trying not to sound defensive. "I couldn't just stick them in the cooler with the rations."

"Maybe he dropped it somewhere," Sawvert said. "Or maybe he gave it to someone who doesn't realize what it is."

"Maybe," Ky said. She felt certain that it was in one of Paison's pockets, and the dead pirate was mocking her still.

But that wasn't where she'd seen something like that part. Where was it?

"What kind of marks would it have on it?" she asked.

"Marks?"

"Any way to identify it? Stripes or something?" She waved at the disassembled beacon. Some of those parts had color-coding stripes, or numbers.

"Sure," Sawvert and Corson said together. They glanced at each other, and Sawvert went on. "It depends on the manufacturer, but basically it'll have a number and a stripe, probably purple. You don't have a parts store that might have it, do you?"

"No . . . but I know I've seen that shape aboard," Ky said. She frowned; something was tugging her toward her cabin, a memory too vague to be recognizable. It couldn't hurt to follow the hunch . . . "I'll be back," she said.

In her cabin, she stood still, trying not to think, not to interfere with whatever memory was trying to find its way to the surface. Nothing showed on the surface but the stains from the cleanup after the . . . the death. No handy part lay in the middle of the floor, or her bunk, or her desk. The shelves to either side of her desk held only the cube reader and one rack of cubes. The desk drawer had her captain's log and its stylus. She pulled open the locker under her bunk, where the brightly wrapped fruitcakes had been stowed. One remained; she hoped they wouldn't have to cut into that one. So far no one had dared complain about the flavor, but Ky still preferred to donate her share to others. No way Paison could have accidentally dropped the part here, but what if he'd hidden it, or had someone hide it, for him? Wouldn't he have chosen the captain's cabin?

It still didn't make sense, the timing of it. He had not had time to disable the beacon and hide a part in her cabin; she knew that. She had been in her cabin when they discovered the beacon wasn't working; she had confronted him too soon after that.

But something was here . . . she knew it. She started with the lockers over her bunk, where she found that things were not quite as she remembered. Of course. The mercs would have searched the cabin and simply shoved things back in, and she'd been too busy since to come in and reorganize. Entertainment and study cubes, clothes folded not quite as neatly as she'd left them. Behind them was a box, somewhat bent. The model . . . the spaceship model. She remembered now having shoved it to the back herself.

Ky pulled the box out—it rattled. When she opened it, a folded note was on top of broken parts. *Sorry,* the note said. *Needle got it. This is most of the pieces.* The needle-round had not reduced the model to its component parts, quite. Some of the assembly was still there. Ky laid the pieces on her bunk, wondering where the round had hit—obvious when she laid them in order—and there it was.

No purple stripe, but molded into the gray cylindrical shape which the assembly directions had told her was a missle was "I–5–239684." The other "missiles" were beige.

Cold chills ran up and down her back. The meaning of MacRobert's cryptic little note suddenly seemed clear. He had, for whatever reason, given her parts to a beacon of some kind and she had been too stupid to recognize them . . .

She grabbed the whole box and raced back down the passage to where Corson and Sawvert were slumped against the bulkhead, contemplating the guts of the beacon.

"Is this one?" she asked, holding out the little cylinder.

Sawvert looked up. "Looks like it—let me see—" She took it, turned it, peered at the inscription. "Yup, that's it. Where'd you find it?"

"In a model kit," Ky said. She put the box down. "Either of you know what the rest of this stuff is?"

"Model kit!" Sawvert leaned over the box. "That's nothing—nor that—but this—and this—and that bit there—all that's the makings of a small pin-beacon. A shouter." She pushed the parts around with her finger. "I don't know if you've got all of it—are there any more pieces?"

"There were, but it was in the way when the mercs shot up my cabin."

"I didn't know about that," Sawvert said.

"You weren't aboard then," Ky said. "Someone we'd picked up off the docks at Prime—someone from home—went crazy and tried to fight with the mercs. They shot him." The less said about that, the better. "So—anything more we can use to fix *this* beacon?"

"Let's just see what this piece does—if it works, the beacon should work. If it doesn't, we have some more bits to try, at least."

Reassembling the beacon took another two hours, but even before they closed the case, Lee reported from the bridge that their passive scan showed the beacon on.

"Only problem is, it's not *our* ID," he said.

"What do you mean, not our ID?"

"It says we're the *Mist Harbor*, serial number XWT–34–693, out of Broadman's Station. I'd guess that scumsucker changed the ID so when he put the part back in, no one would find us."

"And nobody will recognize us for who we are, unless we can change it back." Ky looked at Sawvert and Corson. "Can you change it back?"

"What he probably did," Corson said, "was change out the chip. That's what he did on the other—" He stopped; Ky suspected that her own face had the same expression as Sawvert's, a mix of horror and fury. "It's not my fault; I didn't want to do it," he said in a rush. "It was Paison—he was the captain, I had to—"

"Did you know he'd changed out the chip on this one?" Ky asked.

"No—I swear I didn't. I didn't even know he had one with him; I wouldn't have thought he could, with the mercs just about pushing us out of our ship and into their shuttle." He swallowed. "Do you have a spare ship chip? I can change it back."

"I don't know," Ky said. She'd not ever thought about it. Beacons came with ships, already sealed . . .

"There's a chip," Sawvert said, pointing to a little piece in the box. "Where'd you get this, anyway?"

"I don't know if it's ours," Ky said, about the chip. But if it came from MacRobert, what would it be? Maybe a generic Vatta ID? Maybe Slotter Key spaceforce? "In the meantime, Corson, since you seem to know so much about how Paison operated, what would he have done to our in-system drive?"

"I don't know anything about drives," Corson said. "I really don't."

"Even a fake ID ought to get someone's attention," Sawvert said. "And if I can fix your transmitter—"

"That would certainly help," Ky said. "I'm not at all sure what this chip is—it was in this box of model parts, as you can see—so I'm reluctant to put it in. At least this way someone can get us on scan. Give us a way to talk to them, and we'll be a lot better off."

*   *   *

"Who is *Mist Harbor*?"

The chief scan tech on ISC's bulbous command ship turned to look at the watch officer. "Dunno. Just showed up, but there's no downjump signature."

"Anything running around with no beacon is probably part of the problem," the watch officer said. "We have a missing ship, and now we have an extra ship—let's get a distance, heading, and mass reading on that, and see if it answers us. And if we have one ship that's been running silent, there may be more. How's the system catalog coming?"

"We have the data from Prime's orbital station; we're using that as baseline and plotting against it. So far no anomalies, but we're only thirty-two percent complete. We wouldn't have found this ship for another two or three hours. At a rough guess, it's four to six light-minutes away, judging by signal strength."

"Commit another two units and speed it up. Do you want *Ganges* to site some additional spindles for it?"

"That would help," the scan chief said. "Real-time scans like that would cut it by half, anyway."

"I'll talk to 'em," the watch officer said.

The scan chief turned back to his board, allocated two more computing units to the system catalog, and then increased the power on the active scan beam.

Two hours later, he knew that the *Mist Harbor* was in the same mass range as the missing *Glennys Jones*, that she was 6.1 light-minutes away, not under power, and did not answer a hail. The ISC specialty ship *Ganges*, having dropped four spindle-ansibles in remote reaches of the system, was able to get real-time data from them.

"That's interesting," the scan chief said. "Not only is *Mist Harbor* the same general size as our missing Vatta ship, but there are two other ships out there lying doggo. One's here"—he pointed, as the watch officer came up beside him—"and one there. I do like that fine-resolution scan we added."

"A year ago we wouldn't have spotted them," the watch officer agreed. "Nice work. I'll pass the word up . . . wonder if that is the *Glennys Jones* and she was captured by the bad guys. Doesn't look good for Vatta if that's true."

"Sir!" One of the junior techs waved for the chief's attention. "*Mist Harbor*'s beacon has gone—no, there it is—look at it—"

The beacon icon blinked on and off, in a rhythm not quite regular.

"Power failure? Fuel expended?"

"No, sir. I'd bet my next raise it's a signal code of some kind. There are dozens of those blinker codes on various planets. This one's from— what did the registration say?"

"Assume it's the Vatta ship, from Slotter Key. Can we translate it?"

"Without translating it, it's got to mean that their transmission capability is gone, and they're trying to signal . . . which still doesn't tell us who's in control."

"At least whoever's looking knows a ship is here," Ky said. "They may not care about the *Mist Harbor,* but they're bound to care that a ship appeared out of nowhere with no downjump turbulence. Someone will come investigate."

"In time?" asked Corson. He looked pale.

"We may be very hungry, but we'll be alive, I'm sure," Ky said with more certainty than she felt. Her stomach growled.

"What if one of Paison's ships gets to us first?" he asked.

"Why would they? ISC is here in force; their best move is to lie low or go away quickly."

"They think Paison's on this ship; he's their commander. He'd be trying to rendezvous. When they don't hear from him, they will come looking."

"Honor among thieves, eh?" Ky shook her head. "I don't believe it; I think they'll run off or stay hidden."

"You don't understand how they work," Corson said.

Ky cocked her head at him. "Are you going to explain, or just complain? Either get busy helping Sawvert fix the transmitter, or I'll have you escorted back to the others."

He looked scared, and bent to his work. But a half hour later, he shook his head. "Can't be done," he said.

"He's right," Sawvert said. "The problem here is mechanical as well as parts missing. Things have been bent, ripped—"

"So he didn't plan on using our transmitter," Ky said. "He was more interested in preventing any of us from calling for help. He did plan on using the beacon. How was he going to signal his other ships?" The answer came to her almost as she asked. "The ship chip change. The signal to his allies is the change in the beacon. They would figure that only he could get it back on, and changed to that ID. So basically— we've just been telling them to come and get us."

"That's what I meant," Corson said. "They could be out there right now—"

"We'd see them on scan," Ky said. "Wouldn't we?"

"Not if their beacons are off," Sawvert said. "Though if they're close enough, we might get them on active. He probably left active scan working, for close maneuvering, and he probably also had a small transmitter on him, for the same purpose. Something that would work within a kilometer or so."

Ky scrubbed at her head. "We need to let the ISC know who and where we are, and what's happened. What if we switched the beacon on and off . . . they'd pay attention to that, surely?"

"So would Paison's people," Sawvert said.

"Yes. That's a risk. But the way I see it, they're going to be after us anyway. Quincy—"

"Yes, Captain."

"How well do you know that old code they used in the war? And do you think anyone in the ISC knows it?"

"Probably," Quincy said sourly. "ISC has a database and a half. But I don't. Best thing is to just count out letters. They've got the processing power to decode something that simple."

"Again, maybe too late for us. But at least someone will have the facts as we know them. And I can tell Dad to send someone to Belinta with our cargo."

"Cargo! You're worried about cargo at a time like this?" Corson looked shocked.

"It's a contract," Ky said. "Vatta honors contracts." She could tell by his face that he had no comprehension at all, but her own crew nodded.

It was easier, this time, to crack the cover on the beacon unit, and this time Ky knew exactly which piece to jiggle to disable and enable the beacon. Unfortunately, that still meant wriggling into the cramped compartment in an awkward position that she knew would make her neck and back hurt: she wanted the beacon connected to its running power system. She tested it, sending the ages-old triple-three distress signal, which Lee easily picked up on their own scan equipment. In the meantime, Quincy had written down a simple letter-number list.

"It works in principle," Ky said. "Now for a message." She scribbled down the simplest thing she could: the ship's name, her name, the number of personnel aboard. "Read that to me one letter at a time," she said to Quincy. "Have Lee check that that's what I actually send."

It seemed to take a long time to work through that first simple message, and Ky realized that she should have had someone else do that while she composed a longer one with more details. She wriggled back out, and turned to Sawvert.

"Repeat that message, and I'll be working on more."

Back on the bridge, she glanced at the scan. An ISC beacon was closer now, but she had no way to tell how close. No odd beacons, so if Paison did have stealth ships in the system, they weren't revealing themselves yet. Could ISC pick them up? She shook her head. She had a lot to tell the ISC or whoever got her message, and it needed to be concise and clear.

"*Glennys Jones*, Captain K. Vatta, boarded by members of the Mackensee Military Assistance Corporation, contracted with MMAC to care for passengers . . ." No, strike *passengers*. ". . . captains and senior officers of other civilian ships interned by MMAC." What was most important? "Arly Paison, captain of *Marie*, mutinied, destroyed transmitter, damaged beacon, accused as pirate by former crew, stealth ships in system, involved in ansible attack. Jake Kristoffson, captain of *Empress Rose*, with Paison. One crew dead, three mutineers dead. Rations low. Insystem drive inoperable."

She handed that to Quincy for Sawvert to transmit. Minutes passed; she watched as the outgoing message came up, letter by letter, on her desk. While it was still in progress, the first response came in.

"Ship with beacon *Mist Harbor* now claiming identity *Glennys Jones*: explain discrepancy in ship ID, passenger totals. Mackensee Military Assistance Corporation reported total personnel aboard plus three to your number."

"I just answered that," Ky said to the bridge crew. "What's that put us, about six lights away?"

"Yup. But I think they're closing. They've got something that can microjump." Lee grinned back at her. "I think we might make it after all."

"I wish I knew where Paison's ships were," Ky said. Then she went on with more information. A list of personnel aboard, and their original ship assignment. A brief statement of her own contracts with Belinta and the Mackensee Military Assistance Corporation. The course they'd been on when they dumped cargo; the beacon ID of that cargo. A more detailed accounting of events aboard, starting with their departure from Prime's orbital station. She was uncomfortably aware that Paison's ships could be listening in, and might choose to avenge the death of their boss. If Corson was telling the truth, something she wasn't sure about.

More responses came in from the ISC ship, as they received the messages. Questions, mostly, many of them she could not answer. Who had Paison's local system contacts been? She had no idea. How long had Paison been in the system? She didn't know. How long had he and Kristoffson been connected? She didn't know that, either. Did she know if the Imperial Spacelines was implicated in that connection? Of course she didn't. Had she questioned everyone concerned? Had she had autopsies performed on the deceased crew and passengers?

"They'll be asking if I filled out some form in quadruplicate next," Ky said. "They should have a list from the mercenaries of who was put aboard, and already know that forensic pathologist is not one of the specialties listed. Of course we didn't do autopsies. We know exactly what killed them. I killed them."

That question didn't show up for another hour, during which they asked a host of other questions Ky couldn't answer. She hoped they'd start offering her some useful information soon, such as when they planned to intercept and remove her passengers, something like that.

"Wonder who that is," Lee said. Ky looked at the longscan display, where two new beacons had lit up.

"That's an odd place to downjump into," Ky said. "What's the downjump turbulence give us?"

"No downjump turbulence. It's like he was running quiet, beacon off, and then turned it on."

"Like us, in fact. And we know who else in the system can manipulate beacons."

"Going to warn them?" Corson asked.

Ky considered. "The ISC will have figured it out on their own. Still, we can tell them what we suspect." She scribbled out another message and sent it down for the others to transmit. Her stomach growled again. With the ISC in the system, she was reasonably sure they wouldn't be left to starve, but she still had a shipful of passengers and not enough food.

"Another arrival, if it is an arrival." That one was clearly a downjump transition, the scan blurry and finally steadying to show the now-familiar Mackensee beacons.

*   *   *

He was in the shower when his skullphone went off. Gerard Vatta turned off the water and answered; it had to be high priority.

"Gerry, we located your daughter Ky, and she's alive."

He almost fainted, leaned on the shower wall, and blinked hard to steady his vision.

"She's had some problems; we don't know the whole story yet, but she's fine and the ship's still whole. I'm sure you'll want to send someone—have you already ordered a ship in?"

"Yes . . . Furman with *Katrine Lamont* is closest. He'll be there in a day or so, if I've got the jump span right. Are the ansibles back up?"

"No, and won't be for days. Whoever blew them did a thorough job. We'll put in narrow-channel emergencies, but only for official use—at least we've got more bandwidth than pinbeams now, but not much. Look, it's irregular, but will you accept a credit line for her until your ship gets there? We've frozen monetary transfers in and out of the system, and between planets for the present. We can have our lawyers talk to yours tomorrow, but I thought you'd want to know now."

"Thanks, yes, I will accept it. Whatever she needs, Vatta will stand for it."

He had to tell the rest of the family. He turned the water back on, finished his shower, and came light-footed out to dress. Myris, sipping breakfast tea, turned at his footsteps. "You heard something? Something about Ky?"

"She's alive. All I know for now, but it's enough."

"Stavros?"

"Doesn't know yet. I'm about to call." Normally he hated using the skullphone for calls out; he swore it made his sinuses buzz. But this was special.

CHAPTER
SEVENTEEN

Ky knew that the rescue operation would be neither simple nor quick, but she had not expected to spend another three days nibbling minimal rations. A ship had to match course with theirs; they had to contrive a way to move people and equipment between the ships. And worst of all was the slow, inefficient spelling out of every communication with the beacon. She had the crew taking turns at the improvised transmitter, but they all had painful backs and shoulders by now.

"Send one person with transmitter," she spelled out, after being told that the chase ship was only nine hours away.

"Not top priority," she was told. "What's the condition of your passengers?"

Hungry, weak, cranky. What did they expect?

"Capable of half hour EVA in pressure suit?"

No, of course not. They'd been too hungry for too long. She sent *No* and wished she had a code for an exclamation point. Finally she had the message they were all longing for. Prepare to receive relief party with medical assistance and rations . . .

*　*　*

This whole thing of standing around waiting for boarding parties was getting old. Ky knew she should be grateful for the rescue, but what she felt was not gratitude. She tried to tell herself it was just the natural effect of fatigue and hunger, perfectly ordinary physical causes for irritability, but she knew it went deeper than that. She had set off on what could have been a boring routine trip or a grand adventure, and here she was being rescued like some twit in a story who hadn't had the sense to stay out of trouble. She snarled mentally at the little voice that said, *Well, did you?* Conscience was a wonderful thing except at times like this.

When the knock came on the outer hull, she operated the exterior hatch—by now it worked smoothly—and was surprised to see that the pressure indicator dropped only slightly. The two people who came into the chamber wore only light pressure suits, hoods pushed back. One of them was Master Sergeant Pitt. She opened the inner hatch at Pitt's signal. The mercenaries? Why the mercenaries? She'd expected a civilian rescue team.

"We've got a transfer launch tubed to your hatch, Captain Vatta," Pitt said without preamble. "Should make it easier. Permission to come aboard?"

Ky did not point out that they already were aboard, and nodded. Pitt came into the little antechamber.

"We've got rations enough to last you until we reach the orbital station," Pitt said. "Anyone's in bad enough shape, we can take them now. How are they doing?"

"The live ones are fine," Ky said.

"Some of them died . . . How did that happen?" Pitt's expression didn't change but her tone flattened.

"I guess they didn't tell you," Ky said. Why not? she wondered. What was ISC up to? "The captain and first officer of *Marie*, and the captain of the *Empress Rose*, were involved in piracy—and working with whoever blew the ansible platforms. They tried to mutiny when you folks left the system. That's why we've got the wrong beacon ID and that's how our insystem drive went off."

Pitt's mouth twitched. "And here I thought you'd decided to head for home on your own. Here—let's get the com tech and transmitter aboard, while you tell me—" She signaled, and a man carrying an equipment case edged past them. "To the bridge with him?"

"Sure," Ky said.

"So, how did they manage that?" Pitt asked. It took Ky a moment to realize what she was talking about.

"Tapped into the ship's data lines and subverted the AI. I'd been afraid of something like that, but we didn't have any way to secure the system against people who knew what they were doing. Too many of them, too few of us, and no real way to isolate them from everything."

"I suppose this is payback for the trouble the first time," Pitt said thoughtfully.

"Huh?"

"ISC must've told our commander all that, but nobody told me. Command wasn't overly thrilled with me for mishandling that first boarding; this must be their idea of a joke."

Ky hadn't thought of it that way.

"So, what did you do?" Pitt asked.

"When the ship took off suddenly? Well—I had to stop the mutiny. Paison—*Marie*'s captain—had a member of my crew hostage and was threatening to kill him unless I surrendered the ship to him."

" 'Course you wouldn't do that," Pitt said. Her certainty surprised Ky.

"I didn't, but why are you so sure?"

"You're not the type. Military-trained, even though you hadn't seen action—you wouldn't fall for that. How many did you lose?"

"Only the one," Ky said. Only the one, but someone she'd known off and on, and her father's chosen baby-sitter. "I—had only the pistol bows, Mehar's target kit. I'd been practicing, just in case. Paison and his mate and a few others had knives; the mate had Gary . . . they had a mob behind them. So I shot them." Suddenly she wanted to tell Pitt all about it, get a veteran's response to it. She must not. "They killed Gary; I killed the leaders; the rest weren't that eager."

"Good job, Captain," Pitt said. "Now—let's get the rations aboard, eh?"

"Why is Mackensee doing this?" Ky asked.

"ISC," Pitt said. "Proof of good faith. They still aren't convinced we had nothing to do with the ansible attack, even with what you said. Or so they say. I think they're just being punitive, myself. But nobody argues with ISC."

That was true. Ky dragged her mind away from that and back to the immediate problems. "What about those rations, then?"

"Right, Captain." Pitt muttered into her shoulder mike and said, "If you'll go on to the galley, and have someone ready to direct stowage, I'll stay here and direct the transfer."

Up in the crew rec space, her crew waited, all but the two on the bridge. They stared at her as she came in, not saying anything.

"It's all right," Ky said. "They're about to transfer rations over to us, and we can start feeding right away. Li, you're in charge of stowage of the rations."

The first person in, however, was not carrying ration packs but a bright orange medical kit. "I need to assess physical condition," he said. "And advise you on refeeding schedules to minimize problems. Do you have records of how much and what you were feeding?"

"Yes—but why do we need that?"

"Because refeeding after prolonged starvation or below-subsistence feeding can be tricky. I'll need to check everyone individually for metabolic variations, and then make out a program. If we're lucky we'll only have two or three main groups to worry with. Spacers come from so many different places, though, with so many different metabolic quirks . . ."

"You can't ask people to starve another day or so while you work this out," Ky said. She could feel her neck getting hot.

"No, of course not," he agreed. "But the first refeeding must be small and bland. Small meals and frequent is the best for everyone; the details do matter, especially in the next week, and especially since your environmental system is operating near its limits. The last thing you need is two dozen bouts of diarrhea." Beyond him, troopers were bringing in dollies of ration packs. Ky could hear Li directing them where to put things in storage.

"That's certainly true," she said. "But what can I have the crew fix now, right away? We have forty-odd very hungry passengers."

"I'll check your crew first, and then them. Let's start with you. Planet of origin?"

"Slotter Key—I'm fine, you don't have to worry about me—"

"If the captain goes down, the ship goes down. Put your finger in this." He held out a fat cylinder with a hole in one end, studded with buttons. Ky put her finger in. "Ah. You last ate when? And what?"

Ky had to think hard to remember, and told him. He touched a button on the side of the fat cylinder, then two others.

"Here's yours, and I'm perfectly serious. For best recovery and performance in the meantime, you need to adhere to this schedule. Now, right now, one bread ration and one fruit pack. The rest I'll upload to your system storage."

"But—"

"That's your hunger arguing with me." He turned to the file of people moving the ration packs. "Bring me one of those." At once, one of the men brought over a flat brown package. The medic ran his finger along a ridge on top; the package folded back. Inside were smaller packets, each with a picture label. Ky stared.

"We had to rip those things open with kitchen knives, and it was a job," she said. "Nobody told us—"

"Sorry. Here." He rummaged in the pack and brought out a sealed packet with a picture of fruit on one side, and another with a picture of a round, flat object colored brown and cream. "Take these and eat them now, right this minute."

Clearly this nut wasn't going to let her alone until she did, and she had a lot to do. "All right," Ky said, and opened the packets. She didn't feel that hungry, but she bit off a piece of the breadlike thing and squirted some of the semiliquid fruit onto the rest of the bread. It was vaguely sweet and definitely tart. At least it wasn't Aunt Gracie Lane's fruitcake. She finished the bread, onto which she'd squeezed the last of the fruit mush.

In the meantime, the medic had grabbed one after another of her crew, insisting that they, too, insert their fingers into his device. He came back to her. "The same thing, in two hours. I'll still be here then, and I'll check on you. Now—I need to see the passengers."

Bemused, but already feeling more alert, Ky led him down to the holds and introduced him. Her heart twisted at the sight of the hollow-eyed, listless men and women who lay on their pallets. The medic checked them one by one, and behind him came troopers carrying ration packs, from which they dispensed as he ordered. For these, more malnourished than her crew, squeeze packs of liquid. "They can have one every hour at first," he said to Ky. "These are also loaded with micronutrients. And then after the first twenty-four hours, anyone who's not having gut problems can move up to the phase two rations, which includes solids. I'd expect by the third or fourth day to move them to phase three. It could have been much worse—I've seen it much worse. You made a good decision, back when you cut the rations early on."

Soon the medic was finished with his assessment; Ky headed back to the bridge. There, the new communications gear had been installed, including a viewscreen that took up half the space between her chair and the pilot's. She finally had ordinary voice contact with the outside world. After days of spelling each message out laboriously, that was a relief, even with a Mackensee trooper standing by the com console to emphasize that the equipment belonged to them.

"Colonel Kalin wants you to call," the trooper said as Ky came onto the bridge.

"Are the system ansibles up?" Ky asked.

"I don't know. The Colonel—"

"Wants me to call. I understand." She eyed him, and decided that trying to claim the overriding authority of a ship's captain would probably not work. She would find out the most the fastest by cooperating. "Do you know the channel?"

"Yes, Captain. It's preentered. All the captain needs to do is press that button—" The trooper pointed.

Ky pressed the button, and other telltales turned yellow, then green. In moments a man's face took shape on the viewscreen. He wore the Mackensee uniform and metal shapes whose significance she did not know on his shoulders and lapels. Gray hair cut close, a broad face, green eyes.

"I'm Colonel Eustace Kalin," he said. "I'm in command of the local Mackensee forces. You're Captain Vatta, is that right?"

"Yes, I'm Captain Vatta," Ky said.

"Captain, we have business to discuss, which would best be discussed face-to-face. I'd like you to come aboard—"

Ky shook her head. "Colonel, this is my ship, and the captain does not leave the ship—not willingly that is—while in transit."

His brows went up. "You regret our giving you emergency medical care?"

"Not at all, Colonel," Ky said. "I'm glad you did, and grateful for your surgeons' skill. But now I am healthy. My place is here, aboard my ship, until we are safely docked somewhere. My second-in-command was killed when some of the . . . the passengers . . . attempted to take over the ship."

"I see," he said. "In that case . . . we have been asked by the ISC to tow your ship back to orbit near Sabine Prime. I understand that you have no onboard power?"

"That's correct," Ky said. "The individuals who attempted to gain control of the ship caused the drive to malfunction, and we are out of fuel. However, I am not willing to have this ship treated as a derelict and subject to wreckers' law."

"What would you do if we *didn't* tow you back?" he asked. "You have no FTL drive; you have no working insystem drive . . . Were you planning to get out and paddle? Do you really think you're in a position to make conditions?"

"All situations are negotiable," Ky said, quoting her father. "I could, for instance, hire you myself to tow us back."

He laughed. "You don't scare easily, Captain Vatta. All right. With your permission and not under wreckers' law, making no claim on hull or cargo other than that which we contracted with you to carry, will you permit us to tow you back to Sabine Prime near-orbit where we can carry on this discussion in a less public venue?"

"Thank you," Ky said. "I accept your offer of transport."

"What we need to do then is let your engineering staff talk to my engineering staff about where to grapple on." He shook his head slightly. "I'm beginning to believe what Master Sergeant Pitt and Major Harris said about you, Captain Vatta."

She had no idea what they'd said—what she remembered best were their comments on young women who harbored rescue fantasies and were too susceptible to young men. But the Colonel almost sounded approving, like the Academy Commandant on a good day.

Three hours later, the *Glennys Jones* was snugged up to the flank of a Mackensee warship, and Quincy and her Mackensee counterpart were deep in conversation with hull schematics. A score of pressure-suited troopers were going over the outside of the hull under their direction, applying some kind of test equipment to various points. Ky didn't have a clue what that meant. The medic had been back to the bridge to remind her to eat her bread and fruit mush. He reported that the passengers were all doing well, sucking down the liquid food packets as fast as they were allowed.

Ky finally went to bed when she couldn't stop yawning, only to wake a few hours later when her stomach lurched sideways and then up. She called the bridge.

"Just an adjustment to the artificial gravity," Garlan said. "We had a little trouble synching our AG to the warship's when they tried a micro-jump with us attached. But that bled off a lot of speed."

"What about our hull strength?"

"That's fine, Captain. There's no strain on the linkage, it was just the delta vee surge of the double endim transition. Since you're awake, they wanted to know if they could do it again, to save time on the way back."

"Let me check with the passengers," Ky said. She struggled up, splashed water on her face, and called down to the holds. The medic answered. "How are they doing?" she asked.

"That gravity surge didn't help," he said. "Their guts aren't that stable yet. What happened?"

"Microjump by your ship. They want to do it again."

"Tell 'em to wait twelve hours," he said.

Ky called back to the bridge, and relayed that. Then she sagged against the headboard of her bunk. She was awake, tired, frustrated, and worried.

Twelve hours and fourteen minutes later, the ship seemed to lurch again. This time Ky had been able to warn everyone it was coming, and the medic reported that the passengers had come through without incident. Some of them were now eating bland solids. She had been given permission to try a proper breakfast, which tasted delicious.

They came out of that microjump in close orbit around Sabine Prime. Ky looked at the scan when the screens cleared and felt her stomach clench on the breakfast it had earlier accepted. Prime's orbital station held several civilian ships, including Vatta Transport, Ltd.'s *Katrine Lamont.*

"What—" She swallowed an epithet. "What is that doing there?"

"I don't know," Lee said. "Last I heard, the *Kat* was over on the Beulah Road route."

"I knew they'd have heard," Ky said. "But I didn't think they'd be crazy enough to send a ship in."

"Next scheduled carrier?"

"Not likely. When we were here before I looked that up, and it was four months off the *Elaine of Gault*. It only feels like four months."

The com tech waved at her. "Captain, you've incoming traffic—"

"Right." She sat down in her seat and prepared to grill the colonel to find out what he knew. But the face that came up was not Colonel Kalin. The dour, lined face looking back at her belonged to the captain of *Katrine Lamont*. She knew it all too well. When she'd been an apprentice, shipped out to experience the wonders of space and get her mind off what her mother called "that military nonsense," Josiah Furman had been the captain of that ship, taking obvious pleasure in putting a Vatta youngling to the nastiest and more boring chores. She'd come back more determined than ever not to be stuck in ordinary civilian transport.

She couldn't think of anyone—barring her mother—she wanted to see less.

"You've made a fine mess of things," he said. "You weren't supposed to be anywhere near Sabine . . . but then you never did follow orders."

That was unfair, she had followed many orders, many stupid orders, many boring orders. She had followed most orders, including his. She tried not to see the expression on the Mackensee com tech's face, just as the com tech was very obviously trying not to look at her.

"What did you think you were doing?" he went on, not waiting for an answer, as if he were her actual parent. "First, you make an idiot of yourself at the Academy, and then you can't even carry out a simple, uncomplicated voyage without getting the entire company in an up- roar. Do you have any idea the profits you're costing us by this?"

It was a pause, if not the pause she wanted. "Trade and profit," Ky said, fighting to keep her voice even. "Vatta captains are expected to take advantage of opportunities—"

"Experienced captains," he said. "Captains who know what they're doing. You—I got pulled off my route, with loss of early-delivery bonuses, just because you couldn't do what you were told and deliver that use- less excuse for a ship to the wrecking yard. Because of you," he said, and glared at her.

She was tired, hungry, grieving, and this was totally unfair. All those emotions tangled in her throat, and she could say nothing. Had her fa- ther told Furman to scold her this way? He hadn't scolded her about the Academy . . . Was he angry now?

"My father—," she finally said.

"Your father told me to come pick up the pieces and be sure you were safe. Pulled me right off my route, told me to skip two destinations. So I have to divert, load up your cargo, load your crew, haul your cargo to Belinta, that armpit of the region, before I can get back to my route, and take you home. My customers will be upset—"

"You can't do that," Ky said.

"I don't want to, but your father said—"

"I mean, you can't take our cargo to Belinta. We have cargo there, in storage, for Leonora and Lastway."

"Then it will have to stay there. I am not going to Leonora and Last- way, and neither are you. I've seen the reports—*Glennys Jones* will never make it out of the system. I'll sell it for scrap here—"

"You will do no such thing," Ky said. Her jumbled emotions had set- tled with anger on top, and at that moment she felt she could leap across space and remove his head without a weapon. "With repairs— simple repairs—this ship is quite capable of taking cargo to Belinta and beyond, and that is what I will do. I am in command of this ship, not you." That last came out weaker than she meant.

"You're under tow," Furman said. "You can't even dock with the station—which, by the way, I understand you left illegally, without permission. Your ID beacon is transmitting the wrong data. They won't let you dock." He smirked. On his big, heavy face it looked particularly disgusting.

Ky hadn't thought of that complication. The moment in which she had elected emergency undock over the possibility of being blown up with the station seemed years in the past. Had it only been a few hands of days?

"It was an emergency situation," Ky said. "Other ships also broke loose—"

"But not Vatta ships," he said. "You've damaged our reputation, you've cost us millions, and now you make excuses—enough of this. Your father sent me out here to take care of things, and that's what I'm going to do. I'll sell the ship for scrap, transport your cargo to Belinta and your crew back to a nexus where you can catch a passenger ship home. Get your things and be ready to leave in—"

Ky stabbed at the board and cut the connection before what she thought emerged from her mouth. Her vision hazed.

"That was interesting," Lee said softly. "He seems to think you're still a schoolgirl . . ."

"Apparently," Ky said. She tried to control her breathing, her face, her voice. It would have been so satisfying to throw something breakable at something immovable.

"Who *is* that?" asked the Mackensee com tech.

Ky took a deep breath. "He was captain on the ship where I served my junior apprenticeship," she said. "We did not get along. To be fair, at thirteen I was the typical adolescent brat, and the youngest of my family. I'd been sent off because my parents thought I was spoiled, and they were right. But he . . . did not help."

"And they sent him to help you now?" The tech's face expressed unexpected sympathy.

"Probably he was closest," Ky said. She hoped that was it. She hoped it wasn't an unsubtle message from her father that she had screwed up yet again, and worse. "Look," she said to the tech. "I really need to talk to home—to headquarters—about this. Is there any chance of getting an ansible linkup?"

"Not for another couple of days, they tell me," the tech said. "What do you think, this guy's going beyond his orders?"

"I hope so," Ky said. "And I hope he's wrong about the station refusing dockage. We have to get in there for resupply and repair."

"I reckon ISC will have something to say about that," the tech said.

"ISC—why?"

"When someone messes up their ansibles, they usually hang around and pretty much run things until they find out who did it and punish them. And didn't you find that out?"

"I found out some," Ky said cautiously. "Not everything."

"So ISC ought to be grateful to you," the tech said. "If they want you to get docking access, you will, whatever poison puss says."

"I hope so," Ky said. She sighed. "I wish—" But she couldn't say that aloud, not in front of her crew or these military types. She wished she was military, where everything was cut-and-dried, open and obvious, simple. Well, except for people like Mandy Rocher. Her mind insisted on dragging up every person she'd found to have hidden motives. "I need to check on something," she said instead. "If he calls back, don't accept it."

"What should I tell him?"

"Tell him I'm not discussing company business over an open line," Ky said, wishing she'd thought to say that earlier. She left the bridge and went to talk to the passengers. They were feeling well enough to complain about the delay in returning them to their ships.

"I can't do anything about that," Ky said. "You know I have no shuttles, and we have no independent power. At least we have adequate food now."

"That's all very well, but what about my ship?" one of the captains said. "Is it still in the system? Are my crew all right?"

"I'll find out," Ky said, and dashed back to the bridge. With the exception of *Empress Rose*, all the ships were still in the Sabine system, and crews reported nothing but minor injuries or illnesses. She reported that to her passengers and explained that no, she could not provide them all a secure comlink to their ships, since ISC now controlled all communications and hadn't put a high priority on their needs.

She went through the protocols to request a link to Sabine Station, and to her surprise was put through to the acting stationmaster. This individual wore the gray ISC uniform with the silver lightning flash and introduced himself.

"Ah, Captain Vatta. I understand that you undocked against orders."

"Yes," Ky said. "Emergency situation."

"Quite. Sabine system imposes a fine of five thousand credits for improper undock, and you have an outstanding ship balance due of

2345 credits for docking services." He looked down at something on his desk, then back up. "A counterclaim for failure to recognize a legitimate emergency and facilitate ship's withdrawal from danger will be entertained by the interim authority."

"The interim authority?" Ky was still wondering where she could scrape up another 7345 credits.

He grinned at her. "That's us, Captain Vatta. Should you make such a counterclaim, including, for instance, Sabine Station's failure to complete your refueling and to allow you timely access to repair and replacement parts, it is likely that your debt would be reduced to zero and docking permission could be given in accordance with Sabine law." His grin widened. "We prefer to make use of local law whenever possible."

Ky blinked. "I suppose . . . I should make a counterclaim, then."

"I would recommend it, yes. Your ship suffered damage, did it not, as a result of this station's negligence and lack of cooperation?"

"Er . . . yes."

"ISC has never favored frivolous suits, so unreasonable requests for damages might prejudice your case, but since your ship was preemptively interned for use as a hostage carrier, in large part because you had no functioning deepspace drive and an incomplete fuel load on insystem, I suggest a computation of what it would take to restore your functionality."

Ky just managed not to gape. Surely they were aware that the ship was old and had more wrong with it than one missing drive component.

"I can't of course name a figure—that would be unfair of me, in my capacity as interim stationmaster. I must be impartial—"

If this was impartial, she didn't want to see partial—at least not unless it was on her side.

"But any material damages could be named. Should they not be upheld by a later court, at least you would have some recompense, I'm certain."

Getting docking privileges alone would be worth it, Ky thought. She collected her scattered thoughts. "With permission, Stationmaster, I'll be back with you shortly. I want to prepare an accurate statement."

"Very good, Captain Vatta," he said. The flicker of his eyelid was not quite a wink. "With respect, I suggest you not wait overlong. Soon our tugs and shuttles will be busy here. Oh, and the fee for towing you into a docking slot will be eight hundred fifty, as usual."

"Back in one," Ky said. She looked around at her bridge crew. "Did the rest of you hear what I heard? Was he really telling us to make out an expense account and blame Sabine Station for the past couple of weeks?"

"Sounds like it to me," Quincy said. "And he's right. The station should have facilitated our repairs, or at least sold us the sealed unit. There was no rational reason to think we'd take it to the Secundus rebels or the mercs. And they should have given ships permission for emergency undock, all of 'em. Much more dangerous for the station if ships were there if the station was attacked."

"I'm tempted to just ask for what our back charges are," Ky said. "That way we can't be excessive."

"No!" Quincy said. "Ky—Captain—that's not the way to think. Let me work on it. We had a lot of damage. There's two of our crew dead—one of them was an idiot, true, but the other wasn't. We had all that work to do in the cargo holds, modifying them for emergency quarters—that used up a lot of our reserve parts stock. And some of that will have to be torn out to make room for cargo. Then there's our cargo, floating around out there—"

"Unless Furman grabbed it already," Ky said bitterly.

"Wherever it is, it's not in our holds," Quincy said. "And we've got to retrieve it, unload the other stuff, and reload the holds. That's several days—docking fees for those days shouldn't be due from us, because it's not our fault. Nor should replacement parts, nor the labor cost to re-configure the holds. The sealed unit was already damaged when we came in; I wouldn't gig 'em for that. But the beacon damage, and the control systems—that's going to take a complete purge to get it fixed."

The amount Quincy came up with after a few minutes seemed huge to Ky, but she transmitted it to the Sabine stationmaster's office anyway.

CHAPTER
EIGHTEEN

The answer came back from Sabine Station after a decent interval. Acting Stationmaster Dettin looked serious, but his voice was pleasant.

"On behalf of Sabine Station, I am prepared to accept this counterclaim of damages caused by this station's civilian management. Since the claims made here are substantially larger than the balance due on the fines and docking use fees on the books, it is my decision that *Glennys Jones* be allowed to dock here, and that all tug and docking fees will be waived for a period of twenty days. However, the final decision, and any monetary damages to be paid other than this offsetting, will be determined by a court at some later date. Acceptance of this proposal is not binding in law as later adjudication may choose to impose additional fines, penalties, or costs on either party." That came out in a near monotone, as if he were reciting text from some legal tome. Probably he was.

"Are you willing to accept these terms and defer funds transfer until adjudication is complete?"

"Yes," Ky said.

"Thank you, Captain Vatta," the man said. "Now, do you wish tug services immediately?"

"Yes," Ky said.

"I can assign you . . ." He looked blank for a moment. "You can expect a tug to contact you in about six hours. Estimated time until docking will be . . . nine hours four minutes. Is this acceptable?"

"Yes," Ky said again, beginning to feel like an automaton. "I will inform the passengers," she said. "Thank you."

"Our pleasure," Dettin said. "When you arrive, there are ISC and Mackensee personnel who wish to confer with you at your earliest convenience. And I understand you have remains . . . ?"

Remains. It took her a moment to realize that the stationmaster meant someone's body. Gary's body. "Yes," she said. "Gary Tobai, one of my crewmen . . ."

"We will have a funeral representative ready to receive the remains."

"Thank you," Ky said.

"By the time you've arrived, we will have limited commercial communications service back up; your passengers will be able to contact their vessels from the station. They have been assigned priority-one access."

"They will appreciate that," Ky said. "I'll tell them. If you'll excuse me, I need to ready my ship for docking procedures—"

"Of course, Captain Vatta. There is another Vatta Transport vessel in the system—have they contacted you?"

As if he didn't know. "Yes," she said. "I presume we will communicate more fully later."

"Captain Furman has requested permission to retrieve your cargo; is this permissible?"

"Er . . ." If she said yes, he would have her cargo in his possession and be able to preempt her contract. If she said no, he would be furious and for all she knew her father would be furious, too. She didn't need more enemies. She didn't need to start her career breaking contracts, either. "No," she said, feeling a great hollow opening inside her. "Not at this time. I haven't determined whether I will be able to meet contracted terms without his help. I would prefer to confer with Vatta headquarters before making that decision, after we have a repair estimate on my ship."

"I see." Was that a twitch of amusement? She hoped not, but she could imagine the kinds of things Furman had said about her.

"We'll expect the tug contact in six hours, then," Ky said. She would try to catch a nap before then, and another snack.

*   *   *

By the time the tug's call came, Ky had slept a few hours, eaten again, showered, and started a list of necessary repairs and their projected costs. Refueling the insystem drive. Purging and reinitializing the ship's control systems. Obtaining a new, certified ID chip for the beacon. Replacing the sealed unit of the FTL drive and the damaged liner section. Removing the plumbing fixtures from the cargo holds—she presumed that Mackensee would want their toilet and sink units back, but that could wait. Repairing or replacing the communications modules. The credits mounted up, a few hundred here, a few thousand there. She compared the total to the amount that Mackensee owed her for transporting their prisoners . . . a squeak, but she might make it.

Once they docked at the orbital station, Ky spoke to the station security about unloading her passengers. In only a short time, they were all out of the ship, onto a dock area secured from the media. Ky had begun to relax when a series of dockside calls came in. A Mackensee officer—she had no idea what rank, but he seemed very young—asked permission to come aboard and arranged for the removal of their property. An ISC official also asked permission to come aboard; she named herself "Assistant to the Incident Investigator-General." A representative of the Sabine Prime government's Department of Foreign Affairs wanted to talk with her about her knowledge of the involvement of Captain Paison in the Secundus affair. A representative of Interstellar Transient Transformations wanted information on Gary Tobai's faith and the type of ceremony desired. And an officer from the *Katrine Lamont* claimed to have urgent communications from Captain Furman and Vatta Transport, Ltd.

She groaned inwardly. What she wanted most was an uninterrupted sleep shift, but clearly she wasn't going to get it. She tried to think what should come first.

"Quincy—what kind of service would Gary have wanted?"

The old woman shook her head. "We never talked about it. He was a Modulan, I know that much, but that's all."

"Well . . . what would be best for the crew, then?"

"Modulan's always safe. But you Vatta are something else, aren't you?"

"Saphiric Cyclans, yes, but it doesn't matter about me." Even as she said it she wondered why. Why shouldn't she matter? "What about his family? Did he ever talk about them?"

"Had a granddaughter out in the Necklace Islands; I don't know about the rest."

"We'll do Modulan and have the box made up for her, then. Do you know her name?"

"Angelica," Quincy said.

Ky called Interstellar Transient Transformations and gave them this information.

"Our condolences, Captain, to you and your crew," the ITT representative said. "I'm Selon Bahandar, and I will be assisting you through this sad time. We'll need to discuss chapel availability, once we've collected the . . . er . . . remains."

"Chapel availability?"

"Yes. We have many other services scheduled, you understand . . ."

She didn't. But then, she'd never attended any religious service on a space station.

"It's a matter of finding the open time slot most suitable to you and to his memory."

"I see."

"You are familiar with the process, I presume?"

She wasn't. They hadn't had a funeral in the family since Aunt Pellit's, and that was over on North Coast when she had an ear infection and couldn't fly. "I'm sorry," she said. "But I haven't dealt with this before."

His smile managed to combine extreme sympathy with extreme satisfaction; Ky found it extremely annoying. "My dear Captain Vatta, again let me express our condolences. Interstellar will be happy to assist you in every detail, as I'm sure you all wish to show the utmost respect for your comrade."

"Uh . . ."

"You may not have known that orbital stations usually allot only one space for religious purposes, a holographic chapel which is preprogrammed to offer a variety of religious spaces suitable for practically every faith and ceremony. Now as you've indicated your loved . . . er . . . lost one was himself a Modulan, let me show you the Modulan setting . . ." Up on the screen, a window opened to show the interior of a typical Modulan chapel, very like that at the Academy except for the lack of a Spaceforce seal. The restful curves, even to the seat backs, the soft golden glow of the lighting, the Focus of Faith in gleaming pewter. "If you want to personalize this in some way—" The display flickered, and morphed to an exaggerated style, with banks of pink flowers along the side walls and a beam of light striking down at an angle to rest on the Focus.

"No," Ky said, slightly repelled as always by the Modulan color scheme of soft greens, but even more repelled by the deliberate drama of the variant form.

"Very well. Now about the Box . . ."

The box, Ky knew, was nothing but a symbol, small enough to fit in the hand; Bahandar's tone added the capital and implied extraordinary worth.

"Traditional Modulans still prefer the plain wood with the Focus on the cover," Bahandar said, implying that traditional Modulans were far behind the times. "But we have a very nice selection of boxes—enameled, inlaid—"

"The plain wooden box," Ky said firmly. "Gary was very traditional." She didn't know how traditional he was in the practice of his religion, but she did know how traditional he was about spending money on things that were not necessary to the ship or its cargo. He would come back to haunt her if she indulged in any fancy additions to his service.

"Very well. And the chaplain," Bahandar said. "There's the recorded service, the Interactive service with counseling subroutines . . ."

Ky had never imagined anything like this. "I thought there was just a chaplain—"

"Oh, if you want a live chaplain, that's certainly possible—" His voice warmed. "We have to arrange to bring someone up from Prime—that is a little expensive . . ."

"No, that's all right," Ky said. "I'm sure one of the other methods will do very well. But you'll have to excuse me—I have other commitments to meet here. If you'll collect his body, I can get back with you later."

"It's a good idea to go on and make arrangements early," Bahandar said. "There are still a lot of casualties coming in—"

She hadn't considered that. "What is the schedule then?"

"With a holographic chaplain, or the recorded or AI version of the service, we can fit you in . . . let me see . . . at 1330 hours the day after tomorrow. That includes a one-hour slot in the . . . that's the Modulan basic-plan chapel, with provision for either the recording or the interactive audio service. If you wanted the half hour of grief counseling in the chapel, the first open slot is 0730 three days from now."

"The recorded version," Ky said. "We won't require the grief counseling." If the crew needed grief counseling—she didn't let herself think about whether she did—Vatta Transport could provide it somewhere else, as part of their health coverage. Not from a smarmy little man who was annoying her more by the second.

"Very well. You're entered for 1330, day after tomorrow, that's Senket, in local calendars. Please be sure that you vacate the chapel on time, as there is a service scheduled after yours. The actual recording begins when you press START and takes thirty-four minutes."

"We will be out on time," Ky said.

"And to what account should this be charged?" Bahandar asked.

"Vatta Transport, Ltd.," Ky said. She had no qualms about that; their insurance would cover it.

"Very well. Now—where is the . . . er . . ."

"In the cooler," Ky said. "One of my crew will show your personnel."

"Within the hour," Bahandar said.

She switched off, feeling slightly ill and not sure why. It seemed wrong to treat the end of Gary's life as a series of practical choices such as whether or not to have a hologram or a recording as the chaplain . . . but she'd just done it. In the military, they handled these things better. Tradition took over. If he had been military, his funeral would have fit that final heroism better; she could imagine the draped coffin, the slow march. There would have been no smarmy little man. She rubbed her head hard, trying to stave off tears and think clearly.

What next? Mackensee or ISC? Mackensee—she was fairly sure she knew what they wanted.

Their contact was a fresh-faced young officer, Lieutenant Sanders, as he introduced himself. He seemed inordinately cheerful, and fully familiar with Ky and the situation.

"Captain, we can send a crew over to remove our equipment, starting at 0900 tomorrow."

"That sounds good. I'll need to talk to someone about our contract—"

"That'll be Major Harris; I'll patch you through in a moment. Colonel Kalin would like to see you at 1400—"

It was 1100 local time now. Her eyes felt gritty. "I can't leave the ship," she said.

"Of course. The Colonel knows that. If 1400 is open . . ."

It was open. That was not how she wanted to spend the afternoon which felt like midnight, but she might as well get it over with. "Fourteen hundred is fine," Ky said.

"I'll switch you now to Major Harris," the lieutenant said.

Major Harris, when he answered, smiled less brightly than the lieutenant, but it was a smile.

"I understand you had some problems with a few of the passengers," he said. "Good job, only losing three. Under the circumstances, we're amending the contract, if you agree, to compensate for the extra days, without reference to the smaller number of passengers. We took the liberty of consulting Vatta, Ltd., while we were outsystem, and their legal staff approved the amended contract, pending your agreement. Have you had a chance to confer with them yet?"

"No," Ky said, feeling grumpier than before. "I haven't had access to ansible communication yet."

"Ah. That's right, the system's not completely up yet. Well, we can defer this matter until you have had a chance to talk to them, or I can transfer funds into an account for you now, if you're willing to take my word for it."

The last time she'd taken his word for something, the ten days and docile passengers had turned into several weeks and a mutiny that cost the life of her crewman. "Let me see the amended contract," Ky said. "What's the compensation rate?"

The contract came up onscreen, and the printer hummed—soon she'd have hardcopy. "You'll notice, when you get to the bottom, that there is a Vatta Transport approval seal from their—your—legal department. There's also a release from liability, protecting Vatta from suits referencing experiences aboard your ship, and Mackensee from suits by Vatta against us . . ."

"I . . . see." Ky had scrolled quickly past the familiar paragraphs of the original contract, to the amendments and the compensation. She struggled to keep a straight face. That was a lot of money . . . and the Vatta Transport, Ltd., seal had the right date codes for this quarter. She wanted that money. She wanted every credit of it, in her accounts, right now. Surely if the company's legal department had approved, it was all right . . .

"Of course, your company didn't know all that happened while we were outsystem, and they would probably insist on additional compensation if they knew . . ."

"Ummm." Ky was deep in the fine print: per diem per passenger, damages to ship, delay of delivery of cargo, damages to cargo if proven by independent appraiser, interest to be paid per day for delay of payment . . .

"So I am authorized to offer a two hundred fifty thousand credit additional compensation, but in return would require a statement that this satisfies all debt between us."

Two hundred fifty *thousand*? They must really want Vatta Transport off their backs. Ky wondered what Vatta had said—what her father had said.

"With all due respect," she said, trying to keep her voice from revealing how much she wanted that money, "you do realize I will have to validate the seal on the original, before I can give you a final answer . . ."

"Of course," he said. "But it would help us to know whether you are inclining that way or not."

"With confirmation of my company's approval, and the additional compensation, I feel sure we can come to an agreement," Ky said. And she would have her communications board back, and her beacon, and her FTL unit . . .

"There is one complication," Major Harris said. "Captain Furman, of the Vatta Transport *Katrine Lamont*, insists that he has the right to negotiate in your name, make binding decisions on your behalf, and that any funds should be deposited to the account he names. We were not told of his involvement when we were outsystem. Is he, in fact, acting as your agent?"

"He is not," Ky said. She could hear the anger in her own voice and tried to damp it down. "I believe he was sent here to check on my welfare, but he is neither my boss nor my agent."

"Good. Since you personally negotiated and signed the original contract, the laws we operate under require us to complete it with you, and involving him would mean a whole new round of legal finagling. Which I, for one, would rather avoid."

"I also, Major Harris," Ky said.

"Well, then. Colonel Kalin can bring the amended contract to you when he visits, and if you sign it, we can transfer the funds immediately into—what account did you want to use?"

Not Vatta Transport's general Sabine account . . . Furman would seize on that, she knew, and he was the senior Vatta captain in the system.

"I'll have that for you before then," Ky said. "I'm not sure of the status of all accounts." The accounts she did not yet have, but hoped to acquire.

"Very well. Just let us know."

Ky cut the connection and leaned back with a sigh. She was still tired, and that was only two down, with one coming at 1400—and it was now 1120.

Food would help. And a shower. But first she needed to contact one of the banks and set up an account to receive the transfer. Luckily Sabine Station had a branch of the venerable Crown & Spears Commercial Bank, and it was only too willing to set up an account for Captain

Vatta of Vatta Transport, Ltd., so that she could receive a funds transfer later in the day. Could she come in and validate identity, or should they send a technician to the ship?

"Send someone, please," Ky said. "I need to stay aboard right now; I'm expecting visitors, both civil and military."

"Very well. We can have someone there with an ID reader in about half an hour. Say 1200?"

"Perfect," Ky said.

She pushed back from the board, then, and said, "I'm going to shower and eat something. Call me if there's an emergency, but otherwise . . ."

"We'll take care of it," Lee said. "Don't worry."

After a shower and change of clothes, Ky wolfed down a quick lunch. Then the bank ID tech announced himself at the dockside.

Validating her ID took fifteen minutes: the retinal scan, the gene scan, the fingerprints, all compared to the data she had left on file with the station in her earlier visit. When the tech reported in, the bank replied with her new account number. Ky sent that on to Major Harris. She looked at her list . . . Could she squeeze in someone else before Colonel Kalin arrived? ISC, it would have to be.

The pleasant-looking older woman who came onto the bridge did not look like Ky's notion of an investigator; she looked more like someone's mother. Not her own mother, but someone's. She wore a blue-gray suit, not a uniform; her silvery hair was piled high on her head.

"I'm Sara Illis," she said. "You must be Captain Vatta. I've reviewed the information you were able to send—amazing how much you were able to do with your communications out. A clever idea, using your beacon like that."

"Thank you," Ky said. She felt buffeted by the woman's approval; that made her feel wary.

"Obviously, we're interested in anything more you can tell us about the attack on the ansibles. You were here when it happened, I understand?"

"Yes," Ky said. "But all I know is what was on the newsfeeds."

"Of course. But we are asking everyone—had you heard anything which, in retrospect, might indicate such an attack was coming?"

"No," Ky said. "That trouble was coming, yes. In fact, the Slotter Key embassy asked me to evacuate some crewmen who'd been stranded here. But other than war, nothing specific."

"Right. And once the officers of the other ships came aboard, when did you first become aware of the involvement of this Captain Paison?"

"Not fast enough," Ky said. A wave of guilt almost blacked out her vision. Gullible, susceptible, an easy mark for an experienced manipulator like Paison. Not so easy, she reminded herself: he was dead and she wasn't. She forced her attention back to the conversation. "The captain of the passenger liner was being so difficult that Paison seemed reasonable by comparison. I actually trusted him, until the mutiny. In fact, Paison himself never told me he was involved in the war, or in the attack on the ansibles. That was one of his communications personnel—I gave you his name—"

"Yes, and he's in protective custody." Illis' smile conveyed no amusement. "He is quite concerned that Paison's other associates might come after him. Unfortunately, he does not strike us as particularly trustworthy either, and we wanted to be sure that what he's telling us is the same thing he was telling you."

"Ah. Well, I have that logged. I'll be glad to make a copy for you." She called in Sheryl and asked her to make the copy.

"Exactly what we hoped." The ISC representative smiled at Ky. "Now, about the Mackensee involvement. In your own mind, do you have any feeling, however vague, that they were involved?"

"Not anymore," Ky said. "If you've talked to them, you undoubtedly know that I was injured when they came aboard my ship—not their fault. One of the people I picked up at Sabine Prime was stupid and got himself shot. I spent some time aboard their command ship, being patched up. Everyone—top to bottom—seemed shocked by the attack on the ansibles, and they denied being part of it. Said it would be stupid for them."

"It's stupid for anyone," Illis said, and for an instant her blue eyes chilled to glacial temperature. "That's why we need to find out who doesn't realize that. Was it someone so ignorant or stupid that they thought it would be a good idea to tweak our tail, or was the target actually someone else? Is this an attempt to frame someone?"

"I don't know," Ky said. "But I'd bet on stupid. There's a lot of it going around."

Illis laughed, a throaty chuckle. "So there is. But we are bound to look at more than the simple answer, Captain Vatta. Oh—and while I'm here, I was asked to deliver a message to you, by hand, from your family. You will have realized that they were quite concerned when they learned that you were in this system when the ansibles went out." She passed a data cube across to Ky.

"I was hoping they wouldn't know," Ky said. Her stomach churned.

Illis shook her head. "We provided a list of ships known to be in this system to appropriate authorities on the planets concerned. I suppose they notified your family. At any rate, your family contacted us, and it was agreed that I could deliver this message, since we didn't know . . . how long it would be before ansible service could be restored. There's also a line of credit arranged for you, via ISC, in your family's name. It's direct for you, so if you need anything, just contact us."

They had not known whether she was alive or not when they compiled this message . . . but they had thought to provide for her.

"Thank you," Ky said, past the lump in her throat.

"That other Vatta ship that's in the system," the woman said. "Captain Furman, I believe his name is. He's told us he'll be taking you away as soon as possible . . ."

"Captain Furman and I will have another discussion or two before I decide what to do," Ky said, with a slight emphasis on "I."

"I see." Her smile widened. "Well, in that case, we would like to talk to you again—my boss, the Incident Inspector, in particular—and thank you for your contribution to the solution of this situation."

"I haven't really done anything," Ky said.

"On the contrary. We really had no idea what was going on, until your transmissions started coming in. You gave us a valuable lead, Captain, and we're grateful. Now, if you'll excuse me, I must get back to my boss. He's waiting for my report." She took the copy of the recording Ky gave her, and left. Ky glanced at the chronometer: 1340. Definitely not time enough to see anyone else before Colonel Kalin showed up. With, she hoped, the contract and the money. Time enough, though, to look at the message.

She put it in the cube reader. There on the screen was her father, with the expression she had seen only a few times.

"Kylara . . ." He swallowed. "Ky, I don't know at this time if you will ever receive this, and I'm finding it hard to record knowing that you might . . . might not. But assuming that ISC can find you in time, I wanted you to know that your family is behind you. We understand why you took a contract from Belinta; we are not angry that you went to Sabine. Gary and Quincy may have told you by now that most Vatta captains do go a bit wild with their first commands. We trust you, we love you. Please come back soon, though, because we . . . I . . . really would like to see you in one piece and soon. I understand that something happened to your implant. As soon as possible, I'll be shipping a replacement to you by secure carrier—probably a Vatta ship, hand-carried. It will have all the current codes preloaded. It might be better to let that ship take over your Belinta contract, but that's up to you. And Ky, I'm really sorry to have sent you off ill-prepared, and into such danger . . ."

He hadn't sent her into danger; he'd sent her on what should have been, and probably was, a perfectly safe route, a boring milk run. She herself had made it dangerous by changing plans, by stepping outside his definitions. It wasn't his fault, any more than her trouble at the Academy had been his fault; she hadn't blamed him for that, either.

She knew he had meant this message to be warm, loving, consoling, encouraging. So why was she feeling like a cat with its fur rubbed backward? That was obvious . . . He was still treating her like a feckless girl, who needed protection and guidance and consolation. He was patting her head, putting an arm around her shoulders, as if she had fallen and scraped a knee instead of having faced real danger, death in several forms, and survived by her own abilities.

What had happened to her—to her ship, to her crew—could not be consoled by a father's love and care. Even though a small part of her wanted to run back to his protection, back to Slotter Key to fall weeping in his arms and rest in his understanding . . . she was beyond that. There would be no easy answers, no easy comfort.

This must be the message Captain Furman had had—go rescue my poor helpless daughter. He might have his own reasons for thinking she was a spoiled darling—she had been pretty rotten at thirteen, she admitted to herself, and probably deserved what he thought of her—but she had grown up.

She looked up to find Quincy watching her. "It's from Dad," she said. "There was a lot he didn't know when he recorded this. He's being comforting and protective . . . He wants me to let Furman take my cargo to Belinta and bring me home. He's apologized for letting me get into such a dangerous situation."

Quincy shook her head. "Wasn't his fault. Do you want to go home?"

"No. I mean, I accept that he meant well. But the Belinta contract is my contract, not Furman's. Not even Vatta's, when it comes to that. Mine. And we have cargo there that's due at Leonora and Lastway. All we have to do is repair the ship . . ."

"All?" Quincy's eyebrow quirked. "It's more than just changing a controller board. But what next?" Clearly, she meant more than after the repairs, or even after Belinta.

"After that run? Depends on what we make from it. If we could bring this ship up to code—"

"Hull's sound," Quincy said. "Nothing wrong with the insystem drive that a load of fuel won't fix."

Ky cocked an eye at her. "You think I should do this, then?"

"I think you'll do what you think you should, whatever I say," Quincy said. "Which is as it should be. All I'm doing is giving engineering data."

"Umph."

"Though if you asked my advice—"

"About what?"

"See, that's what I meant. You make up your own mind. If you asked my advice about what to do, I meant."

"You would say what?" Ky persisted.

"I would say nothing," Quincy said. "I would say it's your career, and your decision."

Ky looked at her, trying to read her face.

"Seriously. You're young, yes, but this trip would mature anyone who survived it. I can guess what you might choose to do, but it's only a guess. You'll have to figure out what works for you. If it's any help, I think you've done well."

"Gary . . . ," Ky said, between her teeth.

"Wanted you to save the ship, and you did. You didn't waste his courage, Captain. I haven't criticized you for it, and I never will."

"But you knew him—you were his friend for years." She could not ask directly, but she could not help asking indirectly, and scolded herself for that even as she asked.

"For years, yes. We were friends. I miss him. I've cried, and I'll cry again. I don't blame you. I said that before."

"Yes. You did." Ky took a deep breath, banishing the lump in her throat that threatened to bring on her own tears. "Well. We'll talk later, Quincy. I'd better get ready for Colonel Kalin."

CHAPTER
NINETEEN

Colonel Kalin was prompt, as she'd expected. In person he looked as tough and competent as he had over the comscreen.

"Well, Captain Vatta," he said, extending his hand. She shook it; it was hard, callused. "I'm glad to meet you at last."

"Welcome aboard, Colonel," she said.

"Is there a secure area?" he asked.

"Not really; we can talk in the recreation area with the doors shut, or my cabin—though it's quite small—or the bridge."

"I see. The recreation area, then. I presume it's monitored?"

"Of course. But merchants no more than the military want their affairs talked about. We have some screening capability."

"You will not mind if I add mine . . . ?" It was just barely a question.

"Not at all," Ky said. She led the way to the rec area, and spoke into the intercom. "Bridge, this is the captain. I'll be in conference in the rec room, with screens on. Use a visual flash if we have a situation develop." She pulled out a chair at one of the tables. "Have a seat, Colonel."

"Thanks," he said, sitting down. She sat across from him as he glanced around. "Pardon me for being blunt, but we have a lot to talk about, and we're both busy professionals."

Ky nodded.

"I understand you've spoken to ISC about the ansible attack; they said you've told them we said we weren't involved. And I've seen what you sent by beacon-flash as well. But is there anything, any detail, you haven't included? We've had to post a hefty bond with ISC until they clear us for that action, and the sooner we settle that the better."

"Nothing but the recording of Paison's crewman talking to me," Ky said.

"And you jettisoned his body?"

"Yes. No cold storage," Ky said. Except in with their food, which she didn't think needed saying.

"I wondered if that was why. Did you beacon it?"

"No, the only spare beacon we had aboard was put on our cargo."

"Ah. We're going to have to try to find it, because from what you and his com tech say, some of his contact information was on his person. Can you give us an approximate location?"

"Only with difficulty. We have the elapsed time, of course, but Paison tried to do a complete wipe of our system, so most of the data are suspect. We haven't had time to do a purge and reset, though, so it might be retrievable."

"Just not believable. Oh, well. The next thing is this contract between us. I hope you believe me when I say that we did not foresee any of the difficulties . . ."

"I didn't think so . . . ," Ky said.

"No. We said ten days, and expected to be back for the passengers in seven, actually. Usually that's plenty of leeway. But when our techs couldn't get even the backup ansible working, we knew we had to jump outsystem to get to ISC before they got to us. Again, we thought we would be right back in the system, but ISC wouldn't pass us out of Tangier, and insisted that another commander be appointed. That's when I came aboard this operation."

"You were trying to work on the ansible platforms? I thought only ISC could—"

"We have techs who can restart backup systems," the Colonel said, rapidly and not looking at her. "And yes, ISC knows about it." She wondered anyway. "At any rate, we did not expect to be delayed coming back into Sabine system, and we were quite concerned—and expressed our concerns to ISC—that you would be running short of supplies. May I ask when you began rationing?"

"As soon as we'd cleared off the counters of the food we had no storage for," Ky said. "My—I'd been told one time that it was always wise to have a few days' reserve, so I calculated for twelve days, not ten. That wasn't bad. Then, when you left the system, I cut back again, trying for the maximum survival with what we had. I had to keep crew rations up so they could do their work . . ."

"That must have been tough," the Colonel said again. "But I'm also impressed. You'll pardon me for saying what you know, that you're quite young to be captain, and I would not have expected a civilian captain with so little experience to be that decisive. Your company must provide excellent training."

"Actually, I learned that at the Slotter Key Space Academy," Ky said. Surely he knew that already. Major Harris knew; Harris must have told him. "Before I was kicked out," she added.

"Um, yes, Major Harris said something about that. Typical cadet trouble, he said." Colonel Kalin shook his head. "You would be surprised how many good young'uns have something like that in their pasts. Now—I'd like to hear some details about this mutiny. We had no idea that Captain Paison was going to cause trouble."

Ky wanted some details of the money she'd be getting, but this wasn't the time to bring that up. Instead, she began a concise summary of the mutiny, starting with her realization that the passengers' location in the cargo compartments gave them potential access to the control systems. When she came to the confrontation, the scene was as vivid in her mind as it had been since. She struggled to keep her voice level and her hands still.

"So Gary said 'Don't let them—' and I shot Paison, and his mate cut Gary's throat—"

"Why did you shoot Paison first?" Kalin asked. He sounded like one of her instructors at the Academy taking her back through a tactical problem.

"I didn't have a good shot at the mate—the way he was holding Gary—and Paison was the leader. I thought maybe, if I got him—" Ky shook her head. "It was so fast—"

"You did the right thing," Kalin said. "But again—it's surprising. I'd have to credit your military training. Then what?"

"The mate's arm sagged as Gary died, giving me a target. I shot him, but not fatally. He charged; I fired again, and that time got him in the throat. I thought that would end it—the others behind them were too stunned by the blood, I think. But Kristoffson came at me; my junior engineer and I fired together, and he went down. Then I told them to sit down, and they obeyed me, and—" And then had come the reaction, the surge of nausea, the grief, the need to keep going anyway, keep the control she had regained, save her ship . . . Again she fought back the lump that had appeared in her throat.

Kalin waited a moment before saying anything. Then he said, "If you don't mind my asking, what was your class standing before that?"

Ky looked up, surprised. "The Academy didn't release numerical standings prior to graduation," she said. "But I was in the honor corps." It still hurt, she found, but the tears were easier to control now.

"I don't find that surprising," the Colonel said. "You know, you reacted much more like a military officer than a civilian ship's captain. It was a creditable performance, Captain Vatta, a very creditable performance. If you were a junior officer in my command, I'd be putting you in for a citation."

Ky choked back the "Really?" that wanted to come out in a schoolgirlish squeak. "Thank you, Colonel," she said in what was almost a normal voice. She could not help the internal warmth that she hoped didn't show in her face.

"Now—we have some financial business to conduct. I have the amended contract with me—I understand Major Harris has gone over the provisions with you?"

"Yes, he has," Ky said.

"I understand that your company's legal staff has vetted part of it—the per diem for extra time and a bonus for inconvenience, delay, damage—but since at that time no one knew about the mutiny, we did not include any settlement for the death of a crewmember and so on. If you feel you need to wait until Vatta's legal staff has approved this additional settlement, ISC tells us the communications ansible should be up for limited service in a day or so. Or, we can deposit the amount agreed on by your company's lawyers now, and defer the rest until that part of the contract is approved. It's your call, Captain."

If she waited for approval, what would the company lawyers say? More important, what would her father say? What if he ordered her, in his position as CFO of Vatta Transport, to turn over her cargo to Furman? She was not going to do that. She was absolutely not, *not* going to do that.

"You're right that it's complicated," she said slowly. "My contract with Belinta, to deliver the cargo that was aboard when your people boarded us, was a personal contract, not a Vatta Transport contract—within my discretion, but not committing the company to it. The company would honor it, had I been unable to fulfill it, but that's not the case. However, this ship is presently owned by Vatta Transport, and her crew—barring those I picked up here on Sabine Prime—are employees of Vatta Transport. So that portion of the settlement which pertains to the death of a crewman must reference Vatta Transport, Ltd. I can, as a Vatta captain, make a valid contract in the name of the firm—including a death settlement—but that is in a different category from contracts for carriage." She paused. "I feel that the contract should cite a specific amount as death settlement for Gary Tobai—that is the part of the contract which must be with Vatta Transport, Ltd., rather than with me."

"It doesn't now, but it could," Colonel Kalin said. "I presume you would then want a separate transfer for that amount?"

"Yes. It would make clear to the company that I consider the rest of the contract a personal one."

"Let's talk to Major Harris," the Colonel said. His eyes glazed slightly— his implant, of course. Ky wondered how much he depended on it in combat situations. His gaze returned to her. "He says that makes sense; he suggests one hundred thousand credits as the amount, and says a handwritten emendation, initialed by both of us, will be adequate."

That was about right, Ky knew. On Slotter Key, the standard scale of compensation for unintended death was graduated by age and expertise, but 100,000 covered most cases. "That will do," she said, mentally subtracting 100,000 from the total payment. It still left enough for the repairs she needed. She took the hardcopy of the contract, flipped through the pages, and wrote in the margin an addendum specifying 100,000 credits compensation for the death of crewman Gary Tobai, signed it, and slid it across to Kalin for his initials.

"Send that to Captain Furman," she said. "He is the senior Vatta captain here, and he will be best suited to receive funds due the company. I've already sent Major Harris the account information for my part."

Kalin cocked his head at her. "Captain, I begin to believe you are devious as well as competent. It almost sounds as if you're about to leave Vatta Transport . . ."

"No," Ky said. But her voice carried little conviction. She hadn't had time to think about it, and yet . . . Vatta offered her security, security and ease—as long as she stayed in the narrow lanes they advised.

Kalin leaned back. "You know, Captain, with your background—and considering your performance—you might be better suited for something other than a glorified truck driver."

"I seem to be suited for getting into trouble," Ky said, looking down at her hands.

"Exactly." Kalin nodded. "You get into trouble, but then you get out of it—you survive, and you even prosper. You're not cut out for boring monotony. Just being thrown out of one military academy doesn't preclude going into the military, you know. We might even hire you." He grinned at her.

"Hire me?" Her gaze came back to him; her heart pounded. She could feel the heat in her face. "Why would you hire me?"

"Let's see . . ." He ticked off points on his fingers. "One of my senior NCOs said you handled the boarding well; she wasn't surprised to find out you had a military background. You didn't panic when you woke up in a military sick bay—and yes, though you had meds in your system, I've seen people panic with those same meds onboard. You accepted the challenge of carrying an overload of passengers, and you coped with every emergency they supplied, including a mutiny. You can make quick decisions—and more important, the _right_ quick decisions. You aren't squeamish. And you can kill at need."

And enjoy it came the response she did not want to reveal. For one moment she imagined herself in a Mackensee uniform, commanding a real unit . . . working up to command a real ship, a warship.

"I have a cargo to deliver," she said, trying to push that vision aside. "I promised them."

"Then you have to do what you promised," he said. He said it the way she felt about it, as much a fact as 9 x 3 = 27. "But think about it, Captain Vatta. If you ever change your mind and want to apply, get in touch with me." His gaze unfocused again, then refocused on her. "There. I've instructed Major Harris to make the transfers. That should be complete in a few minutes. I know you'll be busy working on repairs, but you'll be welcome aboard my ship, if you care to visit while we're here. Just call over and we'll set up a time. The officers usually meet for a half hour about 1800, before dinner."

Go aboard a warship again? She wanted to, and she was afraid that her desire showed in her expression. "Thank you," she said. "It will depend on how the repairs go . . ."

"Of course. It's been a pleasure, Captain Vatta." His handshake was military-firm; his expression the one she would like to have seen on her father's face, instead of that worried concern.

When Colonel Kalin left, she still had to face meetings with Sabine

Prime officials and Captain Furman's representative; she didn't look forward to either.

Sabine Prime had sent a woman with the title of "Second Assistant Secretary to the Department of Foreign Affairs." Unlike the ISC representative, Gillian Favor was a vivacious young woman who waved her hands a lot when she talked.

"We have several issues, Captain Vatta," she said. "I suppose you know that we are charged with administering the Universal Commercial Code, so we have to report on your handling of the passengers assigned you by Mackensee and the incidents which resulted in the deaths of . . . er . . ." She looked at a list. "Captain Paison, his mate, Captain Kristoffson, and your two crewmen. Then we also need to know what, if anything, you knew about the plot to blow up the ansibles before you left this station."

"I knew nothing about it—my first knowledge of the attack came when I tried to make an ansible call and the ready light didn't come on, and then the standby light went out."

"Oh, my. We certainly hadn't known you were making a call at the time. Do you have the records of that?"

"No," Ky said. "My communications equipment, including the stored records, was damaged in the mutiny that occurred."

"Oh, that's too bad. Well, let's see. Now, you have some kind of records of the trip, don't you? The court will want to establish whether or not your agreement with the mercenaries qualified as 'cooperation under constraint' or not, and whether the treatment you accorded the passengers was in line with the UCC."

"Yes, I have those records. Do you need them in hardcopy, or do you have a filedump where I can send them?"

"A filedump will be fine, Captain Vatta. Thank you. And let me just say, I am so impressed. I really admire you—"

"Excuse me?"

Favor's smile was brighter than ever. "I mean, I always wanted to go out in space and have adventures, but I didn't know how . . . My family's always gone into government service. I really admire someone who goes out and does things."

Ky opened her mouth to say it was nothing much, and adventures weren't as much fun as they were made out to be, but Favor rattled on.

"I mean, I've been to the adventure resorts and things, you know, with mountains and snow and all that, but space . . . it really is different. When I think about you, all alone out there in the empty dark and cold and all and running out of food, it just gives me the shivers. I mean, I know I could never do it." That finished on a note of near smugness. She was clearly absolving herself of the need to move out of her own comfort zone.

"I suppose not," Ky said, instead of the half-dozen other things she wanted to say. She hadn't intended the sharp tone, but Favor stopped rattling and looked at her.

"I suppose you think I'm silly," Favor said.

"No," Ky said. "But I didn't get into this for the adventure."

"Really? Why did you, then?"

It was a reasonable question. "My family trucks cargo in space ships," Ky said. "Like yours goes into government service."

"You mean—they just expected you to? It wasn't that you wanted to get away, get out into space, see other planets?"

She did not want to talk to this person about her past, about her dreams. "Pretty much," Ky said instead. "And for the most part, it's not all that exciting. Seeing other planets, sure. But the rest of the time it's just business."

"Oh." Favor looked disappointed. "I suppose, if you're used to it—"

"Right." Ky was tired of this detour. "If you don't need anything else, I have other appointments, and it's getting late—"

"Oh. Of course, I'm sorry, I didn't mean to—I was just interested, it sounded so exciting—"

When she had twittered her way out, Ky shook her head. "I'm probably not being fair—"

"To think she's a fluttery featherhead? Possibly not, but she's a good imitation." Quincy had come onto the bridge, and now shook her head.

"And I still have to cope with Captain Furman." Ky let the resentment come into her voice there. Quincy looked at her.

"Didn't you apprentice on his ship?"

"Yes. It was not a happy experience."

"Apprenticeships rarely are. What's wrong? Is he still treating you like a child?"

"Yes. You saw part of it. He's going to want to drag me back home like a trophy failure . . ."

"You need something to eat," Quincy said. "Garlan, go get her something to eat." Garlan nodded and left the bridge.

Ky started to say *You're not my mother*, but her stomach growled and she realized she was feeling hollow.

"All right," she said, sinking back into the seat. "I am hungry."

When they were alone, Quincy leaned forward. "Ky—is there more to that message your father sent?"

"Yes," Ky said. She felt her muscles tense and tried to relax. "Said he was sending a new implant out with a Vatta ship. I suppose that's Furman." She could hear the sharpness in her own voice. "I don't want to go back. I don't want to let Furman take our cargo to Belinta. It's my job—my contract—and I'm quite capable of doing it."

"I agree," Quincy said.

"And I don't need the implant," Ky said.

"I wouldn't want to do without mine," Quincy said. "Makes it a lot easier."

"The implant . . ." Ky stopped, unable to articulate her feelings about it. She tried again. "The implant *is* Vatta, in a way. The Vatta connection: the codes, the propriety databases, the protocols, all preloaded for me. Yes, it's easier to have it all available internally. I really like parts of it. But . . . when I rely on it . . . I'm not really thinking for myself. I can miss solutions I might otherwise come up with. We didn't have them at the Academy. . . . We had to *learn* to learn, remember, analyze, plan, all with our own brains."

"You were doing fine before you were shot," Quincy said.

"Maybe. Maybe not. It was always whispering to me, shaping what I knew . . . and with so much in there, I wasn't as likely to look outside for more information, was I? And after, without it, did I do that much worse?"

"No," Quincy said. "I have to admit you seemed just as competent without it. But everyone has one . . ."

"Most people, certainly spacers, yes. If I could have an empty one and choose what to put in it—"

"You could," Quincy said. "But it seems a waste to me. You need the Vatta protocols." She paused; Ky said nothing. "By the way, are those mercenaries trying to recruit you?"

"Why?" Ky asked, trying to conceal a guilty start.

"Well, Beeah went dockside, to try to link up with some equipment suppliers, and he told me he ran into one of them who said something about how you'd end up in their pockets."

"Not likely," Ky said. "I have a contract to fulfill."

"What are you going to do if Furman orders you to turn over the ship and give him your cargo?"

"I—don't know."

Quincy shook her head. "Now that's not true. I think you know perfectly well. My real question is, are you going to stop with defying Furman, or are you going to break with Vatta as well? Is that the real reason you don't want a Vatta-programmed implant?"

"Break with Vatta? I hadn't even thought of that." But even as she said it, she knew she had . . . at some level.

"The thing is, if you decide to break with Vatta, you need to let the crew know. Those who want to stay with Vatta would probably rather leave now, and go with Furman."

Without the Vatta component of her crew, she had only three crew, the ones she'd picked up here. And even they might not want to stay with her. She thought about them. Two experienced environmental techs, one with some bridge experience. One drives maintenance technician. Hard to run a ship with that. Impossible to run a ship with that, with no pilot, no cargomaster, no . . .

"Oh. Well, I hadn't planned to leave Vatta . . ."

"Can you commit to that beyond Belinta? You don't want to leave anyone stranded."

Of course she didn't want to leave anyone stranded. Her head ached. It was all so blasted complicated. Contracts for this, contracts for that, personnel problems.

"Here, Captain," Garlan said, bringing in a tray. Ky's stomach rumbled at the smell of a hearty soup. She ate quickly, aware of Quincy's worried gaze still resting on her like a heavy weight. When she finished, the problem was still there, and her stomach knotted around the soup.

"I'm not going to abandon my crew anywhere," Ky said. "But I hear what you're saying, that some of the Vatta people may want to go back with Furman."

"As long as you understand . . ."

"What about you?" Ky asked. "Do you want to go back?" Losing an engineering chief would be bad but not impossible, as long as she didn't take all her supports with her.

"I haven't decided," Quincy said. "I'll stay with you through repairs, anyway. But—I could retire now, and it's been a . . . a difficult trip."

"Yes," Ky said. "It has. And you've certainly earned retirement. I'd like it if you stayed, though."

"We'll see," Quincy said. "It all depends . . ."

On what? Ky wanted to ask, but she knew better. "Thanks. I'll go talk to Furman's representative now."

*　　*　　*

Furman's representative was his second in command, a cheerful stocky man in Vatta blue with a small lock-case clipped to his wrist and a large briefcase in his hand.

"Captain Vatta, I'm Bantal Korash," he said. "I have a special package for you from your father. I'm afraid you'll have to validate and sign this—" He pulled a plasfilm receipt from his pocket.

"And I'll have to inspect the seals," Ky said. That was the first, simplest level of validation for both of them.

"Here, then." He handed it over; she turned it over and around in a specific pattern, observing that each seal was unbroken. Then she thumbprinted the receipt, signed it, and he put it back in his pocket. "And I also have some forwarded mail; your father says it's nonurgent but wanted you to have it." He opened his briefcase and handed her a small pile, including one with all too familiar handwriting. Her heart thudded painfully. Hal. What had he said? Had he understood? "Captain Furman would like to get everything straightened out so we can get back to our route. I understand you have cargo for Belinta?"

"Yes. There's no reason to delay you—Captain Furman can take the *Kat* back to his route right away."

He shook his head. "That's not what Captain Furman says. He says he's supposed to make sure you're all right, and in his mind that means making sure you get back to Slotter Key safely."

"I'm fine," Ky said. "You can see that."

"But the ship . . . and didn't someone die?"

"The ship needs repair; we're working on that. Gary Tobai, my cargo-master, was killed during the mutiny. His funeral's day after tomorrow, station time."

"Tobai! I worked with him four years ago, on another ship. What happened?"

"Furman didn't tell you?"

"No."

"The passengers the mercenaries stashed aboard the ship included some troublemakers—some of them tried to take the ship over. They did manage to degrade the system controls, turn on the insystem drive, and destroy our communications transmitters. They took Gary hostage, threatened to kill him if I didn't turn over command of the ship."

"If they'd done that much, why did they need you?" Korash asked.

"I don't know. I do know that I tried to stop them—and killed the two ringleaders—but Gary died. I couldn't stop them in time—"

"But if they had Gary hostage, how could you—"

"I had other crew to think of, and the passengers who weren't involved. That had to come first. He knew it—he told me not to give in."

Korash stared at her, eyes wide. "You saw him?"

"Yes." Ky closed her eyes briefly, where one of the rotating scenes of disaster from this trip passed before her eyes. Skeldon's face, as she just caught sight of him in her cabin before everything went black. Gary Tobai looking her in the eye, and then . . . not.

"How could you—watch—" Now he sounded disgusted, as if she were something contemptible. Anger stirred; Ky pushed it down.

"You're welcome to come to his memorial service," Ky said. "Day after tomorrow, the station chapel. A Modulan service."

"Oh, I couldn't," Korash said. "I'll be back on our ship by then. But how do you feel about it?"

"Horrible," Ky said. "I keep thinking I should have done more to prevent it—more to keep them from getting systems access, from grabbing Gary. But there were a lot of them and few of us. If I'd known who was behind it, I'd have spaced them to start with and saved us all a lot of trouble."

"Spaced—you wouldn't really space anyone—!"

Ky looked at him, a nice decent older man who had never faced what she faced. She tried to soften her voice. "Actually I would, if necessary to save my ship. Mostly it's not necessary."

"That's hard," he said. His face was two shades paler; she could see the sheen of sweat on him. "That's really hard." He swallowed. "I suppose that's the sort of thing you learned in the Academy."

"Yes," Ky said. It saved time trying to explain what couldn't be explained.

"Things are different in the civilian world, you know," he said.

"I know that," Ky said. "But my first responsibility is still to my ship and crew, even under civilian legal codes."

He had an odd expression, somewhere between curiosity and revulsion. "How did you . . . er . . . I mean . . . do you carry a . . . a weapon?"

"You want to know how I killed them, is that what you're asking?"

He flushed, then; "I . . . I guess so."

"I shot them with a pistol bow that one of my crew had—a target bow."

"You did that before?"

"I practiced, once I realized that we might have trouble with our passengers. My crew member taught me how to use it. I suppose that shocks you . . ."

"I couldn't shoot anyone," he said firmly. "I just couldn't."

Her patience snapped. "Then I suppose it's a good thing you've never needed to." Before he could say anything else, she said, "You can tell Captain Furman—or I can contact him myself—I am going to get this ship repaired well enough to take my cargo to Belinta—myself—and he can consider himself free to return to his regular route. I will check and see if any of my crew wish to return with him, and I will prepare a message for my family. I'm assuming you came in by shuttle?"

"Er . . . yes."

"Well, then. When does it leave or was it a charter?"

"A charter . . ."

"You can spend a couple of hours here?"

"Yes . . . but I have to let them know when I want to leave."

"I'll speak to the crew shortly; I'm sure they'll want to stay for Gary's memorial service, at least. So Furman can leave after that, if any of them want to go with him, or earlier if they don't. I can have that answer for you in . . . say . . . three hours. I'm sure you'd enjoy that time more on the station than on a small ship like this . . ."

"Er . . . as you wish . . ."

"You have an implant, yes?"

"Yes."

"Fine. Give me your number; I'll contact you."

At last he left, and gave her a vague sort of salute on his way out. Ky took a deep breath and then tabbed the intercom.

"All crew, come to the rec area, please. I have an announcement."

A few minutes later, they were all there except for Beeah, still out on the station.

"Captain Furman, of the *Katrine Lamont*, wants me to agree to sell this ship for scrap here, take all of you and the cargo aboard his ship, and go back to Slotter Key via Belinta. I'm not going to do that; I'm going to repair the ship with the money Mackensee paid me, take my own cargo to Belinta, and pick up our cargo there, and go on our original route to Leonora and Lastway. However—" She paused. "While I don't have direct orders from Vatta headquarters to do what Captain Furman says, I suspect that his report of my decision will generate some heat. Most of you are long-term Vatta employees. I will understand if you don't want to be involved in a dispute between me and my family's business. I will also understand if you don't trust me as a captain, after the death of a crew member you all knew for a long tme. So I'm giving you the opportunity to transfer to the *Kat* if you want to. I'll give you all an exemplary report for your records."

"If we leave, what will you do for a crew?" Lee said. "We can't just leave you out here alone . . ."

"There are always transients," Ky said.

"Have you looked?" Quincy asked.

"Well . . . no. Not yet. But it's up to you, really. I don't want you staying out of some guilt thing." She yawned; she couldn't help it. "Sorry. I'm going to go get something to drink, give you all a little while to discuss it."

"What about us?" Li asked. "We're not Vatta employees, really . . ."

"Furman says he'll take you at least a lot closer to Slotter Key, a mainline station," Ky said. "Or you can hire on with me, if you're willing to learn cargo work as well as your primary specialty. Talk to Quincy—she can tell you about Vatta, and about me." Ky pushed back her chair and stood. She was seriously tired, the accumulated strain of the past days settling on her shoulders like a sack of wet sand.

CHAPTER
TWENTY

She decided another shower would help—after the days of rationed showers, she enjoyed the opportunity for a long one—and stood under the warm spray for several minutes. She felt better, but also even more sleepy. She meant to sit on her bunk only a moment, but suddenly her beeper was sounding, and she opened her eyes . . . She had slept for an hour.

Not a good sign if the crew had needed an hour to decide what to do. She braced herself to hear that they were all leaving.

"Coming," she said. Even that brief nap had helped; her eyes no longer burned. She finished dressing and returned to the rec area. To her surprise, only Quincy was there. The old woman looked up at her.

"Went to sleep, did you?"

"Sorry . . ."

"You needed it; you were dead on your feet. We would have let you sleep longer, but we heard from Furman's messenger."

"Ah. And?"

"I have to tell you I'm not happy about going against your father's wishes . . . I don't want to lose my retirement because he blames me for your decisions." So her father had told Furman to bring her home?

"I'm the captain; they're my decisions. My father knows me; he should know that I'm stubborn enough to ignore any advice you give me."

"Yes. I am taking that into consideration. But are you willing to tell him that and save my reputation as a reliable baby-sitter?"

"Of course," Ky said.

"It's been a difficult voyage, Captain. For a moment here, I'd like to talk to you in my role as designated grandma, not as crew."

"All right." What was coming now, a lecture about filial duty?

Quincy drew a visible breath and started in. "When your father asked us to crew for you, he told us you were studious, hardworking, smart, and honest. All that sounded good. Then he told us you had a habit of picking up strays and were headstrong as a mule. One of the things he wanted us to do was protect you from the kind of person who'd gotten you in trouble at the Academy. He didn't say much about that, so I don't know if it was a love affair or something else. Watch out for the lame puppies, he said. She'll do something stupid just to help someone."

Ky felt her ears going hot. There it was again, that same assumption . . . that same wrong assumption.

"And we failed," Quincy said. Her eyes glistened. "Gary and I—we were supposed to protect you, and we almost let you get killed by that young idiot. We hadn't kept you from bringing him aboard, and we hadn't kept an eye on him, and when you were carried past, the medics all looking so grim . . . I felt as if my own granddaughter were dying and I'd killed her. Gary felt just as bad."

"It wasn't your fault, either of you," Ky said quickly, reaching for Quincy's hand, but Quincy pulled it out of reach.

"Let me finish, please. So then you didn't die, and you took that contract with the mercenaries . . . doubt you had much choice . . . and you came back just as cool as snow and perfectly professional. I don't know when I've been as proud. You were trying to prevent the trouble you foresaw—and I hadn't spotted it, except with that fancy-pants from the _Rose_—and I realized it was some of my engineering modifications, for the passengers, which gave Paison access to the systems, made his takeover possible. When they grabbed Gary, I was terrified; I could not imagine how we'd get out of it alive, any of us. I know he didn't want to be the reason you didn't act, if you could find any way to act. I'd have felt the same if they'd grabbed me. I wish they had . . . I'm older. But anyway—you knew what to do, and did it, and saved us. I was . . . useless. Not because I'm old, but because I've spent my life on safe

ships traveling safe routes; I haven't been in a fight since I was a child."
Quincy paused, shook her head, and then went on. "So if you were my granddaughter in truth, I'd be so proud of you—and a little scared of you—and yes, I would trust you because you've been right so far. What I don't know is . . . can you trust me? Would you rather I went back, and let Beeah take over as Engineering First? He's qualified, as far as the engineering goes, and I don't think you need a baby-sitter anymore."

Ky leaned forward. "Quincy . . . please. Don't blame yourself. It was not your fault. You've been a wonderful resource, and of course I trust you. But if you want to go back, I'll understand . . ."

Quincy blinked back her tears and managed a shaky grin. "I thought I did . . . I really thought I did. I've never served with anyone who's . . . who's killed someone. At least that I knew about. It was . . . awful. Your face, when you came back to the bridge. But you know, Ky—and I'm calling you Ky in the person of that grandmother—I've decided I'd rather stick with you and find out what you're going to do next. For one thing, I'd miss my shipmates, all of whom want to stay with you except Li, who says she'd rather go somewhere with Furman, if he'll take her."

Ky's throat closed; she swallowed the lump of emotion, and nodded. "Thank you . . . thank you, Grandma Quincy."

"And another thing . . . you've been through a lot—we all have, but you more, because of the injury. You haven't been able to take it easy, as I'm sure you were advised to do by the medical people. Right?"

"Yes . . ."

"So I'm telling you, as the resident grandma, to start taking it easier. Yes, we have repairs to make, a cargo to load, a contract to fulfill. But I want to see you taking regular sleep shifts of adequate length, eating the proper foods, exercising, and letting your now-enlarged crew do its work. Clear?"

"Yes, Grandma," Ky said.

"And expect emotional fallout . . . You've been holding yourself together, which we all needed. What you need now is a chance to let go. Don't fight it too hard or too long."

"Yes, ma'am," Ky said again.

"End of Grandma's lecture," Quincy said. She took a deep breath. "Good heavens, I can't believe I've just been so dramatic. Now, Captain, Beeah has a list of suppliers and prices. I can review them for you, and let you rest, or you can review them, whichever. Keeping in mind the advice I just gave you . . ."

"Quincy, I'd like you to review suppliers, prices, and our needs, and make it all come in under budget. Somehow. We'll also need to resupply the galley—" At the look on Quincy's face, Ky laughed. "All right, all right, Grandma already knows what to do with an egg. I'm going to go send that message to Captain Furman's messenger, then take your advice and get more sleep. In fact, I may sleep until first shift tomorrow."

"Yes, Captain," Quincy said.

Sending the message took only moments; Ky didn't wait for a reply, but went back to her cabin, stripped off her clothes, and fell into the bed without even updating her log. She woke slowly, rising gradually through layers of thought and memory and finally opened her eyes to see that she had, in fact, slept through the rest of second and all of third shift. She stretched, feeling a little stiff but really rested for the first time in . . . well, since she'd come back to the ship the day the ansibles were attacked.

She rolled out of her bunk, showered, dressed, and came out into the corridor where the smell of cooking food drew her to the galley. Garlan was cooking breakfast.

"Captain—you're up."

"Finally," Ky said. "You must have wondered if I'd sleep forever."

"You look better. What do you want for breakfast?"

"Whatever that is—make some more of it. It smells like exactly what I want."

"Sure. Eggs and sausage, easy enough."

Ky ate a full plate of eggs, sausage, potatoes, a slice of fresh melon—she wondered what that had done to the budget—and considered her schedule. She still had to get that machinery back to the station and aboard, locate the parts, have them installed, find out how to get the right ship chip installed in the beacon, get Li transferred to the _Katrine Lamont_, see if ISC had any bandwidth for commercial messages yet so that she could let Belinta know their tractors were, in fact, coming . . . oh, and the mail from home. With the clarity of a full night's sleep, she remembered that she was not supposed to put in an implant without a neuro evaluation, with the recommendation that it not be done for six months, so she didn't have to decide right away whether or not to put in the implant her father had sent.

When she came onto the bridge, Lee nodded to her. "Quincy's put a stack of things on your deskcomp; you'll need to sign off on the orders. Looks good, Captain; she found a supplier for everything we need. There's not a current opening in any of the good refitting yards, but she says we can install the sealed unit ourselves. Insystem drive's fuel price is up, but not impossibly high. She says everyone's being cooperative, so we should hurry up and get out before they change their attitude."

"Good," Ky said. She opened her desk. Sealed unit for FTL, yes. New liner to replace the old cavitation-damaged one. Replacement for communications transmitter. Upgrade for scan—upgrade for scan? She hadn't asked for that . . . but she would like it if they could afford it. Beacon repair. Replacement ship chip . . . unavailable.

The explanation made sense, though it was a pain. Under UCC regulations, no two ships could have the same identifier chip. *Glennys Jones'* original chip couldn't be turned in for a new chip, because it was somewhere in space, probably still in Paison's pocket. Never mind that no one was going to find that chip . . . it had not been turned in, so a chip identifying the ship as *Glennys Jones* could not be issued, even with a replacement registration number. The Universal Commercial Code had very strict requirements; Slotter Key and Sabine Prime were both signatories to the agreements. The ship would have to be reregistered—most easily as out of Sabine Prime, with some difficulty out of Slotter Key, if the Slotter Key embassy would cooperate.

All Vatta ships carried Slotter Key registry. Ky put in a call to the Slotter Key embassy, but it was nighttime there, and it would be hours before the consul saw it. And what would she do if he refused her request? What if Captain Furman got to him first?

And what should she name the ship instead? Certainly not *Mist Harbor.* Finding a unique ship name wasn't easy; the first eight or ten she tried in the database came up with the notation "unavailable: in service." Was it even worth registering a ship that was going to be scrapped anyway?

But it was not going to be scrapped anyway. And finally she thought of a name that no one would have used yet, a name she wanted to honor. She called Quincy on the intercom.

"What?" Her chief engineer was clearly busy and not in the mood to chat.

"We need a new ship name. What about the *Gary Tobai?*"

A long silence. Then Quincy said, "That would do. Yeah. He'd like that."

Ky entered it in the database, and as she expected found no match. She put a reserve tag on it with a three-day permit—surely she'd hear in three days, and she could renew the hold if she had to.

Two hours into day shift for the Slotter Key embassy—and well into second shift for Ky—she heard from the consul. "I hear you lost one of those people we sent you," he said.

"He disobeyed orders and did something stupid," Ky said.

"Why am I not surprised—the young blond one, right?"

"Yes."

"Well, you need to fill out some forms for us. The embassy has to report all injuries and deaths of Slotter Key citizens for the D & A report. I'll have those sent up to you. What about funeral arrangements?"

"He didn't have anything on file with us, but one of the others told me he was a Modulan, so I thought we'd combine his service with the one for one of the other crew."

"Sounds good. I'll notify the family that services were held . . . what date?"

Ky looked at the calendar and answered in terms of the local calendar.

"You'll be in attendance?"

"Of course."

"Good. I'll tell them services were held with the captain in attendance. Remains?"

"I have no idea. I was unconscious and in surgery at the time the remains were disposed of."

"Good enough. The rest of the forms are coming up shortly. Now, what else?"

"I have to reregister the ship," Ky said. "Vatta ships all carry Slotter Key registry. Can we do that?"

"We could," he said, "if your senior captain in system, Captain Furman, hadn't told me that your ship was up for scrap and Vatta would not sanction an offworld licensing fee."

"And how much would that be?" Ky asked.

"You're not going to like the answer," he said.

"Which is . . . ?"

"It's not worth it, really. Two hundred fifty thousand credits for a ship of that mass. You can get a perfectly viable Sabine registration for one hundred thousand—it'd be fifty thousand if you were a Sabine citizen. We charge that much for out-of-system registration just to discourage people . . ."

Ky found her jaw on the floor and yanked it back up with an effort. "Two hundred fifty thousand for a ship chip and a piece of paper?"

"And the honor of the Slotter Key government. Yes. I said it wasn't worth it."

"It's ridiculous. It's outrageous."

"Yes, it is. But it's what I have on my list, so it's what I have to do. So let me know what you want . . ."

Ky had no idea what reputation Sabine Prime ships had in the universe; she'd already discovered that Slotter Key might be a liability. Still, Slotter Key was her planet and her government and she felt uneasy about changing the registration to something else.

The money problem still existed. She had the money for the sealed unit, for the fuel, for resupply of the galley, but she didn't have a spare 100,000 credits, let alone 250,000, for the new license. Another thought occurred, almost as unsettling. She called up the Sabine registration database.

Sure enough, to register the ship under the Sabine flag, it would have to undergo a full inspection and pass as sound. She called up those criteria for the ship's size. As she'd expected the ship would not pass Sabine's very stringent safety inspection, even with all repairs in place. She'd need to install a new communications system, new scans, a more powerful beacon . . . and the combined cost of these quickly surged past the cost of a Slotter Key registration. Slotter Key, on the other hand, required no inspection for offworld registrants.

Ky scrubbed at her head with both hands. Back to square one, again. Money. It was always about the money.

Back in her cabin, she noticed the stack of mail she'd laid aside the day before. She left Hal's for last, hoping the hammering of her heart would slow before she got to it. Please, she thought, please let it be good. Aunt Grace wanted to know if she'd eaten the fruitcakes yet, and advised her to cut small, even slices if serving them to friends. Ky thought of the last fruitcake, now in the galley storage, and shook her head. It would be a long, long time before she cut into that one. She could still taste her share of the first two. Cousin Stella sent a brief note of condolence and the advice to "stick it out; everything passes." MacRobert's note advised her of a source for "equivalent model kits and replacement parts, of higher quality than that found in most toy stores." Her eyebrows went up at that. She still wasn't sure what Mac intended when he gave her a ship model with communications parts in it. Bond Tailoring had sent notice of a sale, now long past; she wondered why it had been forwarded until she saw her mother's notation alongside one of the illustrated dresses: "It suits and they still have your measurements."

And now for Hal. The envelope enclosed some kind of box; she could see its outline. Had he sent a present? Her spirits rose; he had understood, he was still her friend, and maybe . . . She ripped open the envelope and tipped out a little brown-leather-covered box she recognized. Her heart stuttered. It couldn't be . . . She opened it, half-hopeful and half-afraid. A heavy gold ring, the Academy class ring, its crest battered and scarred, almost unrecognizable. Someone had attacked it with a chisel. She plucked it from its slot and looked at the inscription. *Kylara Evangeline Vatta,* with a line gouged through it.

Her vision blurred. He'd sent it back. He'd sent it back defaced.

She clamped her jaw shut on the scream that wanted to come out; her stomach churned; she felt cold and sick and empty all at once. Memory threw up a vivid image of the day they'd exchanged their class rings, the day the rings had been handed out. It wasn't like engagement rings; it had nothing to do with marriage—though, buried deep, she'd had a hope that marriage might come to them someday. It was about trust and honor, not money or sex, a ritual begun, their seniors had told them, before Slotter Key even had a Space Academy, transferred in by those who founded it. Few cadets exchanged class rings, but she and Hal had been so sure of each other, so sure of their abilities, so sure of their friendship . . .

He had stood there, hazel eyes looking into hers. "It would be an honor, Cadet Vatta, to exchange this token with you—" He had asked; she had wanted to but waited, not willing to pressure him.

"And it would be an honor for me," she had said. Formally they had linked arms, and formally passed the boxes hand to hand, and she had considered herself the custodian of his honor as he was of hers. For all that the Academy did not list numerical rank, there were ways of knowing who was at the top, and they both knew they stood number one and number two, and had—sometimes alternating those positions— since their first year. She had taken it seriously, as she took everything seriously . . .

And he had sent her ring back defaced, scarred, even her name scratched across. She did not need the letter to tell her what he now thought of her.

Her hands were shaking. She dropped the ring onto her bunk and unfolded the letter that had come with the box. However bad it was, she had to read it. She had to know why, how he had come to hate her so much. She had understood he might have to cut all ties, never contact her again—she had not imagined that he would turn on her like this.

"Ms. Vatta," the letter began. Hot tears stung her eyes; she blinked them away, trying not to remember the sound of his voice calling her "Ky" and "Kylara" and once—just once—"Kylara-beshi." The letter was . . . even worse than she could have imagined from seeing the ring. She had almost ruined his career, he said. Because he had trusted her, because he had believed her lies—"I never lied to you!" Ky burst out loud. "How could you—!" The cabin's hard surfaces threw the sound back at her. She clamped her lips again and kept her eyes on the letter, reading every word, every word that stabbed her with unfair, untrue accusations. Disloyalty. Dishonesty. Deliberate attempts to sabotage not only his career, but the honor of the service. She had seen him angry before; she knew just how his face would harden, how the muscles along his jaw would swell, the veins throb . . . It was all too easy to see him writing this letter, nostrils flaring, breath coming fast. Hal's outrage built, from the first cold, formal sentences following the salutation, through a series of increasingly angry dissections of every mistake she had made in the Academy, to a furious conclusion that accused her of seducing Mandy Rocher, an innocent youngster who would never have gotten in trouble if it had not been for her influence.

She let the letter fall from her hand when she had read that last sentence instructing her not to attempt a reply; she felt strangely detached, a vast cold gulf inside her that had once been a warm friendship she'd believed would last forever. How could it disappear so completely, how could he change that much that fast? Had it ever been real, then? Probably not. Nothing real could change that fast, surely. He had liked her when they were the best of their year, because liking her enhanced him. But what she had felt—that warm attraction, that love—he had not felt.

Every error of judgment she'd made about people rose up in memory . . . Time after time she had believed that someone needed help, or was friendly, and time after time . . . She fell from shock into a depthless black hole of misery.

She was a fool, and so were those who had misidentified her problem. It wasn't the lost puppies, the seemingly helpless whom she'd tried to help, who caused her the most trouble. No, it was those who seemed sound and solid, the ones she had trusted because anyone would, the ones she'd considered allies, not victims. She hadn't had rescue fantasies about Hal, or Paison. Anyone might have believed they were what they appeared. Yet Paison's apparent goodwill and common sense had been as false as Hal's apparent admiration and affection.

People had died because of her naïve stupid faith in someone not worth it. Slowly, anger seeped in to replace the shock and horror of Hal's attack. Anger at those who had failed her, lied to her, fooled her. Anger at herself for believing them.

She had told herself not to make that mistake again when she'd quit crying about missing her own birthday party. And—whatever her family said, however they had misunderstood her motives on other occasions—she had learned. When she looked at her own motives, case by case, she had barged in to help others only about as often as anyone decent did. Mostly she'd been asked to help because—with the family's certainty that "helping others" was her favorite role, she was the one they turned to.

That had to stop. If nothing else came out of Hal's betrayal, she must somehow convince people—her family, others, herself—that she was who she was, and not who they thought she was.

When she finally fell asleep, hours later, something new and hard had replaced both the cold emptiness and the hot anger.

The next morning, the day of Gary Tobai's funeral, Ky awoke calm, surprising even herself.

The entire crew attended the funeral service; to Ky's surprise, the consul also showed up, just as Ky pressed the button that signaled the start of their service.

"My duty," he said. "You're looking a bit peaked, Captain. Have you heard anything official from Vatta yet?"

"The ansibles aren't repaired yet, are they?"

"Not yet, but we expect them up in a few days. Of course, I keep saying that, echoing ISC . . . just another few days now. But I'll speak with you after the service."

The service itself was properly Modulan, restrained and cozy at the same time. The recorded voice that read from the Book of Changes and paused for their responses had exactly the right blend of sincerity and calm. Ky eyed her crew; nobody burst into tears, nobody looked angry or otherwise upset. The graceful harmonies of Modulan funeral music concluded the service, and then they had ten minutes to socialize before they had to leave the chapel. Ky didn't know what she felt. Her mind shied away from considering her feelings about Hal, and avoiding those feelings kept her safely remote from the ones about Gary or Skeldon. She concentrated on seeing that everyone else was taken care of. The consul had nothing more to say, really, and left before their time was up. When the warning light blinked, she ushered them all out, where they stood in the corridor as the mourners for the next funeral arrived.

"I know what we should do," Beeah said. "We should go eat something onstation."

"Where?" asked Lee.

"There's this place—Tiny's. Not expensive, close by. Unless the captain wants us back on the ship right away?" He looked at Ky. She had no more desire than the rest of them to go back aboard right now.

"No—you're right—let's go eat or something." She hadn't been on the station except in transit to and from the ship and the shuttle lounge, but Beeah would know where to go. "Lead the way," she said.

Tiny's Place was packed with spacers, civilian and mercenary. Ky flinched from the noise level, but it dropped noticeably when her crew came in. She wasn't sure if that was a good sign or a bad sign. Two tables in the left back corner were empty and she headed for them. When the crew had settled in, Ky looked at the order display. Prices were listed in Sabine centas and universal credits—no longer one hundred centas to the credit; the Sabine currency was shaky, she realized. She'd been paid in credits; they could afford to eat just about anything they wanted.

"Get what you want," she said. "It's on me." They nodded. Ky pressed the display to indicate all charges on one check, and added the table number of the other table as well. She looked at the menu, mostly shellfish or fish and vegetables in various combinations. Sabine's brackish swamps produced tons of bayhopper and jitterlegs, genetically modified crayfish, the cheapest protein source on the planet. Ky chose a bayhopper goulash and hoped for the best. Her crew followed suit; nobody ventured to order the outrageously expensive cattlope grill.

It still felt odd to be here, in a place like Tiny's—so obviously a spaceport dive. How many times in her life had she been in a dive? Only the once, tagging along with older cousins and scared she'd be reported to her parents. She looked around, and saw no other captains; she was glad she had folded her captain's cape into its carrying pouch. There were men and women in shipsuits, casual station clothes, and—in the far corner—uniforms. Mackensee uniforms. She looked away. She wasn't going to think about the Colonel's offer, not now.

Their orders had been delivered, and she was just tasting her bayhopper goulash—quite good—when someone bumped hard into her chair. "You! What you doin' in our place?"

Ky swallowed the lump of bayhopper and twisted her neck to look at the person behind her. "What—?" she started to ask when he grabbed her arm.

"Yer in our place—them's our tables—dint they tell yer?" A group of large, rough-looking individuals now stood around her end of the table. Behind them, Ky saw the furtive movement of others slipping away, toward the door.

"No one mentioned," Ky said. "But there are other empty tables."

"Don't want other tables. This's ours, and that'n, too."

The anger she'd been suppressing edged up her throat and into her voice. "Too bad," she heard herself say. "We're here for a funeral dinner, and that's what we're going to have. Sit someplace else."

"You stupid bitch!" The man behind her yanked her chair back with her in it, and grabbed the front of her uniform, lifting her upright. She could smell the liquor on his breath; this wasn't the first bar he'd visited that shift. "You think because you're a damned officer you can come in and give orders to people who aren't even your own crew—" His huge fist was drawn back, ready to pulp her face.

The anger surged through her, banishing any fear. Before he finished the speech she had slammed one hand into his throat, ducked away from the possible blow, and in the same movement put a knee where it could do the most good. He gasped, lost his grip, and she hit the floor, balanced and ready to spring back into action. She had wanted to hit someone for so long—a second man tried to grab her from behind; she rolled with the pull, cracking his shin with a heel and breaking another's nose on the way past, just on spec.

"Ky, be care—" Quincy's voice, now chopped off as the men tried to keep her crew from helping her. Ky reached over someone's shoulder for a bowl of hot bayhopper goulash and flung it in the face of the man who had just pulled a knife, parrying his suddenly blind stab with the dish itself. She heard and felt her crew scrambling to get out of their chairs, heard the gasps and grunts and curses as the fight spread. As she'd discovered in contact games, she could be aware of the whole tangle of motion and for once she didn't have to stick to any rules . . . She punched, rolled, kicked, spun, each time enjoying the solid *thwack* as her strike hit home. Some of her crew—Beeah not surprisingly, and Lee, and Quincy—turned out to be good at this, too. The others dove beneath the table.

The man who'd first grabbed her was back in play now, swinging one of the chairs—steel and plastic, not a storycube prop. Ky grabbed one for herself, and they clashed the legs, glaring at each other. If only she had a spear or something—no that was fictional. Then he pulled out something that looked like a cleaver on steroids. Where had he hidden *that* from station security? It whined through the air, and a leg of her chair hung from a ragged edge. Whatever it was would cut steel . . . He grinned.

"You'll pay for that," he said.

"I doubt it," Ky said. She had no idea what to do to counter his attack, but she wasn't going to go down without a fight.

At that moment, six bodies in military uniform entered the fray as a unit, just in Ky's peripheral vision on the right.

"Advance," said a dry voice that Ky almost recognized.

The man lunged at her again, his weapon slashing at another of the chair legs. Ky squatted quickly, trying to come up inside its arc, but his weight overthrew her; she was flat on the floor, the legs of his chair caging her head for an instant, until he lost his balance and fell sideways, weapon arm outstretched.

Ky rolled toward him and got a hand on his wrist, but he was taller and heavier. She tried to tuck and kick him in the gut, but the chair got in the way. He leered at her, and started to roll up . . . when a booted foot landed hard on his hand.

"Let go," said the voice.

"Go—" the man said, an anatomically impossible suggestion.

The tip of a very sharp blade came into view, beside the boot, resting on the skin of his hand. "You can let go, or I can cut your hand off your blade finger by finger," the voice said. "Your choice."

His hand loosened; someone reached down and removed the weapon, but the blade menacing his fingers never quivered.

"Captain Vatta," the voice said. Ky looked up. She knew that face. Master Sergeant Pitt.

"Need a hand up?" Pitt asked.

"No, thanks," Ky said. She scrambled up, put the damaged chair back where it had come from, and looked around for her crew. The fight was over. Six men lay or sat on the floor, some unconscious and some merely stunned; some of her crew were up, breathing hard, and two were still under the table.

"Sorry to interrupt your meal," Pitt said, "but the dinner conversation seemed to be turning general." Her eyes twinkled. Ky could not help grinning back.

"It wasn't our plan," she said. "We'd just had a funeral . . ."

"I heard," Pitt said. "I'd have come if I could. We missed it by fifteen minutes. He was a good man."

"He was indeed," Ky said. Suddenly her bruises hurt, her head ached, and she wanted very much to sit down and go to sleep. Not much was left of their meal; the table looked as if someone had wallowed on it and maybe someone had.

Pitt looked down at the man who had attacked Ky. "You're off *Marie*, aren't you?" she said. He spat in the direction of her boot but didn't answer. "Not a good choice," Pitt said. "*Marie* crew are supposed to be aboard, waiting for interrogation . . . I think we'll do a little interrogation on my ship." She looked at one of the other soldiers. "Jem—call the ship and get them to send a squad."

More quickly than Ky would have imagined, a squad showed up to shackle the attackers and take them away. Pitt shook her head at the departing brawlers. "Not very good at it, that bunch. Nasty for someone with no training, but you, at least, knew what you were doing. Come on, let's finish that funeral dinner. Charge the damage to *Marie*—I'll back you on the damage report."

Ky wasn't sure she could eat anything but the bayhopper goulash was just as good the second time around, and the raw whiskey Pitt encouraged her to sip took the ache out of her body.

"You know, Captain, you're really wasted on a merchanter," Pitt said quietly. Ky wasn't sure how she'd ended up sitting next to Pitt, between her and another mercenary. "I know, the Colonel said you have some kind of promise thing you have to do first, but . . . you belong with people like us, really, not with people like them—" Her gaze settled on the ones who had dived under the table.

"Not their fault," Ky said. "They haven't had the training." Her blood warmed to the praise, though, and she felt again both the glee and the guilt as the fight replayed in her mind. Pitt, she realized, would not condemn her for what she'd felt when she killed Paison and his mate.

"True but . . . here's something I don't say often, and won't say again. There's some born to it, Captain, and you're one of 'em. I don't know what happened to get you out of that training, but you're someone I'd be glad to serve with. And I can't say more than that."

"Thanks," Ky said. She was aware of a floating disconnect between her brain and body, and hoped she wasn't drunk. Very drunk.

"Cup of black coffee and a good big dessert will cure what ails you,"

Pitt said. "We'll just sit here and talk about nothing much, how's that?" And for the next hour, Pitt told stories of the Mackensee Military Assistance Corporation, every one of which made Ky homesick for a community she hadn't had yet. Ky could tell when the alcohol had mostly left her system; she blinked and the lights didn't flicker. She thanked Pitt and led her crew back to the ship.

And she stared at the battered circle that had been her class ring and felt nothing but vague anger.

CHAPTER TWENTY-ONE

"**F**TL sealed unit's in," Quincy reported. "Custom Parts had an Ames & Handon 4311b in stock, and that's better than the one we took out. I've checked all the calibration; it looks slick."

"What's the damage?" Ky asked.

"Only ten percent higher than before we left, and it's higher quality. You want it, right?"

"Right," Ky said. She watched the figures Quincy sent come up on her deskcomp. "And the liner?"

"Got that, too," Quincy said, with a hint of smugness. "How's the re-licensing coming along?"

"Paperwork and money," Ky said. She had her deskcomp set to display the falling balance in their accounts . . . amazing how fast a lot of money could disappear. She not only had to pay for the registration and the custom ship chip, but for the database search which ensured that no one else had used the name Gary Tobai for a ship. She had to appear in person to take possession of the new ship chip for the beacon, and then spend a sweaty and uncomfortable half hour getting the beacon unit out, seating the new chip, and replacing the unit in its cramped space. A whole new beacon would have cost another 100,000 credits.

Meanwhile, she fended off suggestions from Captain Furman—more like orders than suggestions—that she allow him to audit her books, inspect her ship, check out her financial arrangments with the Sabine branch of Crown & Spears, make arrangements to have the ship scrapped . . .

"For the last time, no," Ky said, hanging onto her temper by the merest fingernail. "I am not selling the ship for scrap here. I have a contract to deliver cargo to Belinta, and that's where I'm going." *And you can't stop me* didn't quite come out of her mouth.

"But your father—"

"Isn't here. Doesn't need to be here. And if he were here, he'd understand my position."

"He'd understand Vatta Transport's position. Damn it, Apprentice—"

Her temper snapped. "I'm not an apprentice, Captain Furman. I'm a captain the same as you are. Get that through your fat stupid head, once and for all—"

"You little—!"

She turned off the comunit, shocked at herself—had she really said that to Furman, senior captain of the Vatta fleet? It felt good; it shouldn't feel good. At least he couldn't ping her skullphone since she didn't have an implant. She had the last word.

"How fast can we leave?" she asked Lee, who happened to be on the bridge just then.

"I'll check, Captain," he said. In a few moments, Quincy appeared on the bridge.

"You want to leave soon?" Quincy asked.

"Yes," Ky said. "As soon as we can."

"Get us clearance, and we're out of here, ma'am. FTL's in, all cavitation damage replaced, cargo loaded and balanced, inspace drive refueled, supplies aboard. Unless there's some niggly paperwork holding us here—"

"There won't be for long," Ky said, feeling a wicked delight bubbling up inside her. They would be on their way, and Furman, she had no doubt, would be stuck where he was until it pleased ISC to let him depart. She called the stationmaster, and in less than two hours they had their clearance for departure. She declined a tug, and in another seventeen minutes forty-two seconds the *Gary Tobai* eased out of its docking bay, maneuvered carefully free of the station and all nearspace traffic, and set a course for the designated jump point.

The ship moved as ponderously as ever; she hadn't had the money to upgrade the insystem drive. But it was her ship again, with no strangers aboard, no one giving her orders. On the communications board, messages from Furman stacked up—she could see the mounting numbers with their origin codes—but she didn't care. He couldn't actually do anything, not without getting permission from the ISC, and right now she had ISC on her side.

As for the military ships, they stayed in tight orbit around both planets. Her new scan showed ships out where the ansibles had been . . . ISC rebuilding its empire, no doubt.

They could stay there till they rotted, all of them, Sabines, mercenaries, ISC, and all, for all she cared. She was free of that. She grinned to herself. She stayed close to the bridge for the first couple of days, then turned it over to the pilots and navigator. If she was going to be a captain—the kind of captain she wanted to be—she needed to trust her people. And she needed to know a lot of things she still didn't know, things a captain needed to know.

Without really thinking about it, she fell into a routine similar to that in the Academy, beginning every main shift with an hour of physical conditioning, and taking another exercise period midway through second shift. She had to be fit; she had to be ready for anything.

On the ninth day, they reached the jump point, and she was back on the bridge for endim transition. The ship barely shivered as the new FTL drive flung them into indetermination; all the telltales stabilized at once in the correct configuration. Quincy was on the bridge as well, running calibration estimates—a first run with a new drive always involved some tinkering and tweaking—but from the grin on her old face, all was going well.

As he'd requested, Gerard Vatta had a ping from the watch station as soon as the Sabine ansibles were back up. He beat Stavros to the communications center by a scant minute; he had just made the connection to the Sabine orbital station when he saw Stavros round the corner. His brother came to the boards and picked up his own headset link.

"This is Gerard Vatta," he said to the com tech on the station. "Patch me through to the Vatta ship *Glennys Jones*, please."

"No such ship is docked at the station," the technician said. "A ship formerly known as the *Glennys Jones*, but reregistered under the Slotter

Key flag as the *Gary Tobai* was docked here but is no longer here and is outside our range. It may already have left the system."

The *Gary Tobai* . . . Ky would have named the ship for Gary only if Gary had died . . . and if Gary had died . . . he had died trying to save her. Gerry squeezed his eyes shut and offered a brief prayer, promising more later.

"The *Katrine Lamont*, then," he said, hoping Furman was still in the system.

"Very good, sir," the tech said.

"*Katrine Lamont* receiving call from Vatta HQ, Slotter Key," the communications officer aboard the ship said, quite properly.

"This is Gerard Vatta; patch me through to Captain Furman."

"Sir, it's—it's third watch . . ."

"And this is an interstellar call, priority. Wake him up."

A faintly hissing silence, then: "Captain Furman here."

"This is Gerry Vatta," he said informally. "What's the situation?" He heard Furman draw in a breath.

"The situation, sir, is that your idiot daughter has stolen a Vatta Transport ship and gone haring off into jumpspace—she says she's on the way to Belinta to deliver a cargo, but for all I know she's on her way to any place you can think of. She hasn't learned one damn thing since she was—"

"Excuse me." Gerard knew that he was being calm; he knew it by the whitening of his knuckles and the fact that he managed that courtesy rather than the bellow of rage he felt. "Did you just call my daughter an idiot and a thief, or perhaps I misunderstood your use of the words *idiot* and *stolen* . . . ?"

An audible gulp. "Sir, I—I misspoke myself. The fact is, despite my attempts to make her see reason, she refused to come aboard this ship with her crew, let me sell off that old hulk for scrap, and bring her home."

"I didn't tell you to do that." He was calm, he was very calm. That, no doubt, was why Stavros now had a firm hand on his shoulder, and why the techs in the communications center were staring at him wide-eyed. "I told you to give her every assistance, to make it clear that she was under Vatta protection."

"You can't protect someone who's acting like an idiot!" Furman blurted. "I tried to talk sense into her—"

"That's the second time you've called my daughter an idiot," Gerard said. Again Furman gulped.

"I didn't mean it like that—I just meant, impetuous, young, head-strong—"

"You should have known," Gerard said. "You had her on her apprentice voyage—" From which she had come back even more determined to enter the Academy, he recalled. Furman had done nothing but drive her farther away back then. Gerard tried to stay calm. It wasn't entirely Furman's fault, but Furman was there, handy, and he wanted so much to tack someone's hide to the wall. He took a deep breath, reminding himself of Furman's years of exemplary service.

"You're not blaming *me*, surely." Furman's voice sounded thick; was it sleepiness or anger? "I'm a senior captain in the Fleet; I disrupted my own important schedule to come get that—her—out of the mess she'd gotten herself into—"

Stavros' hand tightened on Gerard's arm; he realized that the wash of brightness across his vision was another wave of white-hot anger. "She did not get herself into a mess, Captain Furman," he made himself say, rather than *You arrogant asshole, say one more word about my daughter and I'll have you for breakfast . . .* "She happened to be in the system when a war started, and she survived until help arrived. I find that commendable. I would find that commendable even if you had done it."

Something that might have been a splutter came into his headphone.

"I sent you to help her. Not scold her. Not order her around as if she were still a thirteen-year-old apprentice. Help her. And what you've done, apparently, is help her go off again, without my having a chance to talk to her, and you may have convinced her that she's in trouble with me. Now you may be one of our senior captains, and you may have an important and lucrative route, but the fact is, Captain Furman, that you are still a Vatta Transport employee, and your job description does not include insulting my daughter . . ." He knew his voice had risen; he knew that Stavros had a hard grip on his arm, and the faces in the communications center were all shocked, and he should get hold of himself, calm down. "Damn it, man!" That was a shout, the shout that brought him back to himself, his voice all but gone. "If she . . ." If she didn't come back, if she was lost because the drive failed, because she'd hurried the repair because of Furman, if she disappeared into the endless dark reaches of space. . . .

"I'm sorry," Furman said, a distant scratchy voice, irritating even in its submission. "I didn't mean any harm, I just thought . . ."

"Just . . . don't say anything," Gerard said. He felt sick, all the energy of anger drained away, the emptiness of not knowing hollowing his heart. He had hoped . . . he had counted on talking to her himself, hearing her voice, proving—if only for the time the call lasted—that she was alive, that he had been told the truth.

"Do you want me to follow her to Belinta? Make sure she's safe?"

Stavros took the headset from him before he could answer; Gerard leaned on the console with both hands, bracing himself upright, while Stavros' calm voice told Furman what to do: clear up all Vatta accounts in Sabine, report in when he had done so, and then in all likelihood return to his usual route for the present.

Gerard blinked back the tears, tried not to sniff audibly at the congestion in his nose. He should be happy. She was alive. She had not let Furman bully her. She had gone off to do her duty, fulfill the contract, trade and profit, like a true Vatta. He could send a message by ansible to Belinta, telling her he was proud of her. He could reach her while she was there. It was all right now.

He could not believe it. He felt in his own heart the avalanche of disasters that had come to her, one after another, each one tearing her away from the family, rushing her away, out of control, to some disastrous ending. She would not come back. If he saw her again, she would be someone else, a stranger, not his daughter Kylara. A quick cascade of images raced through his mind: infant-toddler-child-preadolescent-teen-young woman. In the future? Nothing.

"Well." That was Stavros, a warm hand once more on his shoulder. "She's alive for sure, our Ky."

Gerard couldn't answer. He forced a deep breath, straightened. Communications techs busied themselves at their consoles, carefully ignoring the senior officers.

"You'll want to leave a message at Belinta," Stavros said. "Letter of credit as well?"

Would she think it was a bribe? Would she think that not leaving one was a ploy to make her come begging? Did she even need the money?

"Everyone needs money," Stavros said. "Even when they have enough."

"A message," Gerard managed to say. "From me." He took another breath, picked up a recording cube from the stack on the console. "I can do it, Stav. I'm fine now." He took the cube into one of the booths they used when they weren't rushing as he had been, and recorded a short, cordial message to be sent to Belinta and left it in the queue for her arrival.

*   *   *

The days wore on, marked only by ship's time. Ky updated the captain's log, scribbling in the margins the things she had not had time to put in before. It might be messy, but it would be complete as she saw it. Her log.

Some things, though, she did not want to put in. Her account of the mutiny was precise, detailed, and accurate so far as it went. It did not include her feelings. It particularly did not include that wholly unmentionable feeling of utter, absolute, complete glee that had taken over when she killed Paison, his mate, and Kristoffson. Oh, she'd thrown up after it was over—and she'd expected that; they'd been told in the Academy that most people did, after a first killing. But even so, even with the horror and revulsion, she'd been aware of something much worse going on underneath.

She had enjoyed it. She had enjoyed the crisis; she had enjoyed the need to make those snap decisions, take that immediate action.

And she had enjoyed killing.

That did not fit with any of her ideas about herself. Kylara the rescuer, yes. Kylara the brave defender, yes. But Kylara the happy killer? What kind of monster was she? And why didn't she feel more like a monster? Was it true, as Master Sergeant Pitt and the Colonel had told her, that she was wasted in civilian life? Was she a born killer, and did that mean she should join up with other born killers? Should she join the mercenaries, where her violent tendencies would be under proper control?

She felt—except when she tried to feel guilty and bad—quite happy. Almost—though she knew this was dangerous—smugly happy. She had had a horrible few months, starting with that morning at the Academy, and yet here she was. People had tried to kill her. She had nearly died. And she was alive and they—at least some of them—were dead. Hal hated her—well, that solved any worry about whether she should ever try to contact him. Mandy Rocher . . . was a nasty little piece of work, and would get his comeuppance someday. She didn't even care that she might not know about it when that happened.

They arrived in Belinta's system four days ahead of schedule—that new FTL drive really was superior—and Ky checked in with the Belinta station. She expected a problem because of the beacon change.

"Vatta Transport *Gary Tobai*, Kylara Vatta commanding, request inbound vector to Belinta station."

"*Gary Tobai*, approved vector relaying to your navigator . . . Captain Vatta, you have ansible messages in queue. Will you accept them now, or wait until your arrival?"

"I'll wait," she said. One would be her father, no doubt. She told herself she didn't care what he said, but she knew she lied.

The ship eased in, day after day. Ky reassured the Economic Development Bureau that she had their ag equipment, every single tractor and implement that could be crammed into their cargo holds. She spoke to the Slotter Key consul in carefully guarded terms about the situation on Sabine, though with the ansibles back up—as the "stations available" list made clear—he could well find out for himself. She made contact with the ISC ship which was patrolling Belinta's outer reaches and carefully did not ask if they thought Belinta's ansible platform was at particular risk.

And finally they arrived, docking neatly at the station. Ky arranged for her escort to meet her at the station downside, and for a room at the Captains' Guild. She planned to accept her ansible mail before talking to Customs, but Customs was already on the horn, demanding her presence. She put on her dress uniform and went out into the dockside area.

"Captain Vatta—it really is you." Not just the Customs Inspector she'd met before, but two men in the uniform of the Economic Development Bureau.

"That's right," Ky said.

"You bought a new ship?"

"No—we ran into a bit of trouble at Sabine, and changed the ship ID chip."

"You weren't . . . doing anything illegal, were you?"

"Not at all," Ky said. She realized suddenly that changing ship chips was the sort of thing pirates did in storycubes. "Someone broke into our beacon, stole the original ship chip, and we had to reregister under a new name. I have the paperwork."

"Oh. Very well. And the inventory of the imports?"

"All here. As you'll see, I bought you new equipment from Farm-Power—"

"Why not used?"

"They aren't selling used there anymore. They've got a war on; the used equipment is all gone. Anyway, all these machines were purchased new on Sabine; I have the inventories ready for you."

"Then we can start unloading today—"

"Not until your payment clears," Ky said.

The EDB representatives scowled at her. "You think we would cheat you?"

"Our contract calls for payment prior to offloading," Ky said. "I'm sorry, but I'm required to adhere to the terms of the contract."

"But we have to inspect it—"

"Of course," Ky said. "I'll escort you to the cargo bays . . ."

There was scarcely room to move in the cargo bays, with diassembled pieces of equipment stowed carefully to make the most use of the available cubage. Ky had to use a hardcopy of the inventory, but the EDB personnel had implants to compare the visible serial numbers.

"How long will it take to unload this?" one of them asked.

"I don't know," Ky said frankly. "My cargomaster was killed in the trouble over near Sabine—"

"Brawling in a bar," said the other EDB man with a sneer.

"No," Ky said. "Taken as hostage by a pirate who had been interned on my ship, and killed when I suppressed the mutiny. That's why I renamed the ship for him. I consider him a hero."

"Oh. Sorry." A moment of embarrassed silence, then: "But how long did it take to load?"

"Without Gary—three days. It was already disassembled, though . . ." She felt tired even before she started, but gave a quick and incomplete recital of what had happened, at least as far as the cargo was concerned.

"You mean it was out there in space, unprotected, for days and days?"

"It was in the same kind of vacuum it would have experienced in any cargo ship's hold," Ky said. "FarmPower assured me that there was no need to keep the holds aired up, or at livable temperature, during transport, and I also have their assurance that ambient radiation while outside the ship would not shorten the working life." She was glad Quincy had thought to ask for that. "Now, as soon as the credits are in my account, you can start unloading . . ."

They dithered another hour or so, but finally authorized the transfer of the agreed amount into her local account, payable without tax in credits. Ky handed over the inventory, told Quincy to supervise the unloading crews, and at last had time to look at her accumulated messages.

As expected, there was one from her father. A full broadband audio-visual that must have cost . . . she didn't want to think. She settled down in her cabin, braced for the worst.

"Kylara, I'm so sorry," was the first thing she heard. Her eyes filled with tears, despite herself. Her father looked exhausted and distraught. "Furman is an idiot, and I wouldn't have sent him if anyone else had been close enough. He was supposed to help you, not cause you more trouble. I'm sorry Gary died—I haven't heard all about it yet, but I'm sure he died trying to help you in some way. I know you were injured . . . Ky, I hope you know that I—that Vatta—were trying to do everything we could to find you, help you, whatever happened. And all I know now is that you must be at Belinta, to have accessed this message—" His voice wavered, then steadied. "Ky, please call me. I've set up a prepaid call; you may not need that option, but just in case . . . please. Please call me. Anytime."

Not the worst, then. Not angry, not like Furman. But—did she want to call home, like a teenager who's gotten herself in a fix and has to call Daddy for help? She had coped with the fix—she had coped with death, with injury. She didn't need him that way.

But he needed her. That tremor in his voice, those circles under his eyes, were not faked.

She went to the bridge and placed the call, using her own now-fatter account. This time the telltales switched promptly from standby to ready to searching to active connection. A brief delay, with a screen message of "reconnecting: mobile unit." That meant he had the skull-phone on.

He answered immediately; the visual was a bouncing green blur, what the skullphone's visual pickup faced. "Yes?" His voice sounded annoyed; Ky flinched inwardly.

"Dad—it's Ky."

A final blur, then motion stopped; the pickup stared at what she could now see was one of the back roads in a tik grove. "Ky! Are you all right?" Not annoyance now, but some combination of eagerness and pleading that saddened her.

"I'm fine, Dad. I'm at Belinta's orbital station . . . you knew that, you left the message . . ." She was babbling, trying to give him time.

"Yes." His breath huffed out; she could almost see his shoulders relax. "You made it . . . not that I didn't think you would, but . . ."

Only a few weeks ago, it seemed, she had been glad to lean into him, feel his comforting arm around her. Now it felt awkward, and not only because he was light-years away. Other kinds of years away, maybe.

"I don't know what you've heard about what happened," Ky said.

"Not enough," her father said. "Not nearly enough. I knew you'd gone rogue—Quincy's probably told you by now we expected something like that on one of your early voyages . . ." It was not quite a question.

"Yes," Ky said. "She and Gary—" Her throat closed; she swallowed and went on. "I knew on the way to Sabine. But they thought it was all right."

"Of course," her father said. "Trade and profit. I was glad for you; it meant—I thought—that you weren't completely shattered by what the Academy did."

"Well . . . the FTL sealed unit failed on downshift into Sabine—"

"It was supposed to be safe—Quincy swore that ship was safe enough for you—" His voice sounded angry again.

"Not her fault," Ky said quickly. "Something she couldn't anticipate. We think it's because there was no cargo on the way to Sabine—we wanted maximum cubage for the pickup. Cargo mass had been damping what was going wrong. Captain's decision."

"All right," he said.

"So then, I was having trouble getting financing for both the equipment and the repairs, and the political situation was getting worse. I was actually trying to call you when the ansibles went out."

"You were . . . good girl!"

He hadn't realized she'd do the sensible thing? He should have known that . . . She pushed from her mind the reluctance she'd had to call for help. "I'd have reached you, too, but the Captains' Guild wouldn't let me put the call through, because they wouldn't charge the Vatta account."

"What!"

"I'd done the Belinta deal as a private contract, not to risk Vatta Transport's image if something went wrong. Besides, my instructions were to take the ship from Belinta to Leonora to Lastway. I didn't know if—what would happen if—"

"We have the highest-rated category of account at the Captains' Guild," her father growled. "Damn them! They have no reason—didn't you tell them who you were? Not that it should make a difference . . . Any Vatta captain should be able to—"

"Dad, I told them who I was, and it made no difference. But a war was starting. Maybe that was it . . ."

"They'll hear from me—from us—," her father said. She could hear his harsh breathing. Then it steadied. "Sorry, Ky. But when I think how scared I—we—were. If we'd gotten that message, at least I'd have known . . ."

"Well, the excitement all came later," Ky said. Before he could reply, she told him what had come next—that she had broken the ship free of the station, moved away from the planet to await events, been hailed and then boarded by mercenaries. How much to tell about her injuries? As little as possible; she was fine. She talked quickly, keeping the recital "clean and lean" as she'd been taught at the Academy. The new contract, the arrival of hostages, the mercenaries' departure, her decision to cut rations, the mutiny.

"That's when Gary was killed, right?" her father asked.

"Yes," Ky said. She wanted—she didn't want—to tell him the details. If she told it all, what would he think of her, his daughter, his own child who could stand by and see a friend killed, and then kill—not once but repeatedly—herself? She certainly couldn't tell him about the discovery—at once terrifying and exhilarating—that she had *enjoyed* killing.

Into that pause he said, "It must have been hard, Ky. I'm sorry you had to face that kind of thing. I'm so glad you lived, that you saved the rest of your crew. I'm so proud of you . . ."

"Thank you," Ky said. "I . . . can't talk about it right now."

"I understand," he said at once. He didn't understand. He couldn't understand. She wondered suddenly if he—the big, warm, safe, father she had grown up with—had ever seen anyone die, had ever killed someone. He cleared his throat, signaling a determined change to another topic. "I have to ask—your Aunt Gracie Lane wants to know—if you've eaten all the fruitcakes yet."

Fruitcakes. Aunt Gracie Lane must be the most single-minded person in the entire universe if she knew anything about what had happened and was worrying about those hideous fruitcakes.

"Two of them, Dad," Ky said. "We shared them out during the— when we were stretching the food supply."

"You still have the third? You know, it would make her really happy, and get her off my back, if I could assure her that you had finished all three. She keeps after me about it, telling me to remind you to serve them in thin, ladylike slices . . ."

Ky tried not to roll her eyes, hard as it was. Fruitcakes! "All right. Tell you what—we'll have it today. As soon as the cargo's offloaded, I'll tell the crew we're having a party and we'll serve Aunt Gracie's fruitcake." Some of them actually liked the horrible stuff.

"Cut it yourself, she tells me," her father said.

"All right, I'll cut it myself. And I'm sending you a written report— about Gary's funeral, and so on, and some paperwork on the contract . . ."

"That's fine," her father said. "Look—I can see by the status line that you're making this call out of your own pocket, but remember that you've got a credit for a call to me anytime."

"Yes, I will. Thank you."

"And—when you know what your plans are—please let me know."

Plans? She had no idea what her plans were; she had cargo for Leonora and Lastway, but most of it was spec.

"I'll let you know," she said. "Good-bye, Dad."

"Farewell, Kylara. You're always in our hearts."

Traditional, and she was blinking back tears as she cut the connection.

So now what? The Belinta station cargo handlers were unloading. She could plan the party, and then, next dayshift, go planetside and see . . . what there was to see.

"It's not that bad, Ky," Quincy said, and Alene, Mehar, and Lee nodded. "I've always liked fruitcake."

Ky shrugged. "All right. I wouldn't make you eat it, but if you want to—and I did promise my father that we'd cut it today."

She put the fruitcake—even heavier than the first two, she thought—on a cake plate, and got out the cake knife and cake fork, each embossed with the Vatta Transport seal. Before, they had just cut off hunks and weighed them . . . but now she put the fork into the cake and poked the tip of the knife in. Hard, dense, difficult . . . the blade slid down, reluctantly it seemed.

And stopped. Ky pressed harder. Nothing happened. She moved the blade over—had Aunt Gracie's vision failed? Had she put in gravel instead of dried fruits and nuts?—and tried again. This time the tip of the blade wouldn't go all the way in. Ky wiggled it around, and suddenly it sank to the plate. That slice worked; she moved over, away from the first attempt, and cut and removed a thin sliver, the thickness Auntie Grace would approve.

Brown, speckled with green and red and yellow and something that looked like a dirty piece of glass. Ky poked it with the knife, prodded it loose, and it fell with a faint clink onto the cake plate.

"Oh, a holiday cake!" Mehar said suddenly. "It's got little presents in it." She picked up the object, wiped it off with a napkin, and they all stared.

Gleaming, flashing, the faceted object lay in her hand . . . several carats of blue-white diamond, perfectly cut.

"Holy . . . whatever," Mehar breathed. She tipped the stone back onto the plate. The crew froze, staring at Ky.

There were, in all, a kilo of diamonds in that fruitcake, most of them over two carats. And a letter, stained by cake batter but quite legible.

The letter said:

My dear Kylara,

I am quite well aware that you do not like my fruitcakes. Therefore I knew you would not hog them down at once, and this little surprise would be available when you truly needed it.

Best wishes, Your loving Aunt Grace.

Ky stared at the diamonds, then at the faces of her crew.

"What do we do now?"

"Eat the fruitcake," Quincy advised, gathering some of the bits and pieces onto her plate. "And tell your aunt it was delicious."